I0732620

UNBROKEN

THE PIRATE & HER PRINCESS
BOOK TWO

ALLI TEMPLE

Copyright © 2022 by Alli Temple
Unbroken
All rights reserved.
ISBN 978-1-7772451-9-1 (ebook)
ISBN 978-1-9907190-0-4 (paperback)

No part of this book may be reproduced in any form or by any electronic or mechanical means, including information storage and retrieval systems, without written permission from the author, except for the use of brief quotations in a book review.

This is a work of fiction. Names, characters, places, and incidents are a product of the author's imagination or are used fictitiously. Any resemblance to actual events, places, or persons, living or dead, is entirely coincidental.

Cover Design: We Got You Covered Book Design
Developmental Editing: Jen Greybeal, Jen Greybeal Author Services
Copy Editing: Adam Mongaya, Tessera Editorial
Proofreading: Lori Parks, LesCourt Author Services

❀ Formatted with Vellum

For you, the reader.
Uncharted felt like such a huge risk when I released it and not only did you read it, you're back for a second adventure. Thank you for making me brave.

For news on future releases, join the A-List, my monthly newsletter.

Content warnings: This book is a fantasy pirate adventure that takes place in a fictional world resembling a historical Earth. It contains the usual levels of piratical violence, consistent with that depicted in *Uncharted*. For additional information, visit the Content Warnings page.

PART I

Watching the woman I love marry someone else is an excellent way to spoil my day.

Being forced to officiate the very same wedding leaves a sour taste in my mouth.

And getting stabbed for my trouble is the perfect ending to an already rotten experience. Not the outcome I would recommend to anyone.

It should be a relief when the doors behind me blow open and the crew I recently left behind charges in, ready to defend and save me.

But all I can see is George.

I press a hand to my bleeding guts and struggle to stand. The prince has a hand in her hair and he's dragging her from the room. I have to go after them, but already my limbs are slow to respond, and the pain is spreading.

The widening terror on George's face is all the warning I get before a shout sounds above me, and I turn in time to see one of Kiril's soldiers bring the blade down toward my neck.

I've faced death so many times I don't flinch, even though I'm unarmed and defenseless.

At the last second, a second blade appears, knocking the descending one away. Maro stands above me, sword held high, mouth arranged in a snarl. And I know everything will be all right, even as I start to shiver from a cold no one else feels.

"George," I say, as the room shudders. "The prince, he took her."

"We have to leave," Maro says, hooking a hand under my arm and hauling me to my feet. I groan with the pain of it, feeling my insides shift, trying to escape through the opening the prince's dagger has left in me. I press tighter, wondering which organ I'm touching.

A second shudder.

"Are you tearing the building down?" I ask.

"We rowed one of the guns up the river."

That's a sensible solution. How many times have I dreamed of blasting this entire wretched fortress into the sky?

"Cinder," a voice rasps behind us. "You gave me your word." Kiril's face, usually so ashen, has turned a mottled purple.

"Did I?" I say, and the effort of speaking leaves me breathless.

"You know what happens to those who go back on their promises to me."

"She didn't." Maro steps between us. "I broke it for her." Their approach toward Kiril is a thing of beauty. That walk, the set of their shoulders, is the final thing so many people have ever witnessed. Does Kiril know it's his last?

But the edges of my vision darken, so I don't get to see the outcome, only hear it. Steel rings out, then the swish of an unmet blade, and then the soft gurgle of a man with his throat slit.

The pain when Maro pulls me to my feet a second time is white-hot, and for a while, it's all I know.

"George." I bob on delirium, and water splashes around me. "We have to go after her."

"You're done making decisions for today."

"No. George." I struggle, or try to, though I'm not sure my arms and legs are working together.

"Stop." Maro's hand on my forehead is ice when the rest of me feels like it's on fire. "You'll tear more, and the doctor won't be able to patch you up. Your princess will be disappointed to hear it."

We find her. Or Maro does. I'm too weak by then to do anything but lie in bed. Not a very impressive sort of pirate. We sail on, and later I hear how my brave princess killed the prince herself. She never needed my help in the first place.

The doctor forces me to stay in bed longer than I want. He says there might be a touch of infection and makes me swallow cups of his foul brews and smears a yellowy paste on the wound. The skin around the crooked stitches is hot and tender, so he might be right. Once, I sneak out of the cabin, if only so I can feel the breeze on my face and smell the salt ocean for a moment, and the effort leaves me so exhausted I have to lean on the rail for support. George finally helps me back to the sofa in my cabin, where she leaves me to get food from Rosie like I'm a helpless child who needs to be fed.

This is how Maro finds me.

"You look like a rotten fish washed up on the beach," they say with no hint of sympathy or humor.

"I feel about the same." It's hard to adjust my position without pulling at my stitches, and I wince when I try to sit up straighter.

"She makes you weak," Maro says, and I don't have to ask who they're talking about. But they're wrong. George makes me better.

"I love her."

For a while, we don't say anything. I sit there, sweating and forcing myself to breathe steadily so Maro can't judge me any further, even though that's all they ever do. They watch me with their steady, assessing gaze that says I can't hide anything.

"We promised each other," they say finally.

I sigh. "I know."

"Never again."

"I know."

"We left Kiril, and we said we would never go back. We are stronger than his games, Cinder."

Right now, I don't feel very strong at all.

"I'm sorry I didn't tell you the plan."

Now their mouth crooks up on one side. "I'd have tied you both to the mast if you had."

"And that's why I didn't tell you."

"The next time I hear of any of the brokers so much as breathing in our direction, it will be war. Do you understand? We don't stop until they're all dead. There's no other way."

I wave vaguely, my strength failing. Maro's convictions are implacable, but we didn't need a war. We're no longer those people.

But I've wondered so many times how we can ever be anything else.

I hold out a hand, and we both pretend we don't see the way I tremble from my fingertips all the way up to my shoulder. When Maro takes it in their firm grip and shakes gently, the knot in my gut under the rude stitches and rancid ointments relaxes ever so slightly.

"Never again," I say.

CHAPTER 1

You would think, after several years of rescuing women desperate to escape various fathers, brothers, husbands, persecutors, and captors, that we would have had it down to a science. Find the woman, help her escape quietly under the cover of darkness, slip away before anyone notices, and bring her safely to a new life with minimal fuss and bother.

Yet, as the shot rang behind me and blew a clump of plaster from the wall past my ear, I had to admit that despite my best intentions, that was not always the case.

"I told you this was a bad idea," Maro hissed in my ear.

"Yes," I said through gritted teeth. "You can tell me all about my failings when we get to the ship."

"Wait!" Lady Amelia, our erstwhile rescuee, said, tugging against the grip I had on her wrist. "My dogs. We have to go back for my dogs."

"No one said anything about dogs." Maro again. You'd never know they enjoyed their work.

"Madam," I said, trying to gain some forward momentum. "We really don't have time." We'd already been forced to wait as she'd gathered an improbable number of possessions from her room and tied them all up in a bedsheet.

To prove my point about timing, nearly ten guards rounded the corner of the hall we were currently racing down. We skidded to a halt and Maro cursed over the slither of steel as they pulled their sword from its sheath.

They glared at me. "This was supposed to be a quiet extraction."

"But my puppies!" Lady Amelia wailed.

After a string of jobs where we had barely gotten out by the skin of our teeth—the fortress with a thirty-foot moat populated by ravenous fish with many rows of serrated teeth and a taste for human flesh had been particularly challenging—we had been promised that the rescue of Lady Amelia would be straightforward. A Paranese noblewoman unable to give her husband the son he wanted. She'd been subsequently shut up in the tallest tower of his country house with only a skeleton staff to attend to her. No one had seen her or asked after her in years. The husband had already moved his mistress into his house in town and she was expected to deliver his first child to great fanfare. The wife was an afterthought. No one would put up a fight.

The detail of the house being protected by half the nobleman's personal guard had been conveniently left out until Maro and I had already scaled the tower under the cover of darkness and were trying to make our egress with the lady in tow. We were halfway clear when one of her tiny dogs had decided to pick a fight with its brother, and a sound like a mourner's chorus had broken out, alerting not only the staff and guard, but no doubt half the county around them.

"Captain!" Maro stood in a narrow doorway, motioning me to follow.

"We have to leave the dogs behind," I said, pulling Lady Amelia along. Her lower lip trembled, and her eyes filled with tears. "It's either them or all of … this." I gestured toward the bedsheet bundle she had slung over one shoulder. She glanced back up the hall, then to me again, and dipped her head once, an apparent capitulation. We continued on.

Maro was several steps ahead of us and threw all their weight against the closest door, forcing it open. Shouts echoed as they charged in, and I followed to find several startled servants in what appeared to be the kitchen.

More importantly, there was a door at the far side of the space, and the small window cut into it said that the outdoors lay beyond.

"Out of the way!" Maro shouted, brandishing their sword. They wouldn't hurt anyone with it—the people here were all frightened and unarmed—but the kitchen staff all scattered, clearing a path as the footsteps clattered in the hall.

Someone shouted orders. But they would be too late.

"Take me with you!"

Maro had the door open when the voice called behind us. A man laughed, but I turned to find a young woman standing ahead of the rest of the cowering servants.

"Excuse me?" I said.

"Take me with you," she said breathlessly. She was skinny, with limp hair that hung in a ragged braid on one shoulder, but she squared her posture and clenched her fists.

"And where do you think we're going?" I asked.

"Captain," Maro warned.

"Anywhere is better than here." She couldn't be more than fourteen.

Lady Amelia hissed. "What are you doing?"

"Captain!"

"Please." The girl rocked on her feet. "My mother died last winter, and if I don't have to serve Lady Amelia anymore, I won't have anything to do. They'll turn me out, and I have nowhere to go."

"Cinder." Maro had come back and grabbed at me, tugging me

toward the door. The girl stumbled after us, and while I didn't tell her not to come, I didn't stop her either. Maro shot me a glance that I ignored. One of us was captain and one was not.

We bolted across a dark stable yard. Lady Amelia's husband must have been confident in the power of the enforcers he had inside the home to repel any invaders, because the property had no gate or wall around it for protection.

For a moment, it seemed as if we were free. I expected the kitchen door to fly open again as we raced toward the trees, but the soldiers didn't come.

At least not on foot.

A few moments later, about halfway to the tree line, hooves thudded behind us. The soldiers had managed to wrangle a few horses and were coming after us.

Maro muttered something that sounded like "This is the last time I—" but the rest was cut off by the pounding of blood in my ears.

"I need you to run faster," I said, pulling Lady Amelia along. She protested, but at least she wore no skirts that would impede her. Sensible boots and trousers. The country of Paranne was archaic enough they still punished women who couldn't provide male heirs, but at least they let them live out their punishment in comfort.

The kitchen girl kept pace with us at least. I was sympathetic to the story she had painted, but we'd been paid to retrieve the lady, not the maid. If she fell behind, I wouldn't stop for her. Maro would have opinions if I did.

Maro disappeared into the trees first, and we were only a few paces behind them. The soldiers called out, but we kept running. The trees thickened around us quickly. I hadn't thought about the possibility of evading riders as we'd come through here earlier in the day, but now I was grateful for the cover. A rider could come through, but not quickly, and since there was no moon to filter light down through the branches, the uneven path would be treacherous.

"Where are we going?" Lady Amelia hissed as we picked our way along a path that only Maro could see. Their years of creeping through the halls and courts of those they'd been paid to kill had left them with certain skills that I would never understand fully but would always appreciate. One of them was their ability to find their way with only the fewest of landmarks to guide them.

"We're headed to safety," I whispered.

"Unless the guards hear that we've stopped for a chat and decide to circle around us," Maro grumbled.

Lady Amelia's hand tightened on my shoulder, but she didn't speak again.

A thin whistle sailed over the air to us. Maro replied with the echoing call, and the whistle came again, a little stronger this time, and my heart relaxed into its usual rhythm. All clear.

Maro moved on.

"This way," I said, and Amelia and the maid followed. Ahead of us, running water babbled a welcome, growing louder as we approached the river that would take us out to safety.

A figure emerged from behind a tree, long and lean like the trunk she'd stood behind. Someone—either Amelia or the maid— gasped in fright.

"She's a friend," I said softly.

So much more than friend. Even if I couldn't see her face right now, my whole being tugged toward her, as it had from the moment she'd been pulled aboard my ship and back into my life after too many years apart.

Maro would have even further opinions about the many soft feelings that floated through me at the sight of George, even if she was barely more than a shadow. Honestly, I had opinions, but the self-preserving instincts to fling myself as far away from

George as possible had been silenced over the past many months. Now I only wanted to keep her as close as possible.

"This way," George whispered. "My lady, nice to meet you."

Lady Amelia made a genteel sound, apparently pleased to find someone who accorded her some respect instead of hauling her around like a sack of grain. Manners were not my strong suit, especially when I was being shot at. George had spent far more time in polite company than I had, and six months at sea was not enough to tarnish her polished way of addressing people. She was beautiful light amid the dark world.

"And another friend for you," I said, trying to draw myself away from those thoughts. Now was not the time. Instead, I prodded the girl in George's direction.

"Who's this?" George asked.

"My name is Elyse," the maid said.

"A complication," Maro grumbled as they climbed into the boat.

"An addition." I couldn't help my grin. Regardless of the circumstances, there was always a perverse joy to be had in Maro's annoyance. It had been the center of our friendship for years.

Case in point: "No oars," I said.

"You can't be serious." Even in the dark, Maro's tired exasperation was obvious. "We're going to drift to safety?"

Trying to get away at any speed would make too much noise, between the splashing as the blades hit the water and the inevitable rattle of the shafts against the gunwales. "The tide is going out. It will pull us to the ocean."

With the others in the longboat, George and I pushed it away from the bank. She climbed in with a silent ease that made me wonder if she'd been taking lessons from Maro when I hadn't been paying attention. I followed after her, ignoring the way the icy water tipped over the inside of my boots and sloshed against my feet.

The consolation was, as the boat drifted downriver, I found a place to slide myself along George's body at the stern. Lady Amelia had been stowed under an oilskin near the bow, and Maro had taken care of Elyse, huddling with her in the boat's middle.

I wrapped an arm over George's side, settling my palm over her stomach. She flinched, but the motion brought her closer against me.

"Your hands are cold," she said.

"You could warm them." I nuzzled at the back of her neck, nose brushing against the slick fabric where she'd tied her hair back in a scarf. Six months aboard the *Crimson Siren* and she'd taken on the salt and tar smell that all sailors had, but underneath there remained a sweetness that I hoped she never lost.

My George. Whatever fates had brought her back to me, I would be in their service forever.

"What will we do with Elyse?" she asked, threading her fingers through mine, drawing them all to her heart.

"We'll figure it out."

For now, I only wanted to be near her. The other questions could wait. We'd been paid to rescue Lady Amelia and bring her back to her parents' house. A stowaway maid was inconsequential.

Then again, we'd been paid once to seize a princess from the prince who had terrorized his people and claimed her as his bride, and she had also come with an unexpected companion. And while I would always love George more, I suspected my crew would place higher value on the loyal maid who had snuck aboard with her. Rosie had since become our cook, saving many of us from bouts of dehydration and intestinal distress that came with her predecessor's never-ending salt fish stew.

"Captain," Maro said softly, but the word still held urgency.

It was hard to know how long we had been drifting. One of

the ribs of the longboat's hull dug into my hip, and even George's skin was cool under my touch now.

"Yes?"

"Lady Amelia's husband appears to be more concerned with her well-being than we were led to believe."

A sound that might have been a snort came from under the tarp. Certainly not very ladylike. I pushed up on my elbow and peered over the side of the longboat.

"Well, that is problematic."

We were coming out of the river's mouth. The beach was a long gray expanse of sand that stretched into the distance. Unfortunately, a hundred yards away from us, a line of lights bobbed in the dark, not unlike the way torches might if they were carried by men riding fast-moving horses. There had to be fifty of them.

"We'll be outnumbered at least ten to one," I said.

"You assume the lady and the maid can fight," Maro said.

"I did say 'at least.'"

"Can we make it to the ocean?" George asked.

I squinted ahead of us. The white demarcation of the breaking waves was still a long way off, and the horses were closing quickly.

Then the boat stopped. It settled with the gentle hiss that said it had buried itself into a sandy embankment.

The horses were getting closer, the sound of their hooves audible now.

This was not at all the job that had been sold to us. One woman no one wanted in a house away from anything.

George was already moving, hopping over the side and pushing against the longboat, trying to guide it back out into the current.

Men's voices called to each other. "They're here. At the river!"

"George, get back in the boat," I said.

A shot cracked through the air. Lady Amelia and Elyse screamed. No one needed to tell them to stay low. George was still on the beach, and even as I went to leap to her side, my whole body froze as panic clawed at my throat. She was so exposed. We all were.

Maro swore and swung over the side, putting their weight into the beached vessel. It gave a little, timbers creaking against the sand. A familiar whistle sang out from over the waves.

"Get down!" I shouted. Maro dropped. George was still pushing on the gunwale. Finally, I flung myself over the edge and tucked an arm around her waist, though now romance was the farthest thing from my mind. I pulled us both down.

The blast as the ball hit the beach shook the world beneath me, vibrating through my chest. George grunted as a wave of wet sand cascaded from the ball's impact and showered over us. Beyond us, horses shrieked and men shouted.

Just as I was about to push myself to my feet and see if the impact had jarred the longboat loose, another whistle sailed over the air. I wrapped both hands over my head, trusting that Ender knew what he was doing at the guns.

The second blast was closer. The screams from the horses were more desperate. Fewer torches lit the night, and the groans of injured and dying men grew louder as their mounts bolted back down the sand.

The three of us put all our weight into the longboat, and it slid back into the water as if it had always meant to be there. This time we rowed as another blast sang through the night. Whether or not it hit anyone, the message was clear, and the men on the shore went from a determined hunting party to a chaotic and disorganized pack as some fled and others shouted for them to hold the line.

George and I put our backs into the oars and carried our small crew out to sea.

"Welcome back, Captain," Ender said, voice relaxed and jovial as I climbed over the rail of the *Crimson Siren*.

"Ender," I said, panting from the exertion of the row back to the ship and the climb up the swinging rope ladder. "Thank you for the intervention."

He smiled, face half shadowed in the lamplight. "We saw those torches and figured you might have had a spot of trouble."

"She wouldn't let us row," Maro said as they helped Lady Amelia on board.

"Too much splashing." Ender stroked his dark red beard sagely, and I threw Maro a look, which they ignored. Ender gave Lady Amelia a friendly salute. "My lady. Welcome aboard the *Crimson Siren*."

She eyed him nervously, mouth working on a question, but whatever she was about to say was cut off as Elyse stumbled over the side and collided with her mistress. They landed in a heap on the deck, and George gave them a bemused glance as she finally came over the rail.

"Who's this?" Ender asked.

"A friend," I said, waiting for Maro's cutting retort, but they had apparently had enough now that we were back on the ship and remained silent. "Take the lady to her cabin."

"And the friend?" Ender asked.

"She can go too."

"I'm not sleeping with a servant," Lady Amelia said as she pushed herself upright.

And we had all been getting along so well.

"Lady," I said, trying to maintain a veneer of respect. "I'm the captain, and the sleeping arrangements will be at my discretion."

"But you can't possibly—" Lady Amelia started.

"I very much can. The cabin has bunks for two. There is no place for class differences on my ship. When you go back to your family, you can—"

"My family?" Her eyes widened.

"Yes. Your parents are very eager—"

"I can't go back there. You'll have to take me somewhere else."

Did we not just discuss that she wasn't in a position to make demands?

"Lady, this is not a pleasure cruise. Your parents—"

She placed her hands on her hips and squared her shoulders in a way I recognized from George when she got an idea fixed in her head. "My parents married me off to that oaf and then let me rot in that house for three years, and today they want me back?" Lady Amelia sneered. "I'm sure what's truly happened is they found another foolish husband looking to earn my father's goodwill by saying he'll have me regardless of the possibility of not gaining an heir. So now I'm worthy enough to return? No." She waved a hand. "I won't go back there. Take me somewhere else."

My spine stiffened at her command, but before I could say anything, George snaked a hand around my waist.

"Of course, my lady." Her voice vibrated gently through my ribs. "We'll talk about a destination in the morning. Ender. Show the lady to her cabin."

Maro's jaw was tight. Their relationship with George was one of tentative mutual respect, but they took exception when George started to issue orders. My ship may not have classes, but we had a hierarchy, and George's place in it was ambiguous.

I glanced at Elyse, who hung back as Ender led Amelia away. "Where do you propose we put her?"

George yawned. "For tonight, she can sleep with us."

I groaned. The bed in my cabin was the most luxurious on the ship, but by any standards it was still a tight fit for the two of us. Adding a third was impossible, not to mention inappropriate.

But George must have seen the confusion on my face because she smiled, pulling on a lock of my hair. "The outer cabin, silly. She can sleep on the sofa, and in the morning, I'll have Rosie find a place for her."

I wanted to protest, mostly on the principle that I didn't like Lady Amelia getting away with her edict that she not sleep with servants. But before I could, George pressed a gentle kiss to my lips, and my objections melted under her touch. She could undo me with the smallest gesture.

She led Elyse away, and I was about to follow when Maro came to stand by my side.

"Are you all right?" they asked.

"Of course." The reply came automatically. "We've escaped worse."

"You hesitated."

I had been about to walk away, and now—once again—I found myself pausing.

"When?"

"On the beach. Before Ender fired."

"I didn't."

"Cinder."

I nearly told them not to call me that. It wasn't my name. George called me Lou. That was who I was, or at least who I was trying to be. Cinder was a creature of the brokers. I'd left Cinder behind when Maro and I had escaped Kiril's service.

But Cinder had also been Maro's friend and captain for years. They'd struggled to accept George among our ranks. I didn't want to make more difficulty for them.

"It was nothing," I said. They waited silently for me to say more, and instead, I left them to the watch. We had nothing more to discuss.

George waited for me in the inner cabin. This room was our haven. Outside, I was the captain. Here, at least, I was Lou. Her Lou.

She hissed as she pulled her shirt over her head.

"What's wrong?" I asked.

George winced as she held her forearm up to inspect. The underside was a long, bloody scrape.

"I caught it on the edge of the longboat when you pulled me down."

I grimaced. I'd only wanted to protect her, and I'd hurt her.

"I'm sorry," I said, taking her hand in mine so I could kiss her wrist. Her fingers against my jaw spoke of forgiveness, and I closed my eyes. So many years had passed without this kindness. I wanted to bathe in it. Soak it into my pores so I would never lose it again.

We lay back to front in the narrow bed, my nose against the nape of George's neck as I had in the longboat. The way I did every night.

She had come back to me and loved me despite the black edges of my soul.

I would protect her at the expense of all else for the rest of my life.

CHAPTER 2

The next day didn't start much better. On the face of it, everyone went about their business undisturbed. George spent the morning working in the infirmary with the doctor, mixing potions and learning his trade, as she often did to pass the time. Around me, the crew worked with the casual precision that could only come from years of repetition. They kept the sails trimmed, the decks clean, and played games like knuckles when time permitted. All was peaceful and as it should be.

On closer inspection though, we had anything but peace, at least in terms of concluding the issue of Lady Amelia's destination.

"I will not be going back to my father's."

In the daylight, with no one shooting at us, it was easier to take in her appearance. She was older than I was by a good ten years, with wispy hair showing early signs of gray and a stubborn set to her jaw that only intensified the longer we argued.

"My lady, I'm sorry, but it's really not up for discussion. Your father paid us, and as a result—"

"He thinks everything can be fixed with money. Have an ugly

daughter? Marry her off to a count with an estate the size of my eyeball. The ugly daughter won't produce an heir? Buy her back and shuttle her off to some other unsuspecting lout who might at least own a few horses."

No one had said anything about her looks. And I didn't find her unattractive. She had a square jaw that added strength to her profile and round hips that held her trousers snug. A man would call them child-bearing hips, and therein lay the problem.

Or one of the problems.

"If she doesn't want to return to her family ..." George said slowly, her back to Amelia and the rest of the crew, who were also doing their dutiful best to pretend they weren't listening.

It was true. Amelia was hardly a lost child. She was a grown woman, and if she didn't want to be forced back under her father's roof, I couldn't argue against it.

Maro came to stand at my other shoulder.

"Captain," they said slowly. "It's unlikely the lady's father will take kindly if we don't return her to him, especially since we have already accepted payment."

There was that. Men like Amelia's father, who thought money was the source of all power, often took exception when their money was taken and goods and services not exchanged. If we left his daughter somewhere else and carried on without a word to him, that might not go well for Maro and me and the rest of our crew.

But the mission of the *Crimson Siren* and the sailors aboard her was to help women in trouble, not transport them from one bad situation to another. And Amelia was a human being with rights and needs of her own, not a horse or a prize pig to be carted wherever the highest bidder asked. My parents had sold me off at twelve for the mere price of not having to feed me anymore. I wouldn't let that happen to any woman of any age ever again.

"We could take her to Davina?" George said.

I couldn't help my laugh. "Somehow, I don't think Lady Amelia would appreciate the offer of employment at Davi's." Davina operated a brothel in Beldridge Landing. By any stretch of the imagination, it was a reputable and well-run establishment, and more than a few of the women who had come aboard the *Siren* had been more than happy for the refuge Davi offered when they'd had no control over their lives previously, but an aristocratic lady like Amelia would likely not feel the same way.

"Not to work there," George said.

"Then to see the sights?" I asked.

George shrugged. "Davi told me she'd helped others move on. Maybe she can do that for Lady Amelia?"

It was worth considering. And there was the question of Elyse. At a place like Beldridge, there was always a means to earn a living, either as one of Davi's girls or as a maid in one of the big houses that lined the periphery of the city. Beldridge was a lively place where people went to start over. Lady Amelia's future wasn't my responsibility. I only had to set her up somewhere she would be safe.

"Let's go visit the Captain's Peg."

BELDRIDGE LANDING always seemed to glow. The buildings along the wharf were covered in a white plaster that was nearly blinding when the sun shone on it at midday. The city was a hub, a port for trade, with fertile fishing grounds offshore that brought fleets from neighboring countries to try their luck.

The last time we'd been to Beldridge, I'd felt pulled so taut I might break. George had been on the Siren for only a few days, and I was terrified to spend too much time with her, lest the illusion of the friend she'd lost be shattered with the creature I'd become. But at the same time, I'd felt the tick of a clock over my head, counting down the waning minutes I had left with her and regretting every one.

Now, months later, she was still here, and the idea that we might enjoy ourselves was so tempting. But first, there was the question of our passengers.

The Captain's Peg sat at the corner of a busy intersection in the middle of Beldridge Landing. Davina, the owner, had been one of the earliest women I'd been hired to bring to a new life, and what a life she'd made it. The brothel was already bustling, men and women leaning out the upper windows and calling to passersby, while customers swaggered in and out. I had always liked the freedom in Beldridge. The people here felt no shame about who they loved and did so openly, to the point that a place like the Peg could operate in the open the way a bakery or tailor's shop might.

A shriek sounded and I tensed, moving George behind me, but then the Peg's door burst open and a flurry of bright blue hair and colored silks burst into the street and right into me.

"Captain!" Davi wrapped herself around me, squealing with delight.

"Hello, Davina. Pleasure as always."

She dropped to her feet, smiling from ear to ear, then her smile grew even wider when she saw George.

"Princess!"

"Davi." George gave her a hug.

"I didn't think I'd see you again."

George blushed, cheeks staining pink in the late day sun. "Yes, well, my previous … difficulty has resolved itself."

Davi raised a playful eyebrow, and her cheek dimpled where she was no doubt chewing on it to suppress her laughter. "Yes, I heard the prince met his end. The details were vague. I gather it's caused quite a stir in your homeland."

"What do you mean?" George asked.

"Power does abhor a vacuum and all that. And the death of the tyrant of Redmere has left a fairly large gap in the power structure. I've heard rumors there's a duke who's trying his hand at ruling. Some talk about him like a great liberator arrived to set his people free. And yet there are a growing number of Redmerians trying to escape to new homes elsewhere, so maybe salvation isn't all it's cracked up to be."

"Davi," I said. We hadn't come all this way to talk about politics in Redmere. Or leave an opportunity open for George to admit to killing her former husband—even if he'd only been a husband for a few hours—in the middle of a busy street.

"Yes, of course," Davi clucked, glancing around at the rest of our party. This wasn't the first time I'd shown up on her doorstep with a desire to keep my business to myself. "Come in. All of you. I have everything you need."

"Captain," Ender said as the rest of us moved toward the Peg's front door.

"Yes?"

"I'll accompany Rosie to the market, if that's all right with you?" He put an arm around Rosie's shoulder. Not that she needed it. Rosie knew how to look after herself. But she allowed Ender to play his role as doting protector. They so rarely had a moment alone. I certainly couldn't deny them now.

"Of course. Find us here when you're finished."

They walked away, melding into the crowd, two red heads together.

Inside the Captain's Peg, Davi seated us around a corner table. Business was swift, and my companions viewed the various couples and groups with various degrees of disinterest, disdain, and intrigue.

"Does this still make you uncomfortable?" I asked George. The heat on her cheeks spread higher, and I wished we were alone so I could kiss the blush of pink off her skin.

"No," she said, ducking her head. "Only now, I know so much better what they're doing and I …" Her gaze drifted up to mine, and immediately, we were both too warm.

"So what can I do for you?" Davi asked, settling into the chair next to mine. Her smile was knowing. She'd always known too much. When we'd been here the last time, I could tell she saw through my indifference toward George. Now she knew immediately what we were thinking and would play it to her advantage as much as possible.

I cleared my throat, trying to muster what few defenses I could. "We're here to find Lady Amelia a new home. She's unimpressed with the options offered by either her husband or her father, and we felt you might have better avenue to help her."

Davi glanced thoughtfully between me and Lady Amelia. "I assume you aren't looking for work in a place like mine."

Lady Amelia didn't say anything, but the tightening of her jaw was answer enough.

Davi turned back to me. "It won't be cheap. With Redmere in turmoil, there are more people leaving the country. It's hard to find caravans and escorts, even this far away, and those who will take a fine lady like your friend here will ask a hefty price."

"We'll pay," I said. "We were paid well to collect her in the first place." If we weren't going to deliver her to the people who had paid us, it only seemed fair to use their funds to help Amelia complete her journey.

"Excellent." Davi snapped a finger, and two serving men appeared, each carrying bottles of wine and trays of food. "Then stay for dinner while we haggle."

"Elyse will need a place too," I said, gesturing toward the girl. She surged forward like she'd been waiting to be summoned.

"Please," she said, speaking directly to Davi. "I can do anything you want."

"Anything?" Davi arched a brow. "How old are you?"

"Fifteen."

"Too young for customers. I don't do that here."

Elyse shook her head. "I can cook. Or clean. Whatever you need."

Davi glanced at me, furrowed forehead questioning. I shrugged. She knew the story. There were girls like Elyse the whole world over. Few were lucky enough to find their way to a place like the Peg.

She sighed and jerked her head. "Go find the kitchen. Tell the cook I sent you. If you haven't broken too many dishes by the end of the week, you can stay."

Elyse scurried away. Davi clapped her hands. "Excellent. Now back to the question of the lady's travels."

"Here." The declaration was followed by a heavy thump as a thick gold bracelet landed on the table we sat around. The group grew quiet as our attention turned one by one to Lady Amelia, who sat with her arms folded over her chest.

"Well, now. That's quite the trinket." Davi was the first to collect herself. It was more than a trinket in fact. Several inches wide and crescent-shaped. It shone in the candlelight.

"A wedding gift," Amelia said. "From my husband. You're welcome to it if you can get me away from here."

Davi grinned. "Generous husband."

"His gifts were the only part of him I liked."

"Are you sure you don't want a job?" Davi taunted gently. "I have a number of clients who would appreciate your talent for telling them exactly how despicable they are."

"I'd rather not," Amelia said.

"Unfortunate. But understandable. In any case"—she rapped the bracelet against the table—"I believe our negotiation is concluded. Should we eat?"

The Captain's Peg may have made their business as a brothel, but if you stayed long enough to get hungry, they also served an excellent dinner. Or perhaps my perspective was skewed after too many years at sea, where meals were cooked using whatever would keep in a damp mess for weeks or months at a time. Either way, by the time we were stuffed full of smoked fowl with sweet fruits and fresh greens, I was too sated to move. Ender and Rosie had joined us after their market trip, and I tried not to make my praise to Davi's cook too loud. Rosie would see it as a challenge to improve what she served us on the ship, and she already took excellent care of us.

Eventually, Davi had one of the servants take Lady Amelia up to an unoccupied room for the night. I wouldn't see her again. I wouldn't wonder what had become of her. My part in her story was done.

Or so I thought.

But later in the evening, full and warm with good wine, I excused myself from the table. Most guests might go relieve themselves in an alley somewhere, but even in a friendly place like this, I didn't like the moment of vulnerability. Instead, I made my way upstairs, looking for an empty room and an unused chamber pot.

"Captain."

I paused at the sound of my name. Amelia stood in the doorway of a room.

"Lady," I said, trying to give her a friendly smile.

"I'm sorry if I was difficult. On the ship. The last few years have been … challenging."

"It's no matter," I said.

"I must seem silly to you. Living in a fine house with all the meals I could want and little dogs to play with."

She was interfering with my easy mood. I said, "I'm happy to bring you to safety."

But she pressed on—and pressed something into my hand. "Thank you. I know it might seem like I didn't need to be rescued from much, but you've changed my life."

"What's this?" The cloth-wrapped bundle was the size of my palm. The material was old and stained.

"Payment. I found it in the house. I had lots of time to explore."

I went to unwrap the twine that held the bundle shut, but she put a hand over mine. "Later. Better to keep it to yourself."

Like the bracelet. She had handed that over like it had no more value than a flower she'd picked in a field. In the wrong place, she wouldn't have left the room alive.

I glanced over her shoulder. The sheet she'd grabbed from her room was spread on the bed. The contents inside had been laid out. Mostly clothes. Leather and wool. But among them, the unmistakable sparkle of jewels and gold.

I whistled softly. "That's quite the going away present, lady."

She smiled wryly. "As I said, my husband was very generous. Perhaps he felt guilty for what he'd done to me. Goodnight, Captain."

She closed the door, leaving me alone in the hall. I hefted the small parcel one more time. Best to heed her words and wait until I had some privacy. I reached into my shirt and pulled out the length of leather tied around my neck. A delicate silver circle was looped through it. I'd found the small bracelet in the dirt beneath an ancient tree when George and I were small. At the time, I thought I'd discovered a hidden treasure. I'd given it to George like a knight seeking to win the beautiful princess's favor. And she'd seen the treasure for what it was, keeping it with her in all the years we were apart and bringing it back to me.

I undid the leather and slipped it through the strings of Amelia's bundle before tying it around my neck again. Time to look at it later. Maybe George and I would find new treasure to share.

As I returned downstairs, my crew and closest friends were obviously settled in. I sat down, and George leaned against my side. She was interrogating Davi about her hair and how she had managed to get it that specific shade of very vibrant blue. George wore her hair uncovered today, though most days on the *Siren* she still wore it tied up in a cloth. She swore it was only for practicality's sake and not any old hang-up from years of living under Redmere's oppressive modesty laws. Despite her reassurances, she still only let it out loose completely when we were alone. Now, it was braided tightly against the nape of her neck. Maybe if Davi could entice her with the thrill of a new color or embellishment, she might find some bravery she hadn't known about.

On my other side, Rosie sat in Ender's lap. They'd been feeding each other bits of cheese and sweets, but now their attention was fixed on a handsome man with violet tattoos on his hands and arms, and twinkling jewels pierced through each nipple. He flirted shamelessly, and while Ender and Rosie were very much a pair on board the ship, neither one of them looked particularly upset at the newcomer's arrival.

Even Maro, who sat across the table from me, was speaking with a young woman who had been circling us slowly all night. She hadn't been able to take her eyes off Maro, and now that our meal was over, she'd taken her chance to sit next to them. The two were engaged in deep conversation and sat closer than new acquaintances would if they were discussing the weather and the cost of cephyr oil. Every so often, Maro would trace a finger along the back of the woman's hand, and once, I thought they were even about to smile.

"Stay the night," Davi said suddenly.

"What?" My attention swung back from the contemplation of my friends.

"I can always make rooms available for you and your crew."

"And room in your coffers, I don't doubt," I said, tightening my arm around George.

Davi grinned. "Your lady paid well, and I'm feeling charitable."

The lump of Lady Amelia's packet hung in my shirt, and I was suddenly very curious as to what it contained. "We'll go back to the *Siren*."

The chorus of protest that came up from around the table surprised me.

"What's one night?" Rosie asked.

"I can pay for a room for me and the little miss," Ender said. The way the tattooed man had a palm on Ender's thigh said it wouldn't be a room for only the two of them.

"Oh, Lou," George said. "Just one night."

I glanced at Maro, expecting them to come to my support, but their hand was laced with the pretty young woman's, and they gave me a one-shouldered shrug that said they'd do as they wished.

George leaned into my side, chin resting on my shoulder so that only I could hear her when she spoke.

"Please," she said again. "Any bed Davi gives us will be so much bigger than ours. Just one night."

Her eyes were huge as I pulled away. A single curl of hair had come loose from its coil and brushed against her cheek. I glanced again at the others, but their attention was already back on their new friends like everything had been settled.

"Well," I said.

"Excellent!" Davi clapped her hands. "I'll have beds made up. You and the princess will have a place of honor. Unless you'd like to share with one of my ladies?"

"A bed for two will be fine," I said rather quickly, and Davi gave me her all-too-knowing smile again.

The evening after that was a blur. Surprisingly, Maro and their young woman disappeared first, but perhaps only because Maro would always value discretion above everything else, while Ender and Rosie seemed to have no such compunctions. The golden man had his hand up Rosie's skirt, and she had her head tipped back to kiss Ender. The three of them didn't care that they were out in the open for anyone to see. Then again, the glittering creatures around them—Davi's employees and the people they befriended for the night—weren't looking, each of them occupied with their own pleasure.

I had a hand in George's hair, fingers worming their way into the tight strands at her nape. She tilted her head back, exposing her throat as she closed her eyes, and it was so tempting to touch her right there. To kiss her and enjoy ourselves like everyone around us was.

She shivered when I grazed my lips across her neck.

"Let's go find that bed," I said, and she practically leapt to her feet and dragged me in the direction Davi indicated.

Whatever modesty George felt in public, when we were alone, she didn't hesitate. Mouth, hands, she was on me in a second, and I was happy to drown in her touch and her kisses. She let me take her hair down and bury my face in the thick strands.

"George."

"I love you."

She said it so often. Nightly. I would never get tired of hearing it. Some days I even believed it. When she let me touch her and didn't recoil, as if she could pretend the blood that would never be fully off my hands wasn't even there, I felt loved.

Davi's sheets must have been soaked in perfume, because after we'd exhausted ourselves, the world spun. I was dizzy on the floral fumes that wafted around us and the intoxicating experience of being the center of George's affection.

"What do you think is happening in Redmere?" she asked. "Davi said there's been some trouble."

My princess certainly knew how to kill a mood when she wanted to.

"I don't think," I said.

"What do you mean?" She rolled, brown hair catching around her shoulders and sliding over her skin.

"I don't think about that place."

"But it's home." She reached for my hand, and instead I pulled my arms over my head as though I needed to stretch.

"Yours, maybe. It hasn't been mine in years."

We'd never talked about this before. Maybe once, in those early days after she'd first come on the ship and all I'd been able to do was use cruelty as a shield to keep her from seeing who I'd become, but that hadn't been a conversation. Only a series of volleyed insults masquerading as self-preservation.

"You never think about going back?" she asked.

"Why would I? I have you here with me." Beldridge was closer to Redmere than we'd been in a while, but that didn't mean we were going to be making a side trip. There was nothing for us there.

"But—"

I stopped whatever she was about to say next with a kiss, one she happily gave in to. For another long while, all thoughts of Redmere were forgotten, until we had twisted Davi's sheets into an unmanageable knot. George, sweat cooling on her skin, made a happy noise as she settled against my side. The food and wine weighed me down.

Sometime later, I woke, and the room was quiet and the bed was cool, even though my skin still held the memory of George's touch.

A sound came from close by, like a single scuff of a foot on the floor, followed by a muffled protest in a woman's soft voice.

George's voice.

I was fully awake in an instant, though I kept my eyes closed, trying to gather what I could remember of the night before. My clothes, the knife I always carried at my hip, they had all been strewn haphazardly about the room. Forgotten because I'd felt safe and at home, surrounded by friends and the woman I loved the most.

And now, when I opened my eyes gently, the same woman was being held by a man who had my very knife held to her throat. Tears streaked her cheeks. One of his hands was clamped over her mouth, and when she made the same frightened sound again, he smiled and pressed the blade against her skin.

Another man appeared, stepping out of the shadows. He moved so slowly I didn't hear him at first, and couldn't stop my flinch as he entered my line of sight. His face was hidden under a hood, but his smile glinted in the thin candlelight of the room.

"Hello, Cinder." His voice curled like a cat who had already trapped the mouse. "It's time we had a talk."

CHAPTER 3

The shadowed man held the candle close to my face, making me squint.

"You're not much to look at, are you?" he asked.

I couldn't tell if he found me unimpressive or unattractive. Neither opinion worried me much. Many had made the mistake of underestimating me. And the only person who I needed to appreciate my looks was George.

But I wouldn't underestimate him. Yes, I'd gotten complacent. Lulled by food and drink, George's body against mine, and the supposed haven that Beldridge represented. Still, he had succeeded where many others had failed, and that made him worthy of a measure of my regard.

I lifted a hand to shade my eyes. "I'd say you're not much to look at either, but I can't see you at all."

He leaned back. The flame flickered and settled as he placed the candle on the small table by the bed. His hair was dark, face tanned. He wore a narrow moustache and a thin tail of hair that curled over one shoulder. As if we had all the time in the world, he lit a pipe off the candle and inhaled slowly. I threw another glance at George, who was watching me with frightened eyes, and the man holding her smiled, tipping her chin up, in case I had missed the blade he held the first time.

"My name is Hafir," the man with the pipe said, bringing my attention back. "You've caused quite a lot of problems."

I did my best to smile, trying to ground myself in the role I had played so many times before.

"What fun would I have if I didn't cause some trouble?"

He shook his head as he puffed on his pipe. "The brokers would have preferred you choose a different sort of trouble."

Anger coiled under my skin. The brokers. That explained a lot. And their involvement said this was truly someone to be respected. I didn't have to like him, but the brokers' agents and assassins excelled at what they did. I should know. Maro and I had been in their place once. The best among us, in fact. These two were lucky they'd broken into our room. If they'd tried Maro's, Hafir and his colleague would already be dead.

"You're here to kill us, then?" I asked. George inhaled sharply. The man with the knife was no doubt trying to make his point felt, but I wouldn't look at him. They already knew George was valuable to me. I wouldn't give them any more information as to how precious she truly was.

Hafir smiled. "If the brokers wanted you executed, I wouldn't have bothered to wake you up."

Assassins were an efficient bunch. Better to slit someone's throat in their sleep and be gone than to risk awakening them so you could revel in their fear. Those who worked for pleasure or notoriety didn't last long. Someone screamed or fought back, other people were alerted, and sooner or later, they were caught as they tried to escape.

"So if you aren't here to kill us …"

He smiled through a ring of smoke. "I'm here to collect your debt."

"I owe the brokers nothing." I had already paid. Maro and I were free.

"Well, you didn't," Hafir said. "Until you killed one of them. They don't take that lightly. A debt is owed."

"I hadn't realized the brokers cared about each other so much." As far as I knew, they were kings with no kingdom. They hoarded gold and power like mythical dragons while taking lives and riches as they willed. I'd delivered wealth and weapons to some of the others occasionally, but apart from these transactions, I'd never known Kiril to have any real connection or affinity to the rest.

The man tsked. "You upset the balance, Cinder. Kiril supplied sailors to the others at a good price."

Yes, I knew about Kiril's sailors too. I had recruited more than my fair share. Frightened fisherman and merchants who chose to sail under his banner rather than be sent to the bottom of the ocean. When Captain Cinder offered you a chance to live, you took it, even if the conditions were less than ideal. They were cheap and abundant labor, if not always completely willing.

"Surely there are other places to hire a crew," I said.

"But not at that price. Very expensive now. Very inconvenient."

"You'll understand if I'm not sympathetic."

"You should be. The shortage is your fault."

His information was bad. Kiril's death was on Maro's hands, not mine. I'd been busy bleeding out on the ground. But at this point, with George and me cornered, Hafir wouldn't care about the minutiae of who killed who, so I didn't correct him. Instead, I let the sheets drop from my chest. I was naked, but the gesture wasn't meant to distract him, it was to remind him that I was not afraid.

"I'm still finding it very hard to commiserate with their inconvenience."

"Well yes, I did expect that. That's why I have my friend here." He gestured at the man who held George. "We needed to make sure we have your attention."

With no warning, the man swung his blade down. It sliced into George's thigh, and she arched. Her cry was muffled under his palm, but still the sound of it cut through me deeper than any knife might.

"Stop," I said, gritting my teeth.

"Are you listening, Cinder?" Hafir asked.

I could barely take my eyes off the line of red that welled up on George's skin and spilled over her leg, but I nodded.

"You know a cut like that isn't severe," he said, puffing new smoke rings into the air like we were talking about old sea battles and fabled monsters. "She'll scar, but she'll live. The next one though—" He nodded at the knife man, who placed the blade against the inside of her thigh. I had kissed that spot only hours ago. And I had also killed more than one man with a wound in the same place. It was fast … too fast for the victim to seek help. The poor failing heart inside would push his life out before he could run a few hundred yards.

"I'm listening," I said, forcing myself to icy calm, even as rage seethed inside me. There would be time for revenge later. When Hafir was comfortable in the thought he'd gotten away with whatever plot he had, I would find him and kill him. For now, though, I would listen.

"Payment," he said, with no further preamble. "You owe the brokers compensation."

I owed them nothing.

"And what is the life of a broker worth?" I asked.

He tilted his head, as if he were doing the mental calculation. As if he had any say in what the brokers wanted. Whoever this man was, he was one of their creatures, like I was. An instrument, but not the musician who drew the bow.

"Thirty thousand gold pieces. Or thereabouts. The equivalent in jewels would be satisfactory, if you prefer."

I snorted. "Is that all?"

The man who held George pressed his thumb against the

wound in her thigh, making fresh blood leak out. She squirmed and whimpered against his crushing hold.

"I'd heard you considered yourself something of a comedian," Hafir said. "But I really don't see that this is something to laugh at. You're lucky we don't take your lady here as collateral."

My scalp prickled at the thought. Kiril and the prince had taken her from me once. Only Maro's quick actions and George's bravery had brought us together again. If they took her a second time, I would set the oceans on fire to find her.

Hafir grinned. "Yes, I see you understand the scope of what we're expecting. Thirty thousand gold coins. A king's ransom to buy safety for you and your princess."

"I don't have that."

"Of course not. We'd know if you did." He stood. His colleague did not, holding tight to George until Hafir was at the door. "You have a month to find the money and deliver it."

"To where?"

He put his hand on the door. "Triere is expecting you."

Triere. I'd heard the name, but never met the owner. But I knew how to find him. He lived in a lavish estate on a lonely island. We'd delivered goods and prisoners to him on Kiril's behalf from time to time but only ever dealt with subordinates.

Hafir must have taken my silence as hesitation, because he said, "We'll find you if you try to disappear."

"You know I don't run," I said, fists clenching.

He shrugged. "I was told you might feel differently now. We found you here. We'll know where you go."

The brokers had eyes everywhere. How long had Hafir been here in Beldridge, waiting for the opportunity to deliver his message?

"I don't run," I said again.

Hafir grinned and tucked his pipe away. "Then I look forward to doing business with you and your crew, Cinder."

The big man finally let George free. She rushed toward me and I gathered her up, holding her tight while Hafir and his friend slipped out the door. The warmth of her body against mine, even as she shook and gulped back sobs, calmed my racing heart.

"I'm sorry. I'm sorry," she said over and over.

"Shh, no. Dear heart. It's fine." I smoothed her hair from her tear-streaked face.

"I should have fought him harder. I didn't hear him."

"No, love. My fault. You're not expected to—"

But the apologies continued to tumble from her lips. George always took blame where none was needed. "We shouldn't have stayed here. I'm sorry for insisting. We should have gone back to the ship. We'd have been safer."

"Shh. You couldn't have known." Though I should have. Staying on land was never safe. The brokers waited in every port. How many times, in Kiril's service, had I come ashore to be met by an agent who told me exactly when and where to find my prey? Someone always knew where you were.

"Let me see your leg." I laid a hand on her thigh and she yelped, flinching away like a frightened animal. The action held so much fear, it broke my heart.

"George?"

A gentle knock came on the door. George scrambled backward, trailing blood on Davi's fine sheets, until she hit the headboard.

"George? Lou?" Rosie's voice came softly through the door. "I heard something. Are you all right?"

"One moment," I said. I found my shirt and tugged it over my head, then pulled the blankets over George. Rosie was her closest friend, but George wouldn't want to be seen like this. *I* didn't want it either. Not when the evidence of my failure to protect her was so clear.

I opened the door partway and Rosie stood there in a gauzy

dressing gown and carrying a candle. The expression on her face was concerned but held no fear or anger.

"Is everything all right?" she asked again. "I heard someone crying."

Her kindness made my throat tighten. She was at risk now too, and she didn't even know it. Ender. Maro. All of them. I'd told Hafir I wouldn't run, and I'd meant it. We might be able to hide, George and I. We could sail off the end of the world and disappear into a jungle where the brokers would never find us again. But in doing so, we'd put a target on the backs of everyone else we cared about. You didn't cross the brokers. I'd enforced that rule too many times to feign ignorance now. Anyone who attempted to run away or fight back wound up in an unmarked grave or washed up on the shore half eaten by the creatures that lurked in the deep, and so did everyone who had helped them or would mourn their passing.

"Nothing," I said to Rosie with a reassuring smile. "A nightmare. Too much wine maybe."

Her frown deepened and she tried to peer over my shoulder, but I held still, blocking her view. One look at George and she'd know we were dealing with no mere nightmare.

Finally, Rosie nodded. The smile she gave in reply to my own was too trusting by half. If she knew what had truly happened, she'd never let George out of her sight again. Rosie loved her nearly as fiercely as I did. But she stepped back and disappeared down the hall, no doubt returning to the place Ender kept warm for her by his side. Maybe their tattooed friend was still there and they could enjoy themselves for a few hours longer.

George was pale when I returned, but her trembling had stopped.

"Let me see," I said as I pulled the covers back. The blood on her thigh was smeared against her pale skin and congealing in a dark line. I'd seen so much blood in my life, but none of it induced the same blistering fear inside me that George's did.

"Why didn't you tell her?" she asked.

"Not tonight." Let them have the rest of this evening in peace. My chance at sleep was over. I'd look out for them, stalking the halls until dawn. Hafir and his friend would be long gone anyway. They needed to give us time to work.

I found George's shirt on the floor and helped her slide into it like a child. The idea that Hafir and the knife man had seen her naked—had touched her—made my hands twitch with the urge to stab someone, and I accidentally tugged at the wound, the darkening blood turning red again. George hissed and I whispered apologies as I bound her leg with strips of cloth torn from the stained sheets.

"But tomorrow? We'll tell the crew? Maro?"

The mention of Maro's name had me jerking again, though I managed to keep from undoing my gentle ministrations this time. If I told Maro what happened, they would want to fight. A war. They were very clear after the last time. They would track Hafir and the big man down and make sure they never made it back to the brokers. Then they'd go after the brokers themselves for daring to retract the promise Kiril had made to us. It would be vicious and bloody, and the risk would be tremendous. With Maro's skills, they might even succeed in finding and killing one or two brokers, but soon enough word would get out to the others, and we'd have an entire ocean of assassins on our trail, ready to murder us all in retribution.

"Lou?" George said softly, and her sweet voice made my chest ache.

I forced a smile as I looked up at her. "Trust me."

"But—"

I bent to kiss her knee where my poor attempt at a bandage ended. She was so alive and warm beneath my lips, and she needed to stay that way. "I'm so sorry this happened."

She gave me her bravest smile. "The perils of loving a pirate."

Her words made my stomach go sour. I nearly told her I

wasn't a pirate, as petulant as the protest might have sounded. George always insisted she wasn't a princess, and perhaps she never truly had been one. But my past identity and deeds couldn't be so easily overlooked. Loving me shouldn't come with risks and dangers I'd incurred in my old life. The last few years, I had worked so hard—if not to undo the hurt I had caused under Kiril's banner, at least to atone for it.

But it seemed that life wasn't done with me yet.

THE FOLLOWING MORNING, we made our way slowly back to the *Siren*. Rosie and Ender were essentially holding each other up. Even Maro moved more gingerly than usual. Davi's wine had done its work. Fortunately, it meant they weren't in any shape to notice if George was also limping slightly. I held her hand and grimaced at every sharp intake of breath, but she insisted she was ready to work as we prepared to depart. Maro gave the orders to the crew to make sail, and I retreated to my cabin before the whirl of my thoughts drowned me.

A month to find enough gold to fill a ship's hold. The easiest place to start would have been to burst into Lady Amelia's rooms and demand the rest of the riches she'd taken from her home. But while her spread of jewels had been impressive, it wasn't enough. Not even close. What the brokers were asking for wasn't something that could be cobbled together robbing careless nobles or paid out in jobs rescuing ladies from towers. Not in the time they had given us, especially not once word got out that we had broken our latest contract and left the lady in question in a brothel. Work would be thin for a few months, so we couldn't rely on legitimate payments to help us raise the money. And any attempts to gain the funds through less than legal means would upset George and go against everything we'd worked so hard for since Maro and I had first left Kiril's service. The brokers expected us to behave like pirates; I would pay them, but I wouldn't stoop to those methods again.

I sighed, then coughed as a waft of perfume hit my nose. A more pleasant reminder of the night at Davi's. But the scent made my head ache and I needed to focus. I went to the small rear chamber, pulling my shirt over my head as I walked. The collar got caught beneath my chin and I struggled, arms trapped over my head, until I managed to wrench myself free. A dull thump caught my attention. The leather loop around my neck had snapped. George's bracelet landed on the blankets, while the bundle Lady Amelia had given me fell to the floor. In my haste to gather up all our belongings and get out of Davi's this morning, I'd essentially forgotten about it. Now, though, I sat at the edge of our narrow bed and pulled the ties loose. The cloth that held it was heavy and folded several times, giving the illusion that the contents inside were larger than they first appeared. But that didn't make them any less impressive. As the last of the wrapping came undone, a lump of gold the size of an egg shone up at me. A ring. It glittered as a hundred tiny diamonds winked up at me, while a thin line of rubies circled the top like a miniature crown.

If the bracelet Amelia had given Davi would be sufficient to buy passage to a new life, this would have set her up in that life where she'd never be beholden to anyone ever again.

Robbing her after we'd gone to all the trouble of getting her out was bad form, but what else had she taken out of that house? And what was left? Perhaps we could go back and search for more.

I went to wrap the ring back up, thoughts whirring, and I nearly missed the markings on the cloth. The lines were faint, but as I spread it back out again, the details in the center were clearer, labeled in a neat hand.

Caged man.

Fire river.

Needle stairs.

"What …" My fingers shook as I passed them over the jagged outline drawn on the cloth. No latitude or longitude, but the perimeter of the landmass was clear. Could it be this easy?

"Captain." Ender entered the outer cabin. He flushed and cleared his throat when he saw me, and I scrambled to pull on a fresh shirt. Close quarters and a minimal number of crew with any medical training meant Ender had seen all the parts of my body at one point or another, but I appreciated his sense of decorum in day-to-day situations.

"What is it?" I asked as I pulled on new pants.

"The princess is injured."

"What?" I banged my shoulder painfully against the door frame in my haste to get to him.

"She's bleeding. Maro sent her down to the infirmary, but I thought you should know."

I grimaced. We'd bought the time we could and the plan forming in my mind was still vague, but we had to tell the others what the future held. I rushed back to the small cabin and gathered up the ring and the map.

Because it *was* a map. No latitude and longitude. This wasn't going to be easy. But it was a solution that sailed us close enough to the wind that we might pay off the brokers without betraying the ideals we'd sought to embrace since leaving them.

"Get Maro and meet me back here," I said.

Ender left and I made my way over the deck, where the crew navigated my ship out of Beldridge with practiced ease. They didn't need instruction or guidance from me. Each was a capable sailor in their own right. They'd be able to sail any ship or under any captain. Someday soon, they might have to.

George was on the narrow cot in the infirmary, trying to keep the doctor at arm's length.

"I'm fine," she said. "It's only a cut. Nothing serious."

Selim Sarkiss, our ship's doctor, harrumphed. He was tightening a kerchief around his forehead. The strip of cloth did a passable job of hiding the wicked scar that crossed from his brow into his hairline. Years ago, he'd taken a shot to the head while serving in the Vestrian navy. The injury had rendered him unfit to serve his country any longer. His hands shook now, making him ill-suited for surgery, but for the crude treatments we needed most often on the *Siren*, he was more than capable.

"Which one of us is a doctor?" he said to George. "I'll be the judge of what's serious and what's not."

And truthfully, the line of dark blood that was spreading into the cloth of her pants did look worrying. He glared at her until she undid them and slid them from her hips, shooting me an apologetic glance as she did it, like it was somehow her fault she hadn't been able to hide the wound for longer.

She'd apologized the night before. Over and over. That she hadn't heard Hafir come into the room. That she hadn't fought back harder. But none of it was her fault. She wasn't meant for this life. Her fear had been my fault. She'd said as much, whether she meant to or not.

"What's this?" Selim asked as he unwound the stained bandage.

"We ran into a friend of a friend," I said simply.

He frowned as he pulled the cloth away, exposing the wound beneath. It was deeper than it had looked the night before, and he grimaced as he examined it.

"I hope you gave them back a gift as generous as this," he said.

We hadn't. And we wouldn't. It would be hard for the doctor and the others to understand, but we weren't going to play that game anymore.

"Come to our cabin when you're done here," I said to George. "I'm gathering the others. We need to talk."

Maro, Ender, and Rosie were waiting for me when I returned. I hadn't explicitly invited Rosie, but she arrived with thin slices of cheese and a glossy purple jam spread onto soft white bread she'd no doubt purchased in Beldridge. By a sailor's standards, it was a feast, and so she was allowed to stay. They all had questions, but I made them wait until George arrived. Her limp was more pronounced now, and she'd had no option but to put her blood-stained trousers back on.

"I'm sorry for all the excitement," she said, with an apologetic smile as she came to sit beside me. "I didn't expect this much attention."

"But how did you hurt yourself?" Rosie asked.

"We had a visitor last night," I said. My stomach bucked like we were lost in a storm, but in the end, I owed our friends the truth. "Two of them, in fact. From the brokers."

George had gone a little paler, and I squeezed her hand, but had to keep from crushing the bones when Maro spoke.

"The brokers?" they spat. "Haven't they learned their lesson? I'd be happy to teach it to them again."

"That sort of approach is how we got into this situation," I said, trying not to sound accusatory. Maro was a weapon, and a well-sharpened one at that. Their methods had always worked well, but we had too much to lose now.

I relayed the details of the night before. Rosie made gasping noises of sympathy, and Ender placed a steadying hand on her shoulder. Maro looked furious.

"You should have woken me," they said. "It'll be that much harder to find this Hafir and kill him now."

"We aren't going to kill anyone," I said.

"But you can't let them think we'll tolerate a threat like this. The brokers only understand one kind of reply."

They did. Blood. I glanced at the line on George's thigh. We couldn't spill more of it. Not George's. Not Ender or Rosie's. Not even Maro's, no matter how much they might want retribution.

"We're going to pay them," I said quietly.

Maro snorted. "You can't be serious."

"We're going to pay them," I repeated, "and then Captain Cinder will retire."

CHAPTER 4

"*R*etire?" This was from Rosie. She sounded mystified.

"That's absurd," Maro scoffed.

"What do you mean to pay them with?" Ender asked, and I smiled with gratitude that he alone was staying focused on the matter at hand.

"It won't be easy," I said.

"We haven't been north of Sevnan in years," Maro said, musing. "If you insist on this course of action, we could be there in a month. Maybe six weeks. Raid the trade routes."

"The brokers gave us a month to pay them."

"A month?" They sounded appalled. "In these waters? There isn't anything nearly valuable enough unless we start sacking cities. Honestly, Cinder. This is humiliating. Forget the money. We'll head north."

"We can't run," I said softly. "I gave my word. You know what will happen if I break it."

"Who said anything about running?" they asked, words clipped. "I know where at least two of the brokers hide out this time of year, and it's not that far north. We could have the first one dead by the end of the week. The second—"

"We aren't pirates anymore," I said, talking over them, trying to blot out the image of brutality and carnage they were painting. Beside me, George was still as a statue.

"Then what exactly do you think we are?" Maro's glare was furious.

"We're …" I floundered for the right word. I'd never been able to put the right label on our new occupation. "Businesspeople."

The awkward silence that followed said I still wasn't successful in naming it.

"What sort of business?" Rosie asked carefully.

"We're in the … business of saving other people." I winced. Even I knew it was flimsy at best.

"But you won't even let us save ourselves," Maro said.

"I will," I insisted. "Only, not the way you want to. It's too dangerous for everyone. Once we've paid the brokers, our debt will be cleared. They left us alone for years after we were finished at Kiril's. It was only after …" The words dried up in my mouth. I nearly said it was only after George had returned to me that we'd come back into the brokers' view, but that was neither true nor fair. I was the one who had gone back to Kiril. The decision had been mine alone. And Maro had been the one to drag the blade over his throat. I tried again. "We'll pay them, and they'll let us go again. Then George and I will leave the *Siren* and disappear, and the rest of you can go about your lives safely."

The silence closed in again. The fury vanished from Maro's face. Rosie and Ender glanced uncomfortably at each other, and even George watched me like she was seeing a stranger.

"What's wrong?" I asked.

"Leave the *Siren*?" she said.

"We'll have new adventures," I said. And with the debt paid, the brokers would have no further reason to come after us or anyone else on the crew.

"This is ridiculous," Maro said, folding their arms over their chest. "You're giving them everything they want and sacrificing everything you have in the process."

Not everything. Not George, who was more important than anything else. Not the safety and well-being of my crew. I would take George away to the life she deserved, where the perils of loving a pirate wouldn't reach us, and the others would be free to live another day.

"If we don't do this," I said carefully, "the next time they come, it won't only be George they threaten. They'll take Rosie. Or the doctor. They know us, Maro. They know who is most vulnerable."

"Which is exactly why—"

"I am captain of this ship," I said. "We do as I say, and I say we treat this as a business arrangement where no one gets hurt, is that understood?"

Rosie and Ender were quick to mutter their assent. I hadn't missed the way Ender had pulled her closer to him when I'd said the brokers would come for her next. Using her as an example was unpleasant but necessary. They needed to understand the threat and why Maro's preferred solution would be impossible if we all wanted to all be alive at the end of it. Maro was skilled. They might make it. The others would not. Not all of them at least.

When I glanced at George, she gave a quick little nod. She'd been mostly silent throughout the whole conversation, which worried me. But I turned back to Maro, who stared at me with hard, narrowed eyes. Rarely did I use the captain's privilege to make decisions, but we had no room for negotiation here.

Finally, they dropped their gaze and knocked their thumb to their forehead. It was the most peevish of salutes, and on many ships, a sailor might be flogged or given extra watches for such disrespect. With Maro, though, the gesture was a profound capitulation.

"Thirty thousand in gold is a lot," Ender said. "Where do we find something like that in less than a month?"

Here, at least, I had an answer. I laid the map out on the table for everyone to see.

"We're going treasure hunting." Perhaps I was spreading my enthusiasm on a bit too thickly, but they all leaned forward, peering at the faded paper. Rosie's mouth was open. Ender's eyebrows were furrowed deep over his face. Even Maro studied the map from a distance. I glanced at George, but she remained seated where she was.

"Look," Rosie said, pointing at the center of the island. "X marks the spot. That's how it works, right?"

"It would certainly seem so." Ender traced the words, following the directions that had been scribbled into the corners.

"Where is it?" Maro asked. "This map has no coordinates."

They *would* be the one to ask the pertinent questions.

"I'm not sure yet."

"You don't know." Their words weren't a question. More a statement of dubiously unimpressed fact.

"I'm not sure *yet*." I pressed against the word and also toward Maro so they understood my meaning. "But between you, me, and Ender, we've seen most of the corners of this ocean. Bring in the doctor and a few of the others, and there aren't many ports we haven't been to. And look at the clues. The needle stairs. The fire river. The caged man. Someone will know where these things are."

"And you think we'll simply sail around in circles until we happen upon the right island? With only a month to do it?"

I clamped my mouth shut. They were still spoiling for a fight, but I wouldn't give it to them. We'd discover the island's location. The clues were too specific to not be identifiable. Better than their suggestion, which would either be cutting a swath through the countryside as we looted houses or running down ships whose only transgression was to sail with the same tides.

But my silence must have looked like uncertainty, because they tossed their hands up in frustration. "For all we know, this is a simple drawing. A doodle. What if it's a fake?"

I pulled the ring from my pocket and let it drop to the table with a substantial thunk.

"Because it came with this, and it's certainly not fake."

The cabin went quiet. George's continued silence still made me uneasy, but the shocked expression on everyone else's face—even Maro's—was very satisfying indeed.

"It's so pretty," Rosie said. "I've never seen anything so big, not even at the palace. George, did you ever see anything like that?"

George shook her head, but no one else seemed to notice her refusal to speak. Ender lifted the ring so he and Rosie could study it, and even in his massive hand, it looked so big.

"So you have a ring and a map of an unknown island," Maro said. Their acid tone was exhausting. Had they always sounded like that when they spoke to me? "Better than no ring, I suppose, but still not much to go on."

"A ring like that didn't come from just anywhere," I said. "Someone will know it. We could go to Vestria. Their jewel market is famous."

"Anain," Ender said, almost to himself. He was holding the ring up to the light and squinting at the inside of the band.

"I'm sorry?" I asked.

"There's something engraved here. Anain? Anoin?"

"Anaïb?" Maro asked softly. Their whole posture changed in an instant, going from tense disdain to something like antic-ipation.

Ender smiled. "Oh yes. That would be a *b*. Yes, Anaïb. Why? Do you know what that is?"

Maro held out a hand—was it possible they shook a little as they did?—and Ender passed them the ring. They lifted it, doing the same as he had done, turning it this way and that so they could better see the inside. "Oh, for pity's sake, Cinder," they muttered through clenched teeth. "I told you to get a better lantern for your cabin."

I rolled my eyes. "Can you read what it says?"

"Anaïb Katalo." They spoke each word in the precise clipped tones that surrounded their speech every day. Here though, the sounds fit, as if the words were made to roll off Maro's tongue.

"Do you know what that means?" I asked.

They continued to study the glittering jewels. "Exactly what it says. It's not a what, it's a who. Anaïb Katalo was the first ruler of my people. But their treasure was lost generations ago."

"Oh, a mystery!" Rosie said excitedly. "I like a mystery."

"And that's their ring?" Ender asked.

Maro let it roll around in their palm. "I have no way of knowing, but it's said they lived in a golden city deep in the mountains. Gold on the walls and jewels everywhere. But there was a coup at the court. One of Anaïb's siblings wanted the gold for themself rather than sharing it among the people. Anaïb was killed and the city ransacked. My ancestors fled, living in caves for years before they dared return."

"And?" Rosie said. "What happened?"

Maro shrugged. "Legend says the city was a husk. The gold was gone, the usurpers too. The people moved on. The city and treasure were cursed, or so they believed. Any place or riches would be when family members betrayed each other."

"And the gold?" I asked, mind spinning. A city's worth of gold would be enough to pay the brokers and still have plenty to escape forever with George. The others could pay their way no matter what they desired. It was even more than I had dared hope for. We could buy our own country if we wanted to. Pay guards to keep the brokers at bay. I would never again wake in the night to find a threat had crept up on us unawares.

"Lost," Maro said. "Never seen again."

"It's somewhere," I said. The ring was proof of that. "We have the map."

"A map that may have already led someone to the ring," Maro said. "Why wouldn't they have taken the rest?"

"If someone found a city's worth of gold, we would have heard about it," Ender said, scratching at his beard. "Even if the news came from a distant port, something like that doesn't stay a secret for long."

"So it's still out there." My pulse was rising with excitement. But we only had a month.

"We'll start with the elders."

"Whose elders?" Maro asked, sounding bored.

"Yours."

They blanched, and I pressed my advantage. "A deposed ruler and a city of gold don't vanish. Tales emerge. Someone knows something. We only have to ask them."

"We don't simply make demands of the elders." Maro shook their head.

"Won't they be pleased to see you?"

Even their lips had gone pale as they licked them. "I haven't been there in fifteen years. I have no idea how we'll be received."

"Excellent!" I popped to my feet and clapped my hands, the plan solidifying in my mind. "Ender."

"Yes, Captain?"

"Set a course for Enomis City."

"Captain." Maro still looked pained. A momentary pang shuddered through me, but the ring fell from their palm and the jewels winked at me in the candlelight, promising wealth and safety, and any guilt I felt passed quickly.

Ender gazed between us for a moment longer, but I didn't change my order, and he finally knocked his brow before he left the cabin, with Rosie following after.

"You're entitled to set our course as you see fit, Captain, but this is a fool's errand," Maro said softly.

I forced myself to hold their gaze. "Prepare yourself. I'm sure your family will be pleased to see you."

They strode out of the cabin. George and I were alone again. The ship carried on, an inanimate object unaware of the voyages she had been on or would take. My home.

But something wasn't right.

"How's your leg?" I asked George.

"Fine." But she put a hand to her thigh and winced. "The doctor put a few stitches in it and gave me a salve to keep it clean. He was very unhappy we didn't come to him sooner."

I didn't respond to that. If I couldn't let Maro dictate orders, I certainly couldn't allow it from the doctor.

And still, George refused to look at me.

"Go on," I said finally. "Say it."

"Say what?" George asked, but her very tone made it clear she knew what I was asking.

"Whatever you've been chewing on this whole time."

"I don't need protection."

Was that all? I'd anticipated something much more serious.

"We all do from time to time. I couldn't keep you safe last night, but I—"

"And I don't need you making decisions for me either."

Here, I was confused. I sat next to her and tried to take her hand, but George pulled it away.

"What decisions?" I asked.

"You're retiring? We're disappearing? We're leaving our friends behind?" She rose and limped in an agitated circle.

"Sit down, you'll tear the stitches."

"Don't tell me what to do, Lou. When were you going to share your plan with me?"

"There wasn't time. I'd only just come up with it when Ender told me you were in the infirmary."

She pinched her lips together, looking unhappy.

"Please," I said. "I'm doing this for us. If we find the treasure, we could be free forever. No running. No one to hide from."

"But what will it cost us?" she said.

"Nothing. It's a lost treasure. Free for the taking."

"That's not what I mean." She sighed, brushing away a stray hair that had slipped free of her kerchief. Her disappointment sat more heavily than any feeling I had toward Maro as they'd stalked out. But, like Maro, George would see I was right. She would understand.

"What about the women?" she asked.

"Which women?"

"The ones who need our help."

It was a valid question. I'd spent a lot of time instilling the virtue of our mission into my crew, and truly, most days it felt like the work would never be done. But the last few jobs had been narrow escapes at best. The information we were given was unreliable. While I still believed in what we did, I wouldn't put the others at risk. And the greatest risk of all was the brokers. That had to be our priority.

"I can't save any of them when someone has a knife to your throat," I said.

George flinched, and perhaps I'd said it the wrong way, but the truth remained. Saving ourselves was more important than any good deed we could do for others. Even if it meant saving my crew and my friends from themselves. George would sacrifice herself to the benefit of others until there was nothing left. Maro would have us all drowning in an ocean of blood. The only way forward that would protect us all was the course I was setting.

George went to the small rear cabin and returned with clean trousers and a loose shirt.

"You didn't want to change back there?" I asked.

"I'm not happy with you."

"George."

She shook her head. "I need to think. And I can't do it so close to you. I'll sleep in the bunks with everyone else."

"George," I reached for her. "You don't need to do that."

But she walked through the door anyway.

~

THE WEATHER STAYED clear with good winds at our back. The morning after our departure, George continued to give me a wide berth, and I let her. We would need to have a reckoning, but I didn't want another argument, so if she needed time and space, I would do my best to give her both, even on a ship that didn't have much space to begin with.

But I couldn't make the same allowances for everyone. Maro had also been avoiding me, sending Ender with messages instead of speaking to me themself. I finally had to corner them at the ship's wheel on our third day at sea.

"How far to Enomis City?" I asked.

They kept their gaze forward. "Another week, if the winds cooperate."

It wasn't ideal. If we were wrong, we'd have wasted a lot of time, but it was the best we had to go on for the moment.

"Thank you," I said.

"For what?"

"For answering my question. It's been days since you said anything nice to me."

"My apologies, Captain. Your boots are looking very well polished this afternoon." They grinned crookedly in the late day sun.

"Very funny," I said.

"No truly. They gleam. You're an example to the rest of us."

I kicked one of my well-polished toes in their direction, and they danced clear. Some of the tension that had hung between us drifted away.

"Are you excited to be heading home?" I asked.

The crooked smile vanished. "It's been a long time."

"How do we find out more about the lost city once we get there?" I asked. "Should we have brought some livestock to sacrifice for the elders?"

Maro rolled their eyes. "They won't talk to you."

"You don't know that." I gave them a roguish smile. "I can be very charming."

"The elders haven't spoken to anyone in decades. They've been sequestered in the great library, reading the ancient texts."

That didn't sound very interesting. I couldn't stifle my yawn, and Maro wrinkled their nose. "There's a reason I left. I was being groomed for a life in the archives."

My yawn turned to a surprised giggle at the mental image of Maro—fierce, terrifying Maro—stuffed into a set of robes and sent up to the tallest tower to read the same stale books for years on end.

"So if we can't walk in and ask to speak to the elders, how do we find out what happened to the lost city?" I asked.

Maro groaned softly. "We'll have to read the old texts."

I groaned as well, more loudly than they had. I'd never had much education, growing up poor with so many siblings on George's father's estate. We were practically feral, and then I'd been shipped off to the navy at twelve and kidnapped by pirates shortly thereafter. Schooling had never been a priority. I could read a chart and write my letters, but the idea of sitting and reading anything for an extended period of time made me tired just thinking about it.

"We don't have to go," Maro said slyly. "I'm sure there's a warlord around here somewhere with riches we could help ourselves to. If his gains are ill-gotten, no one would resent us too much for taking them."

But we couldn't take that option. It wasn't what respectable people did. And storming someone's estate in the hopes of finding treasure could easily go badly, as we'd so recently shown rescuing Lady Amelia. Poring over dusty old texts wasn't exciting, but it would be safe.

"Are you sure the livestock sacrifices won't help?" I asked hopefully. "We could make a small detour to find a goat or two."

"They'll find you highly uncultured if you show up on their doorstep and start slicing up goats," Maro said.

"Even if I also bring you with me?" I put an arm over their shoulders. "They'll be so glad to see you returned to the fold. Prodigal wanderer back from the sea."

To this, they said nothing. At least we'd stopped arguing for the time being.

On the deck below us, George stepped off the rigging. She glanced up at us, and I went to smile at her, but she looked away again just as quickly, before heading down toward the mess.

That was a relationship that still needed repair.

CHAPTER 5

The winds had pushed us closer to Vestrian trade routes than we usually travelled. The Vestrian navy was ferocious. On the few times we'd come this way on a job, the extractions had been meticulously planned to avoid detection and had handsomely compensated us. More than once, we'd only escaped on a lucky wind after several hours of pursuit from an eager Vestrian naval officer out to prove himself.

Which was why my blood chilled when, on the fifth morning, I woke to the distant sound of cannon fire.

I hurried up to the quarterdeck where Maro stood at the wheel.

"What is it?" I asked.

"I can't tell. Neither vessel is flying any colors. But the pursuing ship has her to rights," Maro said, peering through a long glass, which I took from them. Sure enough, the downwind ship seemed to have already been disabled, with her mast split in half. A billowing white shape hung in the water—a lost sail that dragged through the waves, slowing them down. That no one had cut it away was an indication of how poorly the crew must be faring.

"Take us around," I said. "Give them a few miles to sort out their differences."

"But they might need our help," George said as she came up the stairs. "Ender! Get the doctor."

I bit my tongue at her order. She was in no position to be giving them, but Ender marched away like he'd been sent on a sacred mission.

"The fate of those sailors is no concern of ours," I said.

George looked horrified. "They're people, and they're in danger."

"And if that other ship opens fire on us?" I asked.

"Why would they? We haven't done anything to them."

"You don't know that for sure. I might have ruined their king or kidnapped their mother at one point or another." I put the glass up to my eye again, scanning the battle. The worst appeared to be over. The ship was listing badly to one side, taking on water. Only a matter of time before she went down completely. The other ship was clearly uninterested in raiding her or taking any survivors as captives, because it was already pointing north and heading out toward open water.

"Very well. Chart a course to the wreckage," I said, glancing at George, who threw me a grateful smile. She'd still been sleeping among the crew. This was the first interaction we'd had in days, and if I could earn some goodwill, I would take it. She'd been worried about the women we might not be able to save. At the very least, we could rescue a few wayward sailors here.

"Captain, it might be a trap," Maro said, and I gave myself a headache with the effort of not rolling my eyes. Maro and George. They would forever be at the opposite ends of every argument and disagreement, with me in the middle trying to find the best passage.

"We can outrun the attackers if they come around. Tell the crew to be ready. Let's see who we can help. Make sure the doctor is prepared to treat any of the wounded."

The ruined ship was long gone by the time we reached the place where she'd been. But the field of debris left floating on the surface to mark her passing was not insignificant. Broken barrels and splintered wood greeted us as we approached. Among them, sailors in uniforms and others in plain clothes floated facedown in the water. We lowered Ender and a couple other sailors in a longboat to look for survivors, but the silence said we might already be too late.

"What do we do?" George asked where she stood at my side. I took some comfort that, in a crisis, we were still drawn together.

"This one's alive!" Ender shouted as he and the others hauled a body over the side.

"Help!" Another voice called faintly, this one from across the *Siren.* I rushed to follow it, and among the debris fifty yards to starboard, a figure was waving with one arm while he clung to something that floated low in the water.

"George," I said. "Help me lower another longboat." It would be faster to send out a second than wait for Ender, who was still struggling to bring in his survivor. George didn't hesitate. Whatever hurt she was holding on to between us, saving a life was more important.

We rowed as hard as we could. The man in the water continued to wave, though as the minutes passed his movements became slow and sluggish. As we approached, he clung to a piece of ragged flotsam. His other arm didn't seem to be working very well, and he cried out when I took hold of his jacket and tried to pull him over the side of the longboat.

George stowed the oars while I dealt with his injured side, and she grasped his good arm. The heavy wool of his coat weighed him down. He screamed again as George and I heaved him up, but he didn't fight us. We were both soaked through when he was finally aboard. The water was frigid. George fumbled to remove his coat as he curled up on himself.

"Leave that," I said.

"He's freezing."

"We're better to get him back to the *Siren* where the doctor can look at him."

We pushed through the remains—human and wooden—on our return. The sight was gruesome, and we passed no other survivors as we went.

The man we had saved was nearly insensible by the time we came alongside the *Siren*. Someone tossed a rope down to us to help pull him up.

Ender had returned with two wet and shivering women in the time it had taken us to retrieve our survivor. They were wrapped in blankets, and Rosie had brought them both bowls of fish stew.

"The princess," the wet man we'd dragged aboard said through chattering teeth.

"What?" My entire body went on alert. His gaze was unfocused and glassy, swimming between my face and George's.

"We need the princess," he said again.

Rosie approached us, her face serious. "They're from Redmere."

"How do you know?" I asked.

"I asked them."

"The princess," the man said again.

"Selim," I said, and the doctor appeared at my shoulder.

"Yes, Captain?"

"Take this man below. Help get him warm."

Selim knocked a shaky salute. "Of course." He helped the freezing man to his feet and led him away to the infirmary.

If only the uneasy feeling that had settled in my belly would be drawn away as easily.

"Do you know any of them?" George said.

Rosie shook her head. "I don't. They asked about others though. Did you find any others?"

"Only him," I said. "And he seems to know George."

She waved a hand. "He was delirious."

"He called you princess. He knows who you are."

"How though? I don't know him."

"What if he was on the prince's ship? What if he knows you killed Beverly?" We'd never heard any rumors from Redmere about the prince's demise. George had told his crew to sail home and tell everyone he had drowned. But if the truth came out, Redmere would be within their rights to find her and drag her back for trial.

I spun on my heel.

"Where are you going?" George asked.

"To the infirmary."

"Lou, wait." She hurried to follow.

The sailor's chatter was audible before we arrived belowdecks.

"She should be queen. We're going to bring her back to Redmere."

"Lou." George's grip on my hand was firm.

"You served Prince Beverly?" I said, not waiting on ceremony as we entered. Selim took a respectful step back. George hung in the doorway, no doubt prepared to block my way if I tried to drag our new guest up to the decks.

The sailor swallowed hard. "Yes. Yes, ma'am. In a manner of speaking."

"You were there? On his ship?"

He blinked. The color was high on his cheeks, but he still had his hands clasped beneath his armpits, trying to find any flare of warmth to revive himself. He looked to be in his twenties. Too thin by half. The skin under his eyes appeared bruised, though that might only be the cold, and he was missing teeth on the top. Not exactly a fearsome sailor. In fact, he looked on the verge of starvation.

"I worked in the palace gardens."

"That's a long way from sea," George said. "How did you get all the way out here?" I glanced at her, and she shook her head. She still didn't recognize him.

The man shrank anxiously down on himself and his voice dropped to a whisper. "We had to escape."

"Escape what?"

"Duke Aubrey of Stockton." He said it like he thought the answer was obvious. "He's the prince's cousin."

"We've heard about him," I said. "Some self-anointed savior."

The man shook his head, eyes wide with fear. "He's not. He's evil."

"Evil how?" George came to stand by me.

"He'll kill you with kindness. Wants everyone to believe he speaks with gods, but he'll slit your throat if you question him. My brother …" He trailed off, gaze going glassy again as he stared at something or someone only he could see. "There's a man at the harbor. If you pay him, he'll get you out. We gathered everything we could find. My sister and I … He picked us up. But he said there wasn't enough for my mother."

George made a sympathetic noise, but I was not so easily moved.

"And what about this princess?" I asked. "You're thinking she can help?"

His expression brightened in excitement. "Do you know where to find her?"

A silence fell over the infirmary as George, Selim and I all glanced back and forth at each other in confusion. The man watched us all, but either he was a skilled liar or he didn't recognize George at all.

"There's no princess here." I said. "We can bring you as far as Vestria, you and the others we pulled out of the water."

He sagged visibly. "Oh, thank you. We won't be any trouble."

I left the infirmary, taking George with me. Perhaps he only saw a sailor when he looked at her, but I wouldn't give him any more chances to recognize her either.

"Vestria?" Maro asked. After leaving the infirmary, we had once again gathered in my cabin, this time with the doctor.

"It's only a few days from here. The longer they stay with us, the more likely the others are to recognize George. We can stop by the jewel markets in Hilltop and see if anyone there knows about the treasure. Might even spare you from your family reunion. I know you were looking forward to being welcomed back into the fold." I gave them a knowing smile, and they pressed their lips together and looked away.

"I know some of the jewelers in Hilltop," Selim said. "Or I used to, anyway. I can make introductions."

"What about the refugees?" George asked.

"What about them?" I asked.

"What will we do with them?"

The eyes of all the others in the cabin were on me, and I unexpectedly bristled. Saving them had become a risk and an inconvenience.

"Once they're ashore, it's up to the Vestrians."

"We're going to leave them there? Alone?" George looked aghast.

"What would you have me do?" I asked. "Buy them a house, ensure they make new friends?"

Her gaze dropped, taking my heart with it. I was trying to steer the course and make progress on the question of this treasure. We didn't need distractions like a trio of homeless Redmerians. Saving them from drowning was gift enough.

"My son," Selim said slowly. "I haven't seen him in a long time. But he lives in Hilltop. He might be able to take them in or help them start a new life."

"There." I smiled at George. "Selim's son will help. Is that satisfactory?"

She cocked her head. "I suppose so."

"Good. Then that's settled."

But it didn't seem to be. At the end of the day, George returned to our cabin, since the spare berths had been given to our new arrivals. I expected more admonitions, but instead, she came to bed brimming of thoughts that needed to be verbalized at that immediate moment.

"They worked at a paper mill." She paced the room excitedly.

"Who did?"

"The two women we pulled up from the sea."

"I told you to stay away from them. We don't want anyone recognizing you."

"Printers use paper," she said as though I hadn't spoken. "I wonder if they knew Niall?"

I sighed as I climbed into bed, letting the rough sheets drag over my skin. Niall had been George's best—possibly only—friend in Redmere City before she'd left. He'd also been a printer and an agent for the Redmerian resistance. He'd been killed as he helped George escape onto the *Siren*.

"Lots of uses for paper," I said, mildly annoyed when George didn't follow me onto the mattress. Now that she was back, I wanted to fall asleep to the sound of her breathing, not the soft slap of her bare feet on the floor.

"Half their family was rounded up and sent away. No one knows where."

"Come to bed, Georgie." I reached for her, but she continued her circuit of our small cabin.

"What if we went back to Redmere?" Finally, she sat on the edge of the bed's creaking frame and took my hand. Her eyes were bright, her cheeks flushed.

I groaned softly. "We aren't back to that idea again, are we?"

But her tone was all sincerity as she rested her chin on my

shoulder. Her touch had me wanting to melt into her, but I could barely allow myself to trust her unspoken offer of comfort. We'd hardly spoken for days. But as though that were all in the past, she hummed happily as she tugged at the lock of hair tucked behind my ear. "You said we'd have new adventures once we were done with the treasure. They need us."

Honestly, they needed a revolution. A bloody one, though so many innocent people would die in the process. This cycle of ruthless princes and wealthy dukes would never end as long as there were bodies to keep working for them. But we would stay as far from all of that as possible. I wasn't going to avoid Maro's war for revenge only to stride into a war for a country I hadn't set foot in for nearly a decade.

"They don't even know us," I said.

But she squirmed in agitation. "Redmere is our home, and people are hurting."

I pulled on her, tugging her toward me for a kiss. "You are my home. This ship is our home."

"But don't you ever wonder …" She brushed a finger along my collarbone, the lines between her brows furrowing even deeper. I mirrored the action, putting a hand to her chest, feeling the steady rhythm of her heart beneath the layers of flesh and bone. I loved that heart and the woman it powered. She cared so much about so many people, even those she'd never met. Her heart was fierce and fragile and I would protect it with my life, even from herself and the dangerous idea she could and should save everyone.

"Wonder about what?" I asked, kissing the soft skin at the hinge of her jaw.

She sighed, but didn't kiss me back. "About your family?"

"No."

"But they're your family." She laughed in disbelief but inched backward, buying what little space she could on the small bed.

I rolled onto my back. "Do you worry about Jeremy?" For

years after I'd left Redmere, George had lived with her brother. I'd never met him, but by all her accounts, he was a scoundrel, and since he was the one who had tried to marry her off to the prince in the first place, I wouldn't be sorry if the first time he and I met was at the end of my knife.

"I worry he hasn't choked on a chicken bone and died alone in his house yet," she said. "But, yes, I do think about him. You're telling me you never think about your parents? Your brothers and sisters?"

"No."

She pushed up on one elbow. "Never?"

They sent me away.

I stuffed the words down. The last thing I remembered of them was my mother buttoning my coat and telling me not to cry when the wagon came to take me to the city because it would embarrass my father. I'd lived more in the ensuing years than most people ever do. I wasn't the stubborn, frightened girl they'd shipped off. I was myself. I didn't need the glow of nostalgia to help me rise in the morning, and anyway, my best memories as a child were all with George, and I had her now, leaving me no one else to miss.

I rolled onto my side, facing the wall. "Never." There was no need. I had the woman I loved and a crew to protect. Wondering about people who were either long dead or who had moved on with their lives would give me nothing I wanted. "We're not going back. We need to take care of ourselves before we worry about the fates of people we've never even seen."

She didn't say anything after that, but no matter how long I waited, her breathing never deepened and softened the way it did most nights as she fell asleep. So we would each stare at our respective walls then. The silence weighed uncomfortably. Gently, I reached behind me, resting my palm softly on George's hip. Soon enough, her hand found mine, tangling our fingers together.

"I love you," I said.

"I know," came the reply.

I was content with that. I couldn't take her home. But we were building one here together.

67

CHAPTER 6

The capital of Vestria was an ancient seaport called
Hilltop. It appeared to sit above a cliff, but in fact, the
lofty city walls had been built to keep out early invaders. Then,
constrained as it was, the city had grown upward instead of
outward, so that towers peeked over the ramparts in every
direction.

The harbor was busy, with a deep channel that led from the
ocean. Fishing boats sailed in and out in an orderly fashion, and a
line of naval ships sat quietly at anchor, reminding everyone who
passed about the might of their sea power and the queen who
commanded it. Upon our arrival, each spindly mast was decked
out in brightly colored pennants, and the city walls were similarly adorned in festive banners. The entire effect was far more
cheerful than the previous times I'd been through the city.

As we approached the wharf, two smaller boats came alongside us, one to port and the other to starboard. Vessels from the
customs house that guided us to a pier at the east end of the
harbor. Maro and I stood at attention as the officers and marines
came aboard. They were led by an upright official who got
straight to business.

"Name of vessel and port of origin?" he said.

"The *White Swan*," Maro said. "Enomis City." It was the alias we used in most ports. Though the name of the *Crimson Siren* was known across the ocean, the ship herself was intentionally unremarkable. If I'd painted her hull red and her sails black, too many of our quarry would have seen us coming.

The official studied the ship. "She doesn't look like an Enomin vessel."

"She's not," Maro said. "But I am."

"And you're the captain?" He eyed them suspiciously. "What's the purpose of your entry to Hilltop?"

"We're jewel traders. We've come—"

"Deniz?" The question interrupted Maro's reply, and we all turned to find the doctor standing on the deck. He was wringing his hands in agitation.

The customs official scowled, then his jaw dropped open. "Father?"

Selim's face brightened in a smile and he rushed over the deck, pulling the other man into a fierce hug. The other officers and soldiers shifted uneasily, and even the shocked Deniz looked uncomfortable as his father let him go. Selim, for his part, continued to laugh delightedly.

"It's been such a long time. And to have you be the first person we see? It's such good fortune! How is your aunt? Do you think she's still mad at me for spilling wine down her dress at your cousin Rinda's wedding?"

Deniz's mouth worked quietly for a minute. His discomfort was almost comical, contrasting as it did against his stern Vestrian uniform.

But when he collected himself, I wished his discomfort had lasted longer.

"Selim Sarkiss," he said, voice projecting over the deck. "You are ordered to present yourself to the court of Admiral Adaa, High Commander of the Vestrian Navy. I am authorized—"

"What?" I said as the marines pushed past us and took the doctor by both arms. "What's going on?"

"—by her supreme majesty, Queen Cheray, to detain you."

"You're arresting him?" George asked.

Deniz looked smug. "My father is a wanted criminal. He's facing a court martial for dereliction of duty."

"Dereliction?" I asked. "He was kicked out of the navy." But Selim made an uncomfortable warning sound, and I sighed as I faced him. "What? Was that not true?"

His smile was wry. "Technically, I left the country before they could kick me out."

"Lou," George said, "you can't let them take him."

"I think you'll find, my lady," Deniz said, "that the law on those who abandon their posts is very clear."

"Doctor Sarkiss is a member of my crew. You have no jurisdiction over him."

"Enlistment in the Vestrian naval service is a lifetime commitment. And anyway"—he pointed at Maro—"I thought you were the captain."

Now my hand tightened on the knife at my hip. Too many questions. Maro was watching me from the corner of their eye. One word from me, and they'd attack. Ender and the others would follow. The Vestrians would be quick to respond and were nearly as well trained as my own crew. Regardless of the winner, the fierce fight would attract attention we didn't need.

I gave Maro the smallest headshake to let them know we wouldn't be disputing Deniz's allegations. Not now, anyway.

"Captain Anaïb," Maro said, giving him a stiff salute before throwing me a dirty look. "My first mate gets ahead of herself sometimes."

I bit my lip to cover my laughter, but hoped it looked indignant instead. Deniz studied us both closely before snapping his fingers. "Send word to naval command that we've secured a prisoner. We'll need soldiers to help transport him to the justice hall.

And ask for more men to search the ship. Let's make sure they haven't brought any other surprises."

"Is that really necessary?" Maro asked. We didn't have anything to hide, but any captain would protest.

Deniz gave them a flat-eyed stare. "You were harboring a fugitive. Better to be sure. You and your crew will wait here until the search is done."

"In that case," I said, "you should know that we have on board a group of Redmerians whose ship went down. They are afraid to go back to their homeland and claim sanctuary here in Vestria."

This appeared to displease Deniz almost as much as the return of his father, but Maro and I simply waited for him to work through his annoyance in silence, and finally he motioned to one of the guards, who escorted the three homeless Redmerians from the ship, after which, the search began in earnest.

Being patient while others wasted my time was not among my best skills. I preferred action to waiting. But demoted to first mate of an Enomin merchant ship, even a pretend one, I had no other recourse. Maro tried to have Deniz and his marines wait on the quarterdeck, where they might be distracted long enough for a few of us to slip away and start making inquiries in the jewel markets, but Deniz steadfastly insisted on remaining on the main deck until his reinforcements came. And in fact, a whole troupe arrived. More than the handful that would be needed to search the ship. A dozen more armed men came aboard, each carrying a rifle and throwing suspicious glances at each of my crew should they do so much as cough.

"We have to do something," George whispered, face turned away from the Vestrian officers. "We can't let them take the doctor."

"Let's see what happens," I said. "It might be easier to let them take him to jail and break him out later than try to fight our way from the harbor now." Once shots were exchanged or swords crossed, there would be nothing for us to do but leave Hilltop, and we'd already lost time detouring here when we could have been sailing to Enomis City. We had to make the best we could of the situation, even if that meant a few more hours of discomfort for the doctor under the watchful eye of Vestrian justice. I could already hear Maro's scolding that breaking him out would be no mean feat either, but I vastly preferred the challenge to the thought of George striding across the deck to make some heartfelt plea on Selim's behalf. Once she opened her mouth, they would know she was no simple sailor, and someone as upstanding as Deniz would no doubt have more questions about how she had come to find herself mixed in with the rabble around her.

The search was exhaustive. They went down to the mess and the hold and were gone for nearly an hour.

"Do you plan to pry up every plank and go through every bunk?" Maro asked.

"Should we?" Deniz didn't sound at all bothered by the idea.

Finally, though, the report came that there was nothing of note.

"You're sure you're jewel traders?" Deniz asked suspiciously. "You don't seem to have anything to trade."

"They're well hidden in my cabin," Maro said. "It's no dishonor to your men that they weren't able to find them. I can fetch them if you insist, but some are so precious you'll understand if I ask you to continue your inspection in private."

Deniz frowned sourly, looking annoyed and a little uncertain. Even posing as a common merchant, Maro still had the air of someone you didn't want to be alone with for any length of time.

Finally, he gave them a stiff bow. "Captain Anaïb, thank you for your time. The prisoner will remain in our custody. You and your crew are free to go about your business, but we trust it will be brief."

"You're too kind," Maro said, words dripping with insincerity.

Deniz's lips curled in a sneer, but he gave us all a short salute and turned to the gangway.

Yet, as the marines took Selim by his arms, a horn sounded, echoing over the city walls and across the water. The entire Vestrian contingent on our decks turned in surprise to face the city. The horn was followed by a regal fanfare. On the wharf, people scrambled as a procession emerged from the busy streets. A dozen riders, their armored uniforms glinting in the sun, parted the people ahead of them like the prow of a ship through the waves. More riders followed as they continued to trumpet their fanfare, while a single figure road behind them, sitting rod straight in their saddle. The only difference between this person and the others around them was the gold band that circled their brow.

"Queen Cheray," Deniz breathed, like he was seeing a goddess in the flesh.

I had never met the queen, but her reign was legendary. More than twenty years earlier, she'd killed her own father to wrest the crown from him during a famine that had killed hundreds of thousands of people in a single summer. She was beloved, but that adoration was always talked about with an edge of fearful awe.

My entire crew had now gathered on the deck to watch her approach.

"Did they know we were coming?" Rosie asked.

"How could they?" Maro said, but their question made me shift uneasily. If Queen Cheray knew we were here, who else did? Kiril had never been successful embedding more than a handful of spies and assassins in Hilltop, but who knew if the other brokers had more luck or who might be waiting for us now?

George was still next to me, and I couldn't help myself when I slipped my hand in hers as we watched the woman at the head of the procession dismount with purposeful grace.

Behind me, Selim chuckled. "My little princess has grown up well."

I glanced at him, then at Deniz, who was also watching his father, but neither man said anything further in explanation.

My ship was already fairly bursting with Vestrian soldiers, but now even more men in smart green coats and carrying long guns marched up the gangway in quick file. Ender had to stumble out of the way because their progress was so determined that even a man his size would have been trampled.

"Make ready!" the soldier at the head of the line shouted as they spread themselves out, clearing space on the deck. "Behold her magnanimous majesty. The First Lady of Vestria and the Isles. Sovereign and beloved ruler of—"

"Yes, yes, that's enough of that." A weary voice wafted up the gangway.

The crowned woman walked in long purposeful strides, polished boots clicking on the wood. Her coat was a deep navy but carried the same insignias as the men who had preceded her. The band around her head was unadorned, and in fact could stand a decent polish, shining dully against her close-cropped dark hair and her brown-gold skin. Her skin was a few shades darker than most of her subjects', and she arched a jet-black eyebrow at the herald who was still puffing on the words she'd cut off, before giving us all an ironic smile. I wasn't impressed with many people. In awe of fewer. But it would be impossible not to be moved by this queen as she approached.

My crew knelt. They were simple sailors, but they were also well trained. Deniz and the others hadn't deserved this courtesy, but Queen Cheray clearly did. Whatever happened in the next few moments—whether it was to demand the doctor be remanded into her custody or that our ship be burned to the waterline—would be entirely on her terms.

She walked across my deck, searching faces suspiciously.

Compared to her sharply uniformed marines, we were a poor lot to be sure.

"Your Majesty," Deniz said, voice faltering. He motioned toward Maro. "This is Captain Anaïb, from Enomis City."

Maro bowed deeply, but Cheray barely acknowledged them. She continued to survey the rest of us gathered before her, and finally, her gaze landed on me.

"Captain Cinder, I presume." Her voice was like a warm summer breeze swirling over the waves.

My toes curled in my boots and every instinct said to run, but we had nowhere to go, and I would not do her the dishonor of lying to her face. Instead, I dropped my head and pulled on a lock of my hair the way I would to acknowledge any other captain.

"Your Majesty," I said.

When I lifted my gaze, she had already moved on, looking over my shoulder.

"And that would make you the Princess Georgina of Redmere."

I spun, and George's eyes darted from me toward the queen and back again, before she quietly cleared her throat and inclined her head the way I had.

"I am Georgina, Your Majesty. And Redmere is my home. Though I'm not a princess."

But Queen Cheray didn't appear to hear that last part. She clapped a hand to her chest and bent from the waist so that her torso was perfectly parallel to the deck of the *Siren*. The gesture made Deniz gasp, before he and all the other Vestrians followed. It was a sight to see, all these strangers honoring George's arrival, but Cheray's words were what shocked me into silence.

"From one monarch to another," she said gravely. "You are most welcome in Hilltop. We're so pleased you've chosen Vestria as your haven, and we are ready to fight alongside you to win back your country."

CHAPTER 7

*I*t wasn't every day that a queen offered to start a revolution for you. I had once claimed a ship of my own as a birthday present. At the time, it seemed like quite the gift. But it paled in comparison as Queen Cheray made her proclamation. What was a ship compared to an entire kingdom?

The wind blew around my ankles, and everyone around us seemed to lean in, as if to catch the exact words that would be spoken on this momentous occasion.

So of course, all George managed to stammer was, "My country?"

Queen Cheray smiled. "Come to the palace. We'll talk further." She eyed me with a pinch to her lips that said she was less impressed with me than with George, but she still said, "Bring your friends. You are all welcome and will be kept safe so long as you're in Vestria."

"Your Majesty." Deniz stepped forward. "If I may. This is my father. Selim Sarkiss. You might remember—"

"Selim." This time, there was no calculation in the queen's smile, only genuine pleasure. She pulled the doctor into a great hug, slapping his back as she laughed, the way Selim had greeted

Deniz only moments ago. "Yes, I'd heard you were here. It has been too long. What finally brought you back to our shores?"

He chuckled. "I was due for a visit with my family."

"Your Majesty," Deniz tried again, but his face had gone a purple color that said he knew he had already lost this argument.

Queen Cheray gave him a wry look. "Some of the officers in my service are altogether too concerned with the proper way of doing things. I'm sure it's all a misunderstanding. Come!" She held out an arm in a gesture that had undoubtedly been captured and would be copied again and again by court painters and illustrators as they tried to preserve their queen's great moments of benevolence and generosity.

The whole spectacle resumed with new fanfare. Horses were brought for us to ride to the palace. George, Maro, Selim and I disembarked. Ender was left in charge of the ship.

I rode alongside George, despite some very pointed glances from the soldier who had handed me my reins. No doubt they wanted Princess Georgina's triumphant arrival to not be mired by the moral quagmire of a pirate escort. But they could paint me out of the portraits later. I wasn't going anywhere.

Somewhere in the shuffle, as horses were sorted and the order of precedence was determined, Maro disappeared. Being put on display like this would no doubt make them anxious. They would find us later, with the added benefit that they would bring some knowledge on how to extricate ourselves from the palace quietly if the need arose.

Our procession made its way through the streets, and people gathered, bowing to their queen and waving excitedly at George. Our opportunity for an inconspicuous visit to Vestria was long gone.

"I suppose we continue to play along?" George whispered to me. The towers around us gleamed in white limestone, and people waved bright ribbons hung out of windows, cheering as we passed.

"Yes," I said. We were in no immediate danger. Our best option was to play the game until we better understood the rules.

"Do you think she knows what happened with the prince?"

I couldn't begin to guess how far her intelligence reached. Before the question of whether she knew George had killed Beverly was the one of how she'd even known we were here. And even if she did know about how Beverly had met his end, Cheray had killed her own father, and in many respects, Beverly's reign had been far more harmful to his people. She might celebrate George's initiative in ending his life.

"Let's talk about that later."

A chill dripped down my spine as we passed under the arched gate at the palace. The cries from the people faded behind us, but in their place was the rattle of armor and weapons as the palace guard raised their arms in salute.

A tall man with salt-and-pepper hair descended the palace steps. He could have given even the officious Deniz lessons in proper posture and bearing. He strode briskly to where the queen waited on her horse, but he didn't help her down so much as he took her hand while she kicked a leg over the saddle and hopped to the cobbled courtyard with the confidence that came from a lifetime of repetition. The tall man kissed her fingers while she smiled indulgently, then took her arm as she led him over to where we sat.

"Princess Georgina," Cheray said. "Allow me to introduce my consort, Duke Ylvar."

The salt-and-pepper man smiled with a glint in his eye. He had broad shoulders paired with an improbably narrow waist, and the reason for his proportions became apparent when he bowed. What I had assumed to be a silver and navy waistcoat over his white shirt was in fact some sort of corset, with lacing that ran from the nape of his neck all the way to the small of his back. The heavy cord creaked as he straightened, but if he felt any discomfort at the restriction, he didn't show it.

"My lady," he said, holding up an elegant hand. "You are most welcome at our court."

George threw me one glance before she took Ylvar's hand and allowed him to help her down. Her dismount was not as graceful as Cheray's, but she didn't stumble or lean on him too heavily as her feet hit the ground.

If I'd known this was where the day would lead, I'd have set things up differently. George stood between Cheray and Ylvar, the two of them shining like royalty, and she looked very much like she'd spent the last six months doing hard labor aboard a ship on the open ocean. A strand of her dark hair escaped her headscarf, and the neck of her shirt gaped open where one of the laces had broken and she'd never bothered to repair it. The cuffs of her pants were salt-stained, as were her shoes, and her cheeks glowed with the sun's kiss more than a princess's ever would have.

She was beautiful, and she had the manners to fit in at any court, but if I'd known she was to meet monarchs as equals, I'd have made sure she dressed the part.

No one seemed to think the rest of us needed help with our dismount, so Selim and I made our way down to the courtyard and assembled at George's back. We were a motley crew to be sure, but George was no ordinary princess.

"Your Highness." Ylvar bowed again. "Allow me to escort you inside." He offered his arm, and I flinched unexpectedly when she took it without looking back. Even in her faded clothing, when she tipped up her head and smiled at him, she looked every inch the ruler she could have been.

We followed them into the palace, and as soon as the doors closed, Cheray's posture loosened. Ylvar's might have too, though it was nearly impossible to tell in his corset.

"Well." Cheray's smile was distracted. "Now they've seen you. I assume you want to wash and unwind before we speak some more."

I took half a step forward, ready to support George if she needed, but she simply gave the queen an answering smile and said, "Yes. Thank you."

Cheray gave me a brief nod. "I trust that your intentions in my country are entirely honorable?"

I feigned shock, going so far as to put a wounded hand to my chest. "I assure your resplendent majesty that what we told your customs officers is true. We are here simply to trade in your jewel market, and then we will be on our way."

A nervous whisper sounded among the guards and retainers around us, but Cheray merely said, "The markets are closed today for the feast day. I'll have someone escort you tomorrow. Some of the sellers in the market are less than trustworthy."

"Selim knows the way. And he knows people who can help us. Assuming we're free to come and go as we please?"

She knew the challenge for what it was. We studied each other for a moment. The queen of Vestria was powerful. Smart. She was not to be underestimated.

"Very good. You can conduct your business while the princess and I conduct ours."

Unacceptable. However long we were here, I wouldn't be letting George out of my sight.

But once again, George stepped in front of me with an elegant nod of her head and said, "If I may, Your Majesty, how did you even know where to find me?"

Cheray grinned, but the calculating brain behind her gaze was apparent. "I happened to be at the admiralty, talking about the Redmerian situation, when word came of Selim's arrest. My intelligence officers have known for some time he's sailed with Captain Cinder. And we knew she had taken a particular interest in your well-being last year. To have you arrive in our harbor? It seemed like too great an opportunity to miss for a little pageantry, don't you think?" Her eyes sparkled at the last, like we were all sharing a good joke, but all I could think was that Vestria already knew too much, and so did anyone else who was keeping an eye out for them. We couldn't stay here. The sooner we left, the better. We'd all be safer back on the *Siren* and out at sea.

But George only curtseyed. "I look forward to getting to know you better, Your Majesty."

"Excellent." Cheray relaxed. "We'll see you for supper tonight. My court will be delighted to meet you."

I'd forbidden them from going after the brokers, but there was a very real chance Maro was going to kill me. Possibly the queen. Maybe even George. This was all far too public. But we said our goodbyes, and Cheray and Ylvar departed, their retinue trailing behind them.

Selim chuckled. "I knew her when she was a girl. Even then, you could see the queen she would be. A mighty warrior. We'll be fortunate if she sees us as allies. It was a good idea, coming here."

"Once we're left alone, we'll leave," I said.

"What?" George said. "No. We can't do that."

"We have a schedule to keep, and it doesn't involve time to play politics."

She crossed her arms over her chest. "You heard her. The markets are closed. We're here for at least one night."

I didn't have time for this. If George dug her heels in any more, we'd get stuck here chasing battles that weren't ours to fight.

Servants took us up several flights of stairs. The walls were lined with portraits of the kings and queens of Vestria. All bore a striking resemblance to Queen Cheray, from the icy determination in their eyes to the same gold circlet that perched atop their brow, regardless of if they were man or woman. It had been the symbol of their role for centuries.

The guest quarters in the palace were ornate and spacious. Selim practically cackled when he was shown the room he was to stay in. It was appointed with heavy furs and rich colors.

"If that's a bottle of wine from the queen's vineyards, then this is an even better welcome than I could have hoped for," he said as the door slid shut behind him.

"You will stay here," a woman said, eyes downcast, motioning me toward an open door across the hall. Inside, a bed the size of our entire cabin waited invitingly.

"Thank you," I said, stepping aside for George. "After you, Your Highness."

George went to move forward, but the servant politely cleared her throat.

"The royal suite is this way." She pointed up the hall.

"Oh, that's not necessary. I can stay with Captain Cinder."

"But—" The woman looked pained. "The queen asked specifically that you—"

"The princess will stay with me," I said.

"But the queen of Polinavia stayed in the royal suites. They're the finest in the palace." Her discomfort was rapidly becoming true distress.

"Then I'll go with you," I said, at which the maid still looked unhappy, but she led us up the hall to an ornate door, stepping aside once it was open.

Despite its lavish decorations, the room smelled faintly of dust. The Vestrian court didn't entertain visitors very often. The walls were hung in tapestries showing scenes from Vestrian folklore—I recognized some of them from tales the doctor told late at night around a second … or third, or fourth mug of ale—and the grate in the fireplace was spotless, no doubt because summer in Vestria would last for at least another month.

"There's more this way," George said, disappearing down a hall. A dressing room no doubt, though we had no clothes to store there.

Near the empty fireplace was a round table made of brass and etched with intricate swirling patterns. I'd brought the map and ring with me and spread them out on it. The map lay silent and unhelpful. I stared at the words on the island, waiting for them to resolve into something familiar. I'd spent nearly nine years at sea. I'd been to parts of the ocean most had never seen. I knew six ways to kill a man with a quill and the four best places to drop a body in the Great Northern Ocean if you wanted them to stay hidden forever, and two more if you needed the corpse to wash up in no less than a week, but no more than a month. But I had no idea where this one simple island was located.

A telltale tapping came on my door, and I opened it quickly.

"Did you let yourself in the front door then?" I asked as Maro slid like a dark shadow into the room.

"I told the man at the gates I was an assassin in Queen Georgina's service. He didn't seem too inclined to question me after that."

"She's not a queen," I said.

"But she's something. These people think she's here for a reason."

The words were an echo of the conversation George and I'd had on board the *Siren,* and once again the very suggestion made something tighten in my chest.

"We don't owe Redmere anything," I said, then made a point of changing the topic. "Where did you go? Sightseeing?"

"In a manner of speaking." They were walking a slow perimeter around the room, peering behind the tapestries and running their fingers over the seams in the stone. Looking for secret doors or holes where someone might listen.

"What manner is that?" I asked, still glaring down at the map.

"I know a few of the houses the brokers keep in Hilltop. I paid them a visit."

I nearly threw the ring at them. "We talked about this. We leave the brokers alone."

They waved a careless hand, picking at a loose piece of mortar. "There was no one there. The houses were shut up. Like the brokers had abandoned them. If they have anyone in Hilltop, they're well hidden."

Perhaps they meant for their observations to be comforting, to know the brokers housed no significant force here, but it had the opposite effect. I followed behind them, checking all the places they had already been, practically feeling the eyes boring into me from behind the walls.

"Did I not say you aren't allowed to antagonize the brokers?" I asked.

They shrugged, disinterested. "This isn't antagonism, it's self-preservation, which you seem sorely lacking. Who doesn't sail into a new city and acquaint themselves with where trouble might come from?"

"If a group of agents suddenly showed up dead in Hilltop, the brokers will know we were here."

Now their expression turned frosty. "You know I would never leave any indication it was me who did the killing. I don't show off. And anyway, the brokers had no way of knowing we'd be in Hilltop. *We* didn't even know we'd be here until a few days ago."

Still, now that they'd put it into the air, I couldn't shake loose the idea that Hafir was just outside the door, waiting for us to fall asleep or otherwise let our guard down. Maro and I would have to take turns keeping watch tonight.

They rapped a knuckle on the brass table. "Were you communing with the spirits?"

My head spun at the change in subject. "What do you mean?"

"This is a Vestrian summoning table. Mystics use it to speak to the souls of the dead."

"Please." I rolled my eyes. "You know I don't believe in those things."

"You should. Every culture has ghost stories and ways to talk to the dead and those left behind. There would be exceptions if ghosts didn't exist."

"Well, if you know any who can help us find this island, I would love to speak to them."

But Maro was already making another circuit of the room.

They put a hand on the mantle. "I don't like this. There's only one way out."

"Two."

They raised one eyebrow, and I pointed upward. "If it comes to it, we could climb up the chimney."

Maro wrinkled their nose. "I'd rather not. All that soot. Took forever to get it out from under my nails last time."

Such drama. A life at sea meant our fingernails hadn't grown straight in years, and were perpetually caked in a layer of tar, salt and grime. What was a little soot?

"Lou!" George's voice carried from the hall, and she rushed in with flushed cheeks.

"That's a lot of excitement for a dressing room," I said.

She laughed. "It's what's beyond the dressing room that's interesting. There's a bathing chamber, and I swear the bath is bigger than this bed. The maids are already filling it." Her eyes grew round as moons, and she licked her bottom lip with a quick flick of her tongue that could only be an invitation.

I stared down at my gritty nails again, then glanced up at Maro.

"We're stuck here until tomorrow," I said. "Markets are closed."

They gave the weariest of sighs. "Go. I'll keep watch out here. But take a knife. Even if you're intent on letting the brokers live, you need to be able to defend yourself."

George giggled and leaned in to kiss Maro's cheek.

"I'll make sure they bring up more hot water for you when we're done," she said.

"Lead the way, Highness," I said as George's laugh sounded up the hall.

AFTER THE SUN WENT DOWN, we were called for supper. Clothes had been sent up for us, and George was dressed in a smart jacket and long trousers with legs so wide it looked like a skirt. The hems flowed around her ankles when she walked. I'd been given a similar jacket, but my trousers were more fitted. The tall leather boots pinched my toes, so I chose to wear my own scuffed pair instead.

The maids had indeed brought up more hot water for a second bath, and Maro glared at me when I asked if they would be joining us to dine with the queen.

"You won't let me kill anyone. The least you can do is let me soak in peace."

The doctor had also offered his regrets, sending a note to say he was going to seek out other family members in the hopes of a more joyful reunion than the one he'd had with Deniz. So in the end, only George and I went down to meet Cheray's court.

The palace's reception hall was massive. A long table ran through the center of the room, and by my count, it could easily seat sixty. Silver and blue banners with the crest of the Vestrian royal family emblazoned on them were mounted from the walls, and a dozen chandeliers each holding dozens of candles hung from the ceiling, casting light into even the deepest shadows of the corners.

George hesitated at the threshold.

"What's wrong?" I asked.

She smoothed a hand down the front of her borrowed clothes.

"I'm fine," she said, though her voice wasn't completely steady. "But the last time I entered a throne room like this, I was just as confused about what was going on."

"Nothing important will come from this," I said. "We'll eat and listen to what they have to say, then tomorrow, we'll go to the market and be gone. Who knows? You might enjoy yourself this time with nothing to lose." She'd wanted to go back to Redmere.

Maybe a dinner with the Vestrian court would remind her how dreary playing politics really was.

The queen and her consort sat on a dais at the far end of the room, and several others, all dressed similarly to them—the women in smart jackets and tall boots, the men in their corseted vests—milled about talking among each other.

As we reached the halfway mark of our approach, brass horns were lifted to announce our arrival. A herald standing at the edge of the dais clapped her hands.

"My lords and ladies. Please welcome Princess Georgina of Redmere!"

The room grew silent as every head turned toward us. Cheray and Ylvar rose, while all the courtiers bowed formally, then applauded as they straightened.

In front of the dais was a second table that ran perpendicular to the long one. It blocked us from reaching Queen Cheray directly, and when we were four paces from it, George stopped and dipped into her most regal curtsy.

"Your Highness," Queen Cheray said.

"Your Majesty," George said in reply.

We were ushered around the table. The queen and consort sat in the centermost chairs. George sat on the queen's right. A liveried servant tried to seat me next to Ylvar, but I took the place next to George without waiting for permission. Queen Cheray watched me with an arched eyebrow, and I dipped my chin in her direction. The corner of her mouth twitched in what might be the beginning of a smile.

The first course was served, which at least gave me something to do with my mouth other than force awkward conversation with the elderly courtier seated beside me. George did not have the same issue. She and the queen barely touched their food. Their heads were bowed together, speaking with a great deal of intensity.

"I bet you've never been to a feast like this," the old man next to me said.

I gave him a tight smile. "Not one I was invited to." No monarch had ever welcomed me as an honored guest to their table. A few times, I'd snuck in, usually to rob someone or poison their drink. Maro and I had brought down the entire Darvin empire that way, by making it look like the prince of Darva had poisoned the Oarian ambassador at a dinner meant to celebrate a newly signed peace treaty.

As the evening progressed, the people around me seemed to be enjoying themselves immensely. Yet, the longer Cheray and George talked, the more unsettled I became. Whatever they were discussing wasn't boring politics. George's voice, even in a whisper, was animated, and Cheray paid no attention to anyone else around her.

Except, it seemed, to me.

"Is the meal not to your liking?"

The question caught me off guard. We were somewhere in the second course, and the queen watched me with a fresh arch in her eyebrow.

"No, Your Majesty. It's excellent. I'm merely a poor sailor still trying to get the world to stop rocking now that I'm off my ship. My coordination is not so steady on land."

"How long have you been at sea?" Beside Cheray, Ylvar's expression was politely interested, no doubt cultivated from a lifetime of making small talk with various dignitaries and rich merchants at court.

"Since I was twelve," I said, glancing at George, who quietly took my hand under the table.

"Is it true you murdered the prime minister of Mondheim?" a voice called from the long table of courtiers.

The whole room fell silent. My grip tightened around my knife, though I kept it on the table. If this was the beginning of a fight, I would be prepared. It would be my luck that the prime minister had a vengeful cousin in the room somewhere.

But I needn't have worried. Though I couldn't see the speaker, Queen Cheray must have known who it was, because her glare was icy as she stood. Awkward glances cascaded up the table of nobles, until they reached a man with the unmistakable pink of too much wine on his cheeks. His face reddened further, and he bowed his head in a silent regret.

"Ladies and lords," Cheray said, apology apparently accepted. She lifted her glass. The entire court stood as one, their glasses raised as well. "I have been speaking with Princess Georgina, and she agrees with me that what is happening in Redmere is a grave humanitarian crisis that needs our attention."

There was a murmur of agreement in the room, but I could only look at George, who was very pointedly not returning my gaze. Instead, her chin was tipped up in the defiant way she had done it so many times in those first weeks after she had come aboard the *Siren.* Every inch the princess trying to look in control of a situation.

"Vestria is committed," Cheray continued, "to supporting Georgina's claim to Redmere's throne and her return to power."

My knife clattered to my table as my fingers went numb with shock. A claim to the throne? How had we gone from being honored visitors to revolutionaries in the space of one dinner?

Around us, no one seemed to notice my surprise. The Vestrian court cheered, lifting their glasses in precise rhythm and chanting George's name three times, before the room echoed with a vigorous stomping of feet. I couldn't very well drag George away from the masses, but I wanted to. We could be back at the *Siren* in less than an hour and on the ocean before the moon had finished her climb.

Instead, I was trapped, both by the crowds and the queen's plans.

CHAPTER 8

As we walked back to our room, the air between George and I crackled with a tension I hadn't felt since the early days after her arrival on the *Siren*. The fact that she didn't say anything or try to touch me—even to take my hand—while we walked said she felt it too.

Finally, after I'd closed the door behind us, she said, "You're angry."

"I'm not."

"Lou."

I gazed at the brass table. I had no ancestors that I knew of to call on for strength. My mother had never been a patient woman, and my father knew how to communicate only with the animals he looked after in the stables. But I needed to call on someone, because my skin itched with the desire to start a fight.

"I didn't know she was going to do that," George said. "Cheray says people are disappearing in Redmere. That the duke has been traveling the countryside, going from town to town, and after he's gone, whole villages have disappeared, and they're never heard from again."

Was he a duke or a magician? The question was irrelevant. Far less important than the one that tore itself from my lips.

"And why is that of any importance to you?"

She stared at me, looking genuinely confused. "I wanted to help. They're my people."

"Your people? Your *people*?" I couldn't stop the disbelief that poured from my mouth.

"Cheray says—"

"We've known her for less than twelve hours. Whatever she says has nothing to do with us." How many times would we have this conversation before George heard me? We couldn't save Redmere. Not when we had to save ourselves first.

"She cares what happens to them. Just like I do."

"And when that caring gets her killed? Gets *you* killed?" May the seas save me from George's sense of altruism. "I've already got Maro out prowling the streets looking to pick a fight with the brokers. I can't be protecting you from the manipulations of a queen we've only just met and can't possibly trust."

Her eyes narrowed. "Don't talk to me like a child, Lou. I'm not a doll whose face will crack if you set her down too hard. I can look after myself."

I snorted. "Not from what I can see." She'd walked right into Cheray's open arms without even looking for the trap that undoubtedly lay inside.

"When did I ever need protecting?" Despite what she'd said, she'd set her jaw in childish defiance, and my blood boiled.

"When Hafir broke into our room and sliced you open like a joint of meat on a table and I couldn't stop him."

The silence stretched between us, filling the room. George looked startled. My throat ached, as if I'd been screaming or crying—or trying not to do either. Slowly, George approached me, but when she lifted her hand to stroke my cheek, I flinched away. I didn't want her pity. Her comfort. I wanted her under-standing.

"I love you," I said.

"I love you too. And I'm safe." Her smile was bright, like everything was all right in the world again.

But it wasn't all right. And it was time to tell the truth. "But you need to be loved by someone who doesn't put you at risk simply by being near you."

"What do you mean?"

"The perils of loving a pirate." The words were like ash in my mouth. I could barely bring myself to say them out loud, but they'd been festering in my mind like a wound, and the only way to stop the rot was to bleed it out. "You said that. After Hafir left."

She nodded. "I remember. But I didn't mean—"

"I am trying," I said slowly, "not to be that person anymore. I have been trying for years, especially since I found you again. And once we've paid the brokers, we can leave and go somewhere no one knows us. Where they don't know me and who I am and what my life has been and—"

Her kiss was soft. Tender. I still wanted to argue, but I couldn't pull away. Not from her gentle touch or the way the kiss turned fierce until I groaned under her mouth.

"You don't need to hide," she said. "We're too strong to hide. We'll stop the brokers. I'm not running off to Redmere at sunrise. We'll find the treasure first, then we'll live the life we want. Not the safest one. The one we choose. Ours. Together."

Fighting wars in Redmere? Playing courtiers in Vestria? There was too much I couldn't control here. Too many unknowns and threats lurking in the shadows. How long until I came home to find another knife at George's throat? How long until Cheray had gotten whatever she wanted and discarded George as a tool who had served her purpose?

How long until George realized the perils of loving a pirate weren't worth the risk?

Time was slipping away. The brokers were coming, and now

we had Queen Cheray to contend with, yet all I could do was slip into George's embrace and pray for another night together.

THE FOLLOWING MORNING, the doctor took us to Hilltop's market district. True to the queen's word, we weren't stopped as we left the palace, though I couldn't tell if the soldiers who dotted the streets were on a usual patrol or if they had been assigned to watch out for us as we walked through the city. They needn't have bothered. Maro was armed to the teeth, even if everything but their sword was hidden beneath their clothes, while the doctor walked us confidently through a busy thoroughfare where it would be difficult for anyone to ambush us. And George was back in her ship's clothes, though someone had washed them along with mine. I felt too shiny and bright by half, but no one seemed to notice a real live princess walked among them.

"How was your family dinner last night?" I asked the doctor as we walked through Hilltop's busy streets.

Selim grimaced. "I went to my sister's house. Deniz was there. I'm not sure if my son is more upset at my perceived failings as a naval officer or that I was able to circumvent the reach of Vestrian justice because of my familiarity with the queen."

"How is it you know her so well?" George asked.

"My father was doctor to her father. I apprenticed at the palace before the sea called for me."

"And your son didn't have the same calling?"

He sighed. "Deniz was always a very serious boy. A strong sense of right and wrong, but no desire for adventure. If I'd spent more time at home, we might have come to a better understanding, but since I was so often away, he took more after his mother, though she died when he was only ten. I was shot and left the navy not long after. Told my sister to raise him. My fault, then, that we never truly had the opportunity to know one another."

It seemed a shame. The doctor was the kindest among us, at least until George and Rosie joined the crew. For him to be so unwelcomed by his own flesh and blood was unfortunate.

The market district was in the northeast corner of the city, cascading upward along one of the oldest sections of the original city wall. We walked through groups of stalls that sold everything from flowers to fruits, reams of bright cloth, and animals I didn't recognize in small cages.

"The jewel vendors are at the back," Selim said. "It's more protected. If a thief were to steal anything, they'd only have one escape route."

"Unless they go over the wall," Maro said, eyeing the towering stone as we approached the deepest parts of the market. Here, the stalls gave way to elegant buildings with heavy doors and leaded windowpanes. The precious wares inside glinted in the sunlight, inviting people in.

"This way," Selim said, motioning us down a narrow alley. We followed him, and the noise of the street behind us fell away. Here, the shops were plainer. Nothing was displayed behind the glass, and most of the interiors appeared vacant, though every so often, a flash of movement deep inside signaled an occupant.

Selim stopped in front of the second to last door before we hit the wall. The shop's windows were in desperate need of cleaning, no doubt a result of the greasy oil lamps that burned inside. The door was made of thick timbers, and Selim rapped on a heavy iron knocker that echoed back up the way we'd come.

"Hayal is from a family of master jewelers," he said while we waited. "We grew up together. The family had stopped making new pieces before I left Hilltop. Their specialty is more historical. If anyone knows about your ring, Hayal will."

"Are you sure they'll still be here?" George asked.

"If Hayal's alive, this is the place." He knocked again. Maro glanced behind us uneasily. A thief would have only one exit, but so did we. Not their preferred situation. I glanced over my shoulder, half expecting Hafir or some other agent to be peeking out from behind a building, but no one was there.

Finally, though, the door swung open, and a tiny woman peered up at us through a pair of spectacles.

"Yes?" Her voice creaked like the timbers of a ship.

"Hayal." Selim held his arms wide like he hoped she might run into them. Instead, the woman squinted at all of us, her lips pressed into a mistrustful line. If she and the doctor had grown up together, Hayal had aged before her time. The doctor wasn't a young man by any means, but the woman in front of us looked like her life might end with nothing more than a stiff breeze.

"Are you here to buy something?" she asked.

"It's Selim. Selim Sarkiss. Do you remember me?"

"Oh, yes," she said, but her tone said she remembered anything but.

"Good morning," George said, giving Hayal her best curtsy.

Hayal brightened immediately. "Princess. I'd heard you were visiting."

Maro huffed. "Does everyone know who she is?"

But George ignored them. "We're hoping you could look at a ring we have."

"A gift from your handsome prince?"

I snorted, but George shot me a look and held out her hand, gesturing impatiently when I didn't immediately respond.

"Maybe we could come inside?" I'd rather not have passed around the ring in broad daylight. But Hayal continued to watch us all with a vacant expression, as though I hadn't even spoken, and finally, I sighed and produced the small parcel, unwrapping it carefully before I handed the ring to George. The rubies sparkled, even in the dim light of the alley, and when George gave the ring on to Hayal, her smile sparkled almost as brightly, coming alive before our very eyes.

"Oh. You're a pretty one. Haven't seen a piece like this in quite some time." She hefted the ring in her hand before turning back into the store. She didn't speak and made no motion for us to follow, but she left the door wide open, so we trailed in, Maro coming last and making sure the latch was shut behind us.

"Mother? Mother, where did you go?" a voice from farther in the shop called. The old woman didn't respond, talking softly to herself as she turned the ring over and over in her palm. But a younger woman emerged from behind a shelf. Her hair was pulled back tightly and she wore thin-rimmed spectacles. She sagged with relief when she saw Hayal. "Oh, mother. I told you not to wander off."

"But Ehran is here," the old woman said, gesturing toward us vaguely.

"Ehran?" Selim said.

"Do you know who that is?" I asked.

"I'm sorry," the young woman said, putting a hand on her mother's shoulder. "My mother is unwell. She might be confusing you with someone else."

"She is," Selim said. "Ehran was my father."

The young woman eyed him before surprise flooded her expression. "Uncle Selim?"

And Selim's answering smile was all familial delight. "Hello, Gahra. You're all grown up."

She started forward like she meant to hug him, then glanced nervously at her mother, who was staring off in the distance. Gahra settled again, gaze on the floor.

"It's good to see you. My mother would be so happy you're back in Hilltop."

Selim watched Hayal for a moment. The woman looked at him periodically and even smiled once or twice, but her spark of recognition was gone.

"She has the memory sickness?" Selim asked.

Gahra nodded. "Four years now. Some days are better than other. She still knows more about how to cut an opal than I ever will, but names and dates are difficult."

As if to prove the point, Hayal reached up and patted Selim's cheek. "Ehran. So handsome. Your boys will grow up to be strong soldiers."

The doctor smiled sadly. "It's good to see you, my friend."

Maro cleared their throat pointedly, and the three Vestrians broke apart.

"We're hoping you could help us with a ring," I said.

"It's a beautiful piece." Hayal held it up, making it glint in the light, before it rolled off her fingertips. I gasped, but Gahra leapt into action, catching it before it hit the floor.

"This ring?" she said. "It *is* beautiful. And old. They don't set rubies like this anymore. How did you come across it?"

"It was a gift," I said.

Gahra whistled softly as she continued to examine the ring. "Generous gift. The band is scratched here, and the diamonds are smaller than is fashionable right now, but since you're friends with Selim, we can give you a good price."

"We aren't looking to sell it," I said.

She glanced at me in surprise. "Repurpose it then? I can pry out the stones and melt the gold, but again, the diamonds are small and—"

"We're looking for the rest of it."

"The rest?" Gahra looked confused.

"The golden city," Hayal said, now smiling at Maro, who looked uncomfortable at the attention. "The cursed treasure."

"It's only a ring," I said. "It can't hurt anyone."

She shook her head. "So many have died. It's hidden."

"You're treasure hunters?" Gahra asked.

I glanced between us. A former pirate, an assassin, an errant princess, and a ship's surgeon. A motley crew indeed. "Something like that." We were getting off topic. "The ring. Has anyone ever come through with other pieces that look similar? Do you know where they found it?"

But she only shook her head, making my heart sink with

disappointment. "I'm sorry. We see a lot of pieces, but most of it is Vestrian. Old jewels from someone's grandmother. And anyone who was hoping to sell off a lost treasure would keep it quiet."

"But people talk," I said. We should have gone on to Enomis City. Stopping here had been a mistake. Desperation rising, I pulled out the map and spread it on a table. "The fire bridge. Needle stairs. Has anyone ever mentioned these? You must hear things."

Hayal and Gahra studied the map for a moment. Hayal traced the lines with her fingertips like she was retracing steps. Finally, she said, "Sarguilla," and my heart leapt.

"Is that a place?"

Hayal plucked the ring from her daughter's hand. "There was a man from Sarguilla. He tried to sell me a bracelet like this once. The rubies were perfect. Like tiny drops of blood on my wrist."

"Sarguilla is too far. It would take six months hard sailing to reach," Maro said, though I ignored them.

"Do you know how he came to have the bracelet?" I asked instead.

But Hayal's attention was already elsewhere, running her fingers over a case that held collars and cuffs made from pounded silver.

"I'm sorry," Gahra said, passing the ring back to me. "I don't think we can be more help."

"Thank you," I said. "We appreciate you trying."

She took Selim's hand, squeezing it between hers. "It's good to see you, Uncle Selim. If you come back on another day, she might be in a better frame of mind. She'd be very glad to see you."

He patted her arm. "Thank you. But I don't know how long we'll be in Hilltop for. I go where my captain tells me." His fingertips lingered on hers and his gaze was on Hayal. I looked away, as if we were intruding on something personal.

We departed the shop, and the dimness of the alley seemed to press down on our mood. As the shop door shut behind us, Maro's hand went to the sword at their hip.

"What is it?" I said, instinctively putting myself in front of George. If it was the brokers, they wouldn't catch me unaware a second time.

Maro held still for a moment, staring up the alley. The space was empty, and people walked by on the main street without giving a second glance in our direction.

"Nothing," they said, finally. "A shadow, perhaps."

But Maro rarely saw threats that weren't there.

"Be ready," I said to George and Selim. "If I give the signal, you run into the closest shop and cause the most disruptive scene you can. Understood?"

They both nodded. The strategy was far from ideal. The brokers weren't always deterred by public exposure. But it might create enough of a delay that Maro and I could deal with them. The worst outcome would be an angry shopkeeper who called the city guard.

"Do we carry on to Enomis?" George asked, slipping her hand into mine as we rejoined the everyday populace in the main market. Maro made an impatient noise in response, and someday I would need to hear the story of why they were so reluctant to return home, but any teasing question I might have come up with was cut off as someone ran directly into us. George cried out and collided with Maro, taking them both to the ground. I stumbled back against a stone wall, crashing so hard on my elbow that lightning streaked all the way to my fingers, making them go numb.

"George," I said, rolling to my feet and spinning, looking for who had run us over.

"I'm fine." George said as she and Maro untangled themselves. Her cheek was smudged with dirt, but she appeared unharmed. Maro already had a sword out, looking for the perpetrator, but whatever had just happened, the goal hadn't been to hurt us, or at least, not seriously.

I patted myself down, waiting for the tingling in my hand to stop. I was about to say no harm done when my fingers froze over my coat pocket.

"What's wrong?" George asked.

I dug inside, silently praying to find what I had missed, but it wasn't there. None of it.

"The ring and the map. They're gone."

George stared at me in horror. In the distance, a woman shrieked.

"There!" Maro was already moving deeper into the market. I spun, staring through the crowd in the direction the cry had come from. The people there had been disturbed, the patterns of their movements swirling like eddies at the shore, away from the central current of those going about their business. On the other side of the curling disruption, a figure in a dark hood pushed their way through.

"George," I said. "Take the doctor and find a guard, tell them who you are and ask them to escort you back to the palace." Whoever this was, whether petty thief or someone with more sinister motives, I needed to know she was safe.

"Lou!" she called after me, but the thief had a head start, and I couldn't waste any more time.

The market was busy, and people who had been knocked over once were disinclined to be patient as we tried to make our way past them. Maro and I struggled to make progress, and the figure in the hood got farther and farther from us.

"The alley," Maro said. "I'll follow the wall." They darted away.

Ahead, a horse reared up, and someone screamed. People turned to see what the commotion was, which at least helped make my path easier with fewer moving bodies to dodge.

The thief had nearly collided with a cart that was coming out of a side street. The cart had toppled over, the horse going with it. The big animal thrashed, long legs kicking as it tried to rise. People darted out of the way to avoid a kick, and the thief was hard-pressed to get around them.

"Stop!" I shouted.

He turned for half a second. Long enough for me to catch a glimpse of a long nose and a thin mustache under his hood. Then he was running again. But my call had garnered some attention, and a guard stepped forward, calling for the thief to stop, only to be knocked off his feet as the two of them collided. Almost immediately, the thief was on his feet and running again. The guard did not get up. As I ran past him, a pool of blood was forming around his head, oozing from the gash where his throat had been cut.

The edge of the market district loomed. If the thief got through that arch, he'd be out into the city, and then I'd never catch him. At the last moment, a gust of air blew toward us, lifting his cloak. I reached, leaning forward. I couldn't reach him, but if I could get an inch closer, then—

My fingers closed around the heavy fabric and I gripped it, pulling for all I was worth. The thief's head jerked back, and his feet flew upward, leaving him horizontal in midair for a fraction of a second, before he hit the stone street with a crunch.

I was on him in an instant. I turned him over, straddling his body as I rummaged through his clothes, looking for what he had stolen. He groaned, but soon enough, he started to struggle, trying to buck me off.

"None of that," I said, finding his knife and tucking it into my belt before I swung and punched him once for good measure. His hands dropped, and I finally found the scrap of cloth and the heavy weight of the ring inside his vest.

"Lou!" George called out somewhere behind me. We were going to have a talk about following orders.

"What's going on?" Two soldiers in Vestrian uniforms rushed

up, pushing their way through the small crowd that had formed a curious circle around us.

But the thief had stilled underneath me. "Lucy?"

I glanced down. His hood had fallen away, and for a moment, my father stared up at me with an expression of shocked horror on his face. Then the shadows moved and the face changed, so my father was gone. But I still knew the features. The thin nose. Narrow mouth. Dark eyes. Mine were very similar.

"Whitney."

The guards parted us and pulled the thief to his feet. Upright, I could see him clearly. It had been more than a decade, so the face I remembered was younger. Still boyish. He was taller now of course, but so was I. His jaw—already swelling on one side, I noted with some satisfaction—was shadowed in stubble I didn't remember, and he was missing part of one eyebrow, but it would be impossible to not know him when I'd spent so much of my childhood hating him.

"Cinder," Maro approached. They hardly appeared winded. "All right?"

"Yes." I gasped. No. I couldn't say for sure.

"You are under arrest," one of the soldiers said. "Murder is the most deplorable of crimes, and the queen's justice makes no exceptions."

"Wait," I said. "I need to speak to him."

"Are you all right, lady?" the other soldier asked. "Did he hurt you?"

"No, it's fine. He took something, but I got it back. But please. I have to …" I had to what?

"You'll have to take it up with the chief justice. This man has murdered a Vestrian soldier. The queen makes—"

"No exceptions. Yes. I heard you." I put my hands on my hips. I couldn't seem to catch my breath.

Apart from saying my name, the thief hadn't uttered a word

the whole time, and he said nothing now. He simply winked, then allowed himself to be led away.

"You should have killed him," Maro said.

"Did you get the ring? The map?" George asked.

"Yes." I patted my pocket to reassure myself as much as her. With everything else that had happened in the last few minutes, I couldn't trust my memory of anything.

"Then it's fine," she said. "Let's go back to the palace."

"It's not fine. I need to talk to him."

"To the thief?" Maro sounded confused, and I couldn't fault them.

"He's not just a thief." I sighed as my head swam. "He's my brother."

CHAPTER 9

"Is it really him?" George asked as we made our way back through the city. As far as we had come to visit Hayal and Gahra earlier, it seemed the walk back to the palace must have been at least twice as far.

My stomach twisted at her question. "I don't know." But it would be nearly impossible for him to be anyone else.

"He was always such a bully," she said. George so rarely had anything unkind to say about anyone that the observation made me laugh, which helped me feel a little better. "Was he five or six years older than we were?"

I glanced at Maro and Selim, who walked ahead of us. They weren't speaking but were giving the illusion that they weren't listening either, which I appreciated. I could barely keep my thoughts together.

"Six. I think. Maybe even seven." To be honest, I wasn't sure. We'd been in the middle of a brood of fourteen children. Or was it fifteen? More than that, really. Two had died at birth, another before my mother had named him, and my little sister Remi had caught a fever the year I was nine and didn't make it through the winter. But there were never fewer than a dozen living persons in the few small rooms we called a home—not to mention the endless stream of skinny, flea-bitten barn cats my brother Ainsley was forever intent on taming. But for most of my life, Whit had always been one of them, no matter which new baby was born or who got sent off to sea or carried off with a cough. A constant dark shadow always waiting to pull my hair or tease me for being too rough and muddy when my other sisters wanted to play with dolls and braid the ponies' manes in the stables.

"How did he know we were here?"

I laughed, arching my back as I tipped my chin up to the sky. Crescent-winged gulls sailed overhead, and I hoped at least a few were laughing with me. My life had become an endless string of coincidences and uncomfortable reunions. I was ready for a few months of anonymity.

"I don't think we can give Whitney so much credit. He was never one for subtlety or strategy."

Whit had always been a blunt instrument. My father had tried to train him in the stables, but despite their size, horses were sensitive creatures, and Whit only wanted to yank them around by their bridles and holler when one of them stepped on his toes. In the end, he'd been sent to work the fields. My father said a brain like his was best suited to work with a shovel or a spade.

But whatever my certainty of Whit's qualities and failings, I wouldn't be able to leave Vestria without knowing how he'd found me and what he'd wanted. He couldn't simply be a thief who happened upon us in the jewel district.

Speaking to him proved easier said than done however. We went to the justice building, but the first person we spoke to declared they had no idea what we were talking about and that no murderer had been arrested. The second, a humorless man with slicked-back hair who approached when Maro's posture became a fraction too menacing with the first clerk, told us that criminals accused of capital crimes were not permitted visitors, and if we had an issue with it, we would have to take it up with the queen herself.

So we did. Knowing a real-life princess must have some advantages, after all.

"This is pointless," Maro said as we made our way back to the palace. "We should be leaving, not wasting time on a thief."

"Our next stop is Enomis City," I said to them with a grin. "Are you sure you're in such a rush to weigh anchor?"

"I need to see the queen," George said as we entered the palace's grand reception hall.

"Is everything all right?" one of the courtiers asked.

She lifted her chin imperiously. "My friends were attacked. I need to speak with the queen right away."

What a princess wanted, she was given. A flurry of activity followed, before we were led to a private audience room where the queen and Ylvar waited for us.

"Princess Georgina," Cheray said, rising from a high-backed velvet chair as we entered. "What happened?"

"Your Majesty," I said, keeping my tone respectful. "I have a favor to ask."

"What is it?" For the first time since our arrival, she sounded almost annoyed, exposing a tiny crack in her magnanimity. No doubt she was unused to granting favors to pirate captains, regardless of the company they kept. I had no doubt that, once she was confident in her alliance with George, Cheray would not hesitate to find ways to push me aside. My presence muddied the waters in her narrative of benevolent liberation.

"A man was arrested in the market this morning for killing a guard, Majesty. I know him. I have no intention of interrupting the processes of your justice system, but I need very much to speak with him."

"Know him?" Ylvar asked where he still reclined on a tufted sofa. "Is he a pirate?"

"No, my lord." I shifted uncomfortably. Even though I knew their truth, the words were hard to force out. "He's my brother."

Ylvar laughed. "Is he now? The marauding pirate's murderous brother. Such irony."

"Yes." I ignored his amusement and turned my attention back to Cheray. "It's been some time since I've seen him. As I said last night, I've been at sea since I was a child. If I could have even a few moments with him. He's killed someone, and he is subject to your laws, but I'd like to speak with him. If I could." I added the last to make sure there was enough deference in the request. These people meant to take George from me, and I would fight them to my last for her, but for now, I could only rely on their indulgence. And my words were true. I didn't expect a tearful reunion. I hadn't given Whitney more than a passing moment's thought in years. But now that he was so close, I needed to at least speak with him. Was this how George felt when she thought about Redmere? This drive? This curiosity? Like if I didn't get to see him again, he would haunt me forever, no matter where I sailed?

Cheray studied me, then glanced at George. In fact, it was George she was looking at when she said, "Fine. He'll be under guard the whole time he meets with you. We can't have any suggestion of the princess associating with criminals." The words forced me to bite my lip. Anyone listening would assume she was talking about Whit, but the flash of her gaze in my direction said she might as easily be talking about me, especially now that I had confessed the family connection.

"Thank you," George said with a slow nod. "We appreciate your generosity."

Our return to the justice hall brought us to the same two officials we'd spoken to earlier, but the queen's request must have reached them before we did, because this time, they were all solicitous apologies and "please, this way, ladies" as they led George and me down a narrow flight of stairs to the dungeons.

George waited in the corridor. She knew the role she was to play, looping her arm through that of the bored-looking soldier who stood at attention, so that I was able to slip inside and close the door behind me. Whitney waited for me, and even as I entered, the gleam in his eye said there was more going on in that head of his than my father might have given him credit for.

"Hello, Lucy," he said. His arms were bound to the chair he sat in, as were his ankles.

I bit back the protest that rose up on long-forgotten memories. He had always called me Lucy, and I'd always hated it. Lucinda was my grandmother's name, though I'd never met her. It always tasted old in my mouth. Dusty. And Lucy was silly and frivolous. The name for a girl who wore new ribbons in her hair every day and rode a pretty pony in circles around a ring. For a while, before I really met her, I'd thought George might have been a Lucy, but I'd realized my mistake when we'd become friends. I had only ever wanted to be Lou. Then the world had made me Cinder, and she was as far away from ribbons and ponies as one could imagine.

"Whitney." We were separated by a wobbly wooden table, and I took the chair opposite him.

"How long has it been?" Whitney sniffed, wrinkling his nose like he smelled something rotten. He'd aged. Closer to thirty now. His beard was patchy on the left side of his chin and his mustache had been too thinly trimmed, looking more like a smear of dirt than hair above his lip. He wore a silver ring in one ear and another in his nostril. Altogether, he looked entirely disreputable. If he'd been anyone but my brother, I might have bought him a mug of ale and seen where our worlds overlapped. But since he *was* my brother, I'd be as likely to crack the mug over his head.

"You left before my tenth birthday. So a decade. Maybe more." Hopefully, the next interval would be even longer. Already, the smug look on his face annoyed me. I hadn't needed to see him after all. He hadn't changed.

He smiled crookedly. "Gotten up to much?"

I could tell him it was none of his business. Should tell him, in fact. But I couldn't stop the little girl inside me who wanted to impress him.

"The usual. Murder, kidnapping, general piracy. Yourself?"

He tsked disapprovingly before he said, "Thievery, conspiracy, the occasional stint as a bodyguard."

"Until someone paid you more to kill the body you were guarding."

If he could, I was sure he'd have spread his hands to argue his innocence in the ways of the wicked world. "A man has to eat, and the best way to do that is with coins in his pocket. I never killed anyone who didn't deserve it. Been home lately?"

I flinched at the rapid change in subject, and his eyes narrowed. I dug my nails into the worn surface of the table. "How did you know to steal my ring?"

"How could you be so foolish as to have it out in the open? Any passerby who peeked through the window would have seen you like I did. The needle stairs. The caged man." His voice rose to a melodramatic falsetto. "I could hear you from the street. You have to hide your prizes better. Did you learn nothing from the necklace, Lucy?"

I should stab him. The necklace in question had been a gift from George. Or, not a gift exactly. She'd given it to me one winter when we'd been particularly cold and hungry. I'd planned to sell it to buy food, but instead, Whit had found it. He'd never admitted to taking it—even now, he had said as much—but two days after it disappeared, he'd come home wearing a pair of boots made from soft brown leather that shone like even the cow it was made from had never seen so much as a speck of mud its whole life.

"That was a long time ago," I said, holding back a childhood's worth of hurts, big and small, like a flood.

He laughed like we were sharing a good joke or a fond memory. But all I could think of was how much I hated him and his silly boots. How he wore them around the stable yard, cocking his feet this way and that, no doubt hoping he might catch a maid's attention simply by the way he wore his boots.

"How's the lady Georgina?" Whit asked. "I see you're still following after her like a whipped puppy. Is she married? I'm in the market for a gently bred wife. Do you think she noticed me?"

I snorted. "You've never had anything to offer someone like her."

"And you do?"

With every second, I spun deeper and deeper into a dance Whit and I had done our entire youth. He always knew every way to push me into a fury over the littlest things and get away looking like an angel. I'd never told anyone in my family how I felt about George. At twelve, I'd barely understood our connection myself. But Redmere didn't look kindly on a love like ours, and even though he'd been away even longer than I had, Whit could easily share those views.

Time to go. I was doing nothing but torturing myself here. I'd wanted to see if he was the bully I remembered, and he was. "As lovely as this reunion has been, I'm off. I'll make sure the guards find you a cell with extra fleas …" I gave him a pointed look. "Though I doubt it'll make much difference to you."

He scratched at his chin, then seemed to catch himself and dropped his hand into his lap. Whit chuckled and tapped the side of his nose. The tip of his finger was missing. There was a story there. One I didn't need to know.

"Goodbye, brother."

"Good luck with your treasure hunt," he said as I turned away. "Though I doubt it'll help, considering you only have half the map."

"What?"

His chair scraped on the floor, and when I faced him, he leered, hands clasped behind his head. It was only then I realized that somehow, during our conversation, he'd managed to free himself from the bindings around his wrists.

I was going to regret this. Whit always liked to play games. But I couldn't help myself. Not if it meant learning more about the treasure.

"What do you mean, half a map?"

"Your map shows the island, but not where the island is, correct?"

"Did you waste time in your escape going over the details of my map? Is that why you ran into the horse? You're a terrible thief, Whit." How he'd managed to live this long in his chosen profession was baffling. Merely the look on his face had me itching for my knife.

"And you're a terrible pirate if you think you can find this treasure with willpower alone," he said, which only made me want to stamp my foot and call him a liar, like I was six years old all over again.

Instead, I rolled my eyes. "And I suppose you're offering to help."

He steepled his fingers in front of him, like he had any leverage. "I know how to get the other map. I could take you to it."

How I wished for a sword. I could cut off the rest of his fingertips until he told me.

"What do you want?" I asked.

His smile grew. "You have to ask? A fate that doesn't include my neck at the end of a Vestrian noose would be an excellent starting place."

"You could have avoided that by not killing a soldier."

Whit shrugged remorselessly. "My knife slipped."

Such a terrible idea, but also the best chance I had. The alternatives were spending who knew how long among the dusty texts in Enomis City or hoping we could outrun the brokers long enough to make it to Sarguilla in search of a man whose name we didn't even know. At least Maro wasn't here to criticize my negotiations.

"We get you out of here, and you give me the second map," I said.

"I don't have it in Hilltop, but yes, that's the idea. And I want my share of the treasure of course." He folded his hands solemnly on the table.

I ground my teeth. "Fine." Whatever was left after the brokers, we could divide up equitably.

"Excellent." He grinned. "When do we leave?"

The door behind us burst open, making me jump.

"Stay where you are!" a flush-faced soldier shouted, before his eyes widened in shock as he noticed Whit's free hands. In the corridor, George gaped at us in horror, though whether that was also in response to Whit's apparent escape attempt or in embarrassment that she hadn't managed to keep the guard distracted any longer, I couldn't say.

Either way, I pushed back from the chair. "Goodbye, brother."

Whit winked knowingly as the soldier wrestled him to his feet.

WE DIDN'T GO BACK to the palace. The walls had eyes and ears there, and anything we said would get back to the queen in an instant. Instead, we walked to the harbor. The *Siren* had been taken out to anchor, and I yearned to be aboard her, on familiar ground. As we stood, a dark shape emerged from the shadows and joined us.

"Everything all right?" Maro asked. I gave them a single nod. "And your brother? A joyous reunion?"

I sighed. The meeting with Whit had left me off-balance when I needed my bearings most.

"Joyous. Exactly that."

They snorted. "He should have been nicer to you as a child."

"He should have," I agreed. "But that doesn't change the present."

Maro's face was obscured by a dark hood, but even the tone of their voice was enough for me to envision the mistrustful glance they must be giving me.

"And what is that present, Captain?"

I wiped a shaking hand over my face, forcing my nerves to still. The world felt like it was spiraling out of my control, and all I could do was cling to the flotsam that floated at the edges. "We have to break Whit out and escape to sea."

PART II

Maro is a master at their craft. But even they make mistakes from time to time.

We've been hunting Sushna Demarche for the last three months. She's been Kiril's agent in the North Valardo region for over fifteen years, transacting deals for new recruits and mercenaries, and making sure money flows back to Kiril in a discreet manner. But a traitor in her organization has recently brought to light—while I pulled out his fingernails, one at a time—that Sushna keeps a small percentage of the revenue for herself, beyond what has been agreed upon with Kiril.

So now she has to die.

She's well connected, so we aren't surprised when we arrive at her home in Valardo and Sushna is long gone. But a few more persuasive conversations with those who want to redeclare their loyalty to the brokers tells us which way she's headed.

Maro goes inland, and we trail after them from sea. In the bigger ports, other representatives from the brokers relay messages, but even in the small towns there are traces of Sushna's passage and Maro's progress. Houses of known associates are burned to the ground. Her allies stagger into villages missing an eye or a hand. They haven't escaped. These survivors are a warning, in case Sushna thinks she's in the clear. Maro works quickly, but the fact that the work continues means they haven't found her yet.

The night we finally discover her, it's pouring. We've made port in a small fishing town called Goolding, and when Maro and I walk into the town's single inn, Sushna is sitting at a table, an entire feast spread before her.

"Hello, Cinder," she says, voice soft and breathy. "I've been waiting for you."

"You held out longer than most," I say, one hand on my sword.

"I needed time to get my affairs in order."

"And did you?" Already, I'm making a mental list of the associates we haven't tracked down. If she's moved her fortune on to someone else, Kiril will want to know. Colluding with a traitor, even a dead one, is still treason.

Maro is at my side but moves slowly toward the door near the rear. Sushna makes no attempt to escape. She watches us both with disinterested eyes. Resignation like this is common. Kiril's rules are clear, and anyone who crosses him knows they're operating on borrowed time. No one escapes forever. Maro and I are very good at what we do.

Yet, as Sushna lifts her hands to the table and I see the bright red slashes on her wrists, my stomach twists. She's not the first to do this. Poison, hangings, we've come across our share of desperate people who knew we were closing in. But of the ones who weren't dead when we arrived, she's the calmest.

"He's a monster," she says.

"Of course he is." I sit across from her, poking at the untouched plate of food on the table. Preserved fish, greens in a creamy white sauce.

"Cinder," Maro says in warning. The food might be poisoned.

She might be hoping to take at least one of us with her into death. Still, I drag a finger through the gravy, watching it glisten on my fingertip, before I lick it off slowly. It's rich, tasting of butter and white wine, two things we rarely get in the cramped mess of the *Siren*.

"You are too," Sushna says.

"Me? A monster?" I am what I am. What I've needed to be to survive when the world didn't care what happened to me, like it won't care when she's gone. Lives will continue. Businesses. Someone will take her place and live rich for a few years before they get overly ambitious and take more than they should. Then we'll start this dance all over again.

I take another taste of her meal, then wait. For the bitter tang in the back of my palate that says I've made a mistake. For the confusion or the racing heartbeat as the toxin consumes me and I realize she's won. For the fear and regret that this is my ending and I've wasted too many years in the service of a monster only to become one myself.

I feel nothing other than a craving for more. For anything to fill the empty clench of my guts.

She's fading though. Sushna's breathing slows and she lists to one side.

Maro sighs in frustration. "Well, this has all been a waste. She could have saved us a lot of trouble and done it months ago."

"You're angry you lost your favorite knife in that tavern fight last week."

"It was a good blade. You gave it to me."

I did. I bought it at a market in Yagrad last summer. The smith said it would never need sharpening. I guess we'll never know.

The crash of a bottle has us both leaping back to attention. The knife—still lethally sharp, even if all others will forever feel inadequate—is flying from Maro's hand before I have mine out of its sheath. In the few seconds it takes for me to find the threat, it's already over. A girl of no more than fourteen staggers back against the wall, Maro's knife buried deep in her chest. Her face is tear-streaked, like she's been crying for some time, but she slumps silently to the floor as the red stain spills down the front of her apron.

"She must have been hiding behind the bar," Maro says as they go to retrieve their knife.

I watch dispassionately as the light fades from the dead girl's eyes. She has dark hair and a nose that turns up slightly at the end. She reminds me of someone I knew a long time ago.

"We should go," Maro says.

But somehow, I can't stop staring at the girl.

I wait. For the confident certainty that her death was justified. For the repulsion at the sight of her life spilling from her. For the grief that she's most likely never left this town, and now we've taken that chance away from her.

Nothing. It's always nothing. I never give these people a second thought.

For the first time in a long time, the nothing bothers me.

CHAPTER 10

$\mathcal{A}$ pirate crew was not a democracy. The captain's word was as absolute as she wanted it to be.

Perhaps, after all these years, I had been too lenient with Maro. I understood their desire to chase down the brokers, but their general insolence was grating on my nerves.

"You have to be joking," they said.

I scowled. "You know I'm not that funny."

"You want to break your brother out of a Vestrian prison and sneak him out of the city?"

"Precisely. Are you telling me you can't do it?"

They narrowed their eyes. Maro was always sensitive to any implication they couldn't do something, regardless of how many times they told me my ideas were impossible.

"If you insist on this course of action, Captain," they growled softly, "it will take me a few days to find which guards can be bribed and which entry points will be easiest to use. I can have Ender figure out how to get the ship away from the harbor without the customs officers—"

"It needs to happen tonight," I said.

"Cinder!" The single word of exclamation echoed across the

water. A gull that had been half asleep on a piling startled and flapped in irritation over the harbor.

"He has the other map," I said.

"We'll have nothing if the Vestrians catch us. We are in a foreign country—"

"Every country is a foreign country to people like us. You're making excuses."

"I'm being cautious, Cinder. I thought that was what you wanted."

"Please." I put a hand on their shoulder. "I know you can do this."

Tension radiated over Maro, but when I squeezed, they sagged under my touch. Maro would always have opinions, but in the end, we were not a democracy. They continued to glower, and their sigh was long and put upon, but they said, "I have an idea. I'll need the doctor's help."

"Then let's go find him," I said.

"No." They took a step back from me and George. "I'll speak with him. If we continue to go around in a troop movement like this, it will only gather notice. You and Georgina go see the sights. Keep the Vestrians' eyes on you until I have the wheels in motion."

I took George's hand in mine. "We can do that."

Wordlessly, Maro vanished into the shadows.

GEORGE and I made a big production of wandering the city. No one seemed to notice us or care when she slipped an arm around my waist or pressed a kiss to my cheek. To be so unremarkable was freeing. Someday, we might have this. Once we'd paid the brokers and were free, we could go anywhere we wanted and melt into the city or build a home high up on a mountain or deep in a forest where no one would ever find us. George kept talking about going back to Redmere, but we could never be truly free there. People clung to their beliefs, and even if we could liberate them from cruel rulers, teaching them to tolerate what they'd learned for generations was immoral would be a much longer task.

We returned to the palace, but there was no sign of Maro, only a note saying we would need to stay one more night while they set their plan in motion. As a courtesy, George requested a new audience with Cheray.

"I need to tell her we're not staying," she said. "And she has to know it's my decision. If she wants my help in Redmere in the future, it will be as equals, not with me as a nominal figurehead." So I kissed her and let her break the bad news to the warrior queen of Vestria.

I slept poorly, thoughts of Whit and treasure and more swirling in my head. I tossed endlessly, and finally, after another hour of thrashing and turning, George rose from our bed.

"Where are you going?"

"There are bedrooms up and down this floor, but this is the only one with its own growling monster. If this is the last evening I spend in a bed that doesn't rock for a while, I'm getting a good night's sleep."

"I'll go with you," I said, not even realizing what I was saying, and George laughed and placed a gentle kiss on my cheek.

"We've been safe here so far. I'll only be a few doors away."

After she left, the room was silent and empty. I didn't sleep any better once I was alone and took to prowling the halls, watching for anyone who might seek to harm George. At least I had room to think. By tomorrow, we'd have Whit and his map and be away on the *Siren*. Hopefully we wouldn't have far to travel after that, because I didn't know how long I would be able to stand his presence on my ship. The mere memory of his self-satisfied smirk made my toes curl. But he was our best chance. If it came to it, I could keep him tied up in the hold until we'd found the treasure.

Eventually, as the sun began to rise, I retreated to our room and tried to sleep, but only minutes after my head hit the pillow, a soft knock sounded on my door. I was up in an instant, ready for an attack, before I realized the brokers wouldn't knock. When I opened it, the doctor waited in the hallway.

"Selim. Good morning." I rubbed my eyes. The motion felt strangely vulnerable, but Selim was one of the few people I could trust, even in moments like this.

"Good morning, Captain." He gave me a quick salute, which left me in more familiar territory, until he said, "I've decided to stay in Vestria."

My heart sank. Apart from Maro, Selim had been with me the longest.

"Stay?"

"Vestria has changed. The people I knew have changed. Hayal and her family could use my help. My own family doesn't even know me anymore. I think it's time for me to reclaim my home here."

I swallowed hard, unexpected emotion clogging my throat. Most sailors in our world were transient, moving from one port to the next, one crew to the next. That was, if they didn't live a short existence that ended at the bottom of the ocean. I'd known the doctor for a long time.

"You will be missed," I said. "Your place on the *Siren* be will yours should you ever want it back."

"You've been a good captain." He knocked another salute. "I hope you find the treasure you're looking for." Then he surprised me and held out his hand to shake. Handshakes were rare among sailors, where hidden weapons were common and hierarchy—even among the chaotic life of pirates—ruled even the minutiae of day-to-day life. But I took it, then froze at the cool lump clasped against his palm. His gaze was direct, and his voice was pointed when, softly, he said, "For later. Maro has the other half."

The object in my hand was smooth like a glass vial, but his meaningful glance allowed no questions about what it might contain. Instead, I took one last second to remember the lines of his face, before he turned and departed.

George returned shortly after. She said she was going to the bathing chamber to wash her hair one last time before we left, and only moments later, two liveried servants entered the room. One carried in a tray of rich golden pastries and two boiled eggs. The other carried a pitcher of water and a basin to wash in and disappeared down the hall George had gone. The first busied herself setting out the morning's small meal. Although she said nothing, her gaze kept darting toward me when she thought I wasn't looking.

"Something wrong?" I asked.

She jumped, smoothing her hands over the front of her trousers.

"I'm sorry. I—" For a minute, she looked like she might run out of the room, but she bit her lip and made a slightly more successful attempt to meet my eyes. "You're Captain Cinder, aren't you?"

She was far too nervous to be an assassin, so I indulged her. "I am."

The maid twisted at her fingers. "Did you really kidnap the princess from Redmere and force her to marry you?"

My hand dropped unconsciously to the scar in my belly where Prince Beverly had stabbed me.

"The princess is free to come and go as she chooses. I've never forced any woman to come aboard my ship and I never will."

She sighed. "It's so romantic. I'd love to go to sea with you."

I eyed her. "What's your name?"

"Lalle, Captain."

"And where do you live, Lalle?"

"In the city, with my family."

"You have children?" I asked. She wouldn't be the first exhausted and downtrodden mother to dream of escape.

But Lalle laughed. "No. I'm only sixteen. I live with my parents and my brothers and sisters."

"That sounds very cozy. Could you ask the princess if she minds sharing her bath?" I turned and pulled off my shirt, making a show of pulling the material over my shoulders. Lalle gasped behind me. I knew what she saw. My back was mottled with scars from various stabbings, whippings, and beatings. I turned, holding the shirt over my breasts, but making sure it didn't cover the jagged purple line where Beverly's knife had gone in.

"Something wrong?" I asked.

Lalle's face was bright pink, and now she truly was doing everything to look anywhere but at the scars I carried from my romantic life at sea. She bowed stiffly, and her eyes glistened as if she were trying not to cry.

"I'm sorry for bothering you," she said, then hurried back out into the hall.

Another person might have been sorry to scare her the way I had. I wasn't. George had asked me what we'd do to save more women once we were done with the brokers, and maybe this was how. Sometimes salvation came in ways other than a daring rescue from a tower. If this encounter kept Lalle at home, safe in the arms of a family who cared for her, then I had saved her too. There would be others.

Unfortunately, before we could do that, there was still the business of saving my ne'er-do-well brother, whether I wanted to or not.

George returned, looking annoyingly refreshed. Still no sign of Maro, but whatever they had planned was undoubtedly already underway. We'd head to the harbor and meet them there.

As we emerged into the early morning daylight, the courtyard was relatively quiet. Unlike the ceremony on our arrival, no one was here to see us off. No doubt the queen was disappointed in George's departure. Better to save some embarrassment for all parties.

George held my hand as we walked toward the arch that led to the city.

"Stop!" Behind us, a shout rang out.

"Oh, dear," I said. "So close to making our escape."

"What's wrong?" George said.

"I can't imagine."

We both turned as a uniformed soldier strode across the courtyard. "You!"

"Me?" I pointed an incredulous finger at my chest.

"Where are you going?"

"The lady and I have said our goodbyes to your queen. It's time to leave Vestria."

"Lord Ylvar wishes to see you."

I glanced at George. She was watching me, but said nothing. I inclined my head to the guard. "Then lead the way."

We followed him across the courtyard and through the busy streets into the justice building. No overzealous clerk stopped us this time. As we came to the bottom of the stairs, two soldiers passed us, carrying a cloth-shrouded figure on a stretcher. George gasped softly, but no one else seemed to notice anything amiss.

Lord Ylvar stood in the chamber where Whit was bound last night. In fact, Ylvar sat in the very same chair. He appeared deep in thought as we arrived, but a cleared throat behind us brought his attention up, and he focused on me with dark, piercing eyes.

"Captain Cinder," he said.

"My lord."

"I'm sorry to delay your departure."

I forced myself to remain calm. I didn't have all the details of what Maro had planned, but we didn't know what Ylvar knew.

"Your hospitality has been gracious. Staying a moment longer is no trouble at all."

He wasn't distracted by my generous words. "Where have you been this morning?"

George's hand tightened in mine, but my voice was steady when I spoke. "I was in my room."

"Your room," Ylvar said. "Were there any witnesses?"

"Yes. As a matter of fact, Dr. Sarkiss came by earlier. Then the maids brought breakfast and a bath."

"And you were in your room all night?" he asked.

"Yes."

"Any witnesses to that?"

"Yes. Captain Cinder and I have shared a room throughout our time in Hilltop," George said quickly, and I hadn't thought her absence the night before would cause trouble, but I was grateful now for her quick thinking.

Ylvar's lips thinned and his frown returned, like he was puzzling through something complex.

"What is this about?" George asked.

He watched her for another half second, but he must have thought better than to question her further. Even if George wasn't going off to glorious rebellion with his queen, in his eyes she was still a princess, and accusing a lady with limited proof would not look good on him.

Ylvar steepled his fingers and braced his elbows on the arms of the chair that hadn't been enough to hold Whit. "Captain Cinder. I regret to inform you the prisoner died suddenly sometime this morning."

George gasped. "Whitney?"

"Is that all?" I asked.

Ylvar's icy stare hardened. "He was your brother, was he not?"

"Well, yes, but we hadn't seen each other in nearly a decade, and even before then, he took more joy in mashing my face into the mud than he did looking out for me. He killed one of your soldiers. I can't say that any of us will feel his loss."

A silence filled the room. The dungeons smelled of damp and fear, but not mine. Regardless of what investigations Ylvar might make, he would find no relation between me and Whitney's death. And truthfully, if he really was dead, I would only be inconvenienced not knowing what he did about the map. I wouldn't miss him at all.

A guard entered behind us and came to speak with Ylvar, whispering to him in low tones. They both threw us quiet glances, then finally, the soldier bowed and departed again.

"You're free to go," Ylvar said.

"Thank you. My ship and crew are waiting," I said.

"Yes, Cheray told me Princess Georgina wouldn't be staying on."

"I hope we haven't inconvenienced Her Majesty's plans too greatly," I said, not caring at all one way or the other.

But Ylvar waved a careless hand. "There are other ways. We questioned the Redmerians you brought with you. Apparently, they were looking for a princess to save them."

"Yes," I said. In truth, I'd forgotten about them. "And stumbled upon Georgina in the middle of the ocean."

"That's the thing," Ylvar said, sounding distracted. "They weren't looking for Georgina. They claim Beverly had a sister."

"A what?" George asked, sounding shocked.

"It's probably a myth," he said. "Desperate people clinging to the hope of any savior. Cheray will see to their salvation, regardless of who is at her side."

George opened her mouth to speak, no doubt needing to defend her decision to leave, but I jumped ahead of her. "Thank you, Your Grace. Best of luck with your investigation." I bowed once and gently tugged George from the room.

"Another princess?" she asked as we hurried down the street.

"None of our concern," I said, trying to walk as quickly as I could without drawing any attention our way. And she wasn't any of our concern, whether she was real or imaginary. Let the Vestrians chase ghosts. We had other missions to complete.

The *Siren* lay at anchor in the harbor, and we paid a longboat to take us out from the wharf.

"Captain," Ender said with a salute as we came aboard.

"Prepare to make way," I said. "Has Maro arrived yet?"

"No, Captain."

"They'll be here shortly then. As soon as they're aboard, we'll be off."

The ship came alive as sailors climbed the rigging. It was the sort of competent order that eased the tension that always lived in my bones. Everyone knew their place and their role, and the ship only worked as well as her crew.

"There," someone said as a breeze that would put Vestria at our backs started to come up. Sure enough, Maro rowed toward us, an upright shape in black with a longboat loaded down with cargo.

"How long are we going to be gone for?" Rosie asked.

"How much did they buy?" George asked beside her. I didn't know what Maro had in mind, but they had clearly acquired enough provisions to make it clear we had no plans to return.

The longboat came aside, and Maro climbed the ladder to join us, while others went about unloading and securing their goods. They'd bought food and ale, and long bundles of canvas as if we intended to do extensive sail repairs.

"Take it all to the hold," Ender said.

"Except for this one." Maro pointed at the last parcel to come over the rail. It was just over six feet long, irregularly shaped, and wrapped in the same canvas. It took two strong sailors to carry it. "Take it to the infirmary."

"What's in it?" Rosie asked, then gasped. "And where's the doctor?"

That was as good a distraction as any while Maro took care of their prize. If anyone was watching us from shore, we were a crew taking care of stowing cargo. No surprises. Nothing to see here.

"The doctor has decided to remain in Vestria."

"He's not coming back?" Rosie looked stricken, and I wished Selim could see her. He made his own choices, but I hoped he knew how much he would be missed.

"Captain!" Maro called from the hatch that led to the infirmary. "I believe you have something I need."

"Right." I fished the doctor's vial from my coat as I headed toward the infirmary. George and Rosie trailed behind me. No doubt Ender would be along shortly, never far from his lady when he could manage it.

By the time I reached the infirmary, the two sailors had laid the bundle out on the doctor's table. Maro dismissed them, and they gave me a short salute as they went back up to the deck. The infirmary was small and became even more crowded as George and Rosie joined us.

"What's that?" Rosie asked again, as Maro pulled out a short knife and cut away the bindings.

"A lot of trouble," they muttered while they worked.

"It's the key that will lead us to the treasure," I said, which had Maro giving me an annoyed glance.

"The doctor said we only had a few hours. It's already been three," they said.

"A few hours for what?" George asked, peering over my shoulder. She gasped when the ropes finally fell away, and I pulled back the canvas to reveal Whit's still face beneath it. "What's this? You stole his body?"

"Easier to steal a dead body than a live criminal," Maro said.

"He's not really dead," I said.

"He looks dead," Rosie said.

"Here," I said, handing George the vial. I took Whit's chin and tipped his head back, parting his lips. "Pour it down his throat."

The liquid was green and so thick, it took an age before the first drop hit Whit's lip, and the rest dripped into his open mouth.

"What are you doing?" Rosie asked.

"Waking him up," I said.

"But he's dead."

I arched an eyebrow at George, who was watching me expectantly. "Sit him up. We'll make gravity do its work."

Getting Whit's limp body upright was challenging, and finally Ender stepped in, pulling him forward so Whit's torso slumped against Ender's broad chest.

"What did you give him?" George asked.

"I assume it's the other part of a potion Maro snuck in to give him this morning." I glanced at them for confirmation and they nodded.

"It's one of the doctor's creations," they said. "The first will slow a person's heart and breathing to the point where it's nearly impossible to tell if they're dead or alive. The second dose, administered within a certain number of hours, will bring him back to life."

"But why risk it?" George sounded appalled. We were really going to have to have a talk about what she remembered about growing up with Whit, because she remained far too sympathetic to my brother's well-being. "What if he had died?"

"Because, as Maro said, it's easier to steal a body than a murderer, and we didn't have time to come up with a better plan to break Whit from the dungeons. But from the pit where dead prisoners are tossed beyond the city wall? A much simpler scenario."

"What if we're too late?" Rosie asked. She looked suspiciously up at Whit's slack face. "What if you haven't given him the second potion in time?"

As if in answer, Whit convulsed suddenly, his whole body spasming as a rasping groan escaped his throat, followed by a stream of black bile. Ender only had a second of warning before the goo hit the floor rather than his back, and Rosie squeaked as she darted out of the way. Whit coughed and gasped, and Ender had to brace him up by the shoulders while he vomited again.

Finally, we got Whit settled back on the cot. His skin was an alarming shade of gray, lips stained black. George wiped his mouth as he stared blankly up at the ceiling.

"Well, clearly, we got him the antidote in time," Maro said dryly.

"What …" Whit's voice was like thin paper tearing. "What did you do to me?" He winced as I leaned over him and patted his cheek.

"Rescued you from Cheray's wrath and saved your life, dear brother. Now you owe me."

Whit tried to push up on his elbows, but he slipped and flopped down. "I'm starting to wish I'd taken my chances with the Vestrians."

In a flash, Maro had him up by his hair, knife at his throat. "We would be happy to carry out their execution."

"Don't be dramatic," I waved a hand. "Get the ship underway."

"And what course should I set, Captain? Or should we ask the prisoner?" If it were possible for Maro to be petulant, we were seeing it now.

"He's a guest, not a prisoner. Get us out of the harbor before anyone decides to do a final cargo inspection."

Maro sheathed their dagger and let Whit drop unceremoniously to the cot one more time. He groaned, and they gave me a curt nod before departing. Rosie and Ender followed. George hovered anxiously by the doctor's old chest of ointments and potions.

"I have to say, your hospitality leaves a lot to be desired." Whit coughed wetly, but nothing came up.

"Well, you're not really a guest, are you? You're family." I pinched his cheek. "George, can you get my brother something to drink? Go after Rosie and see if she has any broth or gruel we could give him—if he'll keep it down."

"Lady Georgina." Whit gave a sluggish wave. "So nice to be in your graceful presence once again. Taking the orders now instead of receiving them? How times have changed."

George didn't say anything as she left. Whit and I were alone.

"I expect you'll feel better in a few days," I said, pulling up a wobbly stool to sit next to him. "The doctor was very skilled with his creations."

Around us, the ship tilted as the wind lifted her sails and began to pull us away to safety. I prayed that the Vestrians would be so preoccupied with the death in their dungeons, they wouldn't be bothered with a single ship slipping away in broad daylight.

Whit coughed again, wincing. Some of his color had already returned, but without the devilish glint in his eye and his knowing smirk, he looked almost approachable. Not friendly, but at least not someone you expected to relieve you of your valuables if you got too close.

"Where are we headed?" I asked.

"Wherever you want."

I wished for Maro's knife. But my hand would do. I slapped Whit so hard his head rocked on the thin pillow.

"That was uncalled for." He blinked rapidly and opened and closed his mouth, working his jaw.

"We're still in Vestrian waters, and you're a wanted man. I've put my crew in danger for you, but I'll just as easily toss you overboard. Tell me, Whitney. Do you feel like going for a long swim?"

But he only rolled his eyes. "You know you can't drown me until you have the information you want. You'll understand if I only give it to you in pieces."

"Give me the map." I hauled him up by the front of his shirt so he knew I was serious.

In the doorway, George cleared her throat. She carried a mug and a tin bowl. I let Whit settle down again.

"Obviously, I don't have it on me," he said. "But I'll tell you how to get it. Sail southwest for three days. Then I'll give you the next part of the journey. Now if lovely Georgina wouldn't mind helping me sit up, I'm sure whatever you've brought to eat will be a far better welcome than I've received so far."

George eyed me, but I gave her a nod and left the cabin wordlessly.

Three days.

It would be a miracle if Whit and I didn't drown each other before that.

CHAPTER 11

In the end, Whit survived the first leg of the voyage, but only because coming back from the dead was a lengthy process, especially without the doctor to ease the way. Whit remained in the infirmary, hacking up black clots and wasting George's time. She had assigned herself to be his nurse-maid, which delighted Whit and rankled me to no end.

"He's taking us to the treasure," she said. "Why shouldn't I look after him?"

On the third day, the wind finally shifted, and the *Siren* began to make her way more determinedly over the water. But with new progress came my brother, staggering out of the infirmary onto the deck. He lurched around sailors, gripping the rail tight where he could. He was only steps away from me when he turned suddenly and vomited into the ocean.

"Still unwell?" I asked, though I was sure my smile told him exactly how much sympathy I was willing to extend him.

"Seasickness. I hate boats." He wiped at his chin with his cuff. "Never get my legs under me."

"The *Siren* is a ship, not a boat," I said, the words coming out more sullen than I meant for them to. Even feeling poorly as he was, Whit gave me an ironic smile.

"You always were a fiend for the particulars, Lucy."

"Captain," Ender said, coming up behind me. I flushed at the idea he might have heard Whit use the childish name.

"Yes?"

"Now that your brother is up and about, we've followed the course you set. Where should we go now?"

I turned to Whit, who was scowling at the low dark shape of an island ahead of us. When he realized the conversation had died, he redirected his scowl at us.

"What?"

"You said you'd tell us where to go."

"Where are we now?"

"Three days southwest of Vestria."

"Why southwest?"

My mouth dropped open. "But you said—"

"When?"

"Three days ago!" My voice rose, and I struggled to maintain composure. Some of the crew had stopped to see what the commotion was, and their stares bored into my back. To them, I was the captain, but faced with my older brother, I was reduced to a frustrated child.

Whit waved an annoyed hand. "I was still half dead. You shouldn't have believed any of my directions."

I took a deep breath, forcing down the protests and choosing a more direct approach. "Ender."

The giant mate came to stand at my side. "Captain?"

"Throw him overboard."

"Yes, Captain."

"Wait." Whit backed up, hands in front of him to ward off Ender's approach.

"You might want to take off your coat. It will be heavy as you swim to shore. Assuming the currents carry you toward the island instead of out into the open sea."

"If you kill me, you won't find the other map." He looked desperately over his shoulder.

"You've wasted my time for three days. I don't need allies like you."

Ender reached for Whit's coat. My brother squirmed, shrugging out of it and trying to make a break to the more open space of the deck. The crew hemmed him in, and Ender followed him with a slow, relentless pace.

"You'll regret this," Whit said. He pulled a small dagger from his belt—where he'd gotten hold of it, I couldn't say—but Ender swung a heavy fist, connecting with Whit's wrist, and he dropped the knife to the deck, where another sailor scooped it up. Ender was finally close enough that he grabbed hold of Whit's collar, hoisting him up onto his toes.

"Any final words?" I asked.

Whit sneered. "You always were a coward, Lucy. Making others do your dirty work. Hiding behind Georgina's skirts when we were children, and now this."

"This isn't cowardice," I said, nodding to Ender. "It's delegation. Every good captain should know how to do it."

Ender dragged Whit to the rail and had a solid hold on his belt, ready to launch him clean into the air, when suddenly Whit cried out, frightened, "I'm taking you to Aga Serala!"

A hush fell over the ship. Ender froze. Behind me, a few of the crew muttered oaths and breathless prayers.

I stepped forward, crowding into Whit's space where he clung to the rail. His eyes were wide and frightened, his breathing ragged.

"The sea witch?" I asked.

He licked his lips. "She lives on Isla Laurentis. It's not far from here."

"Might be a trap," Ender said.

"It's not," Whit said, swinging his head wildly between us.

"Then why?" The legends of Aga Serala were more terrifying than the ones I'd cultivated about Captain Cinder. Some said she was part fish or part crab. She had one hand that was a giant pincer and was known to pinch the sailors who crossed her in half. She traded favors with sailors in exchange for their souls, which she trapped in the rock of her cave. She lured ships in close to the shoals, then feasted on the guts of the lost, often while they were still alive.

"She has the map," Whit said. "I gave it to her."

"Why?"

"Because she had something I wanted."

"Throw him over," I said to Ender. I didn't have time for this. Now that we knew where the map was, I'd retrieve it myself.

"Wait! You'll never find her on your own!" Whit had lost all pretense of confidence. One of his fingers was bleeding where he'd torn a nail in his desperate efforts to hold on to the rail. "I'll show you. But we need to go to Port Darto first."

I rolled my eyes. Port Darto was a notorious pirate haven. More than likely Whit would take us there, find a dark alley, and have someone stab me in the back.

Two could play that game. Though I had my own knife, I held out a hand, and the sailor who had picked up Whit's dagger came forward and placed it in my palm. I wasted no time pressing the tip beneath his jaw where his pulse beat wildly.

"Take us to the witch."

"Lucy, she won't—"

"I'm the captain of this ship. We go where I say. And right now, I'm saying we're going to visit Aga Serala. She has the map. We aren't taking you on a tour."

"Lou. Stop," George said.

"Yes, Lucy." Whit's eyes twinkled as his voice rose in a mockery of George's. "Stop."

"Take me to the witch." Too much time. We could have been

in Enomis City by now. Every time we made port, it slowed us down, and the brokers always had someone in Darto. They would see us and know we were still looking for ways to pay them. I glared at Whit, silently telling him I'd be more than happy to feed him to the brokers' justice if it would buy us more time.

Finally, he nodded jerkily, moving with care so as not to injure himself.

"Just remember I said it was a bad idea," he said slowly.

He always did need to get the last word. Well, he was about to learn things had changed in the intervening years. I poked him a final time. "And one other thing."

He sighed wearily. "Whatever you want, sister dear."

"My name is not Lucy. It was never Lucy. Do you understand me?"

"Perfectly. What should I call you instead? Lou?" His gaze drifted to George, and my skin prickled at the familiarity.

"Cinder will be fine."

He laughed, then he sobered. "Cinder? Captain Cinder? You're Captain Cinder?"

Was I? Cinder had been a creature of the brokers, and I wasn't that person anymore. But the outward trappings remained the same, from the crew who sailed with me for years right down to the red mark on Whit's throat where the knife hadn't quite pierced his skin. It was the way Cinder had solved so many problems and won even more confessions. I threw a guilty glance in George's direction.

"No more nicknames," I said.

Whit pulled himself up, straightening his clothes. "Yes. Captain. Whatever you say."

IT WAS low tide as we approached Isla Laurentis. We took a longboat, Whit, George, Maro and me. I'd made sure Whit knew any attempt to escape would result in Maro cutting him down at the knees, and whatever games he thought he could play with me, his nervous glance in Maro's direction said he understood exactly what their capabilities were.

"This way," he said, leading us to the edge of the beach and into the trees.

"I expected a sea witch to live closer to the water," George said as we picked our way inland.

"Caves are damp and the lighting is terrible," Whit said. "And by choosing somewhere else to live, Aga Serala has the chance to observe visitors to her island while they splash through the caves along the shoreline looking for her."

Maro and I glanced at each other at the same moment. They'd been strangely silent since Whit had divulged our destination. But the hairs on the back of my neck stood as Whit spoke about unseen watchers.

We came to a clearing, and Whit stumbled to an abrupt halt when a voice said, "Come no further."

We spilled out behind him into the open space. A child sat on a tree stump in the middle of it. She was thin and small, with matted braids that hung from her hair and tanned skin decorated with bright paints or powders that shimmered blue and purple in the sunlight filtering through the trees. Silence reigned as we all watched each other. I cleared my throat and jerked my head in Whit's direction, but he shook his head.

"You're the one who rushed things and insisted we come here. I've done my part."

"Maro," I said, hoping they would take the hint and draw their sword to hurry my reluctant brother along. But their eyes were locked straight ahead, staring at the witch with an unreadable expression.

Making the decision for us, Aga Serala slipped from her perch. Her feet were bare and mud-stained. Her dress was plainly made but rattled as she walked, adorned with shells on thin tassels that swung with the motion of her steps.

This was the monstrous sea witch of legend? Where were her claws? Her seductive song?

Though, as she approached, it became apparent she might not be the girl I had initially thought. Though she was small enough to be a child, her eyes and mouth were crinkled at the edges, and the joints in her fingers were swollen. Her irises were nearly colorless, and the braids at her temples were streaked with silver.

"Aga Serala," I said, "We're looking for—" But the witch silenced me with a single flick of her wrist. She didn't even glance at me, approaching George, who gasped when Serala reached for her hand and held it close for inspection. She trailed a gnarled fingertip over George's palm, tsking when she reached a point of interest.

"Don't be sad. It was a good death," she said. Her voice creaked like trees in the wind, but her words were steady.

"Whose death?" I asked.

Serala's attention flicked to me, and the annoyance in her expression was so profound, I dropped my own gaze to the forest floor, feeling like a child scolded for speaking out of turn. When I looked up again, Serala had released George and moved on to Maro. Here, she reached up to take Maro's cheeks in her palms, then stood up on her toes so that she could kiss them. What started as a polite greeting lingered for a moment too long, then turned hot and passionate. Whit cleared his throat beside me, but Maro was smiling openly when they finally broke apart.

"Hello, old friend," she said, the words dancing in merriment, and Maro actually chuckled. It was a sound I had never heard them make. Dry and deep, speaking of pleasure and fond memories, from within their chest.

"Hello, little friend." Their voice held the warmth of coming home, and I couldn't tell if I was irritated that I didn't know this story or annoyed Maro hadn't thought to disclose they already knew the witch before we'd come ashore.

They gazed at each other for a moment longer. Might have stayed like that for hours, but I elbowed Whit forward. He glared at me one more time, but finally, he said, "Serala, we've come for—"

She kicked him the shins. Whit yelped and hopped away. Perhaps the sea witch and I might be friends after all.

"You took something you weren't supposed to," she said, pointing a crooked finger at him.

"What? I would never!" He bent to rub his injured leg, then had to dance back again as she smacked the top of his head.

"Naughty boy. What did I tell you about taking things that weren't yours?"

I laughed. "Sounds like you missed some lessons in our childhood, Whit."

He started toward me, but when Aga Serala approached him again, he backed up quickly, hands raised in supplication.

"I thought we had an agreement," he said. "A trade."

"You took my things," she hissed, eyes narrow. "My pretty things."

"What's she talking about?" I asked. The more agitated she became, the less likely we'd get our business done quickly.

"This is why I told you we weren't ready to come here," he said.

I sighed heavily. "Whitney. If we avoided every island and port where you'd upset a woman, we'd be at sea for the rest of our lives."

"Give it back!" the witch cried, apparently indifferent to our bickering.

"I told you I gave her the map," he said to me.

"Yes."

"We traded for it."

"We did not!" Serala shrieked, and lunged for him. I stepped in front of her. Despite her small stature, she was surprisingly strong and struggled against me with the ferocity of a wet cat.

"What did you take?" I asked Whit.

"Nothing!"

"Liar!" Serala screamed.

I sighed. "What did you trade for the map?"

He scuffed a booted foot in the dirt and wouldn't meet my eyes. Rightly, he stayed out of Serala's reach, though if he delayed for much longer, I would let her do with him as she would, and we'd take the distraction as an opportunity to find the map ourselves.

Finally, Whit said, "A pendant."

"He took it!" Serala said, but her fury was subsiding. I let her go, and she stumbled away. She went to Maro, who held a hand out to her. The witch's eyes were red with unshed tears.

"I haven't been able to dream since." Serala sniffled piteously. Maro looked furious.

Whit shuffled uncomfortably for a moment, before finally, he said, "It was an opal. The size of a goose egg."

"A dream stone," the witch said. "My visions are gone."

"We'll find it," Maro said. The statement held so much warmth, while the compassion on Maro's face nearly made my heart stop. There was so much history between them. Time I knew nothing about. How was this someone Maro would take care of, when all they did with me was question and push?

"We had an agreement," Whit insisted, unaware of my inner turmoil.

"If we can get your stone back," I said to Serala, "would you be willing to give us the map my brother gave you?"

"I don't think—" Whit said, but no one was listening to him.

"Brother?" Serala tilted her head, eyeing me, then she laughed and clapped delightedly, all her previous agitation forgotten. "Of course. Your brother. Two lives. Two truths." She skipped around in a circle, humming to herself. "You'll have to choose one life and one truth. We all do."

I didn't know what she meant, and my impatience was roiling beneath my skin. I bowed quickly. "I'm sorry for bothering you. We'll return with the stone my brother took from you."

"Lucy. Cinder. I think—" Whit said, but his protest was cut off by a grunt. Hopefully, Maro had kicked some sense into him.

The witch didn't reply, merely spinning away, dancing to a song none of us could hear.

We marched in silence back the way we had come. Whit was well ahead of us, obviously eager to be away from Aga Serala's reach. George was behind him, walking doggedly onward. Maro walked at my shoulder like an angry storm cloud.

"You should have drowned him," they said.

"We need him."

"For what?"

"I made a deal."

"Is he blackmailing you?" they asked.

My pulse fluttered as they poked too close to the truth. Whit wasn't blackmailing me, but the brokers were pulling my strings, and every time I thought we were making progress, we were blown off course yet again.

"Of course not," I said abruptly. "If anything, I'm using *him*."

Maro shook their head as they wobbled over a tree root. "For what? Entertainment?"

"Haven't you had enough?" I asked.

"Of what?"

"All of it. The lies. The tactics. A treasure like this is enough to set us all up for life. George and I can sail away where no one will find us. You can …" I paused, unsure how to finish the sentence. I couldn't imagine Maro doing anything but what they always had. And yet, seeing them with Serala, there was so much I didn't know. Stories. Maybe even ambitions. "You can have the ship, if you like."

They stumbled backward, almost as if I'd struck them. "You'd truly give it up? The *Siren*? The crew? All of it?"

My throat went dry at the thought. The *Siren* was mine. Truly the only thing that I had ever been able to call my own. Giving it up was unthinkable, and yet …

"I owe George a better life than the one we have here."

Maro grabbed hold of my arm, pulling me to a halt. "We've had a good life here. Taken it and owned it. Why are you so keen on giving that up?"

"If you'd ever loved someone as much as I love her, you'd understand," I said, though I wasn't able to meet Maro's eyes. I shivered when they tipped my chin up, forcing my gaze to them. They stared at me, unblinking, before releasing me suddenly and straightening.

"That's the most true thing you've said today."

Up ahead, a branch snapped and Whit tripped, tumbling over a tree stump and down a small hill. George hurried after him, calling his name.

Maro sighed. "Working with him is still a bad idea."

"There were no good ones."

"I still think—"

"It's not an option," I said quickly. We were going to retrieve the witch's opal and come back here.

But Maro wouldn't be put off so easily. "You'd rather sail around in circles at your long-lost brother's whim than take matters into our own hands?"

The day had been a colossal waste of time. I didn't want to add an argument into it.

"I'm taking the most direct route to safety," I said, watching as George helped Whit back onto the path. The beach and the *Siren* lay ahead.

Maro said, "You're going to get someone hurt."

I laughed. "Hopefully Whit."

"Cinder."

"There's too much at stake. A knife to George's throat. Or one in my guts. Have you forgotten?"

"Dragging your body back to the ship? I would never."

"We won't be dragging any more bodies anywhere."

"It's what we do," Maro said.

"No. It's what *you* do. And if you feel that strongly about it, we can let you off at the next port. Or leave you here with the witch, if you'd prefer."

They froze on the path, and their tone was genuinely confused as they spoke. "You want me off the ship?"

"I want you to stop harassing and questioning me at every turn. But if you can't do that, then maybe it's time we parted ways."

They were silent for a long moment. My ears burned, waiting for a reply. I would never actually tell Maro to leave, but I needed them to hear me instead of constantly arguing. Finally, they said, "I'm sorry. I hadn't realized this was weighing on you so much." Then they hurried ahead before I could say anything else.

CHAPTER 12

A ripple of discontent washed over the crew as we returned to the *Siren* without the map. That murmur grew when Whit suggested once again that our next destination be Port Darto.

"What's Port Darto?" George asked.

The crew within earshot made signs to ward off danger and whispered to each other. No doubt, by the end of the day, everyone would know where we were headed.

"If you left the witch's opal in Darto," I said, "it's long gone."

"Oh, no," Whit said quickly. "We won't be getting the opal back. I sold it to a collector from Sevnan. We'll never see it again."

Would the desire to stab my brother at every turn ever cease?

I certainly hoped not.

"So we go into the devil's teeth in Darto? If your plan is to have us all killed—"

He shook his head. "I wouldn't go there if there were any other options. But if Serala really has lost her ability to see the future without her pendant, then I know something we can get in Darto that will work just as well."

Maro made an unhappy noise, and in this case, I couldn't help but agree with them. Port Darto was the primary city on a jungle island that had changed hands so many times in the last two hundred years that it essentially belonged to no one and had thus been claimed as a haven for the nationless and forsaken. Though Maro and I had our own disreputable standing, even we steered clear of the place. Yet time was of the essence. I shrugged at Maro, hoping to placate them. "It's been a few years. The population is fairly transient. We may not be recognized. Whit will pick up whatever he needs, and we'll be back to Laurentis before anyone notices we've arrived."

Maro chewed on my rationalization for a moment. I braced for a fight.

"As you wish, Captain."

I swayed in surprise, but Maro was already going about the business of sailing. They relayed the headings to the crew, who set about weighing anchor and setting the sails.

We didn't speak again about Maro leaving the ship or about going after the brokers. All our conversations were short and businesslike. I'd said I wanted Maro to stop arguing with me, but their detachment was somehow worse.

The winds were in our favor, and we arrived at Port Darto two days later as the sun was setting. The town had been built on the back of a sand bar and always had the appearance that it was about to topple into the sea. Although it had no organized system of government or city management, those that owned the waterfront businesses were in a perpetual cycle of reinforcing the walls and foundations to keep their brothels, taverns, and gambling dens from sinking altogether.

The harbor was a mess of boats and ships of all different sizes and origins, from the simple fishing boats that came from neighboring islands in search of spirits and exotic spices, to the sleek, fast trade schooners from the distant Hasset empire in the south who came to Darto in search of less-than-legal wares. The water was deep enough at the end of the pier that we could have tied the *Siren* to it, but I had Maro anchor us at the edge of the vessels currently at rest in the harbor.

"In case we need to make a quick getaway," I said. "Whit and I will take a longboat into town. Keep an eye out for our return."

"I'll go with you," Maro said.

"No, stay here." The fewer of us on shore, the less time we'd waste trying to get away if we had problems.

"Captain, I really think—"

"Wait here." I belted a sword to my hip. If I let Maro anywhere close to shore, they'd go prowling through the streets and causing trouble we didn't need. "You'll know if we run into trouble."

"Georgina will come with us though," Whit said, and I whirled on him.

"What for?"

"I need her help." He said it plainly, like the answer should be obvious.

"Help?" He was so infuriating. "I've given you my entire ship and crew to sail around in circles. If we need a third person to come, we'll bring Ender."

"Oh, no. He's not nearly pretty enough. Lady Georgina is by far the better distraction. I need a lady on my arm, and you don't look the part."

I bristled at the very suggestion. "I'm not your lady."

"And that's exactly why George needs to come," Whit said.

"I'm not your lady either," she said, crossing her arms over her chest as she came to stand beside me. I swelled with pride.

"No, but people will believe you are," Whit said. "More than sister dear, who looks like she's about to stab someone at all times of the day."

"Only you," I said sweetly.

"The point is," he said, "you draw attention, and the wrong kind in a place like this. Too many people will want to try their hand at besting you, and we don't have time for that. But bring a pretty lady with us, and all eyes will be on her. If you won't let me do this alone, then we go as a threesome."

If he couldn't see there was more to George than her face, that was his loss. Still, whatever he was up to, the faster we got it done, the faster we could be on our way. I'd keep close to protect George and let Whit play out whatever scheme he had in mind.

"Fine. But the second I get more than a whiff of danger"—truly, this whole plan stank of trouble—"I'm taking George and leaving you for dead. Understood?"

George leaned in and kissed me quickly. "I'll be careful."

"It's not you I'm worried about," I said, but Whit was already climbing down to the longboat and didn't hear me.

We made our way into town. Letting Whit lead was uncomfortable, but it gave me a chance to stay alert for possible threats. I wore my hat low to cover my face. If anyone from the brokers was here and watching, hopefully Whit was right and their attention would pull toward him and George who, as promised, had her arm looped through his, and laughed and smiled at everything he said. The very sight of them made my skin crawl, but her act seemed convincing enough.

A few times, as he'd predicted, someone would linger a little too long behind us, giving me a considering eye before falling away. But one man with his hand on a sword in a well-worn leather sheath looked me up and down.

"You look like you know how to handle yourself in a fight," he said with a sneer.

"I know how to handle myself anywhere."

"I'd like to see you try." But before he could get his sword halfway free, I'd grabbed a bottle from a nearby table and flung it at him. It was only a distraction; I didn't need for it to hit him. He yelped and ducked, and I followed, sweeping his legs out from under him so I could kneel on his chest and put the tip of my knife to his throat.

"Now you've seen it," I said.

He lay gasping like a fish as I stood, tucking my knife away again. I had to give him credit for knowing when he should stay down.

"But my wine," someone said, though their protest ended quickly under the heat of my glare. Whit and George had carried on as if I didn't even exist. Most people were still watching me nervously, but those who weren't were gently stepping out of George's path, like they might for a visiting queen. I half expected one man who looked particularly taken with her to bow as she passed, and I shuddered with barely concealed annoyance that Whit's point had made itself so quickly.

The laughter and music of the dockside establishments gave way to a heavy silence as we walked through what might have once been a busy city square, but was now abandoned. At the center stood a fountain so overgrown it could not have run in years. A man the same color of dirt from his bare callused toes to the tips of his greasy hair slept at its edge, mouth agape. A skinny dog licked hopefully at the man's fingers and was rewarded for its optimism with a sharp kick that had it yelping as it darted away.

"This way," Whit said, taking us to a narrow alleyway between two tall buildings. Here, it was too close for him and George to walk side by side, so she slid in between us, where I could best protect her. Whit's shoulders scraped the stone as we went, leaving streaks on his dark coat.

"Is there a market?" George asked.

Whit chuckled. "Not exactly."

Darto had two districts, or it would if it were a more civilized place. The part of town closest to the waterfront was also the most chaotic, with travelers and merchants looking to make money through honest and dishonest means alike.

The farther section into which we emerged was closer to the edges of the jungle and far more dangerous. The more permanent residents plied their trade here, buying and selling only in the wares and ways that were convenient to them. Business was transacted behind closed doors and away from prying eyes. The merriment from the wharf faded to distant conversations and faint music, leaving me with one hand on my sword hilt as I scanned the street and alleys for possible threats and exits.

"You better not be leading us into a trap," I muttered.

"After you nearly killed me in Vestria and have repeatedly threatened to stab or drown me? Dear sister, why would I do that?" Whit didn't look back as we spoke. But he stopped midstride, so George and I collided. While we disentangled, Whit spun in a slow circle, as if he'd suddenly lost his way.

"Something wrong?" I asked.

Whit snapped his fingers, smiling like he'd had a great revelation. "It's this way."

He led us to a building with boarded-over windows. An old wrought iron sign with what looked like four cats twisted into the metal hung over the doorway. When Whit pulled on the door, it swung with a shrieking hinge that spoke of long disuse. Inside, though, was a different story. While we stepped into what looked like a simple shop, sounds of laughter and music drifted toward us.

He led us through a back door and down a narrow set of stairs carved into the dirt. The space smelled damp, but the music grew louder.

"For somewhere so secret, it seems very unguarded," I said.

Whit laughed softly. "They've been watching us since we came out of the alley."

The way at the bottom of the stairs was covered by a curtain of beaded strands that did nothing to stop the strong smell of tobacco or the sounds of men and women laughing. Someone played a whistle and another played a hand drum, keeping a rhythmic tempo.

The room inside was surprisingly big, with a low ceiling and oil lamps that burned a weak smoky light and cast long shadows in dark corners where faceless figures watched us. The center part of the room was packed with people dancing in time with the music, or lounging on a hodgepodge of wobbly chairs and sofas, or perched on old barrels and crates. They laughed raucously and cheered when a barmaid carried a tray laden down with foaming mugs in their midst. She handed them out to whatever hand reached for them, then returned to where a large man in a scraggly black beard and red shirt sat, his back to a number of casks that dripped from recent use.

"Whitney!" A cry went up from the dancing throngs, and it echoed over and over as heads turned toward us. Whit raised his hands and smiled at all the welcomers like a returning hero. He walked through the revelers, shaking hands and shouting jokes that had the whole group rolling with laughter. His easy friendliness irritated me.

"Who are your ladies?" someone shouted.

Without missing a step, Whit wrapped his arm around George's waist, pulling her away from me.

"This is my sister!" he said, then tipped George back and planted a lusty kiss on her lips. I gripped the hilt of my sword, fighting every urge not to run him through right here. When George straightened, her face was bright red, and just as quickly as Whit had dipped her, she slapped him hard across the face, which only led to more laughter and cheers around us.

"You've come at the right time," a man with more rings on his fingers than teeth in his mouth said.

"You have no idea how often I hear that." Even though he still had one arm around George, he reached for a woman's hand and kissed her fingers and gave her a knowing wink that set off more rounds of laughter and jokes.

The toothless man cackled. "Your old friend was here yesterday."

"I have many friends," Whit said. He led us to a table. "You'll have to be more specific."

"Captain Harlow, of course!"

The room dropped to the silence of a tomb. All eyes were on Whit, who was frozen in place. He was halfway to his seat, his knees bent, his body hunched, and all the color had leached from his cheeks.

Fortunately, with everyone's attention on Whit, no one noticed the way I gasped, and there was no one to feel the way my heart crashed to a halt in my chest.

Captain Harlow. I knew him by reputation only. A gentleman sailor who had taken to sea because he had no desire to spend his fortune on property, cards, and women. Instead, he'd purchased a fast ship and a competent crew who had helped his riches grow at the expense of others, until he'd run afoul of one of the brokers. Sensing an opportunity to use Harlow's particular skillset, that broker—I wasn't sure which of them—had set him to work doing what he did best, only now on their behalf. Kiril had ordered me to give him a wide berth while he ransacked towns and plundered ships. I'd heard that he'd eventually come to a new arrangement, largely regaining his independence in exchange for a small percentage to the brokers for their ongoing disinterest.

He was relentless in his pursuit of gold. No ship, country or treasure was safe once he set his mind on it. If he was anywhere nearby, our treasure hunt had become ten times more complicated, and a hundred times more dangerous.

hatever Whit's history with Captain Harlow, he quickly regained his composure and changed the subject. True to his word, George remained the center of attention as the two of them chatted and laughed with revelers.

"Has anyone seen Conrad lately? I was hoping he'd be here." He nodded thanks as mugs of foaming ale were handed over our small table. George sent me a questioning glance, and I wrapped my hands around my drink but gave her a gentle headshake. Too many unknowns. Too many times lately we'd been somewhere I thought we would be safe, only to have the brokers break in, or my own sea-forsaken brother rob me. If I couldn't keep her safe there, we had to be on full alert here.

"You look familiar." The toothless man slid onto a small wooden stool next to me. His breath stank of rotting meat and had a consistency that left me feeling like I'd fallen asleep on the breast of a decaying whale.

"Do you know my brother, friend?" I asked, keeping my voice low and my hand on my knife. Men like him had a tendency to touch things that weren't theirs, including hands, thighs, and other body parts.

He laughed, and his tone dropped too, losing some of its squeaky delirium. "No, I've seen you here without him. You're no petty thief like him. You're someone else. Braver. Deadlier." He pointed a finger at me. "I know you."

I pressed my mug of ale into his hands. "A gift then, friend, for your discretion."

He eyed me, dark pupils too wide even for the low light. But he lifted the mug in a toast, then drank the whole thing down in a single gulp and disappeared back into the crowd.

"Whitney!" At the far end of the room, a man the approximate size of a mountain had entered. His arms were outstretched as if he wished to embrace every single person before him, and his smile was so wide I had no doubt he could swallow us all too if he tried.

A new chorus of cheers went up at the big man's arrival. Conrad, apparently. He moved through the crowd like a tidal bore, people swirling out of his path, even as they greeted him brightly. The whole atmosphere was different from anywhere else I'd ever seen in Darto. While waterfront taverns were often this raucous, there was always an edge of danger to them. Here, everyone seemed delighted to be in everyone else's company, with no ulterior motive.

I didn't like it.

I caught George's gaze and motioned for her to sit beside me while Whit's attention was elsewhere.

"Are you all right?" she asked.

"I was about to ask you the same thing."

She grimaced and wiped at her mouth with her sleeve. "I'd rather not have the taste of Whit on my lips, but I'll survive." She lifted her mug with a smile, but I couldn't return it. The atmosphere had me on edge, and the longer we sat here, the more I could feel the weight of the building above us pressing down. This was why I preferred being on the water. Nothing above you but the open air and sky.

"My friend!" Conrad bellowed, practically lifting Whit out of his chair to crush him to his giant chest in a smothering hug. Although Conrad was fully dressed, both his shirt and trousers looked like they were holding together through sheer desperation alone, the seams straining as his muscles bulged under the thin material. "It's been too long. So good to see you."

"And you," Whit said, a little breathless as he was deposited back on the ground.

"And who are your friends?" Conrad clapped Whit on the shoulder, practically knocking him face first onto the table. "Don't tell me you've finally found a wife. Or two wives?" His eyebrows, as massive as the rest of him, bobbled in amusement.

George twined her fingers with mine possessively. "He wouldn't be able to handle the both of us."

Conrad bellowed a laugh. "Oh, I like you, lady. If you decide you do need a husband, I would be happy to oblige. My other wives wouldn't even mind too much. They like someone with a little bit of spirit."

George flushed and squeezed my hand tighter. Whit chuckled, but he eyed me. I wasn't about to cause a problem, but my patience with this place was wearing thin.

"What brings you here?" Conrad asked, attention turning back to Whit. The big man sat down next to him, and I could practically hear the existential sigh of the chair he claimed.

"We're on our way to see Aga Serala," Whit said.

Conrad's face sobered immediately, and he leaned in, as if suddenly he didn't want to be overheard. "The Mother of Seas," he said reverently. "She wasn't very happy the last time you paid her a visit."

I rolled my eyes. Whit's reputation preceded him.

"I'd like to bring her a peace offering," he said, unruffled. "I was hoping you might have some moss jade to sell?"

The big man's expression, already serious, darkened further. "There are other places you could have acquired that in Darto."

Whit smiled a charming smile, fingers drawing lazy patterns on the worn tabletop. "But no one I like as well as you."

They stared at each other, locked in some wordless battle, even as the merriment around us picked up again. George was squeezing my hand so tight my knuckles popped, and I suspected she was holding her breath.

"It'll cost you," Conrad said.

"We can pay," Whit said. With what money wasn't clear. If he had any funds with him, I didn't know about them. I certainly wasn't giving him any money.

"You'll have to wait here," Conrad said.

Whit lifted his tankard. "If you could have someone send over more refreshments, we'll be happy to do so."

When Conrad moved away from us this time, he did so with no ceremony. The people still moved out of his way, but there were no greetings, no friendly handshakes.

"What was that about?" George asked, loud enough to be heard over the music.

"You need to go," Whit said.

"What?" I asked, senses coming to alert.

"I'll join you shortly, but once Conrad returns with the jade, we'll need to make a hasty exit, and it will be easier if it's only me."

"What have you done?" I asked.

"Nothing. Trust me."

I didn't. Not in the slightest.

"George, wait outside," I said.

"I'm not going without you." Her hand was still in mine.

Whit rolled his eyes. "Ladies, this display of devotion is touching, but I need you to listen to me and leave."

I glanced at George, then at the people around us. Trying to make a fast escape in the crowd would be difficult. Too easy to get separated. Too easy to catch my sword on something—or someone—in the close confines, leaving us vulnerable.

"This better not be a double-cross." I pointed an accusatory finger at Whit.

He pressed a pained hand to his chest, the picture of shocked disappointment before pulling me into a tight and unexpected hug. "You must learn to trust me eventually, little sister."

I squirmed out of his hold, scowling as he grinned.

"Don't keep us waiting," I said.

"I would never," he said, which didn't make me feel any better.

Outside, the street was still deserted, except for a skinny cat that crossed our path as we emerged. The music trailed behind us. I glanced overhead at the empty mouths of windows as they silently observed us. Whit had said we'd been watched from the time we exited the alley, but wherever those watchers might be, I couldn't say for sure.

"What do you think he's doing?" George asked.

"I couldn't begin to speculate." Though if it had been me, I'd already be sneaking out the back and leaving us out to dry.

"Who is Captain Harlow?"

Nerves pricked up my spine. "Can we talk about this when we're safe?"

George whirled, feet scuffing on the ground. "Are we not safe here?"

"I don't know, all right?" Out of habit, I reached for my knife, then froze.

"What is it?" George said.

My knife was gone. I'd belted it at the small of my back to leave room for my sword at my hip, and the small sheath along my spine was empty. I spun, knowing already that if it had simply fallen out on the street, I'd have heard the clatter of the blade on stone. It was still inside. Lifted by roving hands as we'd exited, or pulled away by the toothless man, along with my gift of ale. Better taken for some unknown purpose than buried in my back or—worse—in George's.

"Lou," George said softly.

I sighed heavily. "What?"

"What happened to the music?"

Search for the missing knife forgotten, my whole body strained from my ears to the tips of my toes, trying to find the music that had been there only a second ago. But now it was replaced with only a suffocating silence. On instinct, I placed myself between George and the door. I may not have had a knife, but I still had my sword, and I would defend us both.

"Get ready," I said.

"For what?" She gripped my sleeve.

"Anything."

The only noise that followed was George's breath in my ear. Then—far away, but getting closer quickly—came a roar like a storm crawling over the sea, consuming everything in front of it. And it was coming toward us.

"Lou?" George's voice was uncertain, and I backed up two steps, forcing her back as well.

The sound resolved into shouting, then expanded until it wasn't individual voices, but the growl of a crowd. An angry one. I gripped my sword tighter, even though one blade was no use against an angry mob.

"We should go," I said.

"But what about Whit?"

"He can—" But I didn't get to finish the thought before Whit barreled through the door.

"Run!" he shouted. George and I tangled for a moment as we spun in opposite directions, and Whit dashed past us. A flash of light caught my attention. My knife, tumbling through the air as Whit tossed it toward me. I caught it awkwardly, though at least on the handle side rather than the blade. I flinched at the sticky feeling of the leather, and when I glanced down, both blade and hilt were wet with dark droplets of blood.

"Whit? What did you—" But the question was drowned out by the wild and furious cries of the people coming up the earthen stairs and through the empty shop, and instead of finishing, I grabbed George's hand and bolted, even as the edge of Whit's cloak disappeared down the alley.

"Shit, hells, and fucking balls," I muttered.

"Whit! What did you do?" George shouted, but my brother didn't answer. It was like the day in Hilltop all over again. I had to give him grudging credit. He was fast when the moment necessitated. And right now, as I glanced over my shoulder at the frothing horde that spilled onto the empty street, it was very necessary.

The alley was a tight squeeze, too narrow to move as quickly as I wanted to. It had the one benefit of slowing down our pursuers so that only one or two could enter at a time, but their howls followed us with terrifying speed.

"Murderer! Stop him!"

I could only guess what boneheaded thing Whit had done and who he'd cheated, but now wasn't the time for that. We were only halfway down the alley, and the people closest to us were gaining.

"Whit!" I gasped. "Wait!" If he would slow, I could hand George off to him and tell them to get back to the *Siren*. Alone, I could fight off the most persistent of the crowd and hopefully lose the rest in the twisting streets.

But Whit didn't slow, and behind me, George cried out as she lost her grip on my hand. I turned in time to see a man with frighteningly bright eyes grab for her. They both stumbled, and for a second, George was free, but he recovered faster and grabbed hold of the tail of her headscarf, catching it and the pleated hair beneath. He yanked savagely and she was pulled off her feet.

I ran for her. Or rather, I tried to, but my ankle turned on a loose stone, and I fell. She screamed, feet scuffling on the stones as the man pawed at her. My whole body went cold with fear. It was like the night at Davi's all over again.

"George!" The call came from behind me, and I stumbled to

my feet, grunting. Whit vaulted past me and jammed my shoulder against the wall.

"Murderer!" The man shook George, tearing at her clothes. She kicked and screeched, but he was much bigger, and alone, she'd have been helpless against him.

But Whit launched himself at the large man, shrieking as he landed on the man's back and clung to him. The attacker reared back, and Whit wrapped one arm around his throat. He used the other one to gouge at the man's eye, pressing a thumb in as he gritted his teeth. The man screamed.

"Lucy!" Whit called, and I pushed off the wall, raising my hand as I crashed into them. A fight in tight quarters like this was always messy and dangerous, so I aimed to make it as short-lived as possible. I buried my knife in the man's chest. He'd tried to hurt George. If I could, I'd have put my whole hand through him. He roared, and I pulled the blade out and plunged it in again, twisting hard. He clawed at me, even as blood began to ooze at his eye socket where Whit's thumb was now firmly lodged. One more stab, and he fell to his knees. Whit scrambled away before he was crushed, and I crawled toward George, who was getting to her feet. A spray of red blood painted her face. She stumbled as I shoved her ahead of me, and she ran on.

"Here." I tossed Whit my knife without a second of hesitation. We had to kill two more of the crowd to give us room, but as the second fell, the small pile their bodies made was enough to slow the others temporarily, and I took off running. George was already at the end of the alley. Ahead, the streets began to fill in. These weren't the people from Conrad's den though. They were the tavern-goers and prostitutes from the wharf. We were reaching more familiar territory.

A shot rang out. People screamed, and others ducked for cover, which only left us exposed, still upright as we looked for an escape.

I grabbed George's hand and turned down a side street as a

second shot was fired. Somewhere along the way, Whit had disappeared, but I couldn't think about that. People were running now. The growing chaos would help shield us until we found a new way down to the docks. Let Whit find his own route. If he got lost or fell behind, so be it. We'd make our way on our own.

But, of course, as the street opened up onto the harbor, Whit was already halfway down the pier.

"This way!" he said, as if he'd been leading us the whole time. I pulled George around me, pushing her at the ladder while I undid the lines that held us to the pier. When I checked over my shoulder, people were still running toward us. Their howls had taken on an animal quality, like predators letting kin know they'd found prey. I scrambled down the ladder while George and Whit shoved us away from the pier.

Torches had gathered on the pier. A few of our pursuers were pulling off in longboats, but we had a good head start on them. When I glanced over my shoulder, lamps were brightening on the *Siren,* and the distinctive sound of an anchor chain making its steady voyage from the bottom of the harbor rattled through the night.

"We'll be on our way," I said to Maro as we clambered over the side.

"What happened?" they asked.

"Let's talk about it when we're clear," I said, and they gave me a dark glance before they marched to the wheel, shouting orders in their wake.

Whit lay on the deck gasping, but he had enough sense to lurch to his feet as I stalked toward him.

"What in the seven watery hells did you do?" I asked.

"We needed the jade." He pulled a pouch out of his cloak, letting it drop to the deck.

"You nearly got us killed. Nearly got George killed."

"Lou." George was standing behind me and she put a gentle hand on my shoulder. "He saved me."

"And you!" I said, spinning, anger turning to a burning fury.

"Me?" She danced back.

"How many times have I told you not to wear that damn thing on your head? That it's not safe? He only caught you because of your sea-forsaken scarf. Do you know what he would have done to you if I weren't there?"

"How many times do I need to tell you I don't need your protection, Lou? I can look after myself," she said, her exasperation plain.

"Well, you've done a piss-poor job of it as far as I can see." I practically spat the words at her feet.

The world fell silent again, the three of us breathing heavily while the crew did their best to skirt around us and get the *Siren* underway. Whit shifted uncomfortably. George's eyes sparkled with tears. My ears burned, but the fury was already leaving me. Adrenaline and fear were a dangerous combination.

"Captain," Maro called from the quarterdeck.

I whirled. "What?"

"What course should we set?"

Were they trying to be obtuse? I bit back a dozen frustrated words. "Back to Laurentis. Now."

"Yes, Captain."

When I turned back, George and Whit were nowhere to be seen.

CHAPTER 14

It was only later that I remembered the pouch on the deck. It was surprisingly lighter than I anticipated when I picked it up. I'd expected a stone, but instead the contents were a fine powder.

"Do you know what this is?" I asked Maro when they joined me in my cabin later.

They took the pouch, sniffed it, then threw it back on the table. "Nothing good. Did your brother not tell you what it was?"

"He said it was moss jade."

Maro spat. "Then you're a fool, Captain."

"What?"

"Where is he now?" They rose, prowling the confines of the cabin like a caged tiger.

"Somewhere down below." *With George*, my mind added helpfully, though I had no rational reason to think they had stayed together once we'd been underway. I hadn't seen George either though. My heart still clattered in my ribs at the image of her tumbling to the stones, the man's hand wrapped around her scarf.

"Ender!" Maro called out the cabin door. "Bring the thief. This is your last warning," they said to me. "If Serala doesn't have the map, we're done with this game."

"You don't get to make that decision."

"The time for you to make them is coming to an end. Captains rely on the trust of their crew, and mine is getting desperately thin, Cinder."

"You weren't there," I said.

"When?"

"With George. When she—" But I couldn't even put it into words. Too many events crashed together like a ship on the rocks. In the alley. At Davi's. Even on the beach with Lady Amelia as men on horseback had borne down on George while I'd been frozen in the longboat. The prince's hand in her hair as he'd dragged her away from me.

When exactly did I mean?

"Captain." Ender knocked gently on the cabin door. "Your brother."

Maro hurled the pouch at Whit as he entered, and it bounced off his chest. "What is this?" Maro rarely lost their temper to this degree. They nagged at me, contradicted me, and they had opinions and lines they would not cross, but they were rarely truly angry.

"Hello to you too." Whit grinned through gritted teeth.

"Answer the question," I said, though the situation was already beyond my control.

Silence filled the cabin. Whit moved slowly, bending by degrees until he was able to reach the floor where he picked up the pouch. He dropped it to the table once again, and when traces of powder spilled onto the wood, he dragged a finger through it before pressing it to the inside of his lip. Maro hissed. Whit sighed and slouched onto my sofa, tipping his head back.

"Moss jade is also known as green lady," he said, staring up at the ceiling.

"I thought it was a stone," I said.

"It's actually made from hardened tree sap." He laughed softly to himself. "But more importantly, it's a powerful drug. Ground up and taken in small quantities, it can relieve pain and provide a sense of euphoria."

"It's a poison," Maro said.

Whit opened one eye, lips curling in a bemused smile. Already, the tension in his face had slackened. "Taking too much can cause hallucinations or visions, which is what Aga Serala uses it for. I suppose even more and someone could die."

The joy on the faces the night before returned to me. The sheer pleasure at welcoming friends in their midst. "Is that what the people in the cellar were taking?"

He shrugged. "Most of them, I expect. Possibly other substances. Conrad is well known in Darto for his ability to procure the finest quality products."

"And they were unhappy you stole some it?" I asked.

"Oh, no." Whit giggled. "They were unhappy I killed Conrad."

"What?"

He waved a dismissive hand, head once again lolling over the back of the sofa. "Well, I didn't have enough to pay him, did I? Do you know what this much green lady costs? But the revelers were understandably upset when the purveyor of all their enjoyment was suddenly bleeding on the floor."

I ground my teeth at his callousness. Maybe it was the drugs talking, but he'd been perfectly sober when he'd ended the dealer's life the night before. He'd had to have known that would be the outcome when we'd gone ashore, but he hadn't seen fit to let me know, putting both me and George at risk in the process.

As if he could hear my thoughts, Whit pointed a finger in my general direction, though it wove in lazy circles. "You worry too much, sister. Tomorrow, we'll be back at Laurentis. The map will be ours before the sun goes down."

His hand dropped, and he slowly tipped to one side until he collapsed onto the sofa. His mouth was agape, and he snored gently. Maro and I stared at him for a moment. My whole body tensed, as if he were about to leap up and scare us, like this had all been a practical joke.

Maro opened their mouth to speak, and I held up one hand in warning. "Not now."

"Captain."

"I don't want to hear it." He'd put us at risk, but we'd escaped. There was no sign anyone in Darto was pursuing us. It was behind us, and soon, we'd have the map. "Take him to the hold. Keep him there until we arrive at Laurentis. And Maro?"

"Yes, Captain?"

"No need to be gentle bringing him down there. Let's see how effective his green lady really is."

Maro's eyes narrowed in dark appreciation. Some things would never change between us.

"Of course, Captain."

George had been cool with me since yesterday, even though I'd apologized as we'd gone to bed. When I said only Maro and Ender would accompany Whit and me to see Aga Serala, George didn't protest. Her hair was braided and completely hidden under a kerchief, which she'd taken great pains to pin in place in the morning. Her silent protest filled me with regret. I shouldn't have chosen it as the scab to pick. For her, it was a sign of where she'd come from. For me, it was the tie she refused to cut. But either way, it wasn't a scrap of fabric that had put her in danger. It was Whit, who had insisted she come. And me, because I'd let him do it.

Once again, we rowed to shore. Somehow, I expected Aga Serala to be sitting in the same clearing, perched on the same stump, but she wasn't.

Whit hummed in concern.

"Something wrong?" Maro asked.

"She usually meets me here."

"Perhaps she didn't expect us back so soon?" Ender said.

Whit shook his head. "She always knows when someone arrives on the island."

We stood in silence for a minute. The trees swayed gently in the lingering breeze from last night's storm, and birds chirped their songs at us.

Finally, Maro sighed. "I know where she lives."

"You do?" I rounded on them, one eyebrow arched. They stared back at me with flat, narrowed eyes, daring me to ask for more answers. Such a story there in Maro's time with the witch, however long ago it was. I stepped aside. "Lead the way then."

Maro pushed deeper into the forest, where the trees were denser and the undergrowth pulled at our ankles.

"Is it much farther?" I asked.

"Just up here," Maro said.

"At the top of the hill?" I asked. The trees were too dense here for anyone to build a cottage.

"No." Maro pointed again, directly above them. "Up here."

I tilted my head back and for a moment saw nothing but limbs and leaves. Then, slowly, as the wind blew through the branches, it became clear that some moved while others did not.

"That's certainly unexpected," Ender said, also staring upward.

Among the trees sat a small house. It was more than thirty feet in the air and seemed to have been built directly into the trees themselves, wrapped around at least five trunks that had grown close together.

"No one ever thinks to look up," Maro said. "This way."

A staircase of sorts had been built on the far side of the stoutest tree by wedging branches into the trunk, each one subsequently higher than the last. To the passing eye, it might have seemed natural as they wound their way around and spiraled higher. A vine had been strung in parallel up the trunk, giving the climber something to hang on to like a makeshift railing. All in all, the setup was reasonably sturdy, except for the way the whole construction moved with the wind. It might have seemed not unlike climbing a mast, but whereas the motion of a boat and its mast on the sea was relatively predictable on any but the roughest days, here the trees seemed to rock in any and every direction, meaning in one moment the distance between the steps was relatively uniform and in the next you had to strain to keep from plummeting all the way back down to the forest floor.

Once, a crack sounded behind me, and I turned to find Whit clinging desperately to the vines and straddling a step. His face was white, his mouth agape. I made my careful way back down to him. As I approached, his features relaxed, but at the last minute, I reached inside his coat and found the pouch of moss jade he'd stowed there.

"I'll take this for safekeeping. If you fell, we'd have climbed all the way up here with nothing to offer the witch."

He grumbled a reply that I didn't bother to listen to as I helped him to his feet, and we carried on.

At the top, we were above the surrounding trees. If I looked over my shoulder, I could see the *Siren* waiting patiently for us beyond the beach. The cottage itself was more of a platform with broad leaves hung overhead and animal skins along the sides to keep out the weather.

"Will we be welcomed? Seems unwise to walk into a witch's home uninvited," Ender asked, but since there would have been plenty of opportunity to shoot, curse, or otherwise expel us from her presence while we made our careful way upward, I had to assume that Aga Serala was at least willing to speak with us.

I patted the pouch, now snug inside my shirt. Hopefully, the jade was all we needed to convince her to give up the map.

"Aga Serala?" Whit called, as he pushed the skin back. "Hello? It's Whitney Perelsior."

I snorted at the last name. It wasn't ours. To be honest, I wasn't sure that we'd had one. Not like George, who had the names of five or however many noble lady ancestors attached to hers before we ever got around to naming her family. We'd been too poor and too irrelevant to need differentiating from the other peasants and laborers in the area.

"Something's not right," Maro said, drawing their sword without so much as a whisper of the blade in its sheath.

"Are you saying you know what 'right' feels like in a witch's treehouse?" I asked.

A breeze blew through the cottage, bringing the scents of the small home toward us. Herbs and smoke, something sweet like honey. And above it, the warm, metallic smell of fresh blood.

"It's not that," Maro said.

We moved cautiously, but there was no sign of anyone else. Finally, we came to a long skin hung over a doorway.

"Cinder," Maro said, pointing at the dark puddle that leaked out from under the barrier.

I glanced at Ender and Whit, who waited tensely behind us. Slowly, Maro used the tip of their sword to pull back the curtain.

Aga Serala lay on a bed that looked more like a nest of woven blankets. She appeared strangely at peace, hands folded over her chest, with strings of glass beads wrapped around her fingers. Her skirts were arranged nicely, and small gold chains looped round her ankles. She'd have looked like she was sleeping but for the seeping red stain that spread from the gash on her throat down the front of her blouse.

"No," Ender said, making a gesture in front of him like he was trying to ward off evil spirits. Maro stepped forward, placing a palm on the witch's cheek. They murmured something I couldn't hear, but when they straightened, their expression was serious.

"Still warm," they said. "Whoever did this hasn't been gone very long. We should leave."

"What about the map?" I asked.

"Forget about the map," Maro said, voice sharp.

"It's gone." Whit stood with his hands on his hips, staring through the doorway at the far end of the chamber. It opened onto a balcony facing the sea.

"How can you tell?" I asked. The room—as much as it was a room—was a disaster, and it was impossible to tell if she'd simply liked to live among this level of disarray or if someone had gone through it looking for something, though the presence of the jewelry on the sea witch's hands and feet would say if they were, it was something very specific indeed.

"Because they would have taken it when they killed her." He pointed out toward the ocean, where a ship sat with its sails furled. For a second, I thought we were looking at the *Siren* again. Except we were now standing on the other side of Aga Serala's home, facing the opposite direction we'd come from and, as I watched, the ship began to unfurl those very same sails, revealing broad expanses of black canvas.

"Who is it?" I asked.

"Captain Harlow," Whit said mournfully.

Even Maro sounded alarmed. "Harlow? Here?"

Whit nodded again. "There were people in Darto who knew what I'd done with the map. Someone must have told him."

Conrad. He'd said Aga Serala would demand a heavy price. He'd known what Whit had, at least in part. And Captain Harlow would never forego a treasure the size of a city.

"We need to go," I said. "We need to go after him. Now."

As though they'd heard me, Harlow's crew unfurled their sails. They were getting ready to leave. If we didn't go after them now, the map would be lost.

CHAPTER 15

"**I** think this adventure has run its course," Maro said. They'd gone back to where Aga Serala lay, and the grief on their face was plain. I turned away, letting them have their moment to say goodbye, whatever their full history with the witch might be. Instead, I watched as Captain Harlow's ship found the wind, bow surging into the waves. If I stood here for ten minutes, the ship would grow smaller. Twenty minutes more and she'd be halfway to the horizon. Longer still and she'd be a small black dot that eventually disappeared.

If I was going to get that map, this was my last chance.

"We go back to the *Siren*," I said. Maro sagged in relief, and I regretted their displeasure before it had even happened. "And we're going to be quick about it. We have to get all the way around this island before Harlow's ship is out of sight."

"Captain," Maro said. My throat was dry as we stared each other down. Tension radiated around their lips and in the corners of their eyes.

"This is our last chance," I said. "If we waste time, we'll lose him."

"He works for the brokers."

"Not anymore," I said, but they ignored me.

"This whole time, you've said we had to sail clear of the brokers and their agents, but now that one of them has something you want, you're going to run them down? That's not sensible, Cinder."

"I'll be the judge of what is and isn't sensible. Not sensible is sentencing us all to death for the sake of vengeance. I told you that from the very beginning, and you refuse to listen!"

"And how is this any better? Sailing from port to port. Chasing treasure that might not exist to fulfill a deal with the brokers they may not honor."

"They will honor it," I said, heart pounding an anxious rhythm as Harlow's ship began to lean into the breeze.

"Only as long as it serves their purposes. You know this, Cinder. It's always been like that for them. When they need you once more, they'll come for you and your princess and rip her—"

"Enough!" I shouted. Maro's eyes were alight with fury and I was breathing hard. My pulse was like the rhythm of a clock, marking the time as Captain Harlow escaped. "My ship. My rules. This is the last time I'll say it. If you can't live with that, you can stay here and bury your friend. No doubt someone will come looking for a curse or a wish and find you. You can beg passage if you want, or become the island witch yourself."

Their gaze dropped down to the motionless figure of Aga Serala, and for a second, grief shone through their anger, and with it came my own regret. I was pushing too hard. Maro and I disagreed often, but we rarely made it personal.

But Maro took a knife from their belt and used it to cut free a lock of their black hair. They pressed a soft kiss to it before winding it around one of Aga Serala's hands and brushing a palm over her forehead.

"Rest well, little friend." Then they straightened, and their gaze when it landed on me was flat and emotionless. "I'm sorry,

Captain. I didn't mean to speak out of turn. Your ship, your rules, as you say."

My throat was dry, and I had to clench my hands to keep from fidgeting. I should apologize. Give Maro a moment more to say goodbye. Ender appeared to be doing his very best to make himself as small and unnoticeable as possible—no mean feat given his height and the width of his chest. Even Whit was staring at his shoes. The discomfort among the four of us lingered a second too long, and the opportunity for my apology vanished.

"Let's go back to the *Siren*," I said quietly, and I didn't look to see if the others followed as I made my way to the stairs.

"What's going on?" George asked as we brought the longboat over the rail. The journey back had been a silent one, and now Maro and Ender both immediately set to work with the crew, while Whit hesitated behind me, doing nothing in particular.

"We're going on a hunt," I said, then shouted orders to set the sails. Crew scrambled up the rigging with practiced confidence.

"What about the witch?"

"She was dead." My pulse pounded in my throat. It had been a long time since we'd had a chase, especially one where we were the pursuer. Since Maro and I had left Kiril's service, more often than not we had been the ones looking for the fastest route to escape.

George gasped. "Dead?" But before I could answer, a great flapping filled the air. Overhead, one of the sails had come free of its rigging and shook in the wind.

"What's wrong with you?" I shouted. "Secure that before someone gets hurt! Maro, get us underway."

I rushed to my cabin without waiting for their reply and pulled out charts I hadn't touched in years.

"What are you looking for?" George entered through the main door.

"He won't hesitate to fire back when he realizes we're in

pursuit." Whit had also followed. "Captain Harlow doesn't brook people interfering in his endeavors."

In the years since we'd left Kiril, I'd slowly offloaded many of the *Siren*'s guns. We weren't in the business of sinking ships anymore, and guns weighed us down when we needed to make a clean getaway. We weren't in a position to take on a well-armed ship. And even if we were, opening fire risked sinking her before we had a chance to retrieve the map.

I finally found the charts for this part of the sea. They were old and torn, left behind by the *Siren*'s previous captain. I jabbed a finger at Isla Laurentis.

"We're here. He was heading south-southeast. He'll have to pass through this cluster of islands here, which will slow him down while he's in the lee of the land. If we go this way and the wind holds"—I traced an arc around the other side of his path— "we can get ahead of him."

"A head-on confrontation will be too dangerous," Whit said. "Trust me. I've seen what he can do."

"We aren't going to confront him," I said. "We're making him deliver the map to us."

The plan was simple. Outpace the other ship, then lower our sails and raise a distress signal. If Harlow was the man his reputation said he was, he wouldn't be able to resist coming to our aid, if only to raid our holds.

The plan should have been simple. But unfortunately, the elements were against us.

We made good time into the evening. The wind held and the *Siren* moved over the waves with the confidence that came from years with a well-oiled crew. Occasionally, Harlow's ship was visible at a distance, before vanishing over the edge again, but at least we knew we were heading in the right direction.

Unfortunately, as the night wore on, the stars slowly disappeared, and even the moon was obscured by a thick layer of clouds. We passed the first of the islands, and lights flickered on the horizon, beginning as distant flashes, then becoming distinct fingers as lightning arced from sea to sky.

"We should bear east," Maro said as they stood at the wheel. "Go around it."

"If we go too far, we'll lose the time we've made."

"Then head farther south. Follow the islands so we can take shelter if we need to."

"And have Harlow slip past us in the dark? He won't stop if he doesn't see us."

"If he's sensible, he'll be looking for a place to ride it out too."

I shook my head. "And if he sails on?"

"I'm not a mind reader, Cinder!" Maro's voice rose. The wind swirled around us, making the lantern light flicker. "If I was, I'd know what had scrambled your brains so completely. Until recently, I'd have said it was love, but now ..." They trailed off as they scanned the sea ahead of us.

"Now what?" I asked.

"Never mind."

"No." I nudged them. "Let's hear it. Now I'm what?"

"You're afraid. You've never let fear rule you before."

"It's not—"

"Don't lie to me, Cinder." Their voice cracked as thunder rolled in the distance. "Not after everything." Their face was deeply shadowed. So many years. So many miles. So many lives taken. They never felt the same guilt I did. The same shame. Maybe because they had chosen their profession and gone into it with a full knowledge of what it would entail. I had chosen mine too, but I had thought the only way to escape the torment of being a child among pirates was to become the tormentor. At no point did I regret deciding to live, but late at night when George pulled me close and sighed in her sleep, I wished I'd known there might be other choices.

Finally, I simply shook my head again. "We sail on."

Storms were their own kind of magic. I didn't believe much in mysterious forces that couldn't be seen. But storms drew power from a source beyond anyone's understanding. One moment, after Maro and I traded watches, the storm was off to starboard and it looked like we might sail around it simply by holding our course after all, and the next, a boom of thunder sounded directly overhead, vibrating through the ship's timbers, and the lightning cracked so close, the scent of charred wood filled the air.

"Ender," I said. "Get everyone out of the rigging. Watch too. Get them all down."

"We should reef the sails first, captain."

"Too late for that." I gripped the ship's wheel as she bucked beneath me. The winds had been high for the last hour, but now they picked up significantly, whistling through the lines and causing nearby fittings to rattle.

"Captain, we should at least do the lowest ones. And bring in the mizzenmast," Ender said. "We'll be blown off course otherwise."

With the great roar that was gaining volume ahead of us, we were unlikely to stay on course in any case, but he was right.

"Send a minimum number of crew. And make sure they know to come down the second they hear the bell."

Ender shouted the orders, voice barely audible over the wind, but the words were carried upward from one sailor to the next. A few climbed down, while the others went out on the yards to reef the sails. In a storm like this, a ship under full sail was at the mercy of the winds, pulled in every direction as the waves built. A reef reduced the area and gave us enough power to keep our forward progress without putting too much strain on the ship.

Still, as the sailors overhead were outlined by another streak of lightning, the ship groaned and rocked.

"Sound the bell," I said.

"But the mizzenmast—" Ender started.

"I've sailed in worse and survived." I tightened my grip on the wheel and squared my feet.

"Should I wake Maro?" Ender shuffled nervously on the deck.

"There's no way they're sleeping through this." No one would be. Soon enough, anyone who wasn't on watch would be on the deck as the swinging bunks and churning cabins inside became completely disorienting.

Not that the situation was any better out here. Ender rang the bell, and the remaining crew climbed down. The *Siren* reared up, prow pointed to the clouds, and slammed down again. Shouts echoed, followed by the unmistakable sound of a body hitting the deck, having fallen from a great height. More cries followed, these from lower down where others had already descended.

"Someone get the doctor!" a voice shouted, no doubt remembering too late that we didn't have a doctor anymore. Regardless, whoever had fallen would need more than the doctor's kind attentions to survive.

"Should I get George?" Ender asked. I didn't reply. She wouldn't be able to help either. A fall from as high up as it had sounded would kill someone if they were lucky. If they weren't, they'd be in agony from injuries she'd never be able to heal.

I swallowed hard. "Check on whoever it was. If they're alive, take them to the infirmary, but don't let anyone in."

Ender saluted me and hurried away. He didn't ask what to do if the sailor was dead. In this weather, the only option was to throw the body overboard. Trying to get it down to the hold until we could have a proper burial at sea would only risk more people. Someone would fall down a ladder or hit their head.

Though, as the wind and water plastered strands of hair to my face, the reality was that our situation was rapidly degrading. The *Siren* scaled a new wave, water coming over the bow and washing across the deck.

"You thought you'd run into the belly of the beast?" Maro had appeared as a dark shadow at my side.

"This time, the beast snuck up on me." My feet slipped out from under me as we pitched to starboard, but Maro was there to grab the wheel as it spun wildly, trying to relieve the tremendous pressure as the sea roiled beneath us.

"We need to head out to open water," Maro shouted.

"We'll drift too far from the islands." I took hold of the wheel again, but Maro refused to relinquish their grip.

"You don't know these seas. Where are the shoals? How far are we from land? You seem determined to drown us, but why make it a sure thing by running us aground?"

Lightning flashed, illuminating Maro's face for a split second, and what I saw made my heart stop.

Fear.

The effect of it was so shocking that I could still see it, even when I closed my eyes to ward off a second flash that almost immediately followed the first.

They'd said I never let fear rule me, but I hadn't known they could feel afraid in the first place. When I opened my eyes again, their face had settled back into their usual grim determination. Yet I couldn't shake the memory of what had been there only a moment before and the knowledge that I was responsible for it.

The *Siren* reared up again, more water pouring over the bow. But this time we were pushed suddenly to port, so her nose was forced down and we pitched to one side. Somewhere below, a woman screamed.

"George!" I shouted, leaving Maro at the wheel and rushing down the steps to the main deck. Around me, sailors struggled to their feet as the *Siren* bucked.

"George!"

She lay on the deck near the main hatch, dark hair free and streaming down her back. I had to cling to the rail to keep myself upright. But when I reached her, it was Rosie who pushed herself to her feet.

"The mess is flooded," Rosie said. "Everyone has come up top."

Everyone, it seemed, as I glanced around in the split second of illumination as another finger of lightning forked overhead, except George. My heart stuttered. Had I seen her since we'd returned from the island? Everything had been such a flurry of activity after we'd begun our pursuit that I couldn't say where she'd gotten to.

Rosie crashed into me. The wind howled like a demon, demanding our obedience and quite possibly our souls. The *Siren* rolled again, and we held on to each other as the water dragged us to the rail. The impact was jarring, but we managed to avoid tipping into the hungry ocean below.

"Find Ender," I said. "Make sure the hatches are all shut." They would be, but giving Rosie a task would help her keep the panic at bay.

"But what about George?" she asked.

"I'll find her."

Last year, George had climbed the mast and stayed on the lookout through a storm. The intensity of the wind and rain that night was nothing compared to what we faced tonight, and I had to believe that George understood the risks better now. If she had gone aloft and refused to come down, she was long gone to the depths, flung away with no more care than I might shoo away a bug.

I couldn't think like that. George was safe and still on board. I nearly wrenched the hinges off my cabin door as my feet slid out from under me. Water rushed past me and inside, swallowing the rugs and furniture I had accumulated to make this place mine and then ours.

"George?" I called, but the only reply was the groaning ship. I rushed toward the rear cabin, half expecting to find her cowering by the bed, but she was nowhere to be found. The second I stepped onto the deck again, Maro called for me.

"Captain! We're losing her!"

"Stay the course. I need to—" My next words were cut off by a bang like a cannon blast, followed by a great rustling as though a flock of giant birds were taking flight overhead. One of the sails on the foremast had torn, the great canvas sheet ripped to shreds.

The ship swung around viciously from the loss of pressure on the sail. Maro brought the wheel about, turning it hand over hand.

"Hold steady!" I shouted, but I didn't stop to see if they listened. I had to find George.

The way down to the infirmary was narrow and slick. My palms burned as I grasped at ropes on either side. On a clear day, a good sailor wouldn't even touch these, but tonight, they were the only thing that kept me from pitching headfirst through the hatch.

She was in the infirmary, leaned over the body of a man who had very obviously had his skull bashed in.

"What are you doing?" I gasped.

George looked up at me with a wide mouth and frightened eyes.

So much fear tonight. George's. Rosie's. Maro's. A storm like this required our respect, and if it wasn't given enough, then it would take our fear.

"Ender," George said, practically yelling to be heard over the thundering downpour overhead and the hungry churning of the waves beneath us. "Ender said he fell. From the mast. He asked me if I might—"

"This man is dead." Without entirely meaning to, I jabbed a finger at his head and suddenly found myself knuckle-deep in his cheek. The bone around it had been reduced to mush, no doubt having taken the brunt of the impact when he landed on the deck. "There's nothing anyone can do for him."

George nodded. "I know. But Ender said … I thought I could …" Her chin wobbled, and her voice broke. The infirmary tipped on its ear, and all the jars—the ones so meticulously prepared by the doctor before he left us—plummeted to the floor and exploded into a profusion of tiny ceramic shards and strange-smelling puddles.

"We have to go," I said. "The ship. The storm. Maro is losing her, and I—" I was what? Nowhere to be seen on deck? I'd abandoned my post to find George. I stuffed the thought away.

We had just begun the climb back up to the deck when my feet were lifted in the air, while the deck overhead seemed to slam downward. I hit my head so hard I saw stars, though no doubt the real stars were still lost behind their wall of cloud.

"Lou!" George's shout came from a great distance away, and before I could even turn to see if she had fallen too, the *Siren* bellowed. The sound was so loud, even over the roar of the storm. I climbed the last steps out of the hatch and watched, helpless, as my ship's mainmast split, splinters of wood breaking apart. We rocked, pitching violently, and slowly the mast came down, colliding with the rigging of the mizzenmast before it stripped the starboard spars off like kindling.

"Maro!"

They wouldn't hear me, but they still stood at the wheel, a dark silhouette too far away for me to help, while the mast fell toward the quarterdeck. At the last second, the *Siren* rolled again, and the wreckage tipped away and fell into the ocean.

We were lost. Wounded beyond repair and left to the mercy of the ocean.

CHAPTER 16

A ship the size of the *Siren* was not made to sail with one mast. On a clear day, we would travel too slowly to make any voyage worth the cost in food alone.

In a storm like this …

We rolled for hours, even after the rain had ended. With only a few reefed sails left, we didn't have enough power to maintain our forward progress. Instead, we were forced to endure the whim of ocean and sky. Ender and I braved a treacherous climb up the remaining foremast to let out the reefs and try to regain some control, but all we got for our trouble was another torn sail; Ender took a block to the head as he climbed down again, leaving him with a wicked gash. Here, at least, was a wound George could tend to, though the infirmary was destroyed.

Maro and I spent the dark, sodden hours at the wheel, trying to keep the *Siren* close to the wind and mostly failing. If we were still anywhere near Captain Harlow and the islands, I had no idea. Maybe he had taken shelter or changed course. Maybe he had also sailed straight into the teeth of it and was now at the bottom of the ocean, taking the cursed map with him.

"We'll have to make port as soon as possible," Maro said at one point as the sky began to brighten. It was the only thing they'd said to me for hours, even as we'd stood shoulder to shoulder, trying to save my ship. Our ship. I didn't reply. What port? Who knew how far we'd been blown off course? Even returning to Darto would take weeks under our reduced speed. And what nearby harbor would have the timber and tradespeople necessary for the repairs the *Siren* would need? Shipyards weren't found in every town or city.

And yet, when dawn finally broke and the storm had moved past us, we were still there. Most of us. Maro made a roll call, and three names went unanswered. Swept overboard with no one to notice. At the sound of his name, Whit emerged from who knew where, looking shaken, but still irritatingly vital.

"I have to say—" he said as he came to my side.

"You really don't," I said. Even his grin persisted, much to my annoyance. Every inch of me hurt. My knees, my shoulders. My hands and fingers felt as if they had been permanently forged into claws from trying to hold the wheel steady for so many hours.

Whit laughed as though we shared a great joke. "You always were tough for a girl, but I'm beginning to think you have the largest balls of any person on this ocean."

"It's such a shame—" I started, but the threat brewing on my tongue was pulled up by Rosie's shout.

"Look! Over there!"

Off the starboard side, a three-masted ship with black sails moved confidently over the waves. She showed no signs of damage from the storm.

In a night when nothing had gone right, this was my one chance to salvage some part of it.

"Hoist a distress flag," I said.

"Captain?" Ender asked.

"You heard me. Send up the flag."

"Captain, I have to disagree," Maro said.

"Of course you do," I muttered.

"We're severely damaged."

"Then we're fortunate we won't have to fake our distress. Ender, the flag!"

"We also have no way to escape or defend ourselves. There isn't an ounce of dry powder anywhere on board."

"We still have swords. We'll have to lure them in close anyway. Swords will be better if it comes to it."

"Captain, I think—"

"This is still my ship!" The words came out more sharply than I meant. "And either way, we are in need of assistance. We will play the part of distressed sailors"—behind me someone snorted softly, but I ignored the disrespect of it—"and when the time is right, we will play our hand and take the map from Captain Harlow. Is that understood?"

The assembled crew around me were ghostly silent. Everyone was soaked and exhausted. Rosie and Ender leaned heavily against each other. Ender's head was bandaged and his cheek was crusted in blood. Rosie looked especially small today, but also like she was determined to hold him upright until the last of her strength gave out. George stood off to one side, away from the rest of the group. Her arms were folded over her chest and the scarf around her hair was mottled with salt stains. When our gazes met, her eyes held a thought or a feeling I didn't know, and even though I was thoroughly chilled from the hours of storming, something icy slithered through me. I had to be the one to look away first.

"Well, go on," I said, waving my arms in dismissal. "Raise the flag. Rosie, see if we have anything left to eat. The rest of you, see what we can salvage for repairs."

They moved apart slowly, with muffled words and half-hearted salutes. A few glared openly at me, and I ignored them. Weariness washed over me. If I could, I would have closed my eyes and let sleep take me right there. But with a captain's privilege to give orders also came the responsibility to see that they were carried out.

A throat was cleared politely behind me, and I whirled to see who dared dawdle now that I had made my instructions clear.

Whit.

I sighed. "Yes?"

"Sorry to bother you after everything," he said, tugging at his cuffs like he might right before asking a beautiful woman to dance.

"What is it?"

"Oh, nothing. Only that if you want Captain Harlow to believe your ruse, it would be better if I were out of sight. We've had some previous encounters that were less than friendly."

"Fine." I dismissed him with a wave, too tired for any verbal sparring. "Find somewhere down below. It will all be wet, but it's the best I can do."

"Captain," a voice behind me called as Whit departed.

I sighed, wishing for one moment where no one needed my attention. "Yes?"

Ender was at the wheel. "The other vessel has changed course. They're headed this way."

I glanced around at my ruined ship. The stumps of two masts. The remnants of torn sails, waving lazily like kelp hung upside down. A poor sight indeed. A perfect lure for a pirate with a greedy eye. If Harlow came with force, we were sorely lacking in ways to defend ourselves.

"We'll have to go," I said.

"We won't get very far," Ender said, then made an apologetic noise when I glared at him.

"Not here. With Harlow."

"We'll take his ship?" George asked, coming up to us.

I could barely think. None of the details were clear.

"Go to our cabin," I said.

"What for?"

"Because the map is there. Find a place to hide it."

"But if we—"

"Just do as I say. I'll call you when I need you."

George's eyebrows did a complicated dance as she tried to follow what I was saying, but frankly, even I only had half a plan. All I knew was that Harlow had the map, he was coming closer all the time, and the only way we would be able to continue this voyage would be on his ship. Who would live or die to make that happen was uncertain.

As I looked at my disabled ship, the only thing I knew for sure was that the *Crimson Siren* had sailed her last. And I was the one who had ruined her.

MARO and I watched silently from the quarterdeck as the man I assumed was Harlow made his way between our two ships. A group of about ten sailors came with him. They were each dressed in a uniform of sorts, bright red coats that wouldn't have looked out of place in any number of naval yards around the world and were no doubt meant to lure distressed ships and crews into a false sense of security as they approached. Once they were on board though, the coats had clearly all seen better of days, and the array of scars, bedraggled hair and leering eyes that accompanied them looked thoroughly untrustworthy.

Captain Harlow, for his part, climbed over the rail with all the grace and dignity of a visiting monarch. For a second, I had the thought that we should have prepared George to present herself as the captain to create a meeting of equals, but I shook myself. Despite the disaster of the last twelve hours, I was still captain. Harlow would deal with me and me alone.

I descended the stairs. "Thank you for coming to our aid."

Captain Harlow was a man of about fifty years of age. Curls

of silver hair peeked out from under a felted hat that showed no signs of having recently weathered a storm. For a seafaring man, his skin was noticeably unlined, and his teeth were entirely present and shockingly white when he smiled.

"It is every sailor's duty to ensure their fellow mariners are well and safe, and you"—he glanced around in a way that made me bristle in indignation for my wounded ship—"looked like you could use some assistance."

I did my best to appear gracious. "The storm caught us on the wrong side of the islands. By the time we realized the expanse of the front, it was too late to go around, and we worried about rocks if we sought shelter closer to shore."

He clucked sympathetically, like a concerned parent listening to a child tell them something adults already knew. I blinked, trying to pull my concentration together. I had dealt with men like Harlow for years. Had killed more than a few. But my exhaustion left me feeling so inadequate today.

"You're fortunate we came along then," Harlow said.

"We are." I extended my hand. "Captain Silvaro, at your service."

He whistled softly. "A woman captain. You don't see many of those in this part of the sea."

I gave him a tight smile. "So far I've had no complaints from my crew."

Harlow cast one more glance toward my damaged rigging. The twist of his lips said he suspected that might not be true.

"Where were you headed?" he asked. I opened and closed my mouth. This was a question I hadn't prepared for given our new circumstances. How had I not thought of this? No doubt because yesterday I had planned for the element of surprise to guide much of this encounter. Captain Harlow would come aboard, a scuffle would ensue, and we would find the map then make a hasty retreat aboard the *Siren.* But today was a different day, and there was nothing hasty about my broken lady now.

Captain Harlow, though, didn't seem concerned with my uncertainty.

"How big is your crew?" he asked.

"About thirty." Getting smaller all the time. First, we'd lost the doctor. Then the body lying abandoned in the infirmary and the others who had gone to the ocean. More soon, if Captain Harlow got wind of what I intended.

Yet right now, he was the picture of genteel generosity. "We can take you and your crew as far as Norampar."

"We wouldn't want you to go out of your way, "I said.

"Nonsense." He waved a careless hand, but for the first time, his gaze held an assessing glint. "My crew and I are sailing to Maudane."

My throat tightened. Maudane. I'd never been there. Was that where the treasure was? For the first time since Lady Amelia had handed me the map, we might have a clear destination. I did my best to school my features and hide the tiny flicker of excitement that sparked inside me.

"That is very generous of you, sir," I said.

"Not at all." Another casual wave of his hand, and I had to remind myself of the dead witch lying in a pool of her own blood. Despite outward appearances, Harlow was not a man to be underestimated.

"Of course, while we can resupply in Norampar, it would be helpful if my crew could bring aboard any remaining provisions that might have survived your recent"—his gaze darted aloft with a knowing smile—"misadventures."

My hands, clasped behind my back, balled up into fists, but I kept my smile easy and unassuming.

"Of course," I said. "It's the least we can do in light of your help. I'll have my first mate escort your crew to the hold. And my own crew will be more than happy to help transport anything you think will be useful."

Captain Harlow nodded like I hadn't just given him permission to raid my ship. But while Maro led his men down below, his gaze kept scanning my own bedraggled assembly.

"I don't suppose you happen to have a good cook?" he asked. "Ours died suddenly about a week ago. Poor soul. He wasn't very good company, but he knew his way around a slab of salted cephyr. We've been far worse for wear without him."

A gasp sounded behind me, and when I looked, Ender had a protective arm around Rosie's shoulder.

"I'm afraid we're not ready to give her up," I said, and Captain Harlow's answering smile was predatory.

"I completely understand," he said. "A good cook is worth her weight in gold."

There it was again. The knowing glint in his eye. But what did he know? While he undoubtedly knew of Captain Cinder's reputation, as far as I could recall, our paths had never crossed before. There was always a chance he harbored a grudge against me for an old captain I'd murdered or a cousin I might have ruined on Kiril's behalf.

"Rosie," I said.

"Yes?" She came forward.

"Can you find Lady Cressida"—I used one of George's many middle names—"and let her know we'll be leaving the ship? She'll need to pack everything, right down to her great aunt Amelia's letters. Do you understand?" I tried to keep my tone light, as if orders like this were commonplace. But as I spoke, the finality at the heart of it made me go cold. We were really leaving the ship. Regardless of what happened in the next hour or the next day, we would have to continue on Harlow's ship. The *Siren* was too damaged. We were leaving my home behind.

Rosie glanced nervously between me and Harlow, but she gave me a quick salute. "Right away, Captain."

"Lady Cressida?" Harlow asked.

"A passenger," I said. "We're taking her to the temple at Norampar, so it's very fortunate you happen to be going there.

Her husband passed away, and she's chosen to live her widow-hood in quiet contemplation."

Harlow ran his hand from his forehead to his lips, something I'd seen particularly devout sailors do right before a battle. I wondered if he'd offered any similar blessing to Aga Serala before he'd cut her throat.

Harlow's crew were very thorough in clearing the Siren's hold, thought there wasn't much to save. Along with what balls and wet powder they were able to find in the armory, and the things Maro had acquired to disguise our departure in Hilltop, the sailors brought up trunks that I had largely forgotten about. An explosion of mildewed silk emerged from one. A barrel was dropped halfway across the deck. One side was so rotten it split and spilled all over the deck. The contents might have been pickled fish at one point, but now they left a putrid stench wafting in every direction and had sailors from both crews leaning over the side to retch.

At one point, a commotion erupted from the *Siren*'s main gangway, and one of Harlow's crew went sprawling, having tripped trying to get out of the way of another sailor who was coming up from below decks. It took me a moment to realize the new sailor was Whit. He'd wrapped his head in a greasy cloth that plastered his hair to the sides of his head. One eye was covered with a patch, and he'd fixed his mouth on the other side into a snarl, making him appear lopsided. I held my breath, waiting for someone to shout his name or point an accusatory finger. But as Whit muttered his apologies, Harlow glanced at him once before turning his attention back to the activity of clearing the ship, and Whit melted into the assembled remnants of my crew.

A moment later, George emerged from our cabin and provided further distraction. Somewhere in the short time since Harlow had come aboard, she'd changed her clothes, and the seasoned sailor she'd become had vanished, leaving in its place a sodden and displeased-looking noblewoman who glared at me with disdain I could practically taste. Her hair was uncovered and left to hang loose, and somewhere she'd found a variety of clothes, from a high-necked blouse to a pair of gauzy orange trousers that cuffed at the ankles. I'd worn those once a long time ago in an effort to overwhelm the woman I assumed was a timid Redmerian virgin with an overt display of sexuality. She hadn't been fooled then, but I hoped Harlow was fooled now. She still clung to a basic idea of modesty though, and had slipped into a black coat that she clutched anxiously at the collar.

"Are you here to save us?" she asked Harlow, letting her Redmerian vowels linger extravagantly. Rosie stumbled out of the cabin behind her, now burdened with a number of packs that I could only assume carried every blanket and cushion we had inside, all in an effort to give the illusion of a spoiled aristocrat unused to making concessions to their surroundings and—I hoped—to hide the map somewhere among their contents. "The people here have been no help whatsoever."

Harlow's smile was charmingly oily as he extended a hand to her. "My dear. We are at your service."

George sighed in relief and threw me a nasty look. I wanted to laugh. Maybe kiss her. Instead, I gave her a cool scowl, having obviously suffered through hours of Lady Cressida's hysterics during the worst of the storm the night before.

"Is that everything?" Harlow asked, and I went to answer him but stopped short when one of his crew spoke before me.

"Yes, sir."

"Shall we?" He held out a solicitous arm to George, escorting her to the rail.

The crossing to Harlow's ship was straightforward. I stayed on board the *Siren* until the last. A captain always went down with her ship. Here, the least I could do was stay with her until the bitter end. I hoped she would wash up on some shore, lying against the sand and making fisherman dream up tales of her exploits. Or else someday she might sink to the bottom and provide a home to bright fish and coral.

"Captain," Maro called from the longboat that was serving as a launch between the two ships. It was all they said. There would be no speeches or farewells, but I said a small silent one as we pushed away. She had been my home. The sole thing that had been mine and only mine for all these years. The *Siren* kept me and the people I cared about safe and alive, and I'd done my best to do the same for her, until I'd failed her at the very end.

I yearned for some small comfort, like George taking my hand, but she sat in the bow with Harlow, so in the end I clasped my hands in my lap and counted the strokes of the oars as we rowed away from the remains of my ship.

The decks of Harlow's ship were already busy with activity as I climbed aboard. The mate gave the call to make sail, and within minutes we were pulling away from the *Siren*. I kept my back to her while pain ripped through me. I'd said my goodbyes.

"We'll be a week to Norampar," Harlow said as he came to stand beside me.

"I appreciate your help," I said, feeling numb.

"Would you be opposed to me putting your cook to work while we sail? I'll understand if you want to keep her with you when we make port."

I waved a hand. "Ender, the big red one, will want to go with her. He's very protective."

Harlow chuckled. "A good cook is worth protecting."

I risked a glance over my shoulder, where the *Siren* slowly drifted away from us. A good ship was worth protecting too, and I had failed.

"Allow me to offer you some refreshment in my cabin," Harlow said.

"I should see to my crew."

"They'll be taken care of." He held an inviting arm out, motioning toward his cabin. "If you please, Captain Silvaro."

I didn't have anything left in me to argue. We were safe for the moment. I checked on the others. Most of my surviving crew must have already been taken below to find bunks. Maro and George were standing together near the rail. Ender was following Rosie toward a hatch. Whit was nowhere to be seen.

"Lead the way," I said.

Harlow's cabin was like the man. Stately. Well maintained. He had an entire antique dining set with a round table and carved chairs, and I did my best not to groan as I settled into one. He allowed me the seat facing the door, and I expected him to sit across from me. Instead, he went to the door and asked a sailor to bring us some food and wine. My mouth watered at the thought. I covered my anticipation by glancing around the cabin, trying to guess where he might have put the map. In his desk? On his person? Tucked in a bundle of clothes and blankets like ours was?

"Thank you again," I said as he took the chair next to mine. "Your hospitality is most appreciated."

"Not at all." He waved a careless hand. "You would do the same for a vessel in distress, I know."

"Of course." I glanced out the window behind me, hoping I might catch one last glimpse of the *Siren*, but she was nowhere to be seen.

"How long have you been at sea?" Harlow asked, and suddenly I was back in the reception hall in Hilltop, where Cheray and Ylvar made pleasant small talk. Had that only been days ago?

"We've been making our way from Paranne," I said, choosing a port at random. I hadn't been to Paranne in years, but the details didn't matter.

"And where are you headed?"

I shrugged. Wherever his map led us. "To Norampar for the lady. Then we'll have to see about finding a new ship or joining a crew." The lies tripped off my tongue easily enough, but they were acid on my lips. Assuming we even survived, I couldn't simply pick up a new ship, even one as impressive as Harlow's. A different ship wouldn't be my home. Now more than ever, the only option was to take George and disappear to an entirely new life.

Harlow finally took a seat across from me. "And tell me, Cinder. Why were you following me?"

J gripped the arms of the carved chair, calculating my possible moves. He was between me and the door. He had no visible weapons, but that didn't mean he was unarmed. My knife was at my hip, but throwing from this position, especially with the table between us, would be awkward and unlikely to do any real harm at this distance.

"How did you know?" I asked.

His eyes crinkled in the corners as he smiled with calculating smugness. "One look at your self-satisfied face. You thought you could put one over on me, didn't you, Cinder?"

"By destroying my own ship?" If I could draw him backward, I might be able to get around him and out the door. But then what? He had a whole crew loyal to him out there.

"I'll admit to being impressed with your level of commitment. Did Triere send you?"

"Triere?" My plans skittered to a halt at his mention of the name.

"The brokers certainly are impatient if they're sending someone else out here."

"Are you working for the brokers?" For a moment, my hazy

mind wondered if the brokers were responsible for the loss of my ship, before I reminded myself that, despite their enormous reach, even they couldn't control the weather.

He laughed. "We have a sort of gentleman's agreement. They leave me be, and occasionally I do them a favor or bring them a trinket. Triere will be very happy to see you when this is all over."

"Where's my crew?" I asked. If he knew who I was, they were in as much danger as I was.

He waved a hand. "Alive. Even your lady, though she's not much to look at, is she? A poor disguise. I had them taken down to the brig. Might need them later if you prove uncooperative."

It was what I would have done. Leverage was key in getting hostages to talk, though gazing at Harlow's cool eyes, I doubted he harbored enough feeling for anyone on his crew that torturing any of them would yield the desired result.

For myself though … I swallowed at the thought of a knife to George's throat. Or Rosie's. Ender's, even. Maro could handle themselves, but no one would be foolish enough to start with them when there were alternatives.

"The map," I said. No way to fight my way out, I'd have to negotiate a truce. "You killed the witch. We want the map back."

He laughed, the sound a low threat in my ear. "Another treasure hunter. I'd heard you were out of the murder and mayhem racket. Looking for fame and fortune now?"

"We have the other map," I said. "The one that shows the island and landmarks."

He had to be looking for it, and his hand spasmed slightly on the tabletop, signaling his surprise. Whatever he thought we wanted, it hadn't occurred to him that we might be half a step ahead. But just as quickly, he regained his composure and rose smoothly from his seat.

"On you?" He must have been very sure of his advantage, because he came around the table like a predator, leaving himself the most exposed he'd been. My hand went to the knife on my hip, but he lunged and we both went over the back of the chair. The impact as we crashed to the ground knocked the wind from my lungs. As I gasped, Harlow hauled me up by my hair and I struggled against his grip until a vicious punch to my side had me crumpling in on myself as I desperately tried to breathe.

"Be a good girl," he growled in my ear. "And hold still." We were pressed against a wall, my chest crushed to the wood as he slipped a hand inside my coat, feeling for hidden pockets where I might have concealed the map. He took advantage to feel around for other things too. Once, I'd taken out a man's eye for daring to put his hand up my shirt. Harlow would meet the same fate when I had a chance, but I'd learned to stamp down the need for immediate revenge long ago, replacing it with the satisfaction that would come from his inevitable pain. Revenge served cold was the best dessert, or however people said it.

Harlow pressed his cheek to mine, his breath coming hot against my face. "You know I'll find it. Better to tell me now and save you and your crew the suffering that will come if I have to look for it myself."

"It's still on my ship. If you want to know what was on it, you'll have to keep me alive." I arched, trying to find purchase to crush his instep or drive an elbow into his gut, but he was stronger than his fine appearance and age might had led me to believe.

"I'll keep you alive," he said. "But I didn't expect to have to start killing your crew members quite so quickly."

The door opened, and we both started. A bedraggled pirate in a soft hat and Harlow's signature red coat carried in a tray with a wine bottle and two crystal goblets.

"Captain," the sailor croaked.

"Put it on the table," Harlow said.

"Very good, sir." He walked with a gentle limp that made the glasses rattle as he went. After he set the tray down, he took a few shuffling steps forward and bowed awkwardly. "Will there be anything else?"

"Yes. Have someone bring one of Captain Cinder's crew here. The red-haired cook, perhaps."

"Of course, sir." He straightened slowly, as if the motion pained him. He peered out from beneath the brim of his head, where one eye was covered with a patch. My breath caught in my throat when I recognized the twinkle in Whit's exposed eye. "Though I would thank you to first unhand my sister."

"Wh—" Harlow began to say, but he didn't finish before Whit hurled himself at the two of us. It was a risky move, further limiting my ability to get free, but also so unexpected that Harlow's hold on me slipped for a second—which was all I needed. As Whit and Harlow grappled, I dropped to my knees and rolled out of the fray.

Harlow was bigger and taller than Whit. Without the need to hold me in place, it didn't take him long before he grabbed the collar of Whit's stolen coat, forcing him backward, tripping over the very same chair that had caught us before.

"You. Thief." Harlow snarled. Whit's disguise was no longer enough to hide his identity. "Foolish of you to cross me a second time."

Whit sighed where Harlow pressed him against the table. "You still have something I want. This time, though, I brought reinforcements."

Free, I pulled my knife from my hip and rushed forward. He was so focused on Whit that he didn't have time to turn before I landed on him. I grabbed his fine gray hair and viciously jerked his head up, slashing the knife over his throat, just as he must have done with the witch. The flesh parted beneath my blade, and a spray of red burst forward to cover Whit's surprised face.

Harlow stumbled back when I released him, hand on his neck, but it was too late. His life was over, even if his body didn't know it yet. He stared at us both, wide-eyed. Whit and I watched dispassionately as he staggered toward the door, but his fingers barely brushed the latch before he stumbled and fell to the floor with a soft gurgle.

The cabin fell silent, save for my ragged breaths. Whit casually wiped the blood from his face with the cloth he'd carried in. He did a poor job of it, made all the more gruesome when he lifted his eyepatch to expose the clean skin beneath.

"Are you all right?" he asked.

I nodded. "You?"

He smiled grimly. "No worse than before."

"Where did you get the coat?" I asked.

"I wouldn't be much of a thief if I didn't know how to slip away from a crew being herded toward the brig and subdue a fellow in a gangway to take his clothing, now would I?"

I rolled my eyes. "I guess a flair for the dramatic runs in the family."

Whit nudged a toe at Harlow's corpse. "This was impressive. You knew exactly where to cut, didn't you?"

"I've had lots of practice."

He knocked a thumb to his brow. "Indeed. The exploits of Captain Cinder are well known."

The name rang uncomfortably in my ears. There had never been much question about killing him, despite all my protestations about not interfering with the brokers and their agents. The how and when had been undecided, but men like Harlow didn't give up what they believed was theirs easily. Killing him had been simple in the final moment. No hesitation. No regret or disgust after the fact. A reflex, really, and an expedient one at that. Being Captain Cinder had its advantages, particularly in the face of an imminent threat.

The thought was cut short as the door behind Whit shuddered violently against the latch, as though a body had been thrown against it.

"What was that?" I asked.

"Your crew, I expect, subduing the bastards who tried to drag them below. Maro in particular seemed unhappy with the prospect of confinement." The door rattled again, and Whit had only enough time to move out of the way before it burst in and a man in a red coat tumbled through it, tripping over Harlow and sprawling on the floor.

"Your turn," I said, stepping aside.

"Can I borrow your knife?" Whit asked.

"You stole a coat but didn't bother to get a weapon? You really are a terrible thief."

"Will one of you kill him already?" Maro said, exasperated, from the ruined doorway. I handed Whit my blade, and he advanced on the sailor, who scrambled backward, while I rolled Harlow over and explored inside his coat as he had done mine. I didn't find the map, but I did produce a fat purse of coins, which I tucked inside my shirt, before I followed Maro back out to the deck.

The fight was bloody but brief. Harlow's sailors were well trained and outnumbered us, but in close quarters, numbers didn't always tell the whole story. Maro moved through the skirmishes, taking down the rival crew with practiced ease. Whit and I made our way around the edges, helping where help was needed. I hadn't boarded an enemy ship in years, but the action was exhilarating as always. The clash of steel, the cries of wounded sailors as they fell beneath our attack. It brought back fearsome memories of a life I thought I had left behind, but I slid comfortably into now, like putting on an old coat. Finally, as their numbers dwindled, one by one the survivors threw down their swords.

When it was over, we were still alive.

"Where's George?" I asked.

"Here," came the answer behind me. She and Rosie emerged from a hatch.

"Ender?"

"Here, Captain." He stood at the back of the surrendered crowd. He was bleeding from a cut on his cheek but seemed fine otherwise.

"I'm fine too, thank you for asking," Whit said somewhere beyond Ender, but I only rolled my eyes in response.

"Throw the dead overboard," I said to Maro, who stood beside me.

"Yes, Captain."

"The rest, take them below." I raised my voice so I could be heard over the entire deck. "Your captain is dead. Your lives will be spared. We make port at Norampar, and then you'll be left there to find a new crew or go elsewhere as you see fit." I reached into my shirt and pulled out Harlow's purse, throwing a small handful of coins onto the deck. "We're looking for a map. Harlow stole it from the witch. These are for the man who tells me where it is."

The crew shuffled nervously, gazes bouncing anywhere but in my direction. A few sneered openly, though they weren't brave enough to say or do more. Finally, though, a young man with skinny limbs and pointy elbows shoved his way to the front.

"There's a secret drawer. In Harlow's desk."

"Shut your mouth," someone growled, but Maro took a single step forward, and the others quieted.

"Go on," I said.

"You have to open the top drawer on the right and the bottom drawer on the left." He bent and collected the two coins, stuffing them into his shirt. "Then open the center one. There's a compartment in the back."

"Thank you," I said. "Come with us. Ender, you and Whit make sure the others are suitably accommodated down below."

The young man—really, he was little more than a boy—led us into the captain's cabin. He faltered a bit at the sight of the two bodies on the floor, but with a gentle nudge, he found his feet again and went to the desk. He pulled open the drawers as described. Sure enough, in the back of the center drawer lay a second compartment that, when opened, revealed a carefully folded piece of cloth, along with a second larger purse of coins. I set that aside for later use, whatever that might be.

"Thank you," I said to the boy. "Rosie, take him down to the mess. He's your assistant until we reach Norampar."

His mouth dropped open. "You aren't sending me to the brig?"

"Your fellow crew members would kill you for your coins and for betraying your captain."

The boy blanched and stammered thanks as Rosie led him away.

"George," I said, holding a hand out, and she came to me, producing the other smaller map. How she'd kept it on her through everything, I didn't know, but I'd be sure to thank her properly when we were alone.

I spread the two of them out on the table. The cloth was the same coarse weave, and the markings were in the same fading black. Most importantly, the rough notes were in the same style of writing.

My whole frame relaxed as I stared at the words and took in their meaning. I couldn't contain my smile as I glanced up. Whit was bending over the opposite side of the desk while Maro lurked at the door.

"We have it," I said. "I know where we're going. Let's chart a new course."

Snow Eagle Island.

I had expected monsters. Dire warnings to steer clear of shoals, or a location that was too close to prowling navies looking for ships to plunder.

Instead, it was the smallest island in a cluster of nine that rose up from the ocean like fingertips. It would take a week beyond

Norampar to get there, putting us uncomfortably close against the brokers' deadline. The last miles led through a channel that looked narrow but not impassable.

"Once we find the treasure, how will we get it to the brokers?" George asked. We were lying in the bed Captain Harlow had left behind for us. The soft sheets made me wonder if I had done enough for George. So often as of late we'd found ourselves in accommodations that highlighted how sparse life on board the *Siren* had been.

It hurt to think of our tiny cabin in the past tense, but I forced myself to look to the future. This ship was mine now. This cabin. Soon, we'd have enough gold to buy a better home for me and George.

I closed my eyes and sighed. "Hafir said to take it to Triere. Harlow mentioned the same name. They have a hideout north of Norampar."

Later, after she was long asleep, the strangeness of everything kept me awake, despite how much I wanted to follow her into oblivion for a few hours. From the soft sounds of timbers rubbing together to the way the crew's feet echoed on the deck, the noises were familiar, but not the same as the *Siren*. Finally, when my tossing had caused me to inadvertently bang a knee against the small of George's back and she'd whimpered her dreamy annoyance, I'd given up and gone outside to pace in circles on the quarterdeck.

At least the sky was the same. The rush of waves on wood as we moved over the water. The differences were harder to spot out here.

"We'll both regret this in the morning," a voice said behind me, and I whirled, pulling out my knife. Whit was there, a dark shadow illuminated from behind by a lantern that hung above the wheel.

"You shouldn't sneak up on me," I said.

He tsked. "And just when I thought we were becoming friends."

I scowled, and he laughed softly, but it didn't have its usual undercurrent of fraternal malice.

Perhaps time to extend a small peace offering.

"Thank you," I said. "For before. With Harlow."

Whit nodded. "I'm sure you'd have found a way out of it eventually, but expediting things before the crew could rise to his aid seemed well advised."

"Cold-blooded," I said. "More than what a mere thief would do."

This time his laugh was a loud, short bark. "It's been years, Lucy. I've lived many lives since the last time we saw each other."

How well I knew that. We could spend the rest of the night sharing stories of our adventures and exploits, but instead I shoved at his shoulder. "I told you not to call me Lucy."

"Why?" He shoved back. "Too childish? Too personal?" Whit gasped, eyes wide. "Is it what she calls you when the two of you are alone?"

My ears flamed. "Who?"

"Her Highness. Lady Georgina." There was still some awe in his voice when he said her name, like she was still the master's daughter. Too high, too perfect for us to talk about her.

"She was never a lady. You must remember how many nights we'd come back from the forest covered in mud after spending the day hunting for frogs or racing fish in a pool."

"I remember father beating you for losing one of your boots in the bog."

My laughter faded, and the cool breeze wiped the heat from my cheeks. As I'd limped home that day, I'd known what would happen. George and I had been back hours past sundown because we'd stayed at the bog too long looking for the boot that had slipped from my foot as I chased after her in play. But the mud had sucked it below the surface, and we'd never seen it again.

Of course, my father hadn't cared about the innocence of it or had even been worried about my late return. He'd only seen the cost of buying a new pair and said he'd take it out of my back. There'd been no regret in his eyes as he'd pulled his belt from his waist. No sympathy either when I'd come home the following day with a pair of George's old boots that she'd begged me to take. They'd been made from fine leather and pointed at the toes with small round buttons up the ankle, the way all noblewomen's boots were made. I'd felt beautiful in them, but my father had only scoffed.

"Best you lose those ones too," he'd said. "They'll be torn apart the first time I take you to work in the stalls. Fine leather like that won't keep the shit out from between your toes."

I put a hand to my chest, feeling the cool loop of silver that was George's bracelet as it hung close to my heart. She'd given me so much. I could never repay her.

"When was the last time you were home with them?" I asked Whit. The question sounded uncomfortably like the ones George always wanted to ask, but suddenly, I needed to know his answer.

"Not long after you went away. I hoped I could find a job on the estate, but Georgina's father had died, and there wasn't much left," he said, gazing into the dark ahead of us.

"A job? That sounds so respectable for you."

"There was a girl."

I laughed. "With you, there was always a girl."

"And a child," he said softly, and I stilled. "Or there would have been. We ran away when we found out there was a baby on the way. Her father didn't approve of me, and Redmere's laws being what they were…"

I'd been young when I'd left Redmere, but even then I knew what the penalties were for a woman who was pregnant with no husband.

"Where did you go?" I asked.

"Nowhere. Or … I went to Vestria for a while, then Oaria. But neither of them made it. She caught a fever on the voyage. The ship had no surgeon. No clean water. There never was much hope for her, and then she started to bleed …" He shrugged.

I was strangely moved by his words. I couldn't say why. Whit and I had virtually no relationship, and I had no idea who this woman might be, but I was sorry for his loss all the same.

He sniffed. "That's what I get for following my heart, right?"

I shook my head. Was it any different from what I was doing? Who I was trying to be? Killing Harlow and taking his crew had been easy and necessary. But I didn't want to pursue those means to an end anymore. Because of George. George, who had asked time and again if we could go home. Who wanted to know what the end of the story was in Redmere, even when I insisted it didn't matter.

"Did you ever see them again?" I asked.

"Who?"

I had to swallow a few times before I could speak the words. "Our family?"

He was quiet for a long time. Long enough that I began to feel silly for even asking. I was right. It didn't matter.

I'd almost given up the whole idea entirely when Whit said, "I was in Redmere City a few years ago. I didn't mean to find him, but our father was there, in a tavern by the wharf."

"In the city?" Our father had sworn up and down he would live and die on the land.

"Hard times. He was in his cups and I don't think he even recognized me. I bought him a mug of ale and we traded a few sad stories, much like this." He raised an imaginary toast in my direction. "He said his wife had died a few winters back. Starvation, after they'd moved to the city."

I was holding on to the rail so tightly my knuckles ached. "And our brothers and sisters?"

Whit shook his head. "He didn't even mention them. Like we'd never existed. So I don't know."

Sounded about right. And there would be no way to find out. Not really. All I had to go on was names I could barely call to mind and the hazy memory of hungry childish faces.

Instead, I asked the question I had ignored from George so many times. "Do you ever think about going back? Making a life in Redmere?"

Whit snorted. "Why would I? Redmere has nothing for me. For people like us. We'd starve in a gutter or get shipped off to work in the mines. Why would I choose that when I can roam the seas with you, little sister?" He wrapped an arm around my shoulder, squeezing me so tight that something in my spine popped, though not unpleasantly.

Later, when I crawled back into the bed with George, I felt easier than I had in a long time. Certainly since the night at Davi's. Possibly since George had come aboard my ship and I'd had something to lose. Whit was right. We couldn't go back. The only reason George and I were free to love each other now was because we had escaped the so-called home that would never accept us.

Out here, we had each other, and now, we had the map. Soon we would have the treasure, and then our freedom.

CHAPTER 18

Norampar was a busy port. The city had a bustling livestock market and a temple where scholars from around the world came to study. The temple's green domes stretched over the city's skyline, beckoning visitors.

We wouldn't be staying. But for the first time in a while, I didn't feel the same sense of urgency I had when we'd stopped in other places. It was only a matter of time before the treasure was ours.

"It's beautiful," George said, standing at my side as the crew set the anchor. The day was hot and she wore her hair pinned up but uncovered, exposing the back of her neck. Tiny dark strands curled against her skin.

On a whim, I asked, "Would you like to see it?"

"What?"

"The city. We have a few hours. Maro is taking Harlow's crew ashore, and Rosie needs to resupply." Once we'd had time to further inspect the ship, it turned out Harlow's aura of grandeur had largely been an illusion. Perhaps his treasure hunting had been less successful of late. Their rations were running dangerously low too, and the drinking water was stale and foul.

"Really?" George's smile lit up her entire face, and my heart beat a giddy jig at the sight. I hoped she'd smile more now that our course was clear. The last few weeks had been endlessly tense. It was time for an excursion. To live like everyday people, even for a few hours, instead of running for our lives and checking over our shoulder all the time.

The temple at Norampar was built to worship goddesses of the sun and the moon. The nun who let us in told us in reverent breaths about how the mothers of day and night had met at dusk, and the stars in the sky were the multitudes of children they'd had while they made the universe.

The dome in the sanctuary was even more elaborate than I had imagined. Painted a dark midnight blue, the stars were fine pieces of faceted silver that sparkled as they caught light from the colored glass windows that circled the dome.

"It's so beautiful," George said, face tilted upward. "Think of the worlds the stars must shine on." She wandered away to where Rosie and Ender were talking quietly. They'd joined us once arrangements had been made for fresh provisions to be delivered to the harbor. Now, the three of them stood with the same awestruck faces as they examined the sparkling spectacle overhead.

Normally, I would envy their wonder. Today though, I felt wonder of my own. I'd sailed through so many ports and never stopped to do something like this. Never taken the time, even when there was no new job to go to. It had never felt necessary, perhaps because I'd never had anyone to share the experience with. I couldn't imagine Maro admiring the temple dome or wandering through the ruins of some ancient city, imagining the people who had lived there. But I had someone now. Once we were done with the brokers' games, George and I might backtrack and revisit all the places I had been to but never truly seen.

"You know," a voice said, so close that a puff of breath washed over my ear. "If you climbed up there and started chipping away, you'd bring down what you owe us in a mere matter of months."

"What—" I spun.

The woman standing behind me was so beautiful, she seemed more like a goddess who had come down from the stars themselves. Her hair was a dark curtain draped over one shoulder, and her skin shone like gold. But her cunning eyes and sharp smile told me exactly who she was and why she was here.

"Of course," she said, "denuding the ceiling would take far too long. But since you already seem to feel your assignment can be delayed while you and your princess explore local points of interest, perhaps you think the brokers weren't serious."

The happy feeling that had taken hold as we'd sailed into the harbor vanished like smoke in the wind. Of course they were here. My optimism had been a foolish mistake.

I said, "We needed to resupply. My ship was damaged in a storm."

She practically tapped her toe in impatience. "Yes, I saw that you'd changed vessels when you arrived earlier." Of course they had been watching. "Resupplying. Is that what you call what you're doing now?"

I clenched my fists, keeping an eye on George and the others. They were far enough away that they wouldn't be able to hear us, but I needed a signal to tell them to get back to the safety of the ship.

"The brokers should know that when I commit to something, I'll see it through," I said through clenched teeth.

"You don't work for them anymore, Cinder."

I glared at her, but I kept my voice cool. "Then how do you explain your little visit?"

She grinned and looped her arm through mine, walking me away from the others. To outside observers, we'd appear as close friends marveling at the splendor around us. I could pull back. Cause a scene. But if she was here, then something had changed, and I'd be better to take a few minutes to try to find out what it was.

"Let me rephrase." Her voice had the quality of oil on water. "You are no longer a servant of the brokers, but you have been invited to complete a task on their behalf. When you still worked for Kiril, he allowed you the leeway he felt necessary for your work. That indulgence got him killed. We will not be so patient this time."

I couldn't help it when I rolled my eyes. "Do you think you're one of them? Just because you've been deputized to speak on their behalf doesn't mean you've joined their ranks. The brokers don't welcome new members so easily."

"But they do demand respect, and this little diversion is only another symbol of the disrespect that oozes from you at every turn."

"I've never had to like the brokers to work with them," I said.

"No." Her grip on my arm was tight enough to bruise. "But you need to listen. And we'll make sure you do." She turned me abruptly so we were facing George and the others again. A man who was barely more than a shadow rushed toward them. He was dressed in the dark habit of the temple monks, and the blade in his hand sparkled like the stars on the ceiling.

"No, wait!" I shouted, and George swiveled her head toward me instead of toward the assassin. My blood ran cold. She wouldn't see him coming.

But Ender did. He pushed George aside with a speed one wouldn't expect for a man of his size. His hand was already reaching for his own knife, but he was too late. The assassin's blade landed high on Ender's chest. Rosie screamed. George stumbled and fell to the ground. Ender pushed the man off with a shout. Around us, other visitors turned to look.

"Stop!" a monk called, rushing over the tiled floor. The assassin spun and ran across the sanctuary. It was only as someone pushed past me and I tripped that I realized the golden woman had disappeared as well. Released, I ran forward as Ender sank to the ground.

"Ender!" Rosie clung to him, trying to hold him up.

"What happened? Who was that?" George asked as I approached.

"The brokers."

"But why? We aren't late. We've still got time."

"We have to go. Help me get him up."

Ender grunted as we pulled him to his feet. His shirt was already slick with blood. I staggered under his weight, even with George and Rosie on his other side.

"This way," a monk said, holding a guiding arm toward us. "We have a surgeon. If you come—"

"No," I said. "There's no time. We need to go back to the ship."

"Lou," George said, looking frightened. "He's been stabbed."

"We'll stitch him up."

"The wound looks serious." The monk tugged on his sleeves anxiously.

"We'll get him to the ship and—"

"Captain." Ender's voice was soft, and when I glanced up at him, his face was pale and covered in sweat. "It's bad. I need—" He coughed and sagged so badly I nearly dropped to one knee. A stain of red shone on Ender's lips.

"All right," I said. "Show us the way. Rosie, go back to the harbor and—"

"No." She shook her head and wiped her nose with the back of her hand, smearing some of Ender's blood on her face. "I can't leave him."

"You need to tell Maro that—"

"I won't!" Her voice rose hysterically.

"I'll go," George said.

"No." It wasn't safe for her to be in the city by herself. The brokers' agent and the assassin were still out there. If they came across George alone, there was no telling what they might do. "Rosie will—"

"Rosie's pregnant," George said.

I nearly asked if that meant her feet didn't work, but then I noticed the way Rosie clung to Ender's shirt. Her knuckles were red with his blood and the only emotion on her face was terror. I knew the feeling all too well. It was the same dread that had filled me as the assassin rushed toward George. And if Rosie and Ender were expecting a child, that emotion would only be magnified.

I nodded to the monk. "Take him to your healer. And would you be able to send a messenger to the harbor to tell my first mate we've been delayed?"

The monk led us up a set of stairs to a surgery that would have made Selim swoon with envy if he'd been there to see it. A row of beds. Soft, clean sheets. Monks and nuns moved silently between a handful of patients, but their attention immediately turned to us as we half carried, half dragged Ender's flagging form through the door. They went to work, helping him lie down and stripping his sodden shirt. George held Rosie, who couldn't look away as a monk examined the wound. Someone brought us mugs of bitter tea, though I was the only one to drink it.

"How long have you known you were with child?" I asked, mostly to pull Rosie's attention away from the surgeons as they prepared lengths of fine thread and heavy needles that flashed in the sunlight the way the silver stars on the ceiling had.

Rosie wiped her tear-stained face. "Not long. Since before we rescued Lady Amelia. I told Ender we should wait a bit before we told anyone. Sometimes new babies don't stay. My mother ..." She laid a hand to her stomach, even though there would be nothing to feel yet. "Is it odd that my first thought was that I wished my mother was here? She had so many children. She'd know what to do."

An unexpected lump formed in my throat. Rosie was here of her own volition. From the very first moment she'd followed

George aboard, she'd always chosen to be part of my crew. No obligation held her here. Only her care for George. And Ender. But we were a long way from Redmere and the family that Rosie often spoke fondly of.

If I found myself in her situation, would I miss my mother? She'd never taught me much about maternal affection. Not that I'd ever thought to be a mother myself. I'd only wanted freedom. Though the debate was irrelevant now, since Whit said our mother was dead. Anything I might have hoped for if my story were different was impossible.

The monk who had brought us to the surgery approached us. His face was serious, his hands folded into his heavy sleeves.

"The bleeding is significant," he said. "He's having trouble breathing. There's blood in his lungs, and we haven't found the source yet."

Rosie clasped her hands to her mouth as her tears began to flow freely. George wrapped an arm around her and pulled her close.

"The healers believe they can help him, but his recovery will be slow. The risk of fever if he goes to sea is high."

"But you can give him medications? Salves? To prevent infection." We couldn't stay here. Time was running out, and the brokers knew how to find us.

"It's a question of how weak he will be. He's obviously a strong man, but the wound is serious. On a smaller person"—he glanced at George—"it would have been fatal."

If I ever saw the golden woman again, she would die a painful death.

A nervous ripple washed toward us. Hushed voices spoke urgently, rising as they came up the stairs. Two monks were trying to speak with Maro as they strode implacably through the surgery door.

Who needed a mother? Whatever they thought of my choice, Maro would always look out for me.

The monks finally let them through, and they already had their sword half drawn by the time they reached us.

"What's happening? What's going on?"

"It's under control," I said. "Ender was stabbed—"

"Stabbed? In a temple?" They spun, as if someone might leap out at any moment and resume the battle, then froze as they looked through the infirmary doorway to see Ender's prone body. "What part of that is controlled? He looks halfway dead."

Rosie, who was already sniffling into George's shirt, began to sob loudly.

"Would you keep your voice down?" I said. "You're upsetting Rosie."

"Excuse me," the monk said quietly. "Perhaps if you stepped into the courtyard—"

"This is your fault," Maro said, disregarding him.

"Mine? Someone tried to attack George," I said. "Ender stepped in front of her and—"

"Not that. This, the whole thing. Your fault," they said again.

"I don't—"

"Yes! Cinder, I warned you, and now it's happened." They shoved at me, forcing me to take a step back.

"Please," the monk hissed. "We're trying to save your friend, but if you come to blows, I'm not sure I can convince them to save any of you."

Maro and I glared at each other, but finally they stalked back down the steps, and I followed while George and Rosie trailed after us.

Unfortunately, Maro wasn't any calmer once we reached the walled courtyard.

"You failed us, Cinder," they said, jabbing a finger at me.

"I don't know what you're talking about."

"Of course you do. This attempt to take some moral high road. A bloodless reply to the brokers when all they understand is blood. I've tried to be patient, Cinder, I have, but if Ender doesn't die, someone else will, and soon. You've lost our ship. And for what? If someone's coming after George, then—"

"It's not about George," I said.

"She makes you weak." They circled me like a wolf stalking prey. "Makes you careful when action is called for, and that is a weakness. I don't even recognize you anymore."

"Just because I don't go charging off with my sword drawn—"

"We said we were done with them. We fought our way free."

"We did." Unexpected tears formed in my eyes.

"And then the princess fell into your arms and—"

"I'm not weak," I said.

"Afraid. Weak." They spat. "Hesitation will get you killed, and if it doesn't, it gets others hurt. That's what's happened to Ender. I warned you, and you wouldn't listen. Do you know how much it pains me to be right? But that doesn't change the result. You're the reason he's lying in that surgery."

Rosie had buried her face in George's shoulder, but George was staring at us, eyes wide, mouth agape. Maro's words opened up the sucking feeling of losing control that had plagued me ever since that night in Beldridge. Yes, while I hadn't made all the best choices, the responsibility for Ender's injury didn't lie entirely at my feet.

"It's your fault the brokers came for us in the first place," I said, voice low.

They scoffed. "I wasn't even there that night."

"You were at Kiril's though. You're the one who killed him— or have you forgotten?"

"We were only there because you sailed us right to his front door, like you sailed us into that storm!"

"The knife that cut his throat was still yours. He's dead, and they want vengeance, and you're the one they should be coming for."

"Lou." George tried to intervene, but this wasn't her fight.

Maro twisted their lips in a cruel smile. "You're the captain, remember? Your ship. Your rules. We've lost everything. Captain, you've cost us everything, and for what?"

I stared, speechless. So many firsts in my relationship with Maro. First, their fear at the wheel during the storm. Now, their anger. They were always calm, even when they were angry. Decisive and quick to act. But now, they weren't simply angry. They were hurt. Even without a knife to the guts, I'd wounded Maro too.

"I'm sorry," I said.

"So am I." Their smile was rueful. "We've clearly been sailing against the wind for too long, and I didn't realize it. I won't interfere anymore." With a heavy sigh, they turned away.

"Where are you going?" I asked.

They hung their head, and when they turned back, the hurt had been replaced with regret. "I don't know."

"I don't understand." But a sinking sensation formed in the pit of my stomach.

Maro grimaced. "Yes, you do. I can't trust you, Cinder. And if I can't trust you, I can't sail with you. Not anymore."

Words failed me. The sinking feeling opened up all the way and swallowed my thoughts and words.

"Don't go." It was George who spoke, not me.

Maro walked past me like I didn't exist. They put a strong hand on George's shoulder. "Take care of her, princess. She loves you."

I held myself perfectly still. If I relaxed at all, I might collapse. My ship. My crew. Now Maro.

They didn't say goodbye.

WE STAYED at the temple long after the sun went down. Rosie refused to leave Ender's side, and George wouldn't leave Rosie. The whole time, Maro's words ate at my insides like rot.

You've cost us everything, and for what?

For what? For freedom. Love. Honor. To prove I could be more than someone else's tool and a murderer. But these were ideals. Values. In the most tangible sense, everything we'd worked for and had together was gone. Burned to the waterline and sunk to the bottom.

I'd tried too hard to protect the ideal of who I wanted to be—of who I wanted George to love—that I'd lost everything else that mattered. I'd cost my friends and crew their home and safety. Maybe even cost Ender his life. I should have listened to Maro, and now it was too late. All I had left was George, and still the brokers were out there. I was sailing straight into their arms once again. Playing by their rules had lost me my ship, my best friend, so many of my crew. It might cost Rosie's baby its father before they even had a chance to meet.

I couldn't win back what I had lost, but I had to protect what little I had left. And I could save so many more from falling prey to the brokers' games in the future. But there was only one way to do it. It would be harder to accomplish without Maro, but maybe they would hear of what I'd done one day and know I'd understood in the end.

George and Rosie were slumped in two chairs against the wall. Rosie was asleep, cheek pressed against George's shoulder. Her face was salt-stained and she had one arm around her belly, like she might protect the unborn child within, even in sleep.

George hummed tiredly as I bent to press a kiss to her cheek.

"What's that for?" she asked.

"I have to go down to the harbor and check on the crew," I said. "Stay here with Rosie. The monks will look out for you."

That she didn't argue or ask for more details was an indication of how tired she was too. Only the care for her friend kept her from tumbling into sleep.

"I love you," I said.

She smiled at me, taking my hand and kissing the palm.

"Don't be mad at Maro. They were upset. They'll come around. You'll see."

They wouldn't. Their fury and rejection were completely justified. They knew it, and so did I.

As I walked back to the temple gates, the monk who had first brought us to the infirmary crossed my path.

"Will you look after my friends for a while?" I asked.

"Of course," he answered readily.

"Thank you. Lock the gates tonight."

Now he frowned. "But the gates are never locked. Everyone is welcome in the temple."

I couldn't have that. Not for a few hours anyway. Once I was away, the brokers' attention would shift again from Norampar, and George would be safe in the temple until I returned. But tonight wouldn't be safe for any of us.

"Do you get many visitors at night?" I asked.

"No," the monk said uncertainly.

"Then please. The people who hurt my friend may return. Lock the gates until your goddesses cross paths again at dawn."

He hesitated, but finally the threat to his temple won out, and he bowed.

"It will be as you say."

I went first to the harbor. Maybe part of me hoped George was right and Maro would be waiting on our stolen ship. But only Whit waited for me on the deck. Not another soul to be seen anywhere.

"Did they all leave then?" I asked.

"Word got out about Ender. Then Maro stormed back, gathered their things, and left without a goodbye. I suspect if we were still on your old ship, a few might have stayed, but they were nervous."

A complication. I had business in the city, but when I was done, we'd need to leave as quickly as possible. Before George realized I wasn't coming back to the temple.

"We need a crew," I said. "Round up any able body who is ready to leave tonight."

"Tonight?" For once, he sounded uncertain.

I went to the main cabin. I'd meant to return to collect a selection of knives and other weapons Harlow had been gracious enough to leave behind. Now, I also grabbed the pouch of coins I'd found stashed in the hidden compartment in the desk. I took half for myself, then, as I re-emerged, I tossed the pouch and its remaining contents at Whit.

"Pay them whatever it takes. However many you've signed on by the time I get back, that's our crew."

"How long will you be?" he asked as I headed back down the gangplank.

"As long as I need."

He called after me, but he had his orders. And I had business to take care of.

PART III

It's not every day a girl receives a pirate ship for her birthday.

"This is by far the best birthday gift anyone has ever given me," I say, feeling lightheaded as Maro and I stand on the pier that protrudes from Kiril's fortress.

"Is it even your birthday?" Maro asks, arms folded over their chest.

"Of course it is." Who's to say it isn't? I certainly don't know for sure anymore, and no one else can argue that I'm wrong.

They're staring pensively at the ship's straining prow. My ship. I took it in a battle from a Sevnan trading company, and Kiril said I could keep it. Mine. The very idea fills me with giddy excitement. For the first time in my entire life, I'm in charge of my own destiny. No one can tell me what to do.

"You'll have to pick your crew carefully," Maro says. "Not everyone will want to sail for a woman, much less a girl."

I roll my eyes and sigh heavily. Maro's older than I am, but we're friends, and I hate it when they treat me like a child. "I know that. What am I going to do? Tell Verlov he's now my first mate?"

They laugh softly at the suggestion. Verlov is the oldest man I know. His body is more salt than skin. And he seems to think that with experience comes the privilege of treating me like a possession. He's always throwing looks my way, or getting too close to me when we pass each other in one of Kiril's twisting corridors. I finally cut off two of his fingers in the mess last summer when he pinched my ass under the guise of reaching past me for a slice of bread. Verlov howled and cursed like a wounded bear and promised all sorts of revenge, but I only laughed in his face as he bled. He's given me a wide berth ever since.

"Kiril wants something," Maro says, drawing me back from my glorious revenge on Verlov's impunity.

"He always wants something," I say.

"He wouldn't give you a ship out of the goodness of his heart."

"You think he even has one?" I know who my employer is. He's not a man. More like a greedy husk who thinks everything can be measured in gold and flesh. But he's given me a place and lets me deal with people like Verlov in the way I think best without interference. It's how I've gotten this far. Kiril knows I'll carry out his orders with exacting ruthlessness because it's the way I deal with everyone. It's how I stay safe.

We stand shoulder to shoulder, watching as the ship rocks gently against her lines.

"What will you call her?" Maro asks.

I grin because I've had the name picked out long before Kiril gave me the commission. "The *Crimson Siren.*"

They snort. "Bit on the nose, isn't it?"

"Why not? A ship's name is everything. Pick the right one, and they'll be whispering about you before you ever make port. No one's going to be afraid of the *Lumbering Mud Hog.*"

Maro rolls their eyes. They think I'm young and ridiculous,

but they never treat me like I'm their inferior. So I screw up my courage and ask the thing I've wanted to since Kiril told me about his gift.

"Will you do it?"

"Do what?" They frown as they turn their attention back to me.

"Be my first mate?"

Something strange passes over their face. Maro is never anything but perfectly calm. They don't get flustered. But I grin as the faintest bloom of color washes over their cheeks. I shove at their shoulder, and their discomfort vanishes behind a scowl.

"I'm an assassin, not a sailor."

"You've got better sea sense than half the captains I've had."

They press their lips together, and for a minute, I think they'll say no. I don't like that. If they don't sail with me, I won't get to see them very often. It's hard to have friends here. You never know when Kiril will decide someone has wronged him and send a former crewmate to drown them or string them up from a yard arm. But Maro has been a steady, reliable presence in my time here, and now that I have my own ship, I won't be around as much as before.

"Fine," they say.

"Fine?" I clench my toes in my boots to keep from jumping in excitement. "Is that a yes?"

They sigh. "Yes. I'll be your first mate. Someone has to keep you in line."

I dance in an excited circle on the pier. "That's what you think. I'm the captain. You do what I tell you."

Maro only rolls their eyes again in aggrieved silence. But I know they're pleased. Who else was I going to ask?

We're going to have great adventures. Our names will be whispered across the seas. Cinder and Maro. We will be unstoppable.

CHAPTER 19

The last time I'd entered a strange city intent on killing someone, Maro had been with me. In fact, they'd been there all the other times. Their absence was a stone in my shoe, leaving me unbalanced as I followed the streets to the parts of town where the brokers' agents would typically be found in a city like this one. If Maro were here, they'd know the houses to infiltrate, but I didn't have that information. Or Maro. I stuffed away the pang of regret that splintered in my chest. Yet as I wound my way through a darkened alley, their voice in my head told me I was being dramatic. That for someone who had been so risk-averse of late, I truly was taking unnecessary risks now.

But before I could leave Norampar, I needed to be certain George was safe here. The monks at the temple would do their best, but as long as the golden woman and her colleague walked the streets, the threat lingered.

It took until the third tavern that recognition finally flickered on someone's face when I asked about her. That recognition quickly flickered into fear, then masked neutrality, but the thin man with thinner hair had already given himself away.

"I would of course reward you for your assistance," I said,

placing one of the coins from Harlow's purse on the uneven table between us. I kept one finger pressed to its surface so the man understood the arrangement. He glanced from me to it, chewing on his lip nervously, but the shine of the coin practically reflected in his eyes, and the longer he stared at it, the more I knew he wouldn't be able to resist.

"Third house on the right once you pass the cleric's hall. But you'll have to follow the alley that leads from the north or they'll see you coming."

I left him with the coin and even bought him a fresh pitcher of ale for his trouble. George's voice asked me how I knew he wasn't lying. Maybe the alley was full of traps and I'd be dead before I got within fifty feet of the house. But once upon a time I had been very good at my job, and I had to trust the skills I'd learned with Maro and Kiril would hold me in good stead.

A man sat on the back stoop of the house, watching two cats fight farther down the alley. Maybe he was the assassin from the temple, but I hadn't seen his face. In either case, he didn't hear me coming until my knife was already in his throat. I stepped over him as he fell, and I slipped inside.

The interior was silent. In my experience, there should have been no more than two to three people living here. They weren't an army, simply in the city to keep watch on the goings on, collect debts, and issue threats as needed.

I had a moment of regret as I made my way upstairs, because already my pulse was picking up in anticipation of a fight. I'd tried so hard not to be that person. For George. For myself. Captain Cinder was numb and unfeeling. Confident in the rightness of her actions, no matter how wrong they seemed to the outside world.

My confidence was long gone, like my ship, but in that moment, I knew this was the only way forward.

In the end, the golden woman was in bed with a man. Her complacency astounded me. In the old days, Kiril would have had me kill her for being so distracted that she didn't notice when I entered the room. In truth, she didn't even suspect until the last second, when I pulled the man from her arms and buried my knife in his guts. He cried out and struggled, but after I stabbed him a few more times, he subsided and slumped to the floor.

The woman scrambled to the other side of the bed and gaped at me.

"You miscalculated," I said flatly.

"They said you'd gone soft." She sneered, but her eyes were frightened, and with good reason. A knife in its sheath lay halfway between us on top of a chest of drawers. She glanced from me to it.

"You'll only delay the inevitable," I said, but she let out a growl of frustration as she lunged for the knife.

I wasn't fast enough to grab it from her, but I was fast enough to bring down my own blade on her hand before she could stop me. The point went through, between tight sinew and bone, pinning her to the chest. She cried out, eyes rolling like a frightened animal. All her bravado from the temple was gone.

"Please," she pleaded. "They said to threaten the princess but let you both live. That you'd understand."

I did understand. Too late, but I did. This close, and without the element of surprise, the golden woman wasn't so fierce. She couldn't be older than I was, and her hands had clearly seen less blood than mine. But they had seen Ender's blood. Had called for George's. They had hurt what was mine to protect. Even if she hadn't fully understood her task, she had completed it, and if I didn't silence her, she would go back to the brokers and tell them I wasn't as biddable as they hoped. More agents would come to Norampar, putting George at risk, and then Triere would be waiting for an angry Captain Cinder when I arrived with the treasure.

With that in mind, I twisted the knife, driving the point deeper into the wood, and she whimpered. Her own knife was in easy reach, but it was like she'd forgotten it was even there. Her gaze was locked on mine. She tried to fall to her knees but only managed to pull more on the widening wound, which made her moan pathetically as tears fell from her eyes. I should have killed her, but her terror made my heart beat rapidly, and I had to steel myself to finish the task. Maybe I was weak. The numbness that had helped in the past was absent now, but I couldn't let her run back to the brokers to report on what had happened here.

"Hands are delicate things," I said. "The bones are very small, and the tendons won't reattach without a surgeon once they've been severed."

"Please," she said again, and the word made my stomach turn. So many people had begged, and I'd never shown them any mercy. Killing her now would be the merciful thing, but I couldn't make myself do it. Instead, I pulled the knife down, like chopping a vegetable, so the blade bit further into flesh and bone. She screamed then.

"That hand is ruined," I said. "You'll never hold a knife again. Fire a gun. Your usefulness to the brokers is over. You were only ever a tool to them and now you're broken."

"No." She shook her head miserably, denying the truth.

"You know what they do to agents who serve no purpose." I pulled the knife free, and she crumpled to the floor like a discarded toy, clutching her hand to her chest. She sobbed piteously. I sympathized with her fear, but I wouldn't make it better.

I knelt in front of her. "If you go to them and tell them what happened, they'll know I got the better of you and kill you. If they don't hear that your mission to remotivate me to their purpose was successful, they will come looking and learn the truth anyway. In both cases, your death will not be swift or painless."

She shook her head in despair, her breath coming fast. "Please, just kill me now. I'm sorry. Do it quick. Please."

It was always this way. First, they asked you not to kill them, then when you presented the truth, they begged you to do it after all.

"Your only option is to run. You know you won't escape them forever. No one does. But you might buy a few weeks or months. Get your affairs in order. Secure whatever gold you might have kept for yourself. It won't save you, but it might protect anyone you care about. I'll leave the choice to you."

"No. No, wait." Her words grew in desperation as I stood. She howled as I turned my back on her. I braced, waiting for her attack. Sometimes they fought, trying to goad me into a quick kill. But she only sat on the floor and wept in defeat.

As I stepped back out to the alley, I felt sick. Once I'd have felt nothing, so any reaction at all was a comfort of sorts. Even if I wore Cinder's face now, I wasn't that person. I was glad George couldn't see me though. Or Maro. George wouldn't have understood, and Maro would have wholly disapproved of the spectacle I'd created.

But I didn't have time to dwell on it. If she hadn't already, George would realize soon I wasn't coming back to the temple. Whit and I needed to leave port before she did.

He was pacing in agitation at the bottom of the gangplank as I returned to the harbor.

"Where have you been?" he asked.

"Did you find a crew?"

"About twenty."

Less than I'd like for a ship this size, but beggars couldn't afford to be particular, and Whit and I were especially poor at the moment. Barely enough to cover two watches, and we'd be in trouble if we ran into rough weather again, but we couldn't wait longer to find more.

"Hello, pretty lady," a sailor with greasy hair said, swaggering up to me as I came aboard. "Are you joining our voyage?"

"Stand down, sailor," Whit said, stepping in front of me. "That's Captain Cinder you're addressing."

The sailor spat on the deck. "Is that so? She doesn't sail these waters. Haven't heard much from her in a long time in any port, for that matter. Seems like anyone with a ship and a woman could pretend to be Captain Cinder."

I sighed internally. After the day's events and my evening's work, I was weary, and I hadn't needed to have this sort of conversation in a few years. But I let this new sailor get closer. Even let him pull at a strand of my hair. He leered, showing a gap in his teeth. When his hand drifted lower, over the front of my shirt, I took hold and twisted. He yelped and struggled, but I kicked his feet out from under him and drove him to the deck. Before he could recover, I planted a foot on his throat and pressed down hard enough to make him gasp.

"Captain Cinder, sir. What's your name?"

His eyes were wide and his voice raspy when he said, "Dornen."

"Is that all?"

Around us, sailors were watching, but when I glanced at them, they all dropped their heads and gave me a hasty salute. I leaned down and Dornen gurgled. All of it was too familiar, from the lingering smell of blood in my nostrils to the struggling man beneath my boot. I had played this game too many times when a sailor thought a woman was only put in his path for amusement or terror—or both. But it was expedient, as evidenced by the way the defiant light in Dornan's eyes snuffed out like an empty lantern.

"My name is Dornen … Captain."

"Well done." I made sure to give him one good kick to his ribs before I backed away. "Whit."

"Yes, Captain?" His smile was amused as he came to stand beside me.

"Help our friend Dornen off the ship. We won't be needing his services."

"Very good, Captain."

"Is he the mate then?" a woman in a stained and striped shirt asked, eyeing Whit as he shoved Dornen down the gangway.

The question made me flinch internally. Maro was my first mate. I couldn't imagine anyone else filling that position. Certainly not Whit. He knew as much about sailing as I did about court manners.

"What's your name?" I asked. Her cheeks and nose were flushed from too much time in the sun. Her hair was pulled back into uneven braids and a scar peeked out near her throat at the collar of her shirt. Yet for all she looked far too frail to crew a ship like this, she saluted me with a distinct confidence before answering. "Perdita, Captain."

"How long have you been at sea?"

"My whole life, Captain."

"Oh, really?" Sometimes a year felt like a lifetime on the ocean, and no one told stories like a sailor.

But Perdita held my gaze. "My mother was a ship's cook. My father was a navigator for the Archidian merchant fleet. We never stayed on land for more than a month in the coldest winters."

Like Ender and Rosie's child perhaps. Someday. Assuming Ender survived. If he didn't, where would Rosie go?

For a moment, my resolve nearly cracked. I could have run down to the wharf. But Whit was in my path, and the moment of hesitation was all I needed to remind myself of the mission in front of me. Ender would live. Rosie was safest with him, and George too. But until I dealt with the brokers, I was a risk to everyone around me. I couldn't go back until the perils of loving a pirate were behind me.

"Your father was a navigator," I said to Perdita. "Do you know your stars? How to read a compass?"

She nodded eagerly. "Yes, Captain."

"Congratulations. You're the mate now. Get us underway."

Her mouth dropped open, and I couldn't help but wonder how old she was. Not quite twenty, if I had my guess. No older than the woman I'd left bleeding in her bedroom. The sailors eyed her, and I hoped she knew how to defend herself. She'd have to earn their respect and quickly. But if I intervened, she'd never succeed.

She must have known that though, because she gathered herself quickly and put two fingers to her lips. Her whistle pierced the air, and a few of the closest sailors flinched at the sound.

"All right!" Her voice carried easily across the deck. "You're a sorry lot, but this is your home now, and the captain says it's time to go. Get to the lines and rigging and prepare to make sail."

For a split second, everyone looked uncertain, but then, one by one, they all gave Perdita and then me one more salute and went to work. A few looked confused, and I pointed them out to Whit who, with a friendly arm around their shoulders, helped them to disembark before we shoved off from the pier and pointed our bow to the mouth of the harbor.

No fanfare preceded us as we passed other ships. The dome of the temple grew smaller in the distance. Hopefully George was still there. Maybe she and Rosie had finally fallen asleep and she wouldn't even miss me until morning. I felt her absence like an ache though.

"Where should I set the course to?" Perdita asked.

"Snow Eagle Island," I said absently, watching Norampar shrink away from us.

"Where's that?"

"The Maudane archipelago. South-southwest, past Arbona." I sounded like I knew what I was talking about, but all I had was a tattered map and the knowledge that this plan needed to work.

Harlow's ship was heavier and slower than I expected. The

winds were in our favor, but our progress was less than I liked. The unfamiliar faces working the sails and rigging left me with an uneasy sensation of a threat close by, like the broker's assassin might appear behind me at any moment with a knife aimed at my heart. Before I'd become Cinder in my own right, I'd posed as a sailor looking for work from time to time, just to gain access to an unsuspecting captain. But the golden woman had said they'd wanted me frightened and willing, not dead, so anyone who had snuck aboard my ship was only there to keep watch on me. I was so close to delivering what the brokers wanted. They would make sure I stayed alive long enough to accomplish their goals. That leniency would be their downfall, but no one here knew that, since I hadn't voiced the idea to anyone. I had no one left to share my plans with.

Whit ate with me in the evenings. It wasn't his place. He barely had one among the crew, lacking the seafaring knowledge to be truly useful as we sailed. But eating alone was more uncomfortable. Everything was out of place. The wrong cabin, wrong table. No George. No Maro to remind me of all my failings.

Even the salt fish stew was wrong.

"We should have kept Rosie with us," Whit said, morosely poking at his meal. The previous cook, before Rosie had joined the *Siren*, had been a strong proponent of this culinary delicacy, but where his creations were so salty they were nearly painful to eat, this one was so bland it seemed to settle on one's tongue like paste, making it hard to swallow.

"She needed to stay with Ender," I said without looking up from my disappointing meal. For their future. For their child. If he survived, they could disappear into the world and live a happy life together.

"Can I ask you a question?" he asked, but his words only made me growl. Making interminable small talk with my brother was my idea of eternal damnation.

"If you must."

"What exactly is the plan now?"

What it should have been all along. But I didn't say that. Self-flagellation was for the middle of the night when I couldn't sleep and no one could see me.

"We find the treasure."

"Oh." Whit smiled. "Still that then? For a second, I thought we were going to do something reckless."

"And then we use it to buy access to the brokers and kill them all."

His smile fell. "And there it is. Are you sure that's wise? The sailors here don't all look like the vigilante sort."

They weren't, but we hadn't had time to be discerning. And even if they were all pirates and mercenaries, the money I'd scrounged from Harlow's belongings wasn't enough to pay them for an extended tour of vengeance. For now, all I needed was help sailing to the treasure and then delivering it to Triere's. Assuming we survived, the others could go on their way, perhaps a little more worldly and a fair bit richer. I'd use the rest of Anaïb's treasure to hire the skills I needed, along with better protection for George. It would take a while. Once Triere was dead, the rest of the brokers would either seek retaliation or go to ground. The voyage would be long and bloody and tales of Captain Cinder would sail the tides once again.

But, assuming it all worked out in the end, we would be safe. Truly. Finally. I tried not to think about the alternative.

Whit was clearly attempting to do the same, with about as much success. "I suppose retirement was never in the cards for people like you and me. I'd always hoped for a house on a hill and the love of a disreputable woman. But I'm sure I'd soon grow bored of such idleness. Better to never find out."

I lifted my glass in salute. "To wishful thinking."

He clinked his against mine. "To treasure."

~

THE GROWING pains of forming a new crew were inevitable. I was in Harlow's cabin—I still couldn't bring myself to think of it as mine—when a commotion broke out on the deck. Shouts sounded, and Perdita's whistle cut through the raised voices for a moment, but the argument grew in volume, and when I opened the door to see what the situation was, a heavy body lay on the deck, a knife handle extending from his chest. He groaned, one hand going to the weapon, before he let out a long gasp and his arm fell to the floor, unmoving.

"What is going on?" I shouted, stepping over the dead sailor.

"I'm sorry, Captain. Sir. I mean—" another sailor with dark hair and a scar on his chin said, knocking an apologetic salute.

"You did this?" I asked. The dead sailor was nearly twice this man's size. A knife leveled many odds, but this man would have to be very skilled with his blade for the fight to end so quickly.

"Captain. I wouldn't—" he stammered.

"It wasn't him," Perdita said from farther up the deck. She held a second man—with some support from two other crew members—back as he tried to surge forward. This new sailor was more similar in size to the dead man on the cabin floor, and he had a split lip and bloody knuckles.

I retrieved the knife from the dead man's chest. It was a plain sailor's blade, though the handle had been cleverly carved to resemble one of the great ice whales that swam the northern ocean.

"This is yours?" I asked the bleeding man, who growled a reply.

"It's mine," the smaller man said behind me, but when I glanced at him, he took two stumbling steps back.

I lifted the blade, holding it so it was just out of the bigger man's reach. "I won't repeat myself."

He eyed me, contempt flashing in his gaze, but finally he grunted. "Yes, Captain."

"You need to be more careful. Losing something like this in

another man's chest makes it difficult to find when you need it again."

He didn't look amused. "Easy enough to get it back once he's dead."

"What is your name?" I asked.

"Harald, Captain." He wiped the blood from his lip.

"And why did you decide our crew needed one fewer member, Harald?"

"He cheated at knuckles." Harald spat.

"Cheated you?" I asked.

Here again, he wouldn't meet my gaze. The ship was unnaturally quiet. Those who weren't aloft had gathered to find out what was going on and no doubt to hear the resolution. I needed to prove myself.

"Five lashes," I said, nodding at Perdita, who blanched.

"No!" The small man grabbed at my arm.

"You want to take his place?" I asked.

"Hector," Harald said, tone a warning.

I glanced between the two of them. "What else needs to be said? A man is dead, and I can't let that go unpunished on my ship."

"Me," Hector said, standing by Harald's shoulder. "He cheated me. Harald was only defending me."

"And why would he do that?" I asked, watching the way they quietly jostled for position, each attempting to deflect attention from the other. It wasn't uncommon for relationships between male sailors to form. A long way from home, pairings were made. But we'd been at sea for less than a week, so they must have known each other before they joined up with us. And I certainly wasn't one to look down on these couplings, but friction among lovers in the confines of a ship grew complicated. I only had to admit how badly I'd handled things once George was aboard to see the truth of that.

"We're brothers," Hector said. "He was only looking out for me."

Behind me, Whit muttered something. Hopefully he knew I wouldn't stab a man on his behalf for the winnings in a knuckle game. We were coming to an understanding, but I didn't care enough about him or such a pitiable sum of money to make the struggle worth it.

Regardless, the question of punishment remained. I rarely had sailors flogged. The last time was the day after George arrived on the *Siren*. The entire proceedings were always a bit gruesome for my tastes, and inconvenient too, since those who took their penance most often needed time to recover before they could safely work and climb the rigging again.

Still, everyone was watching, and if I let a man's death go unpunished now, we might face serious conflict once the treasure was recovered.

"There will be no flogging. But nor will there be any more knuckles," I said, pointing at the brothers. Hector slumped. Harald looked unmoved. I raised my voice. "For anyone. If you can't be trusted not to kill each other over something so simple as a game, then we'll have no games."

Protests rose from the crowd. A few grumbled curses under their breath. Perdita put her fingers to her lips, letting her whistle sound over the crowd.

"Captain's orders!" she shouted. "You won't like the alternative."

The complaints subsided, though more than a few angry glances were thrown our way. Perdita ordered them all back to work, and even Harald and Hector slunk through a hatch and out of sight.

"That was very considerate of you," Whit said. "They'll all hate you by sundown."

"Better than sailing with insufficient crew. Their mood will change once we've found the treasure. Gold heals many wounds."

~

WE REACHED the Maudane archipelago toward the tenth day. Harlow's map made it clear the only way to approach Snow Eagle Island was from the north, through an incredibly narrow channel bordered on both sides by a labyrinth of rocks that lay just below the water's surface. The last two days of the voyage, I had a man up the mast calling out directions. As we made our careful way, we came across the remains of others who had not been as savvy in their navigation. Through weather and age, lost ships had been reduced to a few jagged ribs poking upward to the sky.

"Have you ever heard of a snow eagle? Or seen one?" I asked Perdita late one afternoon.

She shook her head, eyes glued ahead of us. She had proven herself an able seawoman and navigator, moving us confidently through the passage. We'd had to anchor in coves overnight, the way being too risky to try for in the dark, but Perdita had been at the wheel every morning at first light, ready to move us ahead again.

"What about you?" I said to Whit.

He grunted. "I try to avoid anywhere with snow. Doesn't sit well with my constitution."

We had our first encounter with the snow eagles later that day. As it turned out, they didn't sit well with anyone's constitution.

Our destination presented itself as we rounded the curve of another narrow, stone-walled channel. The island was as wide as our field of view, with a single cone that rose from the center, stretching toward the sun, populated by leafless gray trees. A crown of white birds circled its apex, making lazy rounds on rising air currents in the heat of the day.

"The very same snow eagles, I expect," Whit said, shading his eyes to look at them.

As if it had heard him, one of the birds peeled off from the invisible air stream and approached. The breadth of its wings easily stretched the height of a person. It flew alongside us for a moment and even seemed to be regarding us with one flat black eye.

Suddenly, a crack sounded over the deck, and the bird exploded in a puff of blood and feathers.

"What was—" I said.

"Sorry, Captain." The cook stood there in a stained apron. He gave me a quick salute, despite the rifle in his hand. "I thought we might have it for our supper, but I must have overdone my powder."

My ears rang, and all I could do was gape at him. To fire a weapon on a ship with no warning was incredibly dangerous. There were too many people, too many moving parts to know that your shot would be a safe one.

Before I could scold him though, a shriek sounded through the air, followed by a rushing sound like wind over waves.

"The birds!" someone cried.

The rush grew louder. It wasn't wind on water, it was wings on air. The birds over the mountain coalesced into a spear tip formation that charged down toward us from on high.

We took too many seconds to react. In all my years at sea, I'd never seen anything like this. They flew at us like avenging angels.

"Get down!" I shouted. "Take cover!"

Everyone sprang into motion at the same time. Some went to the deck, covering their heads with their hands. Others did their best to drop through hatches or slide under an oiled tarpaulin. Two screamed as the eagles arrived, soaring over the main deck with their talons forward, grasping and tearing. One man swung, trying to use his arms to gain some space, and the giant bird took hold of him. It wasn't big enough to lift a person off the ground, but the bird handily tore the man's flesh from his arm with a wet ripping sound. He cried out as blood sprayed him and the bird overhead.

"Get down!" I called again. The birds that passed us the first time were beyond the ship now, but when I turned, they were making a wide arc over the channel we had come through and returning toward the ship.

"Captain!" Perdita called, and I only had a split second to see her coming up the quarterdeck stairs, a rifle—perhaps the same one the cook had used—in her hand. Two other sailors followed, each similarly armed and carrying powder horns.

I dropped to the deck. Whit was already there, and I only had long enough to wonder why he hadn't thought to drag me down with him before the first rifle sounded and I had to put my hands over my ears. Two more shots sounded in quick succession. The deck shook as two birds fell to the wood. There was a great whoosh over my head, followed by the heavy drag of talons along my back, like the birds were looking for purchase. Another volley of shots. A new round of screams from both birds and sailors. Running footsteps sounded on the wood, but I held still. Unarmed as I was, I would be no use to anyone.

Finally, silence descended. I lifted my head carefully. Perdita and the other two riflemen were at the rail. Whit was on his knees. A few others risked attack and lifted their head or opened a hatch to peer out. A half dozen or so dead and dying birds littered the deck, as well as two sailors who lay groaning on the wood, blood soaking through their clothes.

"Right the ship!" I shouted, rushing to the wheel. In the chaos, we'd veered sharply off course, and I struggled to turn us away before we hit the rocks on the starboard side.

"What in the seven hells of Oaria were those?" Whit said breathlessly as he slowly climbed to his feet.

"The snow eagles of Snow Eagle Island?" I said.

"Handy to bury a treasure on an island with natural guardians."

Very useful indeed. Whoever had left the gold here must have known the region.

"Perdita!" I called.

"Yes, Captain?"

"Get those injured seen to. And find the cook. Tell him we'll be having snow eagle stew for dinner after all."

A thin cheer went up from the few above decks, though it didn't speak to much enthusiasm. No doubt they all doubted the cook's abilities to make the snow eagles palatable when he'd been so thoroughly hopeless with the fish stew.

"Well then," Whit said, straightening his cuffs. "Hopefully the eagles were not an omen of things to come."

But I knew the landmarks listed on the smaller map. The caged man. The fire river. Needle stairs. It didn't sound like a simple stroll on a mysterious island.

"Or else the birds are only the beginning," I said.

Everyone came ashore, even those injured from the eagle attack. Along with a healthy assortment of weapons, I'd had Perdita make sure the crew brought with them a variety of ropes and axes. With no idea what we would be facing, it seemed best to bring as much as we could carry.

Time to see if the map was real. First stop was the caged man.

"This way." I pointed into the trees. The others followed wordlessly. The trees were even denser than they'd appeared from the ship. If they'd been alive and green, the path would have been impenetrable, but here they merely provided an obstacle course for us to climb over and around, while the branches grasped and tore at what they could reach.

It was also completely silent. No cries from the birds overhead. No leaves to rustle in the wind. Soon, the gentle rush of the waves on the beach was left behind too. Only the scuff of boots and the heavy breathing of sailors accompanied us as we made our way.

"Should have carried more water," Whit said. His face shone with perspiration.

"You can take a dip in the fire river when we come to it," I said, and he pouted.

"Do you think it's an actual river of fire?" Perdita asked. The quiet awe in her voice reminded me of Rosie, and I half expected George to chime in and tell her they certainly would never see something like that in Redmere. I missed their cheery conversation.

"Let's start with the caged man and see if the interpretation is literal or metaphorical," I said. "That will give us a better idea of what we're facing."

We'd been walking for about an hour, moving slowly uphill, when the dead trees began to thin out. Until then, we'd had to go in a single file, but now the others fanned behind me. Some already had a weapon drawn. Others glanced around with nervous eyes. The silence engulfed us. The trees had provided poor cover, but without them, the bright sun overhead baked into the ground beneath us.

"Captain." Perdita was a few steps ahead of me, and her voice was lower than I'd heard it. She pointed forward. Dark shapes swung from the trees that lined the area.

As it happened, the caged man was not a metaphor.

Each of the cages was shaped from branches and vines. They were suspended from dead tree limbs and swayed lazily in the breeze. Every one contained what appeared to be a heap of rags.

"What do we do?" Whit asked, and for a moment his question annoyed me. My old crew wouldn't have looked to me for every direction. Maro would already be putting people to work, while George and Rosie would be guessing what might be inside.

But they were gone, and we were here. Once we determined a direction, we would be one step closer to the treasure.

Seven cages waved in a gentle breeze. According to the map, our path led somewhere to the right of the caged man, but the other trees weren't included in the drawing. Beyond the cages to the left, the forest grew so thick that our progress would have been painfully slow, twisting and climbing to find the narrow spaces between the old trees. On the right, the path split. One way led steeply up the side of the conical mountain, disappearing over a ridge, while the other led along a trail that fell sharply away. Choosing the wrong way would slow us significantly.

"We'll need to bring these down," I said, walking around each of the trees. Whoever had hung the cages had clearly wanted to make sure they weren't disturbed, as the ropes used to tie them off were cut high above the ground. The bark was smooth like stone, and the only branches were well above our heads. Impossible to climb.

"Captain?" Perdita said.

"Cut them down. Start with the two on the end here." I pointed to the branching path. "We need to know what's inside of them."

They went to work with axes. The trees, though dead, were very dense and determined to withstand our onslaught. Bits of wood chipped away like shards of rock, but slowly the first tree and its cage began to sway, and finally, the trunk gave way with a sharp crack. The cage broke into pieces as it hit the ground. The pile of rags unraveled, and long brown sticks scattered over the stones. Upon closer inspection, they were bones, not sticks. Whit bent to pick one up, then yelped as another tumbled out from beneath it. A human jawbone, including a complete set of teeth, settled at my feet.

"Did you know what was in there?" he asked me.

"I had a feeling." Cages like that were used to torture people or—if the torture wasn't successful, and sometimes even when it was—to leave them to die. How they'd wound up here though …
"Take down the rest."

"But there's a man in this one," Whit said, toeing the jawbone. "So that means we take the path up the hill."

"My ship—" I started to say.

"Your rules," Whit said with a heavy sigh. "Yes, Captain."

The clearing filled with the smell of sweat and the groan of sore muscles. One by one, the trees cracked and toppled. In most, the rags were empty. As the hours wore on, Whit argued again that the first tree had been the correct one, but I ignored him, and we continued. When the last tree fell, the cage and bag within rolled away from us and tumbled down the second path toward the cliff.

"Catch that!" I called, and Whit was already running after it. He nearly had it when his foot caught on a petrified tree root and he stumbled, landing with a grunt and sliding toward the edge and the open space beyond. "Whit!"

He scrambled and twisted, clutching the bag, and at the last minute, his fingers slipped into a small crack between stones. His slide stopped with a painful jerk, but when he looked up at me, he smiled.

"Well, that was exciting," he said.

"Foolhardy," I corrected, dropping to my knees. "Are you all right?"

He grunted as he slowly pushed himself upright. "Never better!"

When we returned to the group, they had laid out the other bones from the first tree. The resulting skeleton was characterized primarily by an unnerving sense of wrongness. The arrangement of the limbs was correct, but they were all too short. The rib cage was too narrow.

"Do the same with these," I said, tossing the sack to Perdita, who organized the crew to repeat the exercise. This time, the head came out of the bag last, and while only part of the jaw was there, it was also very definitely human.

"You see," I said as they laid out the rest of the skeleton next to its tree. "Not as simple as you first thought."

Whit rolled his eyes. "Yes, yes. You were right, little sister."

Even before they had finished, the second set of bones settled into a familiar shape. Long arm and leg bones. Collarbones that curled gently at both ends. The heart-shaped formation at the top of the sternum.

"Now that's a man," I said.

"And the other?" Whit asked.

"No idea. A dog perhaps?"

"With a man's head?"

Around us, sailors muttered and made signs of protections about their chests and heads. I rolled my eyes. The world was full of enough human monsters. We didn't need the mythological ones that filled our minds.

"A trick, most likely, to fool the impatient into taking the wrong path."

He rolled his eyes too. A familial trait apparently. Something we'd learned from our parents. I refused to think it was a part of Whit that had rubbed off on me.

"Fortunately, I've already started to cut a trail for us," he said with a grin, though the corner of his smile twitched nervously as he eyed the narrow downhill path.

I put a hand on his shoulder, but my tone wasn't teasing when I said, "If you're too afraid, you can stay here."

"You're as likely to maroon me here with the dog man."

"I never go back on a deal," I said.

As we descended, the path was so steep as to make our progress very slow. The rocks gave way to sand that made our feet slip. A few of the sailors used the rope to tie themselves together about their waists, but all that resulted in was three of them getting pulled over the edge when the ground gave way beneath the fourth. Only Perdita's quick thinking kept us from losing them all, as she grabbed for the last's foot just before he slithered over the side of the path.

At the bottom of the descent, as my thighs quivered from the endless exertion of keeping myself from pitching forward, we found ourselves in a narrow ravine, with a new wall rising steeply upward in front of us. We walked along the ravine floor.

The space became more confined and the air took on a sour smell. It felt thick and heavy, almost like it curled around our ankles before slowly climbing our bodies and making its lazy way into our lungs.

"What is that?" Whit asked, a hand to his mouth.

"Sulfur," Perdita said. "We had a ship's surgeon who liked to crush it into a powder for poultices and press it into wounds."

I winced at the idea. This smell, coupled with the scent of putrefaction that came when a wound turned bad, would be enough to turn anyone's stomach, or even make the wounded wish for death.

The sun sank below the ravine lip, leaving long shadows that quickly joined each other so our path darkened. We'd brought oil-soaked rags for torches and lit a few to help keep us going. The map had given no sense of size for the island, but it was clearly quite large. We had yet to find the fire river or the needle stairs. We weren't going to make it to the treasure today.

"We should make camp," Perdita said.

"Not here," I said. Every step brought us closer to the treasure. "It's too confined if we need to retreat or defend ourselves from nocturnal predators."

But there was nowhere to stop ahead. Although the ravine had cooled after sunset, we rounded a curve in the rock, and it was as though we'd stepped behind a curtain—the air behind it was so hot, I immediately perspired inside my clothes. The sulfur smell thickened, making me cough.

"Be careful," I said, putting a hand out to steady myself, and the stones under my palm were warm to the touch. Then the ravine wall ahead of us began to glow. The light turned red and orange, rippling and making it hard to focus on an individual point. The sulfur was so strong that a man behind me gagged.

"Captain," Perdita said. "I'm not sure it's safe to continue."

"Let's see how much farther this goes," I said, pushing on. I had to unbutton my coat, but even that offered no relief. The heat was oppressive, almost pulsing off the walls, and the light became painful to look at directly. Sailors coughed and my eyes streamed as we finally arrived at the end of the path. Ahead of us, swirling red and orange molten rock moved in a lazy flow in front of us, following a channel it had melted into the rock ages ago.

"What do we do now?" Perdita asked.

"I don't know."

Somehow, we had to cross this river of fire.

CHAPTER 21

e retreated. I hated to do it. Every step felt like I was leaving George behind all over again, even though she was hopefully still safe at the temple. But it was too dark to proceed and the terrain around the molten river too uncertain.

The others set up camp far enough back that the sulfur smell was bearable, and while it was hot, we wouldn't expire before the morning came. Still, as I lay awake, the others tossed and muttered softly around me. It was not an easy night.

At one point, Harald let out a howl.

"This is impossible!" He spun wildly, pulling at his clothes. His shirt was sodden with sweat. "This heat. No one can bear this."

I'd spent weeks adrift in windless oceans while the sun baked everything it touched. Skin blistered and lips cracked. But not everyone suffered heat well.

Harald began to strip out of his clothes. Hector, his brother, sprang to his feet, trying to corner him.

"Stop," Hector said. "Harald, we're fine. You have to stop."

"We'll be dead by morning," Harald insisted. "She's brought us to our death."

He was delirious, but he couldn't incite the others to panic. Sighing, I pulled my knife from my belt. Hector tried to hold his brother, but Harald was much bigger and threw him off, stumbling away from our camp, though in his disorientation, he headed toward the river, not away from it. I caught his arm and pressed him up against the side of the ravine wall. I put the knife's tip at his throat, just beneath his jaw, and he struggled, eyes wide and rolling. In my head, George's voice told me this threat wasn't necessary, but hysteria could be a suffocating mistress, and breaking her hold needed confident action.

"You will stop this," I said, as pleasantly as possible. "You're upsetting the others and wasting energy better spent fording the river tomorrow."

He shook his head, gasping. "We can't. No one can cross that. We'll all die."

I pressed the tip in farther. It was too dark to see clearly, but years of practice said I hadn't broken the skin.

"If you feared death, you shouldn't have come to sea, friend. But if you trust your captain, you'll see another day."

We stared at each other in the glow. When he finally sagged in my hold, I let the knife drop. I released his arm and he collapsed to the ground, head bowed as he sobbed. Hector joined us, still trying to comfort his bother.

"See that he gets some water," I said, and walked away. No one had slept through Harald's outburst, and they all watched me as I returned to camp. I lay down on the ground, my back to them. They wouldn't be able to hear my racing heartbeat, and I needed them to believe I was in control of the situation, or else they'd all abandon me. The relationship we had as captain and crew was too new and tenuous for a mission like this. Trust was the only thing that held a crew together. More of Maro's wisdom that I had so blatantly ignored.

As soon as the first rays of sunlight peeked over the ravine walls, we broke camp and made our way back to the river. It was still flowing, bubbling and crackling. The river was about fifteen feet below us, and the lava had completely bisected the ravine. On the other way, the path continued, though the rope rock walls were not as high.

"We need to get across," I said.

"There." Perdita pointed. To our right, a small ledge jutted out from the side of the stones, creating a path no wider than a single foot. It dropped down toward the river, but at its end, wide flat rocks protruded out from the burning stone, making a potential path to the other side. The space between those end stones looked wide. It might be passable, but the jumps between steps would be significant.

"Look." Hector pointed upward and to the left. "We could use that." Perhaps fifty yards upriver, a long cord was suspended between the two sides. Experienced sailors could work their way across a secured line like that.

"You go," I said to Hector. "If you find a way across, we'll follow."

His climb was challenging, but not impossible. Within ten minutes, he'd reached the top. Hector waved, then tugged on the line. It held, even as he pulled harder.

"That might actually work," Whit said.

Hector swung one leg over the rope. Slowly, he worked himself forward until he had both hands and ankles wrapped around it, and he hung in open space. We all held our breath as the rope sagged under his weight, but it didn't give way. From this distance, it was hard to see him clearly through the waves of heat, but I thought he might have smiled.

"There better not be any climbing after this," Whit said as Hector reached the midway point. "My shoulders will be done in by the time we reach the other side."

But we never got the chance to find out. Neither did Hector. As he began the second half of the climb, the rope's swaying became more noticeable.

"Slow down," I said softly, but of course he was too far to hear.

In an instant, it seemed as if someone had shaken the rope the way someone might crack a whip. Then the tension was gone as the rope fell away, and he was falling through open air until he hit the orange and black surface below.

"Hector!" Harald called, but his brother was already halfway under, flames consuming him. The fire had taken him even faster than the ocean could drag a man down to the depths. And somehow, we still had to cross it.

"I'm sorry," I said, placing a hand on Harald's arm. His gaze was locked on the place we'd last seen Hector, and he shrugged off my touch.

"This is your fault," he said, slowly turning toward me. "You killed him."

"He made the climb himself," I said.

"You told him to!" He shoved at me, and the others around us shuffled nervously. Some muttered agreement.

"Careful, friend," Whit said, coming to stand at my shoulder.

"Friend?" Harald spat at my shoes. "You're not my friend."

"No," I said. "But I'm your captain."

"You killed my brother!" He jabbed a finger against my chest. If Maro had been here, they'd have taken his hand for the brazenness. The others around him mumbled to each other, but none would meet my gaze.

"You knew there were risks when you signed on. Did you expect a pleasure cruise?"

His grief was plainly evident, but my question stood. A seasoned sailor knew the dangers that came with joining a crew. If it weren't a fire river, then it would have been a rival ship who tried to chase us down, or simply starvation and dehydration when the winds died and left us too far from shore.

Back in my days sailing for Kiril, I'd have been tempted to push him into the river after Hector simply for questioning me.

At the very least, I should make an example of him to the others for daring to defy me. But instead, I simply sighed.

"If you want to go back to the ship, you're free to do so," I said.

The shuffling and mutters stopped.

"Are you sure that's wise?" Whit asked through clenched teeth and with his lips barely moving. "They might leave us here."

There were always risks. The perils of piracy were endless.

"If we're not back two days from now, then you can sail on with no guilt. But you forfeit your payment. If you keep going with me now though, whatever treasure we find at the end of this map will be shared among you. If you work as a crew, you'll be rewarded accordingly."

Harald turned on his heel and started back up the way we had come. A few others trailed after him, including the two men who had been injured by the snow eagles. Whit opened his mouth—possibly to wish them well, but more likely to call them cowards—and I cut him off with a nudge of my toe against his boot. He should be thankful I didn't kick him. We didn't have room for him to shake the remaining crew's confidence. I believed there was a treasure waiting for us at the end of this map, and it would be enough to buy our freedom. But I needed the sailors who were left to carry whatever we found off the island, or we'd never make it back out.

"This way," I said.

The ledge down to the river was even narrower than I'd guessed. I had to walk with my back to the wall, feet turned out wide. There was no place to regroup at the base. To give everyone else room behind me to keep moving, all I could do was take a step out into nothing and wait for the first stone to catch me.

The surface was flat, at least, and big enough that I could jump and land with both feet planted firmly. I glanced behind me, and Whit was watching from the rock ledge. A smudge of soot was smeared over his face, like he'd wiped his nose or brow with a stray sleeve.

No way back. Not with the others behind me. It was onward or death.

I took the next step. The air burned my lungs. Sweat dripped down my back and over my chest. My feet were uncomfortably hot in my boots.

"Lucy!" Whit's voice was strained, and he coughed as I turned. My footing wobbled and I had to flail my arms to keep from pitching to the side.

"What?"

"You're smoking!" He coughed again, burying his face in his arm.

"What?"

"Your coat is smoking!"

The hem of my coat caught fire. I cursed and tore myself out of it, much the way Hector had torn out of his clothes the night before. Small flames singed the hairs on my arm as I tossed the coat into the fire, where it was immediately engulfed as the river carried the ashes away.

My heart shook in my chest, unable to settle its rhythm, and my head swam with the heat. I couldn't find forward again. Could barely find up. The whole world seemed to be tilting and—

Strong arms wrapped around me, keeping me from following my coat into the fire.

"Come on, Lucy," Whit said, holding me tight. "Almost there."

I tried to shake him off. "I'm all right. There isn't room for both of us here."

"Well, clearly there is," he said. "Though it's closer than I like to be to a woman who isn't impressed by my masculine wiles."

If I could have shoved him away, I would have, but it seemed uncharitable to push him to his death when he had saved me from mine.

Slowly, we found the way. There were cries and curses from the crew behind me. A few burned hands and more charred boot soles, but in the end, we all made it.

"How will we make it back?" Perdita asked, and I ignored the question, pushing myself upright.

"Come on. We have to continue."

We found water late in the afternoon. I half expected it to be poisoned or too acidic to be drinkable, but it was cool and refreshing, and we all practically fell into it.

"When we're rich, I'm going to come back here and build a house next to this stream so I can bathe in it every day." Whit was sitting on the sandy bottom, submerged to his chest, and he lay back with a happy sigh and a splash.

It was a nice idea. Not entirely dissimilar to the dreams I had of taking George to some far-off island where no one would ever find us and we could live free like we had when we were small.

Maybe there was no freedom. I'd tried to pay for it over and over and here I was, miles from everyone I cared about—except for perhaps Whit, who I was grudgingly learning to tolerate—and no true sense that we would ever be safe.

Whit emerged from the water with a happy smile on his face that dimmed a little when he looked at me.

"What is it?" he asked.

I studied him, trying to guess at the experiences that had made the face in front of me. Lost love, true, but others. What places had he seen? Lives taken? Would he stay with me as the way got bloodier, or would he leave me like Maro had? Would that be my fault too?

Behind us, a sailor coughed and gagged before spitting a stream of black into the water. It swirled and flowed past my ankles. He muttered an apology and saluted before wading into deeper waters.

Now was not the time for sweet familial feelings.

We hiked uphill for another few hours. My thighs and knees ached and my lungs burned. The crew trailed behind me in a long, struggling single file. Finally, though, we reached the apex of the conical mountain we'd seen as we arrived. From here, the entire island was visible. Our ship waited patiently, a small dark shape at the end of the island channel.

"Now what?" Perdita asked, leaning back to stretch out her spine.

According to the map, we should be at the needle stairs, though with no indication of topography, it was hard to say where to look to find them. I walked around the perimeter of the cone, checking all sides for steps that would lead us down the other side of the mountain. In some places, it was too sheer to be passable. On one side was a very sandy slope that dropped away gradually.

"If I had my choice," Whit said, coming to stand behind me, "I'd go that way. Might even lie down and start to roll and let gravity do its work."

It sounded so appealing. "No stairs though." The map had been correct in its other waypoints. As tempting as it was to tumble down this gentle slope, it wouldn't take us where we needed to be.

"Captain." Perdita was farther up the slope. She lay on her belly and peered over the lip down into the cone. "I think there's something down there."

We scrambled up to join her. The edge of the cone was smooth and flat, like it had been worn away over time. Somehow, I had expected it to contain more of the molten lava from the fire river, but the inside glowed a deep turquoise color with rippling white lines where water mixed with wind far below.

"Where?" I asked. All I saw was blue and a very long drop.

This far, the water would feel like stone to someone who fell, shattering bones on impact.

"There!" Perdita pointed excitedly, and my heart stopped as a flash caught my eye. It was gone again in a second, but reappeared, a yellow-white wink against the far wall of the cave where stone met water.

"What is it?" Perdita asked.

And then it came again, but this time a shaft of light pierced over the water's surface and illuminated the entire chamber. Golden light splashed up toward us, rippling from a million faceted surfaces on the walls of the cavern below.

My heart beat so fast, it was fortunate I was already lying down.

"Perdita," I said. "I believe you've found the lost treasure of Anaïb."

CHAPTER 22

All credit to whoever had hidden the treasure on the island. They did not make it easy to retrieve, even once it was found. The conical cavern's walls sloped outward, making it impossible to scale down. We didn't have enough rope—nor, at this point, strength—to simply drop it over the side and climb down hand over hand, like we might hurry down from a mast. There was a ledge about halfway down one side. From there, someone might be able to safely jump, but the recessed walls meant that even a shorter distance was impossible to reach with a rope.

We had spread out, walking around the edge of the crater, looking for any gentle way down but finding nothing. Then, one moment, Whit was behind me, cheerfully cursing the sailors who had hidden their treasure so well, as well as our parents for birthing a stubborn little sister to drag him across oceans in search of riches he could see but might never reach. The next moment, he shrieked as he was suddenly cut in half. Only his torso and shoulders were still visible over the stone surface. His eyes were wide, and he scrambled to keep himself from disappearing entirely. It took three of us to pull him out of the hole he'd fallen into.

Whit had found the stone ladder.

When he was safe, I crawled over to the gap. It had been partially hidden by a cluster of shrubs on one side, making it look smaller than it was. On the end still partially covered by plants, the space looked endless, deep and open. On the side closest to Whit's foot though, it sloped away more gently, with rounded formations like rocks sticking out from the wall.

Or like stairs. Steep ones like the gangways in a ship rather than the broad ones built in homes. I gathered a handful of pebbles and tossed them inside. They clattered and fell, but if I lay with my face on the ground and ignored the chatter of the people behind me, I could hear their descent. They dropped a long way, bouncing off something solid in a rhythmic descent.

"Perdita," I said. She was still speaking to Whit, her tone growing playful. She had her hand in his, and she almost looked ready to kiss his knuckles. "Perdita!"

She dropped his hand and straightened. "Yes, Captain?"

"Light a torch."

"Right away." She jumped up to follow the order. While she struggled with flint, I walked around to the far side of the open mountaintop where we'd lain before, looking down at the water and the out-of-reach treasure.

"Drop it in the hole," I shouted, and she complied.

Waiting felt like an eternity. I wasn't completely sure what to look for or where to look. In all likelihood, the torch was stuck, or the oil cloths had already been extinguished.

Mercifully though, a flash caught my attention, and the torch reappeared, spinning like a glowing child's toy on the ledge halfway down the cavern.

"There! We go down there!" I rushed to rejoin the others. "Get the ropes. This is the needle and we are the thread."

To call them steps would be generous. At first, the rocks were narrow and slick, with barely enough room for a toehold or fingers to hang. The only thing that kept me from plummeting to a painful death was the rope around my waist, tied off to a petrified tree at the surface. Twice, the rope got stuck, and I had to climb back up to find the ledge it had wrapped itself over. But finally, as my legs shook and the stones bit into my fingertips despite years of calluses, a breeze rushed behind me, brushing under my shirt and along my sweaty back.

At the ledge, I untied myself and gave the rope two hard tugs —the signal to Perdita to send the next person down. The ledge was sandy, and I sank to the ground, sitting cross-legged at the edge. In front of me sparkled a wall of such wealth. The gold climbed from the waterline all the way to the top of the chamber, as though the person who brought it here had hoped to recreate the lost city.

I missed George. I'd found the treasure, and she wasn't here to see it.

To the left was an opening like a long tunnel through which the sun shone dimly. I was distracted from further scrutiny by a scattering of small stones that signaled the arrival of the next person down the shaft. Whit. He tumbled more than emerged, but when he finally righted himself, he was no worse off than the last time I'd seen him.

"Thieving is never as exciting as this. Get in, get out. Sometimes you might scale a wall. Woo a bored countess to gain access."

I laughed softly and rolled my eyes.

"But you, sister." He dangled his legs over the ledge a few feet away me, shaking rocks out of his boots. "You certainly know how to keep things interesting. At least you've found us a boat so we don't have to climb back up this way."

"What?" I said, but I followed Whit's gaze, where he peered over the edge. I'd been so focused on the riches before me that I hadn't had a moment to orient myself.

Beneath us though, hidden deep in the shadows, was the unmistakable prow of a ship.

It FELT like it took hours for the others to descend, but finally, Perdita was the last to come down.

"Oh, that's much closer now, isn't it? You could jump and swim for it." She sounded breathless but entirely pleased with herself.

The other sailors who had stuck with us stood, eyes gone bright with the splendor. No doubt they dreamed of the lives just this section of the wall could buy them.

"Let's see what we're dealing with," I said. "Set up the ropes to lower our equipment down." Not all of the tools we'd brought from Harlow's ship had made it to the cavern, but we still had a few axes and shovels with us. Enough to start removing the gold from the wall. We'd need to find a way to convey it to the ship.

"Yes, Captain," Perdita said.

I stepped off the ledge and fell.

The water was a shock, colder than I expected. Even from the lower ledge, the impact was still jarring, sending spikes of pain through my legs and up my spine. But as I floated back to the surface, gasping for new air, I kicked easily, moving through the water and away from the ledge. Splashes behind me said others had followed. We were committed now. Sink or swim.

Perdita set a few sailors to work. Whit and the remaining crew jumped and swam toward the glittering wall, no doubt eager to confirm the truth of what was plain before our own eyes. I made my way back toward the figurehead that peered out from behind the rock ledge.

The ship was old, built in a style my forebears would have appreciated. The scrollwork at the base of the woman's feet was intricate and seemed to glow from rich-colored paint, even in the dim light. A long chain, with links the length of my arm and the width of my torso, extended from the bow into the water below, anchoring the silent vessel in place. It also provided an adequate opportunity to climb aboard, though the route was awkward. My hands were too small to grip all the way around the metal, and the surface was slick with what must have been years of seaweed growth as the tide had gone in and out.

On board, she swayed with a familiar indifference. Although the prow extended beyond the column, most of the ship was tucked away in a secondary chamber, almost like it had been hollowed out to fit her dimensions exactly. The decks were smooth and the fixtures had turned green with age. The sails in the rigging looked to be in place, and we'd only know if they were serviceable or if they'd gone black with rot once we unfurled them.

I had a hand on a hatch that would lead belowdecks when a fight broke out near the cavern's opposite wall.

"Glass! It's all glass!" someone shouted, but before I could see who it was, there was a splash as several men all fell into the water together. Whit was standing on the far side of the space, hand on the glittering wall.

"What's going on?" I called, coming to the ship's bow.

Whit shook his head and pulled a pistol from his belt. The powder was hopelessly beyond saving, but he took the butt and swung forcefully at the jeweled wall. A musical sound of tiny shards falling to the rocky ground echoed toward me, and Whit repeated the action several more times, with the same result.

"It's all glass," he said, and even his tone sounded flat. "A wall of glass."

My heart sank. "But what about the treasure?" It had to be here. The map had been too accurate for us to be in the wrong place.

One of the sailors roared and picked up a rock the size of his head. He hurled it at the sparkling wall, and more of it fell, raining fine pieces of glass on everyone, making them duck and cover their heads. There was a cracking sound, like ice on the coldest of days, and more of the glass fell, this time from higher overhead.

"All this way for nothing!" the sailor shouted.

I shook at the anger in his voice. All this way. So much lost in the process. The map had led us to the right place, but it had all been for nothing. I would have to go to Triere empty-handed, which meant I wouldn't even be able to get close to him. I had no better way to protect George than when I'd left Norampar.

Each fallen glass shard felt like it lodged in my chest. Nothing. Worthless. Wasted time and effort, friends and even my home lost. For nothing.

The sailors bellowed and cursed. Whit stood with his hands on his hips, staring up at the wall. Perdita was still on the ledge, surveying the disaster unfurling before us. No doubt she was considering if she could make it back up the needle stairs and find her way to Harlow's ship before they left tomorrow. It was what I would do. But those of us in the lowest part of the cavern were stuck. Our only option was to sail out in this old ship and figure out what to do next.

"Send someone down the tunnel," I said. "See if there are any secondary passages on either side." The real treasure had to be here. There had to be a way to salvage this.

As Perdita called orders and others protested, I took a step back until I was out of sight. What if I'd failed? Spent weeks and lost my crew—and was now risking a mutiny for a second—all for the sake of a prize that never existed? I'd been too proud and too stubborn to listen to Maro until it was too late, and too desperate to protect George to consider any other options.

Mired in questions, I slid back the hatch. If nothing else, we needed to know if this poor old ship was seaworthy. The aged brass fittings ground and flaked off where the salt air had tried to fuse them. Finally, though, I stared into the blackness below. No sense waiting for anyone else. The ship was either abandoned or inhabited by a mythical sea creature waiting to pounce on the first unlucky soul to descend. But while the air inside smelled stale, there was no evidence of any inhabitants—human or otherwise.

Climbing down felt like coming home. I could go up and down steps like these in my sleep. The dark presented no challenge at all. When my feet hit solid wood below instead of water or rot, I breathed a sigh of relief. At least we weren't trapped. We could sail out. I would find another way to stop the brokers.

I was midship. Probably a gun deck, though as I felt my way around, I found no artillery. Nothing at all, though the footing became uneven. No matter which way I stepped, the entire space was vacant. Once, I found what I initially thought was a mast, but the surface was rough and cool, more like the stone outside than the weathered wood of a ship.

There had to be a porthole or a gun hatch. Even if the weapons had been removed, there would be openings. I pressed against the irregular surface of the wall until something gave way. A splash of light spilled over my feet. As I pushed the hatch open farther, a hundred colors threatened to swamp my senses.

I stood in a palace. One of the great temples of antiquity. The walls were gilt and crusted with jewels. Even the mast glittered in a serpentine pattern as rubies spiraled and crisscrossed around each other.

"Oh, you sweet beauty," I muttered. So many stones. Not left in the hold, but embedded into the ship. Trunks and casks could be lifted. To purge this ship of her precious cargo would be an entirely different undertaking. Everywhere, as I opened more hatches to bring the light in, were more riches. They covered the decks, leaving only narrow paths for feet to follow, and the ceiling overhead shone so brightly in long chains of stones and gold links that one barely missed the presence of the oil lamps that would undoubtedly tarnish all this beauty.

I explored breathlessly. The lower decks were the same. Even the old iron stove had jeweled feet. I found battered pots and swung them against the wall, half expecting them to shatter like the glass decoys outside, but while a few tumbled to the ground, they all stayed intact, forged with the strength that eons in their stone birthplaces had given them.

"George," I whispered, hoping that even all these miles and miles apart, she would hear me. She always said she felt connected to me, even during those years she'd thought I was dead. "I found it."

I'd found the treasure that would set us all free.

 hit was the first one to climb aboard. He shrugged out of his sodden coat and wrung it out on the deck.

"They're not very pleased with you, Lucy," he said.

I would never break him of that habit, but I could buy his goodwill and that of the crew. I could buy anything I wanted. It wasn't an entire city's worth of gold, but even the amount stowed below would be more than most of them could dream of.

"We'll see about that," I said. The others were climbing over the rail as one, even Perdita. They were a mass of sour faces and soggy clothes.

"You did this," one of them said, pointing a crooked finger at me. "Brought us all the way out here, and now we've got nothing."

The others muttered their agreement. Whit took a quiet step closer to me. Perdita looked anxious, with one hand on her belt like she might have to draw her sword at any moment. If Maro were here, they'd have brought them all to attention with a single snap of their fingers. But I was on my own, so I opened my palm to show them the handful of sparkling stones inside.

A moment of silence filled the space. One sailor tripped forward, like he might grab the jewels from my palm, before he scoffed.

"Another trick," he said. "It's all worthless."

"Look again." I threw a green gem up in the air, letting it catch the light as it arced above us. Several hands reached for it, and a brief moment of shoving broke out as it landed on the deck with a dull thud.

Finally, a gnarled sailor, older than the others, stepped forward with the jewel in his hand.

"There's more?" he asked.

"Much more," I said. "Just beneath our feet. Enough for us all to live like empresses and kings into our old age. You're each entitled to your share, but to do that, we need to get off this island."

The mood had lightened immediately. The sailors answered with a round of salutes and a muttered "Yes, Captain." How quickly I could fall back into their good graces. If only they knew what I had to ask of them next. We would all live rich and happy … if we survived the brokers.

A secret thrill filled me as we finally emerged from the cave. I'd been right that the rock around the ship had been hewn to exact specifications. The tunnel to daylight was no different. Mere feet separated the apex from the top of the mast, and the width of it was so narrow that we were able to touch the walls in places as we slowly made our way forward. Only the receding tide made it possible for us to make any progress.

The cave expelled us from the far side of the island out into the open sea. Perdita set the crew to catching enough of the silvery speckled fish that swam below the surface of the waves to keep us fed, however meagerly. The cook had been one of the ones to turn back, though that was no real loss. A brief rain shower as the sun sank below the horizon gave us enough to drink that we wouldn't perish within the next few days if we were careful.

"Where are you planning to drop the crew off?" Whit asked me as we went through a laughable charade of a captain's dinner that evening. The aft cabin sported the same gaudily encrusted decor as the rest of the ship, but was very poor in actual functional furnishings. We ate thin slices of oily raw fish while perched on a pair of bejeweled crates that had been brought up from the hold.

"Why would I do that?"

With some effort, Whit pried a pearl the size of an eyeball from the table between us. "This is a lot of temptation for a poor sailor."

"They'll be paid well for their service. But not until the voyage is done. We talked about this after we left Norampar." I sent him a pointed glance. "We still have a ship to sail and the brokers to face." I hadn't been explicit with the crew on where we were headed next and who waited for us. Most would have never heard of the brokers. No need to make them uneasy.

Whit coughed uncomfortably. "So I suppose it would be too much to ask that you let me carry on my way?"

I choked on a greasy lump of fish. "Excuse me?"

"Lucy." His charming smile was back. "I'm a thief, not a sailor. We had a bargain, and from what you've said, these brokers aren't someone I'd like to come face to face with."

Something like panic rose up inside me when I least expected it. Why should Whit's departure bother me? We were nothing to each other. Our bargain was met, and he was free to go where he would. But somehow, I'd thought our paths might mingle for a while longer.

"We don't have time for detours," I said, not quite meeting his gaze. "We'll deliver the treasure, and then anyone who wants to go will be dropped off in port."

With any luck, Triere wouldn't see us coming, and I could be quick in sending him to his death. Then I'd have to get back to George before the surviving brokers did and make sure she was taken care of over a longer term. Hunting down the others would be hard, and putting together a crew better suited to the task wouldn't be cheap. I dragged a hand over the sparkling window frame to my left. I'd have to find somewhere to hide all of this. Perhaps that was what the sailor who'd hidden this ship had done. Hidden the contents of the ransacked city in caves and on the walls of lost vessels around the world, where at least some of it would hopefully remain safe from greedy hands.

Whit started to speak again. "Lu—"

"Stop calling me Lucy."

"Lou." He traced the facets of an emerald with a fingertip. "You certainly grew up strong, didn't you?"

I chewed on another piece of odious fish. Statements like this always made me uncomfortable. It was the same reason I'd never wanted to talk about the past with George. I hadn't grown up. I'd survived. Was still surviving, even when I thought I'd found my way out. The thing that had gotten me through was Maro. Their obstinacy. Their skills. Then George. Her kindness. Her optimism. Maybe Whit was part of this voyage too. He'd stayed steadfast this long.

We sailed on, making do with the few provisions we could catch. The crew, though sparse, was capable, and Perdita was a reliable mate. There were few enough left of us that most of the sailors slept on the deck, but when I went down below, there were noticeable blank spots in the wood where gems had been removed. Not enough to cause a problem in my future plans, but the crew would definitely be well paid for their time, even if they never received a single coin from me.

When we arrived at our destination, I was struck with the difference in Triere's home versus Kiril's. Deep upriver and cobbled together with old ship's timbers, Kiril's place of residence was more lair than palace, as warped and decayed as he was. By comparison, Triere's home was an estate. A guardhouse was perched on the rocks as we rounded the last edge of land. It was a tall, thin tower with a rounded golden dome. As we passed by, a flash of light came from the window at the top, but instead of facing out toward sea like the towers meant to keep lost sailors from crashing on the rocks, this one flickered inland, toward the sprawling home that lay on the hill. It was built in the same style as the tower, but the columns that supported the roof above the main verandah were taller than the guard tower itself, and gold flashed from around the windows as well as the sloping roof. Red and gold banners waved in the breeze, and an answering flicker of light winked at us and the tower, indicating the signal had been received. They knew we were here.

"Do you think this Triere person has taken decorating tips from our ship's builder?" Whit asked. "They certainly don't shy away from opulence, do they?"

Nor did they hide. Kiril had always lurked in the shadows and sent others to do his bidding. Triere's home seemed to welcome anyone and everyone with open arms.

"We'll leave Perdita and the crew on the ship," I said. "It'll be easier to escape with fewer of us ashore."

"But you want me to come with you?" Whit asked.

I grinned at him. "Too late for cold feet, brother. Triere will expect me to bring a second. If you're lucky, after we kill him, you can help yourself to a few of his treasures. An insurance fund in case your share of the jewels here won't buy everything your thieving heart desires."

"How exactly do you mean to kill him?"

I stared at the great house, its doors and windows flung open like a dozen hungry mouths. So many people had walked in and never left alive again.

"We'll wait until we're inside and see what options are available." They were expecting our arrival, and there was no way to sneak onto the island. Better to walk in through the front door and wait for our chance.

The crew hadn't even finished furling the sails when a long-boat was already on its way out from the shore.

"Whit. With me. Perdita. The ship is yours."

She gave me a sharp salute. "Yes, Captain."

"If you can, try to keep Triere's guards from going below until I return. No sense in letting them see the extent of our spoils if we can. Wouldn't want word getting out."

"Very good, Captain. I'll tell them we have sailors with the fever below. That usually keeps prying eyes at bay, at least for a little while."

The simplest lies were often the best. Wherever we went next, I hoped Perdita would stay with us. She was a good ally, assuming she had the stomach for what would follow today.

The longboat came alongside, and of course, Hafir was the first over the rail. The sight of him made my blood boil. But in broad daylight and without the element of surprise, he was simply another man. His smile was unpleasant, his mustache too finely curled as if he'd been tugging at the ends in anticipation of my further humiliation. I'd let him best me, and he was no more formidable than anyone else I had ever faced.

"Hello, Cinder," he said. "We'd begun to think you'd decided to run after all. Quite the mess you left behind you in Norampar too. Where's your lady friend? I was anxious to see her."

Blood rushed in my ears. They hadn't found George. I had to force my hands to steady as I reached into my shirt and threw Lady Amelia's ring toward him. The lump of red and gold sparkled in the sunlight. Hafir gave me a narrow-eyed glare before he bent to retrieve it, holding it up between two fingers to see it sparkle in the sun.

"We've brought your payment," I said. "Before I give it to you, I want to see Triere."

He tsked, attention still on the ring. "An audience wasn't part of our agreement."

Without waiting for more, I strode over the boards, three quick steps that had me in front of him before he'd even taken his gaze from the ring. He never had a chance to see my fist coming, and it connected with his nose. The satisfying crunch of flesh and bone sent him sprawling onto his ass with a shocked howl.

"Now you listen to me, you little toad," I said, leaning over him. "We both know you're only a messenger who's getting above himself. Take me to Triere. The brokers will have their treasure. None of it is yours." I collected the ring that he'd lost track of in his pain and tucked it back inside my shirt.

As I approached the rail, the other two sailors that had come aboard with Hafir glanced at him nervously, but they stepped out of the way. One even gave me a shaky salute, which I returned. Without another word, I swung a leg over the rail and climbed down to the longboat. Whit followed silently after. The others, including a groaning Hafir, soon did the same. They didn't even leave anyone aboard with Perdita and the others. Overconfident shits. If it had been me, I'd have searched the entire ship from top to bottom before I left it and probably sent more men out to guard it, else Perdita and crew get ideas about escaping with the treasure in tow before Triere and I had settled our dealings.

On shore, we were led up a path made from slabs of a golden stone so smooth it was slippery where the slope became too great. Once, a boot scuffed behind me, and Whit swore softly. I reached backward, and to my surprise, he took my hand. His grip was warm against mine. I nearly choked when he squeezed my fingers. The gesture was so simple. So strangely comforting. Even when we'd been young and hadn't known what sadness and cruelty the world really contained, he wouldn't have done something like that. I nearly glanced over my shoulder to see if he was trying to say something. Warn me in some way. But Hafir coughed and said, "Triere is busy this afternoon. We'll—"

"No," I said. "Triere was clearly anxious for me to arrive or he wouldn't have sent someone after us in Norampar. We'll go now."

Hafir might have looked unhappy, but his face was so mottled with blood and rapidly spreading bruises that it would be nearly impossible to say for sure. Finally, he sighed, coughing uncomfortably.

"This way, if you please."

Whit and I followed wordlessly. At the door, they searched us for weapons and removed each one with no promise of returning them before leading us inside. The main hall glittered almost as brightly as the inside of my ship. Gilt frames and jeweled mirrors lined both sides. Spoils of war, no doubt. The serious nobles and wealthy heiresses who watched from their paintings as we passed were far more likely to be Triere's victims than relations, though I supposed they might be both.

Occasionally, I would catch a glimpse of myself in a mirror as we walked by. Dark hair and serious eyes. Too thin, perhaps. I didn't see my reflection very often, other than as a wavy image in the water, and I flinched at the sight of the woman who stared back at me.

I looked like my mother. I hadn't seen her in nearly a decade, but she was there in the shape of my nose and the thin set of my lips.

I couldn't hold that woman's gaze.

Ahead of us, muted laughter rang out, followed by a chorus of amusement. I immediately forgot about the woman in the mirror. We could become reacquainted when this was over. For now, we were about to face Triere and whatever guests were in attendance, and that needed all my attention.

Hafir opened the door, and we passed into a vast banquet hall. The entire space was golden, from the glittering panels on the walls to the sparkling crystal chandeliers that glowed overhead, to the mirrored floor and ceiling that reflected all the opulence back at itself for eternity.

At the far end of the hall, a group of people gathered around a table entirely too small for the room. It seated the seven of them comfortably, with one empty chair at the foot, but in the grandeur around them, they appeared unnaturally small.

Yet, as their laughter cut off and seven heads turned toward us, my heart grew cold. Not so small after all. Each scrutinized me with the intensity of a predator sizing up a meal.

"Cinder," a woman sitting in the center of the group said, her voice tinkling like glass breaking. "You've arrived. I am Triere. We've been waiting for you."

She was a woman. It shouldn't have surprised me. Power and evil were without gender. But somehow, perhaps because of all my years with the men who had been my captains, and then with Kiril, I had assumed all the brokers were men. Triere was dressed in flowing gold robes to match the room. Her hair was adorned in shimmering strands of gold that swirled among her coppery red curls, making her stand out even against the ornate decor. Her eyes flashed like diamonds as we took each other in.

"I was summoned," I said, keeping my spine mast straight to cover my surprise. I scanned the table, looking among the roasted meats and rich sauces, cataloging the knives and forks that had been left strewn carelessly on the table. Each was a weapon. One I could use, or one that could be used against me.

Triere pouted. She was older than I was but must have used at least a portion of her riches to keep her skin and face looking as young as possible. She practically glowed. Her eyelids were painted gold, and her cheeks were flushed a healthy pink.

"Someone as renowned as you," she said. "At best, we could only request your assistance."

"At a knife's point," I said. Somewhere to my left, Hafir wheezed on a chuckle, and as tempting as it was to kick him again, I held my place.

Triere didn't seem moved. "We all know how the world

works. You most of all, Cinder, or Kiril's chair at our table would not be empty."

I glanced from her to the vacant seat to the other diners who were all eyeing me silently. They were all men of varying ages, sizes and colors. Some wore thick beards. One had no visible hair to speak of at all. A few tapped fingers adorned with stones and thick gold bands impatiently. All carried an air of disinterested malevolence that rolled off them like fog at the coast after a storm, thick and unmoving. I knew the taste of it, just like I knew the twist of their mouths as they observed me and thought only of the skills I could bring them and the ends I would serve.

They were the brokers. All of them. Kiril's brethren. The ones I had sworn to kill before I could return to George.

And they were all in the same room.

For some reason, I'd always thought there were six brokers. Kiril had only ever mentioned a few by name. Each traded in different goods. He had been most interested in the cost of human lives—buying and selling them, destroying those that crossed him. As I understood it, Triere functioned essentially as a banker, obsessed as she was with gold and coin. There were others who dealt in weapons. Land.

For there to be eight of them, their reach and power was even greater than I had imagined.

"Have you done what we've requested?" one of the brokers, an old man with skin like a dead fish's and one eye that swam lazily after the other, asked.

My heart dropped. They watched me like a monster of legend. Seven heads. Fourteen—or so—eyes. Around them, guards and attendants clustered like scavengers, waiting for their share of the spoils.

I didn't dare glance at Whit, but hopefully he knew just as well how badly the odds were turned against us. I couldn't kill them all. Not here. One—Triere—perhaps, while the element of surprise was with me. The others slowly, over time. I knew their faces now.

"Cinder?" the fish man prompted.

I swallowed. "I've found a treasure."

A ripple flowed over the assembled brokers. Relief? Pleasure? It seemed unimaginable that any of these rulers of the sea had been uncertain about my success.

Still … better to test the waters.

"I don't have it here," I said.

"What?" Triere said. "Why not?"

The ripple came again, more agitated this time. Soft words were murmured to each other.

"It's very large. Too big for one ship to hold. I lost the *Siren* in a storm—"

"Kiril would be very disappointed to hear that," one of the others observed, though they spoke too quickly for me to find which of them it was.

"Kiril is dead," I said. "And if you want the wealth you asked for, you'll need to provide me with new ships."

The fish man pushed to his feet. He was very old, but once both his eyes had focused on a single point, the sharpness of his gaze said he was still not to be underestimated.

"You failed," he said.

"We have brought what we could." I made sure to say this directly to Triere. If I could buy her grace with the possibility of vast riches, she might sway the others and let Whit and I leave. Every move I made right now needed to be about time and regaining some distance from the brokers so I could act safely. "With more ships, I would—"

"We don't have time for this," said a man at the far end of the table with a beard that nearly fell into his wine.

"Who doesn't have time for greater wealth?" I asked. "Hafir said that since Kiril's death, you were struggling to—"

"We do not struggle," Triere said, but her previously gloating tone had turned brittle, and she sent an icy glare in her agent's direction.

"No, of course not." I did not drop my gaze. They might believe my desire to help in the name of saving my own skin or buying favor, but if I were too subservient, questions would arise. They'd known Kiril. They knew the legends of Cinder.

Triere snapped her fingers, and Hafir took a step forward. The brokers would not be denied.

"Search the ship," Triere said. "Bring this treasure she says she has. Question the crew about where they found it and how much more there might be."

"Right away, Lady." Hafir bowed stiffly and backed away, always facing the table, as though Triere herself were a queen.

"Cinder," Triere said, drawing my attention from Hafir's parting form.

"Yes?" I narrowed my eyes as she studied me.

"We have a proposition for you."

Now, I glanced at Whit. I should have let him go when he'd asked. A broker's proposition was not something you said no to, and the results were often drawn out and bloody. Maro had been right. Of course they had. The brokers would never leave us alone. I'd made a mistake and played into their hands once again, and now I'd drawn Whit into it with me.

"What do you ask?" With any luck, they would send me off somewhere far away so that I had lots of time to make my way back and dispatch them one at a time.

"We need you to buy a country."

Better than leading a revolution, I supposed. I was no general. And purchasing one would be easier than poisoning a king to overthrow him. No doubt Triere had aspirations to sit on a true throne, rather than in her hidden palace here at the ends of civilization.

"Which country?" I asked.

"Redmere."

Something inside me clattered into silence. The brokers leaned forward as one, sensing their advantage. Of all the places in the world they could acquire with their vast wealth, they chose to turn their attention to Redmere?

"Oh?" I said, forcing my voice to maintain its steadiness.

"The time is right. When the prince died, we lost an ally and business partner. The new duke has aspirations of remaking the country for his own means, and we cannot have that. We will claim Redmere as our own."

Oh, George. It was as though she stood at my shoulder, telling me what to do. That we had to stop this. That we should fight. But deposing a ruler was one thing. To buy a country outright was entirely another. The brokers meant to step into the open, and Redmere was an ideal means. The people were poor and accustomed to oppressors. The brokers could provide the duke with however much wealth he desired and still have enough to introduce themselves as powerful partners in trade and battle to any other allies who might approach.

"We thank you for your service," Triere said, with the same slow pleasure Kiril used to speak in. That word. "Service." It always came with the implication of easy willingness, and for so long, my service had been exactly that. "In return, we are pleased to offer you a seat at our table."

The world tilted.

I glanced at the empty seat. Kiril's seat.

"By rights," Triere said, "it's yours, since you killed him."

I hadn't. Maro had. I'd been wounded and lying in my own blood, but regardless, the offer was impossible to accept. To do so meant I could never go back to George. Yes to refuse meant I would never be truly free. The brokers would always look for ways to regain my service.

"I cannot." The words scraped over my throat, tripping on years of regret and anger and grief. Scars the brokers had left me with. But I would take no more. I would fight for my freedom in any way I could. "I will pay you what you say I owe, and then I will leave, as per our agreement." The answer was hopeless, but all I needed was enough distance to regroup before I started picking them off one by one.

Triere sighed, but she appeared neither surprised nor disappointed. The brokers would have another way to achieve their goals. Another proxy. Kiril always had a secondary plan. If one assassin failed, there was another to send. If they couldn't win me over with the offer of power, they'd force me into the chair by using whatever leverage they could find. Fortunately, George was not here, so they would have very little to work with.

"Whitney." Triere's voice echoed off the gold and glass. "It is so good to have you back again."

A sound came from my right, like a body being dragged over stones, but it was only Whit's boots as he took a staggering step forward. I nearly asked him what he was doing, but when he was two paces in front of me, he bowed stiffly. His hands were balled into fists and his movement as he rose again was unsteady, as though his joints could not function simultaneously.

"It's a pleasure to be home," he said.

CHAPTER 24

My knees went weak. The knuckles in my hands popped as I curled my hands into fists. For two seconds, the world around me spun, lights wheeling off the ceiling and floor like a hundred balls of flame all being juggled at once. Then everything straightened as Triere said, "Did you do as you were ordered?"

"The ship at anchor contains more jewels and gold than I've ever seen in my life. And ..." He turned, and for a moment, an apology flickered across his face. "I've brought the legendary Captain Cinder back into the fold."

My throat was dry. Rage colored my cheeks. He was lying. He'd always been a liar, and now he was doing what he needed to escape the brokers, like I was.

But his words didn't make sense in that context. Neither did the way he completed his path to Triere's side and bent to kiss her. His lips grazed her cheek, but she turned her head and reached up to his neck, bringing him back down to kiss him again. Slower this time. Like a lover.

He'd lied, all right. To me.

It was everything I could do not to grab a weapon from the

nearest guard and rush at him. The fury inside me blazed. He'd lied. A lifetime of hurts and resentments balled together and demanded that—finally—I get my revenge.

And instead, I stood completely still and processed this new betrayal.

He'd wormed his way onto my ship, earned my trust until we obtained the treasure, then brought me back into the fold.

Had it been his plan from the beginning? He'd stolen the map, and I'd assumed he was a common thief looking to claim an advantage while I was in an unfamiliar city. The brokers had eyes everywhere, but never once had I considered those eyes might include my own brother's.

"You bastard," I said through gritted teeth, then instantly regretted it. Any show of emotion would only weaken me in front of the others.

Whit looked chagrined for a second, but Triere twined her fingers with his and pushed her lips into a fresh pout.

"Heartbroken?" she asked. "What did he promise you? A comfortable home? His undying adoration?"

Whit cleared his throat uncomfortably. "Captain Cinder wouldn't be swayed by such pedestrian enticements."

No, but at the heart of it, I'd believed Whit—if not exactly on my side—had no motive but to enrich himself. I'd even begun to believe there might be a future where we weren't strangers, but in the end, it seemed I'd never known him at all.

The words shook as I said, "You must have been in Triere's service for quite some time if you were entrusted with a mission like this."

Triere grinned. "Whitney has been my dearest one for the last six years, haven't you?"

My heart didn't break. It ripped itself to a hundred little pieces, one for every hurt he'd inflicted while we were small, and one large shredded fragment that was the hope that had grown over the last few weeks with him.

Whit's smile in Triere's direction was hollow.

"I have a request," he said.

She patted his hand. "Yes, pet?"

He grimaced, but then pulled himself straighter and tipped his chin down the table. "I'd like the eighth chair."

The breath left my lungs. Of course. Of course he would. Whit had only ever been interested in himself, and now he wanted absolute power. Everything he'd done had been about joining the brokers' ranks. Everything he'd said had probably been a lie, right down to the lost love and child he'd told me about. Whit would have left her on the shore to suffer the consequences of his indiscretion as his boat sailed away.

I knocked a stiff salute in his direction. "Well played." He didn't meet my gaze, and a flush of pink spread over his cheeks. Regret? Embarrassment? Anger at being mocked in front of the people who held his fate? If he joined their ranks, I'd have to kill him like the rest, but unlike the others, I'd enjoy it.

Triere tsked. "My dear. That's quite the request."

The color spread farther over Whit's face. "I think I've earned it. Haven't I done everything you asked?"

She considered. The others murmured. He couldn't join them. Their darkness had twisted them and destroyed their humanity. Somewhere, Whit still had his. He had to. I'd spent too much time with him for it all to be an act.

"We'll give you Redmere," she said. "Yours to rule on our behalf."

I burned at the suggestion. Not that I wanted the offer, but it wasn't theirs to give. Or Whit's to take. I wasn't even sure it was George's, but it should at least belong to someone who knew what the people's suffering had been.

Finally, Whit glanced at me, as if he could hear the roar of thoughts in my head. The swirl of emotion in his eyes was inscrutable. He said, "I would prefer the seat."

There was no ripple of conversation this time. Only silence in the cavernous empty room. I held my breath.

Finally, Triere plucked at her golden clothing in annoyance and said, "You'll have to kill Cinder for the honor."

Whit froze. My hand went to the hilt of a sword that wasn't there. The brokers watched us with wordless but perverse amusement. If Whit came for me, if my life was truly in danger, he had to know I'd fight tooth and nail, regardless of who we were to each other.

"I'd rather use her," he said, voice hoarse.

"Use her?" Triere tilted her head.

"In my service. As a broker, I'm allowed to employ whoever I want to serve my purposes, correct?"

She pursed her lips and tapped a finger on the table. The man sitting closest to her leaned toward her, whispering gently in her ear. Her gaze jumped from me to Whit and back again, and finally, she laughed softly, the sound barely leaving the back of her throat.

"You're not a broker yet, pet, and Cinder has become far too difficult to control. To prove your commitment, we need to you to take down your predecessor's murderer. This shouldn't be difficult."

Everything was a transaction for them. He had to know that. I squared my shoulders, hands in front, ready for whatever he would bring.

"Come on then," I said. "I've been waiting to do this since I was a girl. You always were a bully."

But Whit stayed rooted to the spot where he stood. His jaw worked, but he remained speechless. Something passed over the line of brokers, different than before. A faint crack in their self-assurance.

"I can't," Whit said finally, and the regret in his voice was obvious now. "I won't. She's my sister."

All eyes turned to me. I glared back. It took a lot to catch the brokers unaware, but despite the fact that their reach was endless, here, at least, was something their spies hadn't been able to tell them.

The silence was shattered by a wet gagging sound. The fish man was laughing. His whole body shook with it. Beside him, the others joined him, one at a time. Triere alone remained silent, but her eyes danced with delight.

"That's very unfortunate, pet," she said. "Considering, when you first came to us, you assured me there was no one in the world who would miss you."

And no one they could use against him. Just like me when I'd first gone to Kiril's. And now, all these years later, we'd formed this tenuous connection that would be our undoing.

"You'll do it, won't you?" Whit asked, speaking to me. His words were coming quickly, like he knew he only had a moment to plead his case, even though every word cost his standing with the monsters he hoped to join. The brokers didn't beg. "When I take Kiril's place. You served him all those years. You could do the same for me, couldn't you?"

I didn't expect the tears that formed in my eyes as I shook my head. Because he might be my brother, but I wouldn't serve him. Not like that. Too many people waited for me. George. Perhaps Ender and Rosie. Maro, who I might never see again, but who I hoped might wonder occasionally what had become of me.

"It doesn't matter if you say yes," Whit said, desperation growing. "You'll do as you're told. Look at you. This is who you are. You'll always—" But his words were cut off as a line of red spread along the base of his throat. I hadn't seen Triere move, but she stood at his shoulder. The dagger in her hand winked in the candlelight, and a single drop of red blood fell to the glass floor.

You knew exactly where to cut, didn't you?

Whit had asked me that as he'd examined Harlow's cooling corpse. One glance at Triere's icy expression confirmed she undoubtedly knew too.

His mouth fell open, and terror filled his eyes. Whit grabbed desperately at his throat, trying to contain the crimson flood that spilled from him, but the effort was hopeless. He had a few seconds left. He staggered forward, reaching his free hand out to me. I took it, going with him as he fell to the floor while the brokers watched the spectacle.

"It's all right," I said. "All right. Nearly over. Whitney. Listen." His rolling eyes settled on mine, and I squeezed his hand. "You're going now. To see your woman. Your child. Our mother. Say hello to her for me." She and I owed each other nothing, and maybe the unknown woman and baby were only imaginary, but if it brought him comfort, that was all I needed. "Say hello."

A heavy gurgling sound rattled in his chest. Blood filled his lungs. I'd told George once that drowning was easy. You simply had to let go. Here, Whit didn't even have a choice. I smoothed a hand over his forehead. Let the brokers watch this moment of tenderness. They were nothing to me. More, they were dead. All of them. For this. For everything they'd done to me and mine.

But as Whit's body finally fell still, the pressure of their gazes weighed down on me. Triere was formidable. I couldn't rush her and hope to gain possession of the dagger. Maro had always said to wait for my opportunity, and this moment was not it.

Triere sank down into her chair again, looking bored. She took a sip of wine from her jeweled goblet and waved a negligent hand. Attendants appeared to wordlessly carry Whit's body away with little ceremony. I stayed where I was, one hand in a puddle of congealing blood on the floor.

"You'll stay with us," Triere said, and I realized she was addressing me.

"I've fulfilled my obligations," I said.

"You remain useful. It would be in your best interests for that not to change."

It was also in their best interests to keep me as close as possible. Free, I would have a chance to pursue them each at my leisure. Clasped to their collective bosoms, I had less room to strike.

"Kiril gave me my freedom." They would find my ready acceptance suspicious.

"And you killed him for it." She snapped a finger, and two more guards—these ones heavily armed—broke from the ranks along the wall. "Take her down to the cellar. A little time to reflect will do you good, won't it, Cinder?"

I didn't reply. She can't have expected me to. Captain Cinder did not beg. One of the soldiers reached for my arm, and I shook him off. He tried again, and I spun, using the heel of my hand to smash against his face. His nose caved in with a crunch. This was becoming a habit, but it truly was the most effective way to make a point. The solider shouted, hands to his nose, and his colleague surged forward, sword halfway out of its scabbard.

"Enough." Triere rapped on the table. "Cinder. Behave."

Like a child. Someone to be controlled with a few harsh words. Their mistake. I had never been a child. Kiril had never controlled me. He had harnessed my rage and used it to his purpose. But now it was mine to direct as I would.

The cellar, as it turned out, was a dignified euphemism for a dungeon, carved out of the island's rock. A reeking pit with only one door on ancient hinges that squealed as they were pulled shut. No light, no matter how long I sat in the dark.

I should have been planning my next step, but I couldn't get my mind to settle. For a while, I felt nothing but fury and self-recrimination. Whit's deception had been complete, but I hadn't done anything to look through it either. From the first moment, all I'd seen was the lout and the bully I'd grown up with. It had never occurred to me that he'd be anyone else.

Slowly though, the fury gave way to a sad loneliness. Over and over, I thought of the people I'd left behind. George. Maro. Even Whit, in the end, or the version of Whit I'd been coming to appreciate at least. I'd been so certain that I could control every situation and knew exactly who to trust. But my conceit had undone me entirely. Even if I escaped here, all I had was a crew I didn't know and who had every right to be wary of me. A relic of a ship, assuming the brokers hadn't yet found what she carried and stripped her down to sawdust. No one to trust. Drowning would be easier, but I couldn't make myself let go of the fight, even trapped underground as I was with the brokers plotting overhead. George was still out there somewhere. Now, more than ever, I had to get back to her.

Sometime later, my knees had begun to ache. No matter how I positioned myself, seated or standing, against a wall or free in the middle of the tiny cell, there didn't seem to be anywhere for me to get comfortable. I paced in small circles, toe catching occasionally on an uneven surface. My mind was equally circular, picking apart small details of what happened, making guesses as to what would be and how long it would take before someone came to—

The bang against the door made me jump. A second one followed close after, like someone had thrown themselves against the wood. For a split second, I thought it might be Whit. Maybe he had survived. Escaped. Maybe it had all been a charade, and he'd never been with the brokers to begin with.

But that wasn't reality. Whit was dead. I would have never allowed myself such wishful thinking before.

Another shudder as the door shook from the outside. No other sounds. No indication of a fight or someone trying to subdue a guard.

For a long time after, there was nothing. I stood in a position I thought faced the door, ready to defend myself. No time to relax. Whoever was out there, I couldn't take any chances.

Slowly, the hinges swung open with a renewed squeal. The light that poured in had me squinting after too many hours in the dark. I'd used the same tactic to my advantage so many times before. Charged below decks to subdue the sailors below before they could react.

This time, though, no rush came. I did not shrink back or press myself against the rock. I was not afraid.

"Since you had no way of knowing if the person opening the door was friend or foe, you really should have at least tried to kill me by now. You'd have failed. But the lack of initiative is truly disappointing." The deeply accented voice made my heart race. I blinked rapidly, trying to clear my vision.

"I'm sorry for disappointing you," I said, allowing myself a smile as I glanced at the prone bodies of two guards lying on the floor.

"We'll have to start your training over then."

Between me and the unmoving guards, Maro stood, with an all-too-familiar look of tired exasperation on their face.

CHAPTER 25

In my head, our reunion involved a joyous leap across the space and a hearty embrace. In reality, I took two stumbling steps forward and pulled Maro into an awkward hug. Their return was little more than a gentle pat on the back, but I felt it all the way through my bones. When I stepped away, they handed me a dagger and a sword. Maro was nothing if not ever-practical.

"How are you here?" I asked.

"How did it take you so long to arrive? I've been waiting for more than a week."

I laughed in a short burst. Of course they'd come here. Snuck in and waited in the shadows. Always looking for the opportunity. I still had so much to learn from Maro.

"Triere killed Whit," I said, as if they didn't know. No doubt they'd been lurking in a corner or hidden behind a secret panel that had long been forgotten.

"He wasn't the brokers' agent," they said, "At least, not fully. I heard Triere and the others talking. They sent others to the ports we might have gone to after we left Beldridge. They wanted to keep an eye on you. Triere seemed infatuated with Whit, but the plan was an uneasy one, and many of the others didn't believe he would come back."

"Did they know he was—" The words failed me. Whit's stricken face as he'd confessed I was his sister played in my memory. "Did they know we were family?"

Maro shrugged. "I don't know. No one spoke of it. The other brokers only arrived yesterday. At most, I believe they thought he might charm his way into your good graces, then steal the treasure out from under you and run with it."

Instead, he'd asked me to leave him in port as we'd made our way here. Had he known? When had he realized he couldn't win with them? When the knife had breached his throat? When they'd sent him after me? Or years earlier?

My fate would be different.

"We need to go." Maro pulled me toward the narrow stone steps that would lead us back up to the main part of the house.

"No." I caught the edge of their sleeve. "I can't leave."

Maro sighed. "I'm happy to see you alive again, but let's not start bickering before we're safe, all right?"

"No," I said again. "We can't be safe until they're all dead. Maro, please. I need your help."

Their smile was a startling line of white teeth in the gloom. "I hope you're asking what I think you're asking."

"We have to kill the brokers. All of them. They're all here. We'll never have this chance again."

The smile turned predatory. Maro let out a relieved breath and clapped me on the shoulder. "I'm so glad to hear you say this, Cinder."

"I know." I dropped my head in shame. "I should have listened to you an age ago."

"No. You did what you thought was right." They laughed softly. "But I'm glad to hear you've changed your mind, because I already killed one getting in here. Old Plintoc was halfway down the stairs. No idea what he was doing. I didn't bother finding out."

With no further comment, they headed up the stairs, and sure enough, the crumpled form of one of the men from the table lay about halfway up.

"Shouldn't we hide him?" I asked, though there were no convenient alcoves or windows for the purpose.

Maro gave him an authoritative shove with a booted foot, and he tumbled down the stairs.

"Why waste time with that when we could get to the good parts?"

I followed as they resumed climbing. "I get the distinct impression you've been planning this."

"I've been listening to them scheme for less than a day and I can't stand a minute more. They're so odious. So self-assured in their power. Even if you hadn't suggested it, I'd have made you wait while I took care of them. It's past time someone did."

It was. We should have done it ages ago.

"You were right all along. About everything," I said. "I'm sorry."

They rolled their eyes. "Don't be so sentimental."

The mirrored room was empty. Apart from the door we'd been led through, there were two others at the end, on opposite sides of the table where the brokers had sat. Maro's feet were silent as they crossed the room, and I did my best to follow in the same manner, though I would never match their abilities.

"The bedrooms are in two wings," Maro said. "With Plintoc dead, there will be three in each."

"Which way is Triere?" Regardless of our history and whether or not he'd truly betrayed me, Whit was my brother, and she'd killed him. I'd earned the right to claim revenge.

"That way. Triere and two others." Maro scowled. "If you alert them by making a production out of this, you know we'll lose at least one or two. I'm tired, Cinder. I've spent too many hours eavesdropping on their foulness. Our next destination better have a bath and fresh food. I don't want to spend the next months or years prowling one broker's den after another."

I gave them a grin and a sharp salute. "Understood. I'll behave."

"I'll meet you at the ship," Maro said.

"The mate's name is Perdita."

They screwed up their face. "You have a new mate."

"I couldn't sail without one. The whole crew left when you did."

"They always did like me better than you."

Maro had been my rudder and my keel for years. I should have seen that. Now it was my turn to give a quick salute, then we parted ways.

Through the door was another stone staircase, though this one was grander than the one up from the so-called cellar. Here, windows were installed every few steps, giving a view of the beach and the full moon that hung heavy over the waves.

The hall at the top of the stairs was empty. I'd expected there to be a few sentries, but the brokers must have been so comfortable in their relative isolation that none were posted. No wonder Maro had been free to roam the halls and listen around doorways for a week.

Four doors lined the corridor. One was open, and inside, the bed lay empty. Old Plintoc's room, perhaps. His neighbor, when I pressed an ear to the wood, was silent, and no glow of light shone beneath the door. Still, I pushed it open slowly, waiting for a creak or groan of hinges that would give me away.

I wasn't prepared for the crash as a stack of tin cups crashed to the floor. They must have been propped up with something that rested against the door, and when the tower gave way, the clamor seemed like a roar in the silent hall.

The fish man had been in bed, but he sprang upright at the sound, lips slapping together.

"Who's there?" he asked.

I didn't give him a chance to find out. The dagger flew from my hand. Knife work was more Maro's specialty than mine, but this time my throw was true, and it buried itself deep in his chest. He collapsed back, gasping as he pawed at the hilt protruding from his flesh, but even as I approached, the red stain spread over his shirt, and the gurgle in his breathing grew.

I put a hand over his mouth as I pulled the dagger free. Blood poured forth. I plunged the blade down a few more times to make sure the work was done.

When he was still and his flat eyes vacant, I covered him with the fine sheets of his bed and paused at the door, listening for signs anyone had heard me. But no one came.

Across the hall, laughter filtered through the next door, and light was clearly visible beneath it. I wiped the bloody dagger against my thigh and made my way to the door. This time, there was no makeshift alarm, but the heavy scent of perfume greeted me as I pushed my way in. This room was much larger than the other, with the bed on the far side, visible behind a gauzy curtain that hung from the ceiling and spanned the entire width of the space.

A man and a woman were on the bed, naked and embracing. Periodically, she would laugh, a high squealing sound that verged on hysteria. The man laved her nipples and pulled on her hair to force her head back.

"Put your hands around her throat." The speaker was obscured, sitting in a high-backed chair that faced the bed and away from the door.

"Sir?" the man said, suddenly sounding unsure.

"You heard me."

As I approached, a pair of thick, hairy thighs became visible around the edge of the chair, then bare feet with toes curled into a fine carpet.

The man complied, even as the woman's face went white with fear. He was obviously reluctant, but then the third person in the chair stood up.

"Would you rather I do it?" he asked.

"No. No, sir." He kissed his partner once, gently, softly, like lovers did. Then he wrapped his strong hands around her throat, thumbs at the delicate soft center beneath her jaw.

I pulled the chair back, dancing away as it crashed to the floor. The broker with the beard spun.

"What's going on?" He was fully naked and his cock stood at engorged attention, swollen and throbbing. His eyes narrowed when he saw me, and I grabbed his wrist and pulled him toward me, using his momentum to catch him off guard.

As he fell past me, I plunged the dagger into the spot where his throat met his shoulder and followed him down, straddling him as he hit the floor. I didn't hesitate as once again I pulled the knife free and turned him over. He was frightened and gasping, but his hands came up, clasping the blade between his palms as I brought it down again. He was strong, but as his life poured out of the first wound, his grip slipped, and soon enough, the resistance of hands and flesh gave way as I cut through the fragile parts of his windpipe.

My hands were clammy as I wiped my brow, and I nearly slipped when I tried to stand. I'd planted my foot in a growing dark red puddle.

The man and woman clung to each other on the bed, looking frightened.

"Go," I said. "Tell no one. Wait at the beach. Stay out of sight. If you're there when I come, we'll take you to safety."

The woman gaped at me, but the man nodded, pulling her from the bed. She started to cry, but he wrapped an arm around her waist and guided her away. As they passed me, I caught a glimpse of fading green and brown bruises around her throat. Not the first night then. My stomach turned, but I didn't have time for sentiment right now. This was the world the brokers created, and tonight, I would end it.

When I returned to the hall, the last door was open. A crystal candelabra like a miniature of the great chandelier downstairs sat on a table, carrying dozens of lit candles. The heat practically radiated down the hall.

I drew my sword and approached slowly, dagger in the other hand. Somewhere, a gull called, and when I stood at the threshold, the windows across from me were open, making the fine curtains wave lazily in the evening breeze.

"Are you coming in, then?" a voice said to my left, and when I turned, Triere was sitting in an ornate chair almost like a throne. She wore a golden robe, with billowing sleeves that trailed right down to her fingertips, but was unfastened below her waist, so that one leg was exposed to the knee and draped over the other. Her toes pointed elegantly to the floor. She'd painted her lips bright red, and it made her skin look even paler. I raised my sword in her direction, and she gave me a sad smile as she tilted her head. "Is that the best you can do?"

Her face and attire were right out of the stories sailors told in the evenings as the drink was passed around. The temptress who lured men from their watch and left them to drown when their night together was over.

"I think you have enough dramatic flair for the both of us."

She glanced over my shoulder. "Are the rest of them dead, then?"

"Yes." No doubt Maro had already finished their rounds in the other wing.

Triere nodded, as if she'd expected as much. "Old, lecherous pigs, all of them. You've done the world a favor."

"And one more," I said, "when I'm finished with you."

"He talked of you often," she said, like I hadn't spoken. Her words caught me so off guard that I hesitated.

"Who?"

"Kiril. He was so proud of what you'd become."

My stomach rolled at the insinuation. "He took the worst parts of me and twisted them until they were monstrous."

She shook her head. "He made you strong. Just like he made me strong."

I'd have said we were nothing alike, but the lie was too obvious, written in the blood I'd smeared down the hall while I stood here feeling next to nothing. I'd spent too long sailing on the brokers' tides to be untouched.

"He took me, you know, when I wasn't much older than you were," Triere said. "Raised me up from the miserable fate my two dead parents had left me to. Eventually, I exceeded his control like you did, and he let me take my rightful place with the others."

"To hurt and destroy as you saw fit?"

She laughed, a deep, throaty sound that spoke of years of knowing she was the most powerful woman in the room. "My dear, all I did was survive. You can't blame me for surviving."

But she hadn't. I remembered survival. The fear. Desperation. The knowledge that, even if I did everything right, I might still not make it until the end of the day. Since then, I'd chosen to live. To fight. To love. Living outside the brokers' hold would always be better than surviving in their grip.

Triere rose, folds of her robe falling around her. "I don't usually make an offer twice, but for you I'll make an exception. Join me. We can remake the world. My people tell me the ship you sailed in on carries enough treasure that we can take hold of my former colleagues' operations with limited fuss and bother. We'd rule the oceans."

"You'll understand if I decline," I said.

She nodded, pursing her lips. "Disappointing. Your brother would have said yes in time."

I lifted my sword, sighing heavily. I wouldn't let her play on my emotions and regrets. "Can we skip to the part where one of us is dead and the other is not?"

Triere grinned and, in a lightning-fast motion, pulled a knife from one of her sleeves. I stumbled backward, knocking the flying blade aside with the flat of my sword. The knife clattered to the ground, and I dove to pick it up. Leaving an unattended weapon on the floor was a guaranteed way to find it in your back soon after. When I straightened, Triere had left her throne and now stood by the bed, a pointed sword in her hand. She gripped it with confident ease.

"Kiril never fought his own battles," she said. "But I assure you I am more than capable of winning mine."

I tucked the extra knife in my belt and prepared to fight. As she lunged forward, blade flashing, I had to dance back quickly to avoid her attack. Despite the size of the room, the space was suddenly cramped with adornments and furnishings, and I tripped over a small low stool. Triere grinned, seeing the advantage. She rushed toward me, and I scrambled back, bumping against a table. It rocked, and the candelabra tumbled over. I had to cover my head as candles rolled off the table and tumbled to the floor. I grabbed one and threw it at Triere, who batted it away, but not before the flames caught the edge of her sleeve. She hissed as the orange tongues licked over the shining fabric, and she had to retreat long enough to shed the smoldering garment. Beneath, she wore only a simple black slip of a dress.

"That robe was a gift," she said.

"People like you don't receive gifts," I said, pulling myself to stand. "They receive tributes. Payment."

Triere lifted her blade. "Should we continue?"

I rolled my head, so very tired of all this. Smoke clung in my nose. "No more distractions."

This time, her advance came even faster, freed of the billowing confines of her robe. She truly knew how to use her weapon of choice. I was capable, but not a master. All I could do was grit my teeth and try to hold her off until she made a mistake.

She didn't. The flick of her blade over my cheek burned where she cut the skin.

Triere grinned. "So you do bleed."

Sometimes, I felt like all I did was bleed for the brokers. I swung at her with a scream.

"You've taken everything from me," I snarled.

"We only took what you offered. You know that."

I swiped again, but she avoided me with practiced grace.

"I was a child," I said.

"So was I. And look at where I am now." She was toying with me. When her blade came down this time, it glanced off my forearm, leaving a wide cut. It would have been easy enough for her to have aimed higher, incapacitating my sword arm at the shoulder. Instead, she laughed. "Pretty pirate queen. Did you honestly think you could win?"

I had. I'd believed I was right. That the brokers deserved their punishment. That I loved George enough I would see her again. But I might have been wrong on so many fronts.

The opportunity, when it came, was over in an instant. One moment, she was advancing on me, the next, a popping sound to my right drew both our attention. One of the candles had rolled to the wall, and the curtains caught fire. Blue flames rushed upward, and Triere's second of distraction would be my only chance. I rushed at her, sword gripped tight in both hands, and her whole body bowed with the impact of the blade into her guts.

Triere gasped, astonished gaze going from my face down to the sword that had invaded her body. She laughed once. "Kiril did truly train you well."

"I didn't learn this from him." Maro had taught me everything I needed to know. "And by outliving you all, I've won." Then I pushed the sword the rest of the way in. Her eyes widened. Blood foamed at her lips, but slowly, her whole body went limp. I let her slump down. Her gaze went dull, though it remained trained on my face as the last of her life left her. As her muscles relaxed, the monster beneath her skin vanished, leaving only a woman. I might see her in any port. Pass her in any market. And I'd never recognize her as anything remarkable.

I pulled the sword free, paying close attention to the slick slide of the blade as it left flesh, waiting for any flinch or inhale that would say she was still alive. But none came. She was dead. If I trusted Maro—and I did absolutely—the others were too. We were free.

A riot of emotions rose up in me, and in the end, I grabbed the upended candelabra from the table and smashed it to the floor by the bed. Candles bounced free of their holders, and two landed against the soft covers that hung from the bed's edge. Within a few seconds, flames licked up the side, then spread in blue-orange fingers that clawed toward the ceiling. I watched, mesmerized for a moment, before allowing myself a final glance at Triere's corpse. Her head dropped to one side, and her hands lay limp at her sides.

Over.

Smoke curled at my ankles as I made my way down the hall, but I didn't hurry. The fire would consume Triere's room and the other brokers before it came for me.

Maro was waiting on the beach. The couple from the bearded man's room—now dressed—was there too. A few others stood off to one side, looking uncertain. None appeared to be armed, and none approached me as I walked across the sand.

Except Maro.

"You always need to have the last word, don't you?" they said, glancing beyond me to the house where flames had begun to lick at the window frames and smoke rose from the roof.

"I was never much of a reader," I said. "Not much call for that skill the way I grew up. But George tried to teach me. And the thing I remember most is the importance of proper punctuation."

They were already squinting at the small ship that lay at anchor in the bay as I put a hand on their shoulder.

"Not much of a vessel," they said. "Wouldn't you have been better off to keep Harlow's ship?"

I squeezed their shoulder. "Wait until you see the inside."

CHAPTER 26

Our reunion was not entirely sweet. Once on board, Maro did grudgingly admit that the ship's plain exterior was excellent camouflage for the riches that lay inside. However, they felt the ornamentation altogether too gaudy and insisted that we put the two survivors from Triere's to work removing it, since we were so sparsely crewed we couldn't spare any sailors to do it. The treasure was stored safely in the hold, piled from floor to ceiling. Maro and Perdita took turns guarding it.

I'd never sought riches. My goals had been revenge. Power. Absolution. Now I had those—perhaps—and a war chest to boot. Or a retirement fund. As we sailed away, Whit's plans came back to me. A house on a hill. A woman who loved me. Quiet idleness until I couldn't stand it anymore and went back to sea now and again. That wouldn't be so terrible. We had enough money now to buy respectability, and there would be no brokers to come for us ever again.

Still, even with the brokers gone, Maro disliked this plan. "I'd rather have my eyes gouged out with sharpened reeds than spend my time hosting parties and buying horses."

"You didn't even listen to my entire vision." I pouted over a bowl of inedibly bland fish stew. "There would also be such scintillating hobbies as poetry readings and—"

Maro threw their spoon across the cabin in disgust. "If we don't get Rosie back, life isn't even worth living."

I froze. Maro hadn't spoken of the others since we'd come on board.

"I wasn't even sure you knew Rosie's name," I said with a grin I knew irritated them to no end.

They rolled their eyes. "She's exactly the woman for Ender, and a far better cook than any of us deserve. The best thing you ever did was bring her aboard. Her and George."

"I thought you said George made me weak." I couldn't stop the petty protest from escaping my lips.

"I'm sorry for that," Maro said. I could hardly believe my ears.

"Did you just apologize? When have you ever apologized for anything?"

More eye rolling, this time followed by some awkward throat clearing. "She's stronger than you think though."

I left my gloating unfinished. "I know." She was everything. Anything she wanted to be. And she was safe now. I'd secured that, no matter how ham-fisted my approach had been. She wouldn't want to retire either. How many times had she told me so? Her only goal was to return to Redmere and help the people she felt she'd left behind.

"Do you know where she is?" Maro asked.

"Norampar, I hope." If she wasn't … If she'd already gone to Redmere, this would be a long and unpleasant chase.

The voyage was slow. The jeweled ship was too small and too laden down to travel with any great speed. The wind was against us, and whereas it would have taken the *Siren* only a few weeks to cover the distance, in the treasure ship, the journey pushed into a month. Every day was torture, feeling like we would never get back to Norampar and to George.

"You really ought to give her a name," Maro said one night as we took over the watch from Perdita.

"I think Perdita's a perfectly lovely name," I said with a smile.

They nudged me gently in the ribs. "Not the girl. The ship."

I bit my lip. Naming her felt important. Permanent. The future was so uncertain. Tying our fortunes to a ship that I still didn't see as mine felt hasty.

"I'll let George choose," I said. "When we see her."

Maro snorted gently. "I believe it's more customary to offer one's intended a simple ring. Not an entire fortune."

I froze, tightening my hands on the wheel. "Intended?"

"She'll want you to marry her, sooner or later. Regardless of the time she's spent with us, she was raised with certain expectations, and those include marriage."

My stomach twisted at the thought. The last wedding I'd been to was George's to odious Prince Beverly. He'd seen fit to stab me for my trouble when I thought I'd done a fine job of performing the ceremony.

I wanted to be with her forever, however she would have me. But if someday she found herself leading a revolution as the new queen of Redmere, it would be difficult for me to hold a place in the light at her side.

I looked away, even though I could hide nothing from Maro. "We don't need anything so fancy as a wedding."

"Doesn't mean you can't have one. If you want it."

I suddenly found the particular shade of blue sky above us very interesting.

Despite all our misadventures, when we finally sailed into Norampar, the day was bright and warm. The temple dome shone a greeting at us, and a fussy customs officer met us on the wharf.

"What is the purpose of your arrival?" he asked, making notes with quill and ink in a heavy leather book.

"We're here to see friends at the temple," I said.

The officer eyed us. "Do you have an invitation?"

Maro shifted impatiently. "I thought the temple was open to everyone."

The man dipped his quill and made more notes. "Most days, yes. Today, though … Without an invitation, I'm afraid—"

"An invitation for what?" I asked.

He gave the weariest of sighs. "For today's wedding festivities. If you were not invited, then—"

"Perdita," I said. "Perhaps you could give our friend here a tour of the hold? Maybe let him sample our wares?"

Perdita gave me a knowing look, and she bowed elegantly. "Of course, Captain. Right this way, sir. If you'd like to inspect what we've brought into the harbor today …" Her voice faded as she led the officer down toward the hold. As soon as they were out of sight, we hurried up the wharf.

I could barely contain myself as we entered the city. Norampar still gleamed with its welcoming glow. As we approached the temple though, the air grew even more festive. The gates were decorated with banners—both the silver and gold of the goddesses, and something not unlike the black and silver of Redmere, though the crest was different.

I approached two brothers standing at the gate and greeted them with a broad smile. "Hello, friends. We've come for the wedding."

One of them gave me a silent inspection. The look on his face said he was left wanting. "Are you from Redmere?"

My smile wilted somewhat in surprise, but I did my best to bluff my way through. "Yes. I'm Redmerian."

His eyes narrowed further. "Are you part of the wedding party?"

"The wedding …" I couldn't fit all the pieces of what he was saying together.

"Seems highly inappropriate for a fine lady to be getting married without more attendants." He cleared his throat.

"Pardon my saying so. I was talking to one of the sisters who dressed her this morning. She said she only had one other lady to—"

"Excuse me," I pushed past them. The brother called after me, but Maro said something to him quietly, and he didn't pursue us.

"What was that about?" Maro asked, hurrying after me.

"How many other Redmerian ladies do you think there are lying around waiting to get married?"

"How many—" Maro's eyes widened. "You mean George is—"

The idea hurt. She wouldn't do it willingly. But if she thought I'd left her, especially if Ender had died and she and Rosie were truly alone in the world … I couldn't believe she would simply accept the next man to cross her path, but safety was of the utmost importance. In so many parts of the world, a man's protection could offer—

"Faster," I said. "Walk faster."

We hurried through the temple doors with no interruption. Monks and sisters were scurrying back and forth, carrying flowers and bright ribbons. None stopped us to ask where we were going, and so I practically ran to the stairs that led to the infirmary, as if she'd still be waiting for me in the hall where I'd last left her more than a month ago.

"What are you going to do?" Maro asked, easily keeping up with me as we climbed. "Burst through the doors and announce your objections? Kidnap her—again—and sail away?"

"If I have to."

"You don't honestly believe—"

"I can't very well take the chance, now, can I?" I snapped as we rounded the last landing and started down the hall.

"You're being ridiculous."

I might be. But all I could think of was her hand in Beverly's. The tears on her face as she believed she was doing the right thing. With the right persuasions, particularly when she believed I'd abandoned her, she might do it again.

The infirmary was empty when we arrived. Not a single patient in any of the beds, not a brother or a sister to help us.

"George! George, are you in here?" I called, and my voice echoed uselessly off the hall. She wasn't here.

"Someone will know where she is," Maro said, a hand on my shoulder.

"Lou? Is that you?"

She stood in the doorway. She held a bouquet of flowers that were such a deep purple they were nearly black and wore a white gown that exposed her shoulders and a deep V of her chest while swallowing her legs and ankles in stiff folds of silk. More flowers adorned her hair, white against the dark curls, and I realized her hair was unbound and left down, brushing over her skin. I ached to touch it. To smell its sweetness.

"George?" I swallowed on a lump.

She let out a happy cry and hurried toward us, though her skirts impeded her progress. I was too stunned at the vision in front of me to move. Finally, she dropped the flowers to the floor and gathered up the silk in great handfuls so she could run the last few steps before launching herself at me, catching me up in a fierce hug. She pressed her lips to mine, and her kiss turned hungry the second I responded.

"What are you doing here?" she asked. "What about the treasure? The brokers?"

"It's done," I said in the split second I could tear myself away from her mouth.

"Over? All of it?"

I threaded my fingers in her hair and inhaled. There were her scents, bright and clean, and there was the aroma of the flowers. The effect was dizzying.

"We're here for the wedding," Maro said.

George shrieked and abandoned me to throw herself at them.

"Maro! It's so good to see you." She spun, glancing around excitedly. "Where's Whitney?"

I wasn't expecting my heart to catch in my throat at the sound of his name. I hadn't thought about him much as we'd sailed back to Hilltop. Not in the way I'd thought about George. I didn't necessarily miss him. In the end, I hadn't known him. But I missed that we would never become the people who might think about each other on occasion. That we'd never have memories to look back on. I'd left my family behind a long time ago, but losing Whit somehow felt like losing them all over again.

George's face fell—even though she couldn't know the true story—and if she spoke to me too softly or sympathetically, I might crack and burst into tears right there in the hallway. Instead, she clutched Maro's hand and reached for mine. "Come on. We're going to be late. Lou, pick up my flowers."

"Wait," I said, shuddering as the wave of grief rolled back again. And it *was* grief. Something I was still unfamiliar with. Part of me wanted to wait for the next rush and examine it more closely. But George was like a hurricane, impossible to escape now we were in her path. I nearly tripped as I bent to scoop up her bouquet. Some of the stems were broken.

"Your timing is perfect," she said. "The others will be so glad to see you. I'd come back to my room to—"

"George. Wait." I pulled on her hand, forcing us to stop. "What's going on? You don't have to do this."

She furrowed her brow. "Have to do what?"

"Marry a …" I struggled with my explanation. "I'm back. George, I found the treasure. It's in the harbor."

"I'm not getting married." She pushed her hair from her face.

We all stared at each other, a triangle of confusion. Somehow, Maro was now holding the bouquet and attempting to find the best angle to hold it so the flowers didn't appear entirely crushed.

"But the brother at the gate said—" I tried. "He said a Redmerian lady was—"

George laughed. "It's Rosie! Rosie's getting married."

I blinked several times, waiting for comprehension to settle. Rosie? Rosie was getting married?

"But your dress," I said weakly.

"Oh." George gave a quick twirl, but sighed tiredly. "It's a bit much, isn't it. Apparently, it's a temple tradition for the bride's attendants to wear white."

"But Rosie … A lady?"

George began walking again, as though everything had been settled, and we followed after her like ducklings. "The brothers and sisters at the temple have been very kind to us, but we can't live off their hospitality forever. I've begun getting to know some of the nobility in the city, looking for people whose influence we could use to get back to Redmere. I thought we'd be better treated if Rosie was a highborn lady too, rather than a maid and a cook. She's now the Duchess of Snowham. I gave her the title. What do you think?"

I could barely think at all. "Snowham. Wasn't that—"

"My grandfather, yes." She took the steps with ease despite the volume of her skirts. "And now my uncle has the title. But we've heard he's aligned himself with Duke Aubrey, so he's a traitor to what I stand for. Our conversations have been successful so far. Of course, we're a long way from Redmere City, but people have connections. I'll introduce you." She continued to rattle off her plans and visions for the future, but I could barely keep up, both mentally and physically. It was like she was traveling on a cloud, and I was stuck in the mud. I nearly tripped as we hit the last stair, and she was already across the hall toward the sanctuary.

"Seems like she's been busy," Maro said as they walked beside me.

Finally, she led us through a corridor with tall windows that faced an ornamental garden. The hedges and shrubs were all decorated in ribbons and feathers, and a crowd had gathered.

"Rosie picked out the decorations herself," George said, before pulling open a door that led outside.

"George!"

Once again, recognition nearly failed me as the woman in the flowing deep purple gown hurried toward us. It was only the cloud of copper hair, bound up in a net of pearls, that identified Rosie, and I gasped. She was truly every inch the lady that George was.

"I'm sorry," George said. "I forgot my flowers, then when I left my room—" She gestured back at us, and Rosie's mouth dropped open.

"Lou! Maro! Did you come back just for me?"

I'd run out of words, so I simply gaped. I felt impossibly scruffy next to George and Rosie. They were so elegant, and I was so seaworn and plain.

"You look beautiful," Maro said smoothly, and Rosie gave her a happy giggle.

"Do you think so?" She smoothed a hand over her front. "I know it's too early to really have much to show, but I feel like I've been squished into this dress like a sausage."

"Duchess." A sister in a blue and green robe bobbed a short bow as she approached Rosie. "Are we ready to begin?"

George kissed my cheek. "Go have a seat. We'll talk when this is over."

"No." I hung back. "We'll stand here. I wouldn't want to—"

"Of course not. Rosie and Ender want you here."

I was back among friends. The thought made me unexpectedly emotional. George smiled at me like I'd never been gone at all, and I lifted her hand to kiss the back of her knuckles. "I've missed you terribly."

She looked like she was about to say something else, but the sister cleared her throat, and George hopped forward, stepping in front of Rosie and desperately trying to pull her bouquet together. Maro and I threaded our way through the crowd—mostly temple inhabitants, but there were a few people in fine clothes who must have been deemed worthy of the spectacle—and found two seats near the front.

A thrumming horn sounded, and we turned to watch as a tall man dressed all in black walked slowly toward the front. My blood went cold, and even Maro gasped.

"Ender," they said.

We might be back among friends, but the last few months weren't without their cost, and the evidence was plain. Ender's movements were slower, and he walked with the gait of a much older man. He was thinner than he should have been, his face drawn. Still recovering from his wound. Even so, seeing him standing lightened my heart. When he stood at the center of the garden, his gaze landed on us, and new color spread to his cheeks, making him look a little healthier. His smile under his red beard warmed his face further.

We were diminished, but we had survived.

Another fanfare sounded, and George and Rosie made their way through the assembled crowd. George looked ecstatic, and Rosie fairly glowed as she placed her hand in Ender's. He stood up a little straighter in return as he stared down at her. He had been smitten with her from the moment he'd found her in the brig with George. Yet, as a priestess stepped forward and began to speak to her people about the requirements and advantages of marriage, I couldn't expect Ender had ever dreamed that he'd get to wed his little redheaded lady in such a grand place as this.

The marriage ceremony was relatively quick. The reception was long. Endless rounds of food and dancing, speeches made—even though hardly anyone in the room could really know either the bride or the groom—then more toasts to everyone's health and happiness and words of thanks to the two goddesses who had made this happy day possible. Ender tired quickly, and he and Rosie made an early departure, but the revelers continued late into the night. Somewhere along the way, Maro vanished—either to ensure we faced no possible threats in the city, or to find the company of a willing body away from the noise of the party, I couldn't say and wouldn't ask when they returned.

George moved about the room, speaking with clerics and nobles. She'd been busy. Everyone seemed charmed with her. A queen without a country, though hopefully we would change that soon. With the brokers gone, we were free to seek out the adventures she desired so fiercely.

Finally, she took my hand and led me from the room. We only made it up the first flight of stairs before she pulled me into an alcove and pressed me against the wall. Her lips on mine were possessive now, and her fingers pulled hurriedly at my clothes.

"I missed you," she said.

"I'm so glad you didn't marry some rich nobleman for the sake of politics."

She laughed as she slid a hand into the front of my trousers, and I spread my legs to give her better access. Her touch was demanding, and I grew hot with need.

"Never," she said, biting at my earlobe. "I would never. Not any man. Only you."

A sister scurried by, and whether she recognized us or not, the stain of pink on her face said she knew very well what we were doing. I gripped George's wrist, stilling her.

"Let's go to your room," I said, kissing her when she pouted. "I don't want to share this with anyone else."

The rooms for temple visitors were hardly more elaborate than our old cabin on the *Siren*, but we didn't care. We stripped each other and fell into the bed, tumbling and rolling together. She pulled my hair as I mapped every inch of her body with my lips. I caressed her skin as she sucked on my nipples. She cried out and clung to me as I took her apart the way she liked to be touched. Mine. My princess. Then she climbed down my body until her head was between my thighs to return the favor, and all I could do was stare up at the ceiling and try not to tear too many fingernails as I clung to the headboard.

Finally, sated and spent, we stilled, wound up around each other. George's hair fanned over us like the finest blanket, and I pulled her closer, content in the knowledge that she was safe and with me once again.

"I'm sorry for leaving," I said.

"You had to," she said, kissing my skin. "I was holding you back."

"You weren't. You never do. You challenge me and frighten me, but you're never a burden."

"Would you have killed the brokers if I was there?"

Would I? Perhaps. But it would have been harder. Leaving her here had given me the room to go through with it as quickly as Maro and I had.

"They're dead," I said. "Maro and I are free, and we have more wealth than you've ever seen in your life."

George nodded against my chest. "I don't know what happens next."

"I thought you wanted to go to Redmere."

"I want to help, but it's a whole country. We can't simply sail up to the door and ask to be let in. I'm not much of a princess, no matter what the people here are willing to believe. Beverly and I were barely engaged for a few days and only married for a few hours. No one outside the prince's circle would have even heard of me. I was thinking it would help the cause if we found this other princess. The one Duke Ylvar mentioned. Beverly's sister. I don't know if she exists, but she would have a real claim to the throne. Not like me."

I'd forgotten about the second princess. But I squeezed George tightly. "You're my princess." It was a sentimental thing to say, but in the privacy of this small room, with the doors closed, there was no one to see this moment of softness.

George was still thinking however. "We can't be sure people will follow me when the real struggle comes. And we'll only get one chance to stop the duke. A sister—a true princess—would—"

"If she exists."

"She would help our cause. Or we could go back to Vestria. Take the support I've gathered here and bring it to Cheray. She would be a powerful ally if we can prove we're useful to her."

So much uncertainty. But one thing I knew for sure.

I pulled away long enough to raise our combined hands and kiss her knuckles. "Princess Georgina, I love you. Wherever you go, I will go with you."

"Anywhere?" The way her voice lifted hopefully at the end could not be ignored.

"Anywhere."

She wrapped herself around me. "I don't know where we'll go tomorrow, but in the end, I want to go home."

"We'll get there. I promise." I closed my eyes. What she didn't know was I was home already. Wherever we sailed, whatever we faced, as long as she was with me, I would always be home.

THE END

THANK YOU!

Thank you so much for reading *Unbroken*.

Sign up for The A-List, my monthly newsletter for new releases, giveaways, and recommendations.

WANT MORE?

The adventures of George, Lou and the crew of the *Crimson Siren* continue in Unleashed.

ABOUT THE AUTHOR

Alli lives in Toronto with her very patient husband and a growing pack of rescue pets. She tries to split her time between writing, exploring Toronto's parks, queueing online for K-Pop concert tickets, and traveling anywhere that has good wine. Tragically, this leaves no time to clean the house.

LGBTQ+ FANTASY BY ALLI TEMPLE

Afterlife Incorporated

Only Mostly Dead

Hate To Haunt You

Vacation From Hell

The Pirate & Her Princess

Uncharted

Unbroken

Unleashed

www.ingramcontent.com/pod-product-compliance
Lightning Source LLC
Chambersburg PA
CBHW030800210726
48290CB00002B/346